NIGHT SHIFT

AN UNEXPECTED MATES PARANORMAL ROMANCE

THE MAGIC OF WISHES & DREAMS
BOOK NINE

ALLIE MCCORMACK

Night Shift / Allie McCormack

Cover Art designed by Dar Albert at
Wicked Smart Designs

Formatted with Vellum

Acknowledgments

This book owes its strength to my extraordinary Beta Reader Team. Their sharp insights, honest critiques, and enthusiastic support have shaped every page. To those dedicated souls who read through multiple drafts, offering fresh eyes and invaluable feedback each time—your commitment to helping me tell the best story possible means everything.

Heids Van Vuuren
Jaycee Madison
Kathleen Crapse
Lorraine Gibbes
Margery Tipton
Riet de Bruin-Strijker

And special thanks to my daughter, Chrissy Bixby, whose creative mind and endless encouragement help bring my stories to life. Her enthusiasm for my wild plot ideas and her knack for solving story problems make her an invaluable part of my writing journey.

Who's Who in
The Magic of Wishes & Dreams

Alessandra Taylor -- Hospice worker and volunteer at domestic abuse safe house. Married to Julian. (Wishes in a Bottle)

Angus Johnston -- Mysterious innkeeper of the West Side Inn. Powerful magical being, of unknown type. Married to Renee.

Becca Castellano -- Rescued by Remi from 1692 Salem where she was to be tried as a witch. Married to Jake. (A Witch in Time)

Beth Kerrigan – Clouded Leopard shifter, veterinary assistant. Chosen of Tyr (Night Shift)

Douglas McCandliss -- Veterinary partner in the Country Vet Clinic. Married to Jacinth. (A Gift of Jacinth)

Harper O'Neill -- Fox shifter, works in banking. Engaged to Nathan. (Foxy Lady)

Jacinth Khayyam -- A charming, cheerful Djinn. Married to Douglas. (A Gift of Jacinth)

Jake Malloy -- Wolf shifter, works as security guard. Married to Becca. (A Witch in Time)

Julian DiConti -- Mage from 14th century Genoa, bound to a Djinn vessel for 600 years. Married to Alessandra. (Wishes in a Bottle)

Katerina Kazakis -- Maine Coon shifter. Former fashion designer, now animal portrait artist. Married to Troy. (A Cat for Troy)

Kester Kazakis -- Maine Coon shifter. Owns the Kazakis Greek Deli. Married to Tamera. (Coveted Mate)

Kieran -- Ancient Djinn prince and statesman. Chosen of Mandy. (A Prince of the Djinn)

Liam McConnnell -- Great Pyrenees shifter. Both physician and veterinarian. Married to Naomi. (Reluctant Rogue)

Mandy Dupont -- Disabled, elderly woman, romance writer. Kieran's Chosen. (A Prince of the Djinn)

Maroulla Kazakis -- Greek-American Kazakis matriarch, Maroulla is the Warden to the Shifter Council for the Northeastern US. She lives in Maine.

Naomi Kerrigan -- Clouded Leopard shifter, librarian. Married to Liam. (Reluctant Rogue)

Nathan Burke -- Musician, cellist and music teacher. Kahu of the jackalope baby, Jill. Engaged to Harper. (Foxy Lady)

Remi -- Mischievous young Djinn who has been time traveling from the 16th century to visit Jacinth. After shifters are outed, he ceases his time traveling so his 21st century self can come be a part of the community.

Renee Johnston -- Mysterious innkeeper of the West Side Inn. Powerful magical being, of unknown type. She's in charge of the dining side of the inn. Married to Angus.

Talya -- Caracal shifter. One of the rescues from the Morocco compound. Adopted daughter of Douglas and Jacinth.

Tamera Austen -- Caracal shifter, vet clinic receptionist. Married to Kester.(Coveted Mate)

Troy Shelton -- Veterinary partner. Married to Katerina. (A Cat for Troy)

Tyr Lindstrom -- Vampire. Builds custom motorcycles. Chosen of Beth (Night Shift)

CHAPTER 1

Beth Kerrigan stood before the mirror in her en suite, smoothing down the dark green scrubs she'd chosen for her first day working at the Country Veterinary Clinic. For now, she'd work the regular day shift while training, but next week she'd begin covering the evening clinic hours, then staying overnight to monitor the boarding animals and post-surgical patients.

"You can do this," she whispered to her reflection. The woman staring back looked healthier than she had a year ago - her body had filled out, no longer gaunt and skeletal, her face regaining its natural softness, and her pale blonde hair had reclaimed its thick, lustrous shine. Her eyes, the color of storm clouds, no longer held that haunted look. Well, not as much anyway.

From the hallway, the sound of footsteps approached her door. "Beth? You okay in there?" Naomi's concerned voice carried through.

"I'm fine." Beth took a deep breath, gathering her courage. "Just nervous."

Her sister's face peeked around the door frame, anxiety in the blue-grey eyes so exactly like Beth's own. "Want me to drive you?"

"No." Beth picked up her bag, checking one last time that she had everything. "I need to do this myself."

This job at the clinic was more than just work - it was her transition from simply surviving to truly living again. The past year here in the safety of the shifter community in the Hudson Valley had been spent healing, studying, and slowly rebuilding herself. Now it was time to venture back into the world... even if the thought made her stomach flutter with butterflies.

Her fingers brushed against her textbooks stacked on her desk. She'd been studying veterinary medicine intensively, determined to make this work. The veterinary partners at the Country Vet Clinic had been kind enough to give her this chance, and she wouldn't let them down.

Beth squared her shoulders, managing a small smile for her twin. "I'm ready. I'm picking up Layla on my way. It's her first day, too, so we can be nervous wrecks together."

Naomi pulled her into a quick hug. "You'll both do great. Have a fabulous day!" Her sister's confidence helped steady Beth's nerves.

Beth headed out to her car, the morning air crisp and cold against her face. She inhaled deeply, loving the scents of fall... crisp leaves and fireplaces. So different from Miami where she'd grown up. She couldn't wait for snow. Last year had been her first time experiencing winter, and she and her twin couldn't get enough of playing in the snow in their clouded leopard forms, as well as Liam, Naomi's husband, who Changed into a Great Pyrenees.

As she backed out of the driveway, Beth caught a glimpse of Naomi waving from the doorway. The unwavering support of her sister and brother-in-law, Liam, over the past year had been her anchor. She'd needed that time to heal, to find her footing again, but she couldn't hide in their protective shadow forever. Three years ago, she'd lost more than her fiance, Neil, when he was murdered—she'd lost herself. Today she would take her first real step toward becoming someone new—even if that someone remained a mystery.

When she pulled up to the sprawling wolf pack house in her green Prius, Layla was already waiting on the wraparound porch. The pretty caracal shifter practically bounced down the steps, her dark red hair catching the morning sunlight. Like many of the women rescued from the compound in Morocco two years ago, Layla had flourished in her newfound freedom. She and Beth had formed an instant connection - two survivors learning to live again, rebuilding their lives.

"I couldn't sleep at all." Layla slid into the passenger seat, smoothing her new navy shirt dress. "I've never worked before. What if I mess up?"

"You'll do great. Don't worry." Beth navigated down the winding driveway. She smiled in reassurance, remembering how quickly her friend had adapted to modern life after years of isolation. "The clinic staff understands this is your first job. They're not expecting you to know everything on day one."

"But what if a client asks me something and I don't understand?" Layla bit her lip nervously.

"Your sister says Barbara's amazing at training new people." Beth steered onto the main road, the early morning sun streaming through the trees. "And Holly and Anna are super patient. It's going to be okay. I promise."

Layla's shoulders relaxed slightly. "Tamera does say they're wonderful. Especially when they found out about..." She paused, taking a deep breath. "About the compound."

"Exactly. They know your background, and they want to help." Beth reached over to squeeze Layla's hand. "Plus, you've picked up everything else so quickly. Remember how fast you learned to use your phone? You're sending group texts like a pro now."

A small smile tugged at Layla's lips. "That's true. And I do love learning new things."

"See? This is just one more adventure. And you've got all of us backing you up."

"And speaking of new jobs..." Beth kept her eyes on the road, her voice softening. "This is my first full-time position too. I mean, I worked through college, but those were just campus jobs. Twenty hours max per week at the library or the campus bookstore."

Her words trailed off as memories of what came after college threatened to surface. The dark period she tried so hard not to think about. The Sanctuary. The isolation. The...

A warm hand covered hers on the steering wheel, pulling her back to the present. Layla's fingers intertwined with hers in a gentle squeeze. Beth blinked rapidly, grateful for the anchor of her friend's touch.

"We start together then," Layla murmured. "Supporting each other."

Beth squeezed back, drawing strength from their shared connection. She was so lucky to have Layla and her sister in her life, who truly understood what it meant to rebuild a life from broken pieces.

She navigated the turn and curving drive into the clinic's parking lot, the brick building's green shutters matching the dense foliage of the surrounding woods. Beth parked in the employee section behind the U-shaped building, her own excitement growing. After everything that happened, beginning this job felt like reclaiming a piece of herself.

"Ready?" Beth grabbed her lunch bag from the backseat.

"As I'll ever be." Layla took a deep breath, squaring her shoulders. "Tamera says I should pretend everyone is family. That makes it less scary."

"You're absolutely right." Beth linked arms with her friend as they walked around the building to the front of the clinic.

"It's like a supernatural family tree in there—Djinn, shifters, and humans all connected through marriage and friendship. Between the partners' marriages to Djinn and shifters, and our own connections through Tamera and Liam, I think most everyone at this clinic is related somehow—by blood, marriage, or magic. I swear, we need a chart to keep track of everyone's relationships. So now... let's go start our new lives!"

"I like that. Starting a new life." Layla's smile brightened her entire face as they approached the glass doors.

The familiar chime of the entry bell rang as Beth pushed open the door. Barbara glanced up from behind the reception desk, her silvering blonde hair neatly styled as always.

"Good morning, ladies!" Barbara's warm voice carried across the waiting room. She bustled around the desk to greet them. "Ready for your first day?"

Beth nodded, grateful for the office manager's enthusiastic welcome. Beside her, Layla was a mass of nerves.

"Welcome to the team." Barbara's eyes crinkled with warmth as she hugged first Beth, then Layla. "Though I suppose you're both already part of the family here. There's fresh coffee in the break room, and Liam brought in those cranberry scones you love, Beth. He said something about celebrating his favorite sister-in-law's coming to work here."

"His only sister-in-law," Beth chuckled. "He has to stay on my good side."

"Tamera's already here." Barbara glanced at her watch. "She came in early to help Dr. McCandliss with a sick ferret."

Layla perked up at the mention of her sister. "Maybe I can peek in and say hi before we start?"

"Of course, dear. Exam room three." Barbara turned to Beth as Layla hurried off down the hall. "It's a relief to finally have another veterinary assistant. We haven't been able to find a suitable tech since - well." She broke off, giving Beth an apologetic glance for bringing up Beth's quasi-aunt who had held the position a couple of years before. An unrepentant rogue shifter, Beatrice was now a lifetime inmate at the Sanctuary.

Layla returned just then, declaring herself ready to go.

"Wonderful. Let me show you where to put your things." Barbara led them through the door marked 'Staff Only' and down a short hallway to the break room. "We've got your lockers all set up."

The break room smelled of coffee and cinnamon, someone's breakfast pastry lingering in the air. Barbara pointed to two lockers along the far wall, already labeled with their names in neat block letters.

"These are yours. The combination is set to 1-2-3-4 for now, but you can change it whenever you'd like." Barbara demonstrated the mechanism. "There's a shelf for your lunch, hooks for your coat or sweater, and plenty of room for whatever else you need to store. And speaking of combinations, we'll get you the access code to the staff entrances tomorrow. There was no point giving them to you now, since we're changing the access codes regularly, and we'll have a new one tomorrow."

"Oh, that's smart," Beth agreed.

She opened her locker, running her fingers over the smooth metal door. Such a simple thing, having her own space at work, but it made everything feel more real. More permanent. She hung up her light cardigan and placed her lunch on the shelf, watching as Layla did the same.

Beth took a deep breath, then let it out slowly, letting excitement begin to creep in. She was really doing this! Her hands smoothed down her scrubs one final time as Barbara led them toward the reception area.

"Holly will show you the reception desk systems," she told Layla. "And Beth, Dr. Shelton is waiting for you in exam room two. He's got a busy day scheduled and could use the extra hands. Remember," she added with a warm smile for both of them. "Everyone here started as a beginner once. Just ask if you need help."

Beth squared her shoulders, drawing strength from Barbara's encouragement. After everything she'd survived, learning a new job shouldn't be scary. Yet her pulse quickened with a different kind of excitement as she headed down the hallway. This was her chance to build something new, something meaningful.

She could do this. She would do this.

The whole day stretched ahead, full of possibility. Beth felt a smile tugging at her lips as she approached exam room two, ready to begin.

BETH'S MUSCLES ached as she walked to her car at the end of her shift, but her heart felt lighter than it had in years. The day had flown by in a whirlwind of learning new procedures, meeting patients, and working in the feline wing of the clinic alongside Dr. Shelton. The veterinarian's warm manner and patient teaching style had put Beth at ease immediately.

She couldn't face going straight home. Not when she felt this alive, this accomplished. Layla had already headed out with Tamera, the sisters having plans to celebrate her first day on the job. They'd invited Beth, but she'd had enough of people for the day, and made a polite excuse to decline.

A local bistro caught her eye as she drove through the small downtown area - she'd been meaning to try it since it opened a month or so ago.

Going inside, the hostess seated her at a cozy corner booth. Beth ordered the chicken marsala and settled back with her Kindle while she waited. The familiar comfort of losing herself in a book wrapped around her like a warm blanket. She'd forgotten this simple pleasure—dining alone, losing herself in words while flavors bloomed on her tongue.

Long after her plate was cleared, Beth remained in the booth, legs crossed at the ankles, completely absorbed in her novel. The wait staff didn't seem to mind, keeping her water glass filled as the dinner crowd thinned out. For the first time in too long, she felt like herself again - the Beth who used to spend hours in coffee shops and bookstores, the Beth who had dreams and plans before everything fell apart.

Today felt like the first real step toward reclaiming that person. Not just surviving, but living again.

Beth startled at the time displayed on her Kindle - nearly eight o'clock. The bistro had emptied considerably while she'd been lost in her book. Guilt nagged at her as she quickly gathered her things and settled the bill, leaving a generous tip for her waitress.

The night air held a slight chill as she hurried to her car. She hadn't meant to stay out so late, especially not on a work night. The streets were quiet as she drove home, streetlights casting pools of yellow light on the empty sidewalks.

Naomi met her at the door before Beth could even get her key in the lock. Her twin's eyes, the same silver-flecked blue, sparkled with amusement.

"There you are! I was starting to wonder if you'd gotten lost." Naomi pulled her into a quick hug. "Did you forget how to check your phone?"

"I'm sorry." Beth fumbled for her phone, wincing at the missed text notifications. "I stopped for dinner on my way home, and got caught up reading."

Naomi held the door wider, waiting for Beth to step inside. "So tell me how your first day went," she invited.

Beth smiled at her twin. "It was actually really good. Dr. Shelton is-"

The thunderous roar of motorcycles shattered the evening quiet, cutting off her response. Beth spun around, the sound vibrating through her chest as her heart hammered against her ribs. Two sleek bikes charged down the street, their engines growling in perfect harmony before roaring to a stop directly in front of the house. The sudden silence felt almost as startling as the noise had been.

The matching black motorcycles gleamed under the streetlights, their chrome accents catching the glow. Beth found herself frozen on the doorstep, watching the riders dismount with fluid grace. Their movements mirrored each other perfectly.

Beth watched, transfixed, as the riders pulled off their black helmets in perfect synchronization. Long, pale blond hair spilled free, catching the streetlight like spun silver. Their fair skin seemed to glow in the evening darkness.

The two men came together in an enthusiastic high-five, their matching grins lighting up identical faces.

"Beat our record by three minutes!" one crowed.

"Told you taking Miller Road would shave off time," the other responded with a laugh.

As they turned toward the house, Beth caught her breath. They were stunning - like mirror images of each other, with brilliant blue eyes and chiseled features that reminded her of Chris Hemsworth from those Thor movies. But their coloring was even lighter, more ethereal, like the elves from Lord of the Rings with their luminous pale skin and silvery-blonde hair.

Beth couldn't tear her gaze from the identical men approaching their doorstep. Beside her, Naomi murmured "Whoa" in a stunned voice that perfectly echoed Beth's own thoughts.

"Who are they?" Beth whispered, mesmerized by their fluid, synchronized movements.

Naomi shook herself, as if breaking free from a spell. "If you'd bothered to check your texts, you'd know." Her voice took on a pointed tone. "They're here to install security systems - both for the house and Liam's shifter clinic in the carriage house."

Beth frowned, her brow furrowing as she turned to her sister. "But we already have security systems. Liam had them installed way back when you two bought the place."

"We need more than basic alarms now. We need cybersecurity." Liam's voice came from behind them as he stepped onto the porch. His tall frame blocked the porch light, casting shadows across the wooden boards. "We have to protect not just ourselves, but all our client information too."

“The clinic records?" Beth's brow furrowed. "But we don't treat shifters at the Country Clinic - just regular pets. What would anyone want with vaccination records and spay appointments?"

Liam ran a hand through his brown hair, hints of auburn catching in the light. "Medical records, client addresses, staff information - it's all data that could be dangerous in the wrong hands. With shifters now exposed to the world, hackers might target the clinic looking for connections or clues about who might be a shifter. We need top-level security on our computer systems to protect everyone associated with the clinic."

"But no one even knows about your shifter clinic here," Beth protested. "It's on your private property, completely separate from the Country Vet Clinic."

"True," Liam acknowledged, "but I still work as a veterinarian there. Anti-shifter groups might scrutinize everyone connected to the clinic more carefully now, especially the staff. With Troy's wife publicly out as a shifter, anyone associated with the clinic could become a target for investigation. They'd be looking for any connections, any patterns that might lead them to more shifters."

Beth hadn't considered that angle. The thought of strangers digging into their lives, hunting for their secrets, sent a chill down her spine.

She glanced back at the twins, seeing them in a new light. Their casual stance and matching grins belied what must be serious expertise if Liam trusted them with such critical security needs. Still, she'd had enough of strangers for the day.

Slipping past her sister and Liam, she retreated into the house. Her social energy had drained completely after the long first day at work. Meeting the mysterious twins would have to wait.

She had a moment of regret, remembering her old self. When she'd been in college, she'd loved meeting new people. Her psychology classes had fascinated her, leading to endless conversations with classmates about human nature and behavior. She'd been the one organizing study groups, planning coffee meetups, bringing people together.

Now the mere thought of facing strangers made her heart race. The young men from the security company looked nice enough - their matching grins and synchronized movements spoke of a playful nature. But the idea of going back out there, of making conversation and being social, sent cold tendrils of anxiety through her chest.

She knew she needed to push past this. Dr. Shelton and the clinic staff had shown her such kindness today. Their gentle acceptance helped ease her back into interacting with others. But it was still exhausting, requiring constant effort to keep her anxiety in check.

Toeing off her shoes at the front door, the hardwood floors warmed her feet through her socks as she padded down the hallway to her room. Living in Florida, she'd never even heard of radiant heating until they moved in here. Now she was a total fan.

Closing the door with a soft click, she leaned against it for a moment before pushing away to change. She peeled off her work clothes, replacing them with soft yoga pants and an oversized sweater that hung past her hips.

That done, she opened her bedroom door, in case Naomi wanted to pop in as she often did. Climbing onto the high queen size bed with its memory foam mattress and cool gel top, Beth pulled her knees to her chest, wrapping her arms around them. She'd been working so hard in therapy to overcome these fears. To stop letting her past control her present. But some days, like today, it felt safer to retreat to her room than face new people.

"Baby steps," she whispered to herself, echoing her therapist's frequent reminder. She'd managed a full day at work. She'd even eaten alone at a restaurant without panic. Those were victories worth celebrating.

Beth folded her legs beneath her, to sit cross-legged in the center of her plush bed. She closed her eyes, letting her breathing slow and deepen. She found that quiet place inside herself, the one she'd discovered during her recovery. Her shoulders relaxed as tension melted away. Each breath brought more peace, pushing away the lingering anxiety from a full day of meeting new people. In this moment, she was safe. Protected. Healing.

A light knock at her door frame pulled Beth from her meditation. Her eyes fluttered open to find one of the identical men standing in the doorway, his tall frame nearly filling it. Up close, his features were even more striking - high cheekbones, straight nose, and those brilliant blue eyes that seemed to glow in the dim light.

"I'm Tyr Lindström." His voice was softer than it had been outside, all business now rather than playful enthusiasm. "I need to check the security points on your doors and windows, if that's alright?"

Beth nodded, gesturing for him to enter. She uncurled from her cross-legged position but remained perched on the bed, watching as he moved to examine the French doors leading to her private patio. His movements were precise and efficient as he tested the locks and hinges, making notes on a sleek tablet.

He worked in silence, moving from the doors to the large window that overlooked the garden. His fingers traced the window frame, testing the integrity of the locks and seals. The tablet made soft clicking sounds as he typed his observations.

Though his presence filled the room, Beth found herself relaxing slightly. There was something reassuring about his methodical inspection, the way he took such care checking every potential point of entry. His earlier boisterous personality had shifted to quiet professionalism that put her at ease.

Beth couldn't help studying him as he worked. The way his dark green henley stretched across broad shoulders, how his dark jeans hugged powerful thighs. Even the graceful way his hands moved as he examined the window frames drew her attention. His presence filled her sanctuary with an energy she hadn't felt in years.

Her inner leopard stirred, rising from its usual watchful crouch to pad closer in her mind. The small cat's curiosity matched her own, wanting to investigate this stranger who radiated such compelling strength. Urging her to move closer, wanting to brush against his legs and mark him with her scent.

Stop it, she told Whisper firmly. She couldn't help peeking, though, as Tyr bent to check the baseboards, his shirt riding up to reveal a strip of pale skin above his waistband.

Her leopard purred, the sound almost escaping her human throat. Beth swallowed hard, shocked by her own response. She'd worked so hard to keep her walls up, to protect herself. Yet something about this man called to both her human and animal sides, making her want to lower those carefully constructed barriers.

"Good locks. Could be better though." Tyr's quiet murmur barely carried across the room. Beth wasn't sure if he was speaking to her or making notes to himself as his fingers traced the window frame.

He turned suddenly, those brilliant blue eyes focusing on her. "Do you keep them locked?"

"Yes, always." Beth pulled her sweater sleeves over her hands. "Well, except at night. I sleep with the window open."

She tensed, expecting a lecture. Everyone else - Liam, Naomi, even her therapist - had strong opinions about her needing her windows open. But Tyr just nodded, his expression neutral as he made another note on his tablet. No judgment, no warnings, just quiet acceptance of her admission. Something tight in Beth's chest loosened slightly at his lack of reaction.

Tyr's fingers traced along the window frame once more, his expression thoughtful. "We can install perimeter sensors outside," he said, his voice still carrying that quiet, professional tone. "They'd create a detection grid around your patio and window. Anyone approaching would trigger silent alerts to security and your phone before they got within ten feet."

Relief washed through Beth's chest. "You mean... I could keep sleeping with the window open?"

He nodded, making another note on his tablet. "Fresh air is important. We'll make sure you can keep your window open safely. The sensors would give you plenty of warning if anyone tried to get close. We can set different alert levels too - wildlife versus human movement."

Beth felt tension she hadn't even realized she was carrying melt from her shoulders. Everyone else had tried to convince her to sleep with the windows locked. But she needed cool, moving air on her face when she slept—it seemed to keep the night terrors and panic episodes at bay. The fresh air grounded her when the PTSD symptoms threatened to overwhelm her in the darkness. Tyr offered a solution that would let her feel both safe and comfortable.

Instead of the lecture she'd braced for—the one she'd heard countless times from Liam about security risks, from Naomi about her safety, even from her therapist about establishing proper boundaries—Tyr had simply accepted her need and offered a solution. No judgment in his eyes, no disapproving frown, just quiet understanding that this mattered to her. The knot of defensive arguments she'd prepared unraveled, unnecessary in the face of his acceptance.

Tyr's gaze continued to sweep the room, landing on the partially open door near the corner. "En suite?"

"Yes." Beth's fingers twisted in her sweater sleeves. "There's a window in there too."

He strode toward the bathroom, tablet in hand. The moment he disappeared through the doorway, Beth sagged against her headboard, drawing in a shaky breath. What was wrong with her? She hadn't felt this kind of instant attraction to anyone for years... not since Neil. The thought of her dead fiancé should have doused these unexpected feelings, but instead they burned brighter. Her skin tingled with awareness of Tyr moving around in the next room, the soft tap of his boots on tile setting her nerves dancing.

Beth pressed her hands to her heated cheeks, trying to calm her racing pulse. She was being ridiculous. He was just here to do a job - checking security measures and installing sensors. Nothing more. She needed to get herself under control before he came back.

The sounds of his movements in the bathroom helped ground her: the click of his tablet, the slide of the window, the quiet murmur of his voice as he made notes to himself. Each sound helped restore her equilibrium, reminding her that this was just a normal security inspection. Nothing to get worked up about.

Tyr emerged from the bathroom, his tablet tucked against his side. His gaze landed on the desktop setup in the corner of her room, the dual monitors gleaming in the soft lamplight.

"What's your computer setup?" He gestured toward the desk.

"That's my gaming PC." Beth shifted on the bed. "And I have a laptop too - that ASUS over there." She pointed to the sleek laptop charging on her nightstand.

Tyr seemed to hesitate, his fingers tapping against his tablet. "Since you're using the house WiFi network, we should probably put security measures on those as well. To protect the whole system."

"Yes, absolutely." Beth nodded emphatically, relief flooding through her. She hadn't even thought about computer security, but with all the clinic data potentially accessible through their network... "Whatever you need to do. I want everything as secure as possible."

Beth swallowed hard, her fingers twisting in her sweater sleeves. "Do you... do you think we're really in danger?"

Tyr lowered his tablet, turning to face her fully. Those intense blue eyes focused on her with laser precision, making her heart skip.

"It's unlikely," he said, his voice gentle but firm. "Your family isn't out publicly. But since both you and Liam work at the Country Vet Clinic, there's a possibility - though faint - that you could be targeted simply for working there."

He shifted his weight, tucking the tablet under his arm. "We're also installing cybersecurity measures at the vet clinic. The goal is to protect everyone - staff, patients, and their families."

A voice called from elsewhere in the house. "Tyr! Need you out here!"

"On my way!" Tyr tucked his tablet under his arm. "I'll be back in a few days to install everything. We'll make sure you're completely secure." He gave Beth a slight bow before striding from the room.

The front door opened and closed moments later. Beth released a breath she hadn't realized she'd been holding. Her bed dipped as Naomi flopped down beside her, making Beth bounce slightly. "They seem nice. Very professional."

"Isn't it kind of late for them to be working?" Beth glanced at her bedside clock showing after nine PM.

Naomi's laugh tinkled through the room. "Beth, they're vampires. This is early evening for them."

Beth's eyes widened as she stared at her sister.

"V-vampires?" Her voice came out in a mouse-like squeak, her heart thundering in her chest as she stared at her sister. "There were vampires in our house?"

"Oh, right, I forgot you didn't read my texts. They work for Lord Damien's clan." Naomi stretched out on Beth's bed, completely unfazed. "Didn't you notice how pale they were? Or how they moved?"

Looking back at the encounter, Beth remembered Tyr's fluid grace, the intense blue eyes that seemed to glow... She groaned and buried her face in her hands. "I thought they were just really good-looking!"

"Well, that too." Naomi rolled onto her side, propping her head on her hand. "They're European, I think. Just from a really, really long time ago. They're part of the clan's security company. That's why Maroulla hired them to handle our systems - they're the best."

Beth peeked through her fingers at her twin. "And you're okay with this? Having vampires install our security?"

"After everything we've been through with the rogues and our un-family, vampires seem pretty tame." Naomi shrugged. "Plus, Lord Damien's Chosen, Alyssa, is pals with Jacinth. That's how they got involved with us," she explained. "A bunch of vamps from his clan volunteered to come up here and provide night-time security at businesses that might be at risk."

Right, she knew Jacinth was a Djinn, and married to Dr. McCandliss, one of the partners at the vet clinic.

Naomi frowned at her. "Anyway, I thought I told you all this."

Feeling heat flood her cheeks, Beth looked down. "I guess I forgot. Or wasn't paying attention when you told me."

Her sister's silvery laugh filled the room as she pulled Beth into a tight hug. "Get some sleep, sis." She slipped off the bed and padded to the door, closing it softly behind her.

Beth took her time in the shower, letting the hot water soothe away the lingering tension from her first day at work. She changed into her favorite silk pajamas, the cool fabric sliding against her skin as she slipped beneath her covers.

Snuggling deeper into her pillow, Beth closed her eyes. But instead of drifting straight to sleep, her mind kept circling back to Tyr. The way his henley had stretched across those broad shoulders. How his long fingers had looked against the window frames as he measured. That intense blue gaze when he'd looked directly at her.

Whisper purred contentedly as Beth buried her face deeper in the pillow, remembering the fluid grace of his movements. Even knowing he was a vampire didn't diminish the attraction she'd felt. She drifted off to sleep with the image of Tyr's handsome face floating in her mind, his lithe form moving through her dreams.

CHAPTER 2

Astride his sleek black motorcycle, Tyr paused before pulling on his helmet. The night air was cool against his face as he watched his twin brother cock an eyebrow at him.

"Something's bothering you," Tobi said, his voice pitched low enough that only vampire hearing could catch it.

"The girl - Beth." Tyr frowned, troubled by the unexpected pull she stirred in him. "There's something about her. She feels... fragile. Wounded somehow."

"Ah." Tobi's expression shifted to understanding. "Beth and Naomi. They're the twins."

"Well yes, obviously they're twins." Tyr rolled his eyes at his brother. "I do have functioning eyesight."

"No, you idiot." Tobi shook his head. "They're THE twins. The ones everyone was talking about a couple years ago. The rogues?"

Tyr went still, his helmet forgotten in his hands as the implications sank in. He remembered now - the whispered conversations, the rumors that had circulated through supernatural circles about the twin clouded leopard shifter women who had been raised by rogues.

"She'd been engaged to some normal human guy while they were in college. Their sisters - the other ones, not Naomi - drugged her and killed the guy while they slept. Set it up to make Beth think she'd done it in some kind of rogue frenzy." Tobi's face hardened. "She got locked up in that Sanctuary place - the compound for shifter criminals - until Liam and Naomi figured out what really happened."

"Man, that's fucked up." Tyr ran a hand through his hair. "And people think vampires are sick and twisted!"

"People don't know about vampires, remember?" Tobi snickered.

"Yeah, yeah. Just sayin'."

Everything crystallized with brutal clarity - her wariness, the need for open windows, the way trauma clung to her scent like smoke. Rage burned through him, primitive and fierce. His hands clenched around the helmet as the urge to hunt down her tormentors clawed at his chest. But that wasn't his place. His job was to make her feel safe in her home. He could do that much at least.

Tyr's protective thoughts scattered as Tobi's phone chimed with an incoming text. His twin pulled out the device, the screen's glow illuminating his face in the darkness.

"Joe needs us at the warehouse." Tobi glanced up from his phone. "Says they've got some questions about the renovation."

"Race you there." Tyr's lips curved into a challenging grin. The familiar spark of competition with his brother pushed aside his brooding thoughts about Beth. "Loser buys breakfast at that diner on Main Street."

"You're on!" Tobi shouted as he jammed his helmet over his head.

Tyr barely got his own helmet secured before gunning his bike's engine. The powerful machine roared to life beneath him, vibrating with barely contained energy. Twin motorcycles peeled away from the curb in perfect sync, their riders leaning into the first turn as one.

The night blurred around them as they raced through the streets, engines growling in competition. Tyr hunched low over his handlebars, the wind buffeting his jacket as he pushed his custom machine to its limits. Tobi's headlight remained stubbornly present in his peripheral vision, neither brother willing to concede an inch. They weaved through the sparse late-night traffic, taking corners with practiced precision, their motorcycles extensions of their bodies after decades of riding.

The warehouse materialized ahead, its industrial silhouette cutting against the night sky. With a final burst of speed, Tyr edged ahead on the final stretch, his front wheel crossing the invisible finish line a fraction of a second before his brother's.

Tyr killed the engine, satisfaction thrumming through him as he pulled off his helmet. He'd beaten Tobi by mere inches, but a win was a win. The old warehouse loomed before them, its weathered brick glowing warmly under the harsh construction lights.

"Breakfast is on you," he called out as Tobi rolled to a stop beside him.

His twin grumbled good-naturedly while dismounting. "Lucky break with that delivery truck. You'd have eaten my dust otherwise."

"Keep telling yourself that."

Tobi flipped the kickstand down with his boot, fair hair catching the harsh construction lights. "Besides, we're vampires. We don't eat, remember?"

"It's the principle of the thing," Tyr snickered. He ran an appreciative hand over his bike's sleek frame. The custom machine purred like a dream, every modification perfectly tuned.

Their reputation for building exceptional motorcycles had grown steadily over the decades. When Lord Damien asked for volunteers to come up here, Tyr and his brother had jumped at the opportunity to expand their business from the cramped quarters they'd had in New York City. This warehouse offered endless potential for their custom motorcycle operation on the ground floor. The two upper floors were being converted into apartments, with steel-shuttered windows making them safe for vampires. As an additional precaution, hidden passages would lead down to a secure bunker in the basement. None of those extra modifications would show in any blueprints, as the construction company was owned by the local alpha wolf shifter, and the entire construction crew was made up of shifters.

Tyr followed his brother into the warehouse, their boots echoing on the concrete floor. Joe Malloy's tall frame emerged from the shadows near the back office, blueprints rolled under his arm.

"Evening, Tobi, Tyr." The alpha wolf's deep voice carried across the space. "Got someone I want you to meet."

A stocky man with salt-and-pepper hair stepped out behind Joe. His weathered face spoke of years working construction sites.

"Alex Metaxas, my foreman." Joe clapped the man on the shoulder. "He'll be your go-to if I'm tied up with pack business. His wife, Lydia, is the manager at Carter's Bank. I expect you've heard they're going public as shifter friendly, next month."

Tyr exchanged quick handshakes with Alex, noting the man's firm grip and steady gaze.

"We need to prioritize the living quarters and bunker," Tyr said, examining the blueprints as Joe spread them across a makeshift table. "The bike shop can wait."

Tobi nodded in agreement. "More vamps are coming up from the city next month. We're going to all need somewhere secure to stay."

"Not a problem." Alex traced a finger along the upper floor plans. "We can focus the crew on the apartments first, then tackle the bunker while the finishing work's being done upstairs."

"The bunker needs to be absolutely secure," Tyr emphasized. "And completely off the official plans."

Joe's eyes gleamed with understanding. "Alex knows how to keep things quiet. We've been handling special projects for the pack for years."

"You boys show me what you need," Alex said. "I'll make it happen."

THE COOL NIGHT air carried hints of pine and loam as Tyr strode toward the tree line, his boots silent on the packed earth. He extended his vampire senses, scanning the surrounding area. No heartbeats except for small wildlife. No human scents on the breeze. Perfect.

Rolling his shoulders, Tyr let his body flow into his alternate form. Bones shifted and realigned as feathers sprouted across his skin. His vision sharpened dramatically as his eyes transformed to those of a raptor. Within seconds, a peregrine falcon perched where the vampire had stood.

Tyr spread his wings, the moonlight gleaming off his plumage, perfect camouflage against the night sky. With a powerful downstroke, he launched himself skyward.

The air currents caught his wings, lifting him higher above the warehouse. His keen raptor eyes picked out every detail below - the construction equipment scattered across the lot, the fresh tire tracks from their motorcycles, even a mouse scurrying along the foundation.

Banking into a thermal, Tyr soared higher, letting the peaceful solitude of flight wash over him. Up here, he could think clearly without the distractions of scents and sounds from the ground. The night belonged to him, a creature of air and shadow.

From his vantage point high above the city, Tyr's keen falcon sight caught a familiar flash of green - Beth's Prius parked in the driveway of her home. His wings tilted automatically, adjusting his flight path before his mind fully registered the decision.

The cool night air rushed past as he spiraled lower, his keen vision picking out every detail of the property. Security lights illuminated the wraparound porch. The French doors to Beth's room stood partially open, gauzy curtains shifting in the breeze. He'd have to talk to her about that; those needed to be closed and locked once she went to bed.

He folded his wings, dropping into a controlled dive toward the rooftop. His talons clicked softly against the shingles as he landed on the peak. The angle gave him a perfect view of both the front and back of the house. From here, he could monitor all approaches to Beth's room while remaining completely hidden in the shadows. In the stillness, his enhanced hearing picked up three steady heartbeats from within - Beth, Naomi, and Liam.

He told himself he was just doing his job - assessing security vulnerabilities from all angles. But the way his heart quickened when he caught Beth's scent drifting up from her open window suggested otherwise. His falcon ruffled its feathers, settling in to watch over her sanctuary.

A flash of white caught his eye as another bird landed beside him. Tyr turned his head, then did a double-take at the sight of his brother's chosen form. The white gyrfalcon stood out starkly against the dark roof, its pale plumage almost glowing in the moonlight.

Really? Tyr sent the thought to his twin. *An arctic raptor? Could you be any more conspicuous?*

Tyr watched as Tobi meticulously groomed his ridiculous white feathers, taking his time before acknowledging Tyr. The gyrfalcon's movements were deliberately slow and precise, drawing out the moment in that particularly annoying way only siblings could manage.

Stalker, much? Tobi's mental voice dripped with amusement as he surveyed the house below them.

Rage and embarrassment flooded through Tyr. With an indignant screech, he lunged sideways, his sharp beak finding purchase in Tobi's pristine plumage. He yanked, satisfaction coursing through him as several feathers came loose in his grip.

Tobi's wings slammed into him, nearly knocking him off his perch. *You absolute ass!*

They grappled on the rooftop, wings beating and talons scraping against shingles as each one tried to get the upper hand. Tyr managed to pluck another few feathers before Tobi's wing caught him square in the face.

Finally, both breathing hard, they settled back onto their perches side by side. A small scatter of white and blue-grey feathers drifted away on the night breeze, evidence of their brief battle.

Tyr shifted his weight, talons gripping the shingles as he stared at his twin's pristine white form. *You're going to get yourself shot.*

Actually... Tobi's thought held that particular tone that always meant trouble. *Think about it. Humans are all worked up about shifters now. They see an unusual bird, especially one that's not native to the area, and what do they assume?*

Understanding dawned as Tyr processed Tobi's logic. *They'll think you're a shifter.*

Exactly. Tobi preened with smug satisfaction. *They'll be so busy trying to trap the mysterious gyrfalcon shifter, they won't notice the actual shifters right under their noses. Perfect distraction.*

Tyr gazed at his brother in stunned appreciation. Trust Tobi to turn what seemed like a liability into a tactical advantage. Tobi's mind had always worked in wonderfully twisted ways.

Devious, Tyr acknowledged, impressed despite himself. *But if you get yourself stuffed and mounted on someone's wall, I'm not explaining it to Lord Damien.*

Speaking of conspicuous... Tobi preened a pristine wing with his beak, the deliberate motion emphasizing his point. *Hawks aren't exactly nocturnal, brother. Any human with basic bird knowledge will notice that.*

At least my feathers blend with the night sky, Tyr countered, ruffling his rich brown plumage. The moonlight barely caught the soft blue-ish tones, letting him fade into the shadows. Unlike his brother's ridiculous white form that practically glowed like a beacon. *Besides, peregrine falcons are common enough around here that no one looks twice.*

Tobi's snicker rippled through their connection. *Keep telling yourself that. At least I have an excuse - white gyrfalcon "shifter" and all that. You're just a lovesick vampire mooning around in falcon form at night.*

Tyr's wings flared in annoyance. He wasn't mooning. He was doing his job, assessing security vulnerabilities. The fact that Beth's peaceful heartbeat below drew him like a lodestone had nothing to do with it. Nothing at all.

Tyr shifted his weight on the rooftop, his talons scraping against the rough shingles. The night breeze ruffled his feathers as he kept his gaze fixed on Beth's patio below.

Speaking of trouble... Tobi adopted that insufferably knowing tone that made Tyr's talons twitch. *What are we doing here, anyway?*

Tyr's wings twitched in agitation. He didn't have a good answer - at least not one he wanted to examine too closely. *I don't know,* he admitted finally. *I just... wanted to be sure Beth was safe.*

The admission hung between them in the cool night air. Tyr could feel his brother's curiosity and concern bleeding through their telepathic link, but he kept his own thoughts carefully shielded. He wasn't ready to analyze why Beth's vulnerability called to something deep inside him, why the thought of her sleeping unprotected made his protective instincts surge.

A flicker of movement below snapped Tyr's attention from his brother. His enhanced vision zeroed in on Beth's patio as a small shadow detached itself from the deeper darkness near her French doors.

The clouded leopard moved with liquid grace, the large cloud-shaped splotches on her coat blending perfectly with the dappled shadows. Even with his enhanced vision, Tyr might have missed her if he hadn't been watching so intently. Her compact form was smaller than he'd expected for a leopard, roughly the size of a spaniel.

Beth's feline shape paused at the edge of her patio, her rounded ears swiveling to catch every nighttime sound. Her long tail curved gracefully behind her as she settled onto her haunches, face tilted up toward the star-filled sky.

Tyr found himself mesmerized by her peaceful stillness. The trauma and anxiety that clung to her human form seemed absent in her leopard shape. She looked... content. In this form, the weight of human trauma seemed to lift from her shoulders. Here, she was pure grace and instinct.

She's beautiful. Awe colored Tobi's thoughts. *I didn't realize clouded leopards were so different from regular ones.*

Yeah, Tyr agreed, watching Beth's graceful movements. *She's not much bigger than a house cat.*

Well, a pretty big house cat, Tobi amended. *But yeah.*

They fell silent as Beth gathered herself, muscles bunching beneath her luxuriant coat. She launched upward in a fluid leap, catching the lowest branch of the massive oak tree beside her patio. Her claws found easy purchase in the bark as she pulled herself up, moving with the natural confidence of a born climber.

Tyr tracked her progress as she emerged onto a thick horizontal branch about fifteen feet up. Moonlight filtered through the leaves, casting dappled patterns across her rosette-marked fur as she prowled along the branch. Her long tail provided perfect balance, barely twitching as she moved.

Finding a spot she liked, Beth stretched out along the branch, her spotted form draping gracefully over the rough bark. Her head rested on her crossed paws while her tail hung lazily below, swaying slightly in the night breeze.

Aww, she's adorable! Enthusiasm bubbled through Tobi's thoughts. *I just want to scoop her up and hug her and squeeze her and call her George!*

She's not some stuffed animal, you idiot. Tyr's wings snapped out in irritation, and he lunged at his brother, beak aimed for those pristine white feathers again.

Tobi danced sideways, nearly sliding off the roof peak. *Aww, is someone feeling protective of the cute little kitty cat?*

That did it. Tyr launched himself at his twin, talons extended. They tumbled across the rooftop in a flurry of brown and white feathers, each trying to get the upper hand. Tobi's wing caught him in the face while Tyr managed to yank out another chunk of that ridiculous white plumage.

You're just jealous because you look like a common hawk, Tobi taunted, pecking at Tyr's wing.

That's falcon to you! And better than looking like an overgrown cockatoo, Tyr shot back, dodging his brother's attack.

Below them, Beth's leopard lifted her head from her paws, ears swiveling toward their scuffling sounds. Her luminous eyes reflected the moonlight as she scanned the rooftop above.

The brothers froze mid-wrestle.

Tyr reacted on pure instinct, his wings spreading wide as he shifted position to shield Tobi's bright form from Beth's searching gaze. His darker plumage blended perfectly with the night shadows, while Tobi's white feathers stood out like a beacon against the dark roof.

Stay still, you idiot, he commanded along their twin bond, keeping his own form motionless as the leopard's eyes swept across their perch.

Tobi, for once, listened without argument. The gyrfalcon's warmth pressed against Tyr's side as they waited, barely breathing, while Beth's keen gaze lingered on their position. Her spotted ears remained focused upward, clearly having caught some hint of their presence.

After what felt like an eternity, Beth's head lowered back to her paws. Her eyes drifted closed, though her ears still twitched occasionally toward any nighttime sounds.

Too close. A hint of sheepishness crept into Tobi's thoughts. *Sorry about the teasing.*

Just... be more careful, Tyr responded. *If she realizes we're here, she's going to think we're stalking her.*

Aren't you though? Tobi's smugness radiated through their link. *Stalking her, I mean.*

Idiot, Tyr projected back, his feathers bristling with irritation. He kept his larger form positioned to shield his brother's ridiculous white plumage from Beth's occasional upward glances.

Well, have fun playing guardian angel. I'm off to check the vet clinic's perimeter again. With a nearly silent rustle of wings, Tobi launched himself from the rooftop. His white form quickly disappeared against the star-filled sky, leaving Tyr alone with his thoughts.

Below, the sleek clouded leopard remained stretched along the oak branch, her spotted tail swaying gently in the night breeze. The peaceful rise and fall of her breathing carried clearly to Tyr's enhanced senses.

Tyr settled more comfortably on his perch. He told himself he was just doing his job - assessing security vulnerabilities and protecting a potential target. But the way his heart quickened whenever Beth's luminous eyes swept past his hiding spot suggested otherwise.

CHAPTER 3

Beth sprawled across her bed, legs raised toward the ceiling as she wiggled her bare toes. The pale pink polish from last week had started chipping, and she'd been contemplating trying out the nail art kit Naomi had given her. Little silver stars and moons waited in their plastic case, promising a bit of whimsy for her toenails.

Her phone chimed from its spot on her pillow. Beth grabbed it, expecting another text from Naomi about dinner plans. Instead, she found herself added to a group chat with Jacinth and Layla.

«Let's take Molly and Yousuf to Nathan's for a play date and picnic!» Jacinth's message bubbled with her usual enthusiasm. *«Molly's kindergarten class is only half day and she's been asking to see Yousuf»*

«Yes! Yousuf will be very excited» Layla responded.

Another message popped up from Jacinth: *«Beth, you should join us! I'm bringing my special hummus and pita bread»*

Beth's fingers flew across her phone screen. *«I'd love to! I can bring a fruit salad»* She bounced off her bed, already mentally cataloging the fresh berries and melon in her fridge.

An hour later, Beth pulled her green Prius up to Nathan's house, a large bowl of mixed fruit on the passenger seat. The sweet scent of strawberries, citrus, and melon filled the car.

Jacinth materialized beside Beth's car door in a shimmer of magic, making her jump slightly. The Djinn's long black hair cascaded over her shoulders as she leaned down with a bright smile.

"Come around to the side gate," Jacinth said, gesturing toward a wooden fence. "Nathan and Harper are in the city for some concert thing, but they said we're welcome to use the yard."

Beth followed Jacinth through the gate, her sandals crunching on the gravel path. As they rounded the corner into the backyard, she stopped dead in her tracks, nearly dropping her fruit salad.

A massive wooden play structure dominated the space - three stories of interconnected platforms, bridges, and towers that would put most park playgrounds to shame. Swings of every variety hung from thick beams - traditional seats, a tire swing, even a rope swing that looked straight out of a Tarzan movie. A twisting slide curved down one side while a rope climbing net covered another.

"Whoa! This wasn't here when I came last month!"

"Impressive, right?" Jacinth grinned at Beth's stunned expression. "The construction crew came over and built it all in one weekend. With so many kids visiting the jackalopes these days, Nathan mentioned needing a play area. Next thing he knew, the whole crew showed up with lumber and tools."

"It's incredible," Beth breathed, watching Molly and Yousuf scramble up the rope net. "They really outdid themselves this time."

"The crew said something about every kid deserving a cool fort." Jacinth eyed the structure with satisfaction.

Beth set her fruit salad on a nearby picnic table as Jacinth laughed. "I think there might have been some wish fulfillment involved. The guys kept arguing about what they'd wanted in their dream fort as kids. Next thing I knew, they were adding a second level. Then a third."

The late morning sun warmed Beth's shoulders as she took in the scene. A patchwork quilt spread beneath a maple tree created a cozy picnic spot where Layla reclined, her dark red hair gleaming in the dappled sunlight.

A movement from the large enclosure caught Beth's eye. Through the mesh fencing, she spotted a small form hopping toward the gate. The latch clicked as tiny paws pushed it open with practiced ease.

Beth's heart melted as Jill emerged, the jackalope's antlers barely more than fuzzy nubs sprouting from her head. The American Sable's rich brown coat gleamed in the sunlight as she bounded across the grass, her long ears swiveling to catch every sound.

Jill paused near their picnic blanket, rising onto her hind legs. Her pink nose twitched rapidly as she scented the air, probably catching whiffs of Jacinth's hummus and Beth's fruit salad. The jackalope's presence felt completely natural now, though Beth remembered the shock that had gone through the supernatural community when the baby jackalope had first shown up on Nathan's doorstep a few months ago.

"Hello, beautiful girl," Layla cooed softly. She'd fallen in love with Jill during her first visit to Nathan's, spending hours watching the magical creature explore her enclosure.

She held out a crisp lettuce leaf to Jill, who nibbled delicately with tiny bites. The jackalope's soft brown fur ruffled in the breeze coming through the open gate of her enclosure.

"Again! Again!" Molly's excited voice rang out as she zoomed down the twisting slide, her dark curls flying. Yousuf waited at the top, bouncing on his toes until she cleared the bottom. His previous shyness seemed forgotten as he launched himself down after her, squealing with delight.

"They've been at it for twenty minutes straight," Layla said, smiling as she watched her son. "I don't think he's ever had this much fun." Her voice held a touch of wonder, and Beth's heart squeezed, remembering what she knew of their past in the compound.

Excited shrieks echoed across the yard as they raced back up the steps for another turn. Jill's long ears perked up at their voices, but she remained contentedly munching her lettuce beside Layla.

Beth glanced around the yard, noticing the absence of Jill's mother. "Where's Sage?"

Layla's musical laugh rang out as she pointed toward the house. "I think it's mommy jackalope time out. She's been sulking by the sliding glass door since we arrived."

Following Layla's gesture, Beth spotted Sage lounging in a patch of sunlight near the glass doors. Her rich brown fur gleamed with hints of silver, the impressive antlers casting delicate shadows on the ground.

The mother jackalope maintained a dignified pose, deliberately facing away from the play area where her daughter socialized.

Sage's ears twitched, clearly catching their conversation. The mother jackalope's nose twitched with what Beth could have sworn was indignation, but she maintained her aloof position by the door.

"Aww, who can blame her?" Beth gathered a few pieces of watermelon rind from her fruit bowl. "Every mom needs a break sometimes."

She crossed the yard, her sandals whispering through the grass. Sage's ears pivoted toward the sound of her approach, though the jackalope maintained her dignified pose facing the sliding glass doors.

"I brought you something special." Beth crouched beside Sage, holding out the pale green rind. The jackalope's nose twitched, whiskers quivering as she caught the sweet scent.

Sage finally turned her head, large dark eyes assessing Beth for a moment before delicately accepting the offering. Her teeth made soft crunching sounds as she nibbled the juicy rind. Beth smiled, reaching out to stroke the thick fur between Sage's impressive antlers. The jackalope's coat felt like velvet beneath her fingers, softer than she'd expected.

"You're such a good mama," Beth murmured, scratching gently behind Sage's ears. Sage's eyes half-closed in pleasure as she continued munching her treat.

After a few more moments of petting, Beth rose and made her way back to where Jacinth and Layla lounged on the patchwork quilt. She settled onto a sunny patch of blanket, crossing her legs beneath her as children's laughter rang out from the play structure behind them.

Beth settled more comfortably on the blanket as she watched Jacinth unpack containers from a wicker basket. The rich scent of garlic and lemon wafted from an enormous bowl of creamy hummus, making her mouth water.

"This smells amazing," Beth said, reaching for a piece of warm pita bread. She dragged it through the hummus, scooping up a generous portion. The first bite melted on her tongue, drawing an appreciative moan. "Oh my god, Jacinth. What do you put in this?"

Layla pulled out a stack of peanut butter and jelly sandwiches wrapped in wax paper, along with two bags of potato chips. "I brought these for the children," she said, arranging the food on paper plates. "And of course they'll want some of the fruit. Oh! And I made deviled eggs."

"Speaking of hungry..." Jacinth's eyes sparkled with mischief as she produced a bottle of champagne from her basket. With practiced ease, she poured the champagne into three plastic cups, the bubbles fizzing merrily in the sunlight, then pulled out a bottle of orange juice and tipped some into each cup.

"Mimosas? At a playdate?" Beth accepted her cup with a laugh, the cool plastic smooth against her fingers.

"It's never too early for a little celebration," Jacinth declared, passing the second cup to Layla. "Here's to your first week at your new jobs!"

"Here, here!" Layla raised her cup, the bubbles catching the sunlight.

Beth echoed the toast, taking a sip of the crisp, citrusy drink. The fizz tickled her nose as the sweet-tart flavor spread across her tongue.

"So how is it going?" Jacinth leaned back on one elbow, her long dark hair spilling over her shoulder. "The new jobs, I mean."

"Wonderfully!" Layla's face lit up. "I'll be starting working the evening shift with Beth on Monday. They've been so accommodating about my schedule with Yousuf. I'll work from four until eight, so I can get home in time for his bedtime. The other staff will stay later to close up."

Beth nodded, watching the children chase each other around the play structure. "I'm doing five to five. After the clinic closes at eight, I'll stay on to get everything set up for morning, and take care of the overnight patients."

Molly and Yousuf came racing across the grass, their faces flushed from playing.

"I'm starving!" Molly flopped onto the blanket beside Jacinth. "Can we have lunch now?"

"Me too!" Yousuf settled next to Layla, his dark eyes bright with excitement.

Jill hopped closer, her nose twitching at the scent of food. Beth helped Layla distribute the sandwiches and chips while Jacinth poured cups of lemonade for the children.

Molly took a big bite of her peanut butter and jelly sandwich, then held out a piece toward Jill. "Here bunny, want some?"

"No, sweetie." Jacinth gently caught her daughter's hand. "Jill needs special food. Here..." She selected a plump raspberry from Beth's fruit salad. "You can give her this instead."

Molly beamed as she offered the berry to Jill. The baby jackalope's whiskers quivered as she eagerly accepted the treat, drawing giggles from both children.

"Mama!" Yousuf turned to Layla between bites of his sandwich. "Molly says kindergarten is so much fun! She gets to paint and sing songs and everything!" He bounced in place, scattering potato chip crumbs. "When can I go to kindergarten too?"

Beth saw Layla's face freeze, pain flashing through her eyes before she carefully smoothed her expression. "We'll talk about that later, *habibi*."

"Okay!" Yousuf stuffed the last bite of sandwich in his mouth and jumped to his feet. "Come on, Molly! Let's go back to the fort!"

Molly scrambled up, nearly tripping over her own feet in her haste to follow. Their excited chatter faded as they raced back to the play structure, leaving their paper plates scattered on the blanket.

An uncomfortable silence fell over the blanket as Beth gathered the scattered paper plates.

Jacinth set down her mimosa, her expression gentle. "You know... the school would put him in Molly's class. They'd be together." She reached out to touch Layla's hand. "He'd make new friends, have other children to play with."

Tears welled in Layla's blue eyes, spilling down her cheeks. She brushed them away with trembling fingers. "I know. I want that for him, so much." Her voice cracked. "When he's with Tamera, or at Sasha's house playing with her children, I'm fine. I know he's safe with them."

Beth's heart ached as Layla drew in a shaky breath, her hands twisting in her lap. "But when I think about leaving him at school..." She pressed a hand to her chest. "The panic hits like a fist. I can't breathe, can't think past the terror of losing him too.

Her shoulders curved inward, as if trying to protect herself from invisible blows. "I know I have to. He's six now - it's the law. And I want him to have friends, to learn and grow." She wrapped her arms around herself. "But I panic. Every time I try to even think of it, I am filled with so much terror."

Watching Layla's pain, Beth felt the familiar ache of recognition. Her own experiences with therapy after escaping the rogues had helped her heal, taught her how to cope with the panic attacks and nightmares.

"Have you... have you thought about talking to someone?" Beth kept her voice soft. "Like a therapist?"

Layla's shoulders tensed, her spine going rigid. "They offered that when we first came here. To all of us from the compound." Her fingers twisted in the blanket's fabric. "I didn't go."

"Can I ask why?" Beth maintained her gentle, non-judgmental tone.

Pain laced through Layla's voice as she responded. "How can talking about it help? Will words erase what happened?" Her voice cracked. "Will they bring back my other sons? Will they make the nightmares stop?" She shook her head firmly. "Talking only brings the pain back to the surface."

Beth's heart ached at the raw hurt in her friend's voice. She understood that resistance - she'd felt it herself in those early weeks after her rescue from the Sanctuary. The fear that speaking about the trauma would somehow make it more real, more present. "The point isn't to make the past disappear. Trust me, I tried that - pretending it never happened, burying it deep inside. But it doesn't work. Therapy helped me understand that healing isn't about erasing what happened. It's about learning to carry it differently."

She searched for the right words. "I couldn't sleep, or when I did, I woke with terrible nightmares. I could barely eat, barely function. The memories and pain were like this huge boulder crushing me. But my therapist taught me ways to cope. How to process what happened without letting it control my life."

Layla's eyes flickered to Beth's face, a hint of interest breaking through her resistance.

"The past will always be there," Beth continued softly. "But therapy gives you tools to handle it. Like learning to swim instead of drowning. And most importantly, it helps you find ways to be happy again, to enjoy moments like this with Yousuf without the fear overwhelming everything else."

Her hand found Layla's, squeezing gently. "The pain doesn't disappear. But you learn to breathe around it, to function despite it. And you learn that it's okay to feel joy again, to build a new life."

Jacinth nodded, her mahogany eyes warm with centuries of understanding. "I've watched countless humans struggle with grief and trauma. The ones who heal aren't those who forget their pain, who push it down and try to pretend it never happened—they're the ones who learn to make space for both joy and sorrow to exist together."

"You're right," Layla whispered, squeezing Beth's hand. "I will try. For Yousuf. I want him to have friends his age, to go to school, to be... normal." She drew in a shaky breath. "Can you... would you help me find someone to talk to? Someone who understands about shifters?"

"Of course." Relief flooded through Beth's chest. "Dr. Harrison, my therapist, she is a shifter like us. She's amazing - she helped me work through so much of my own trauma. I can give you her number."

Jacinth's face lit up with sudden inspiration. The Djinn sat forward, her dark hair swaying with the movement.

"Oh! I almost forgot - the kindergarten class always needs parent volunteers." Jacinth's eyes sparkled as she turned to Layla. "You could help out two or three mornings a week. That way you'd be right there in the classroom with him."

Layla's fingers stilled their nervous twisting of the blanket. "I could... stay with him?"

"Absolutely! They love having parents help with art projects and reading time." Jacinth's enthusiasm bubbled through her words. "You'd get to see firsthand how the school handles security, meet the teachers and parents... watch how they interact with the children."

Beth stared at Jacinth in amazement, wondering how she hadn't thought of this perfect solution herself. The idea was brilliant - letting Layla ease into the school environment while staying close to Yousuf.

She could experience everything alongside him, building her own comfort level gradually.

"That's genius," Beth breathed, watching hope bloom across Layla's face. "You could be there to see exactly how they keep the children safe."

"And by participating," Jacinth continued, "you'll become more comfortable with the whole routine. Plus, Yousuf will love having you there."

Layla's shoulders relaxed slightly as she considered the possibility. "I... I think I could do that. Start slowly, like you said." Her gaze drifted to where Yousuf and Molly were taking turns on the tire swing, their delighted squeals punctuating the afternoon air. "He deserves to have this - friends, school, normal things."

Beth reached for her mimosa, taking a sip before deliberately lightening her tone. "So... speaking of new experiences, we had some interesting visitors at the house the other day."

"Oh?" Jacinth's eyes sparkled with interest.

"Security experts - vampires." Beth felt her cheeks warm at the memory. "Tyr and Tobi. They came to check out the house and property to see what's needed."

"Striking doesn't begin to cover it." Beth fanned herself dramatically, drawing giggles from both women. "Tall, gorgeous, with these incredible blue eyes. And the way they move..." She sighed. "Like dancers or something."

"And there's two of them?" Jacinth's grin turned wicked.

"Identical twins." Beth nodded, her face growing warmer. "Though Tyr seems more serious than his brother. Tobi was cracking jokes the whole time they were measuring windows and checking sight lines."

"Lord Damien's security team is the best," Jacinth said. "Though I suspect you're more interested in their... other qualities."

"Can you blame me?" Beth laughed, tucking her legs beneath her. "You should have seen Tyr in this fitted henley..." She trailed off, remembering how the fabric had stretched across his broad shoulders.

"And?" Layla prompted, clearly enjoying Beth's flustered state.

"And nothing! They're vampires, for heaven's sake. I barely know them." Beth buried her face in her hands, but couldn't stop grinning. "Though Tyr did say they'd be back to install the new security system..."

"Mama! Come push me!" Yousuf called out from the swings. Beside him, Molly bounced excitedly.

"Me too!" Molly shouted, waving both arms at Jacinth.

A genuine smile broke across Layla's face as she stood. "Coming, *habibi*!" She turned to Beth and Jacinth. "Thank you. For understanding. For showing me there's hope."

Jacinth rose with fluid grace, mischief dancing in her expression. "Come on," she said, extending her hands to both women. "I believe we've been summoned. Those swings won't swing themselves."

CHAPTER 4

Beth pulled into the familiar parking lot of the West Side Inn, nostalgia washing over her. The restored Victorian's welcoming porch lights glowed in the early evening darkness, just as they had almost two years ago, when she'd first arrived here, scared and uncertain after her release from the Sanctuary.

The inn's front door opened before she reached the steps, spilling warm light across the wraparound porch. Renee's elegant figure filled the doorway, her dark eyes sparkling with warmth.

"Beth, honey! Come in out of the cold." Renee enfolded her in a tight hug that smelled of vanilla and fresh-baked cookies.

"It's so good to see you," Beth murmured, letting herself relax into the embrace. Renee had been like a surrogate mother during those first difficult weeks of freedom.

"Look who's here, Angus!" Renee called over her shoulder as she ushered Beth inside.

Through the open doorway between the lobby and lounge, Beth could see the warm glow from the fireplace. Angus's tall frame appeared in the doorway, silhouetted against the dancing flames. His white teeth flashed in a broad smile as he crossed the lobby to greet her.

"Welcome back, Miss Beth." His deep voice carried the same calm reassurance she remembered. "You're looking well."

Beth ducked her head at the praise, warmth flooding her cheeks. "Thank you. I'm feeling much better these days."

"As you should." Angus gestured toward the lounge. "The others are gathering in there. But first..." He exchanged a knowing look with his wife. "Renee just pulled a batch of her famous snickerdoodles from the oven."

"Can't have a proper meeting without cookies," Renee declared, already steering Beth toward the lounge.

Beth hung her coat and knit hat on the wooden pegs along the wall, grateful for the warmth radiating from the crackling fireplace in the lounge, just through the door from the lobby. The flames cast dancing shadows across the polished hardwood floors, bringing back memories of countless evenings spent in this welcoming space during her recovery.

Beth followed Renee through into the dining room where people were already gathering around a grouping of tables that had been pushed together to form one long table. She waved at everyone as Renee led her past the swinging door into the kitchen, breathing in the heavenly scent of cinnamon and sugar. The industrial-sized kitchen gleamed with spotless stainless steel, but somehow still managed to feel cozy and welcoming. A cooling rack on the center island held rows of perfectly golden snickerdoodles.

"Here, dear." Renee handed her a silver platter piled high with the still-warm cookies. "Make sure these get put out on the buffet table." She fixed Beth with a stern look, though her dark eyes twinkled. "And be sure to keep some for yourself before they all disappear. You know how quickly they go."

"Yes ma'am." Beth couldn't help but smile, remembering how these same cookies had helped coax her out of her shell during those first difficult weeks at the inn.

"Angus and I won't be here for the meeting tonight." Renee wiped her hands on her apron. "We have some business to attend to elsewhere. But Katerina promised to keep us in the loop about everything discussed." She patted Beth's arm reassuringly. "That girl notices everything - she won't miss a single detail."

Beth balanced the heavy platter carefully as she nodded. The cookies' sweet aroma made her mouth water, bringing back memories of late-night conversations in this very kitchen, when nightmares had driven her from her bed and Renee had always seemed to know exactly when to appear with fresh-baked comfort.

Heading back into the dining room with the platter of cookies, Beth's gaze swept across the familiar faces. The veterinary partners from the clinic where there - Troy Shelton deep in conversation with Suzanne MacPherson, while Douglas McCandliss listened intently to something his wife Jacinth was saying, her dark eyes animated as she gestured.

Sliding the cookies onto the buffet, and nabbing a couple for herself before finding a seat, Beth smiled at her friend's enthusiasm. It still amazed her sometimes that Douglas had actually married a Djinn - how did that work, she wondered, loving someone who would never age, never die? And what must it be like for Jacinth, falling in love with a mortal, knowing she'd have to watch him grow old and leave her behind?

Beth's pulse quickened when she spotted Tyr and Tobi among the group. The vampire twins stood near the window, their fair hair catching the warm light from the crystal chandelier overhead. Her mind flashed back to their encounter the other night, how carefully Tyr had examined her security needs without making her feel vulnerable or broken.

She offered them a small smile as their brilliant blue gazes found hers. Tobi grinned broadly in response while Tyr's expression remained more reserved, though his eyes held a warmth that made her cheeks heat slightly.

Beth's mouth fell open as she took in the twins' t-shirts. She hadn't noticed their casual attire at first, too caught up in their striking features and intense blue eyes. But now that she looked closer...

Tyr's black shirt had "Blood Type: Yes, please" emblazoned across the chest in bold red letters. The fitted cotton showed off his broad shoulders, making Beth's mouth go dry. But it was the slogan that had her pressing her lips together to hold back laughter.

Tobi's shirt was even worse - or better, depending on your perspective - "Vampires Do It In The Dark" stretched across his chest in gothic script. When he caught her looking, he waggled his eyebrows suggestively, causing Beth to lose her battle with composure. A giggle escaped before she could stop it, and she ducked her head, trying to get her giggles under control.

"Beth! Over here!" Katerina Shelton sat beside her husband Troy, and waved, beckoning her over to them.

Beth made her way over to where Katerina sat, settling into the empty chair beside her. The Maine Coon shifter leaned close, her wild dark hair brushing Beth's shoulder.

"I thought this was going to be more casual," Katerina whispered, her golden eyes sparkling with amusement. "You know, everyone standing around with cookies and coffee, getting to know each other. Not so..." She gestured vaguely at the formal table arrangement.

Beth nodded in agreement as she scanned the dining room. Beyond the familiar faces from the clinic, she counted at least six people she didn't recognize.

The sharp sound of hands clapping cut through the quiet chatter. Beth turned to see Jacinth standing at the head of the table arrangement, her long black hair gleaming in the chandelier light.

"Thank you all for coming tonight," Jacinth's melodic voice carried easily through the room as conversations fell silent.

Jacinth's gaze swept across the gathered faces, her dark eyes warm and welcoming. "We're here tonight so all our teams can get acquainted - security, veterinary staff, and support personnel. It's vital we work together smoothly, especially with vampires joining our community security forces."

At the mention of vampires, Beth noticed several people shift uneasily in their chairs. Dr. MacPherson's shoulders tensed slightly, though she maintained her professional smile. Even Joe seemed wary, gripping his coffee mug tighter, his knuckles whitening.

Only Douglas appeared completely at ease, probably due to being married to a Djinn. He sat beside Jacinth, nodding encouragingly as she spoke. Troy and Katerina also seemed relaxed, though Beth remembered they'd had more time to adjust to supernatural revelations.

Beth's gaze drifted to where Tyr and Tobi sat side by side a few chairs down from her. If they noticed the undercurrent of tension their presence caused, they didn't show it. Tobi maintained his easy smile while Tyr's expression remained neutral, though Beth caught a slight tightening around his eyes as he observed the room's reactions.

She understood how people could be wary - vampires had been the stuff of horror stories until recently. But after meeting Tyr and sensing his genuine desire to help protect them, she couldn't quite share their fear.

Joe rose from his seat, his tall frame commanding attention. The wolf shifter alpha's presence filled the room as he cleared his throat.

"I know this is unprecedented - vampires coming to our aid, shifters and vampires working together." His deep voice carried easily through the quiet room. A wry smile touched his lips. "Well, at least since the 16th century."

Soft chuckles rippled from where Tyr and Tobi sat, their blue eyes dancing with private amusement. Beth wondered what memories that date stirred for them, how many centuries of history they'd witnessed.

Joe's expression grew more serious as he continued. "I realize many of you may have doubts about the vampires offering their help." His gaze swept across the gathered faces, acknowledging their concerns. "But Lord Damien has worked tirelessly for centuries to keep vampires hidden from humans. And if there is one thing he can be counted on, it is his word, his honor."

Joe's voice rang with quiet conviction. "So when he offered the assistance of the vampires, the Shifter Council had no hesitation in accepting."

He glanced toward Jacinth, inclining his head. "With that said... I'll pass the floor back to you."

Jacinth smoothed her long dark hair behind her shoulders, her warm smile encompassing them all. "Let's keep introductions brief so we can move on to the important matters."

She gestured to Douglas beside her. "My husband, Dr. Douglas McCandliss." His blue eyes crinkled as he gave a small wave. "Dr. Troy Shelton and his wife Katerina." The Maine Coon shifter's wild dark hair bounced as she grinned and wiggled her fingers in greeting. "And Dr. Suzanne MacPherson. Douglas, Troy and Suzanne are the clinic's veterinary partners."

Jacinth turned slightly, indicating an elderly man with silver-streaked hair sitting near her. "This is Arthur, a fellow Djinn and dear friend." His weathered face creased in a grandfatherly smile that made Beth feel instantly at ease.

"And this young troublemaker," Jacinth's tone held fond exasperation as she gestured to her other side, where a young man sat who looked to be about in his early twenties, "is Remi, also a Djinn."

Remi flashed a bright, mischievous grin at the group, his dark eyes dancing with barely contained energy. Despite his youthful appearance, Beth had heard that Remi was actually several centuries old. The concept of immortal beings who could appear any age still made her head spin sometimes.

Joe Malloy rose from his seat, his tall frame commanding attention. His deep voice carried easily across the room as he introduced himself as the local wolf pack alpha.

Her gaze shifted to Jake beside him as Joe gestured to his brother. Despite their family resemblance, Jake's features held a gentler cast than Joe's more commanding presence. Beth remembered hearing he worked security at one of the local banks.

"Jake will be coordinating our shifter security teams," Joe explained, his hand resting on his brother's shoulder. "He's got experience with both civilian and shifter protection protocols."

Liam stood next when Joe indicated him, his lean frame straight and professional. "Dr. Liam McConnell," he said in his slight Irish lilt. "I'm both a veterinarian and physician, which gives me unique insight into treating both human and shifter patients."

Liam turned his attention to her. "And this is Beth Kerrigan, one of our new vet techs at the clinic."

She managed a small wave, grateful when Joe quickly moved on to indicate a group sitting together at the far end of the table arrangement.

Beth counted four men and three women, none of whom she recognized.

"These are the rest of our security team members," Joe said. "All experienced in protection detail and crisis response."

Beth's attention shifted as another figure rose from the table - tall and commanding with shaggy blond hair and dark green eyes that swept the room with a predatory alertness that made her wild cat's instincts prickle.

"I am Aleksei, second in command to Lord Damien," he stated, his voice carrying a hint of an accent Beth couldn't quite place. "These are Antonio and Dimitri." He gestured to two vampires seated near him - one with Mediterranean features, the other with the caramel skin and flashing dark eyes of desert peoples.

"Tyr and Tobi you all know already." Aleksei nodded toward the twins before continuing. "More of our clan will be joining us from New York City once the living quarters are completed."

Aleksei's commanding presence held everyone's attention. His dark green eyes swept across the gathered faces as he outlined their priorities. Watching how professionally Aleksei conducted himself, how seriously these vampires all seemed to take their protection duties, she couldn't help but be impressed. These weren't at all the monsters of legend - they were highly trained security professionals who happened to be vampires.

She couldn't help but marvel at how much had changed in the past year. The vampires' decision to emerge from centuries of isolation had shocked the supernatural community. Their own laws had demanded absolute secrecy, yet when shifters were exposed to the human world, the vampires had stepped forward without hesitation.

Lord Damien himself had appeared at an emergency council meeting, pledging his clan's resources and expertise to help keep exposed shifter communities safe. The vampires' vast wealth and centuries of experience living undetected among humans had proved invaluable during those chaotic early days.

Beth's gaze drifted to Tyr, noting how intently he focused on Aleksei's briefing. These vampires could have maintained their secret existence, letting the shifters handle their own crisis. Instead, they'd risked exposure themselves to help protect complete strangers. She'd heard through Naomi that several vampire clans across the country had followed Lord Damien's lead, reaching out to local shifter communities to offer assistance.

The gravity of that decision wasn't lost on Beth. Vampires had survived for millennia by staying hidden, their laws regarding secrecy absolute. Breaking that tradition, especially for beings they'd historically kept their distance from, spoke volumes about their commitment to protecting the supernatural community as a whole.

"For now, our primary focus will be the veterinary clinic and Kazakis Restaurant," Aleksei continued, his accent giving the words a crisp precision. "Both locations have drawn increased scrutiny since Katerina's television appearance."

Katerina nodded. "It took them exactly zero days to figure out that Kester is my brother, and owns the restaurant," the Maine Coon shifter explained. "But we expected that, and were prepared. So far, there haven't been any issues, although," she grinned, "a few groupies are making Kester nervous."

"We'll expand coverage to include Carter Bank once Lydia makes her public statement," Aleksei continued. "By then, the additional members of our clan should have taken up residence here."

Movement caught Beth's eye as Jake exchanged a meaningful look with his brother. Joe gave a slight nod, and Jake rose to his feet, his expression grave.

"Actually," Jake's voice carried a note of concern, "we've already had one reporter track down Harper, the fox shifter from the Yosemite video. She relocated here, and works at the bank." He ran a hand through his hair. "The Djinn helped modify the reporter's memory, but I think we should include the bank in security measures from the start. Just to be safe."

Jacinth rose to her feet, her warm, chocolate-brown eyes sparkling with determination, drawing everyone's attention.

“I'd like to ask for help regarding Nathan and Harper's jackalopes," Jacinth began, her tone serious yet compelling. "As you know, they have a mother and baby living in their backyard pen, and..."

Tyr's head snapped up. "Jackalopes? Those are real?"

Jacinth nodded, her dark eyes brightening with enthusiasm. "Yes, they're real. Last year, Nathan found an injured baby jackalope in his yard. The mother appeared shortly after—as if sensing her baby was being cared for. They simply... stayed." She paused, her voice softening with wonder. "We thought they'd vanished from the world decades ago. Extinct. Finding two alive has been extraordinary."

She brushed a strand of silky black hair behind her ear. "Nathan and Harper became their kahu—their guardians. The jackalopes trust them completely."

"On weekends," Jacinth continued, "shifter children visit to see them. I've woven magical protections throughout the property. Humans peering over the fence see nothing but an ordinary yard with playground equipment, and security cameras capture the same illusion. The children can play freely in either form without worry. My magic also creates barriers against natural predators—no coyotes, hawks, or foxes can enter to harm Sage and Jill."

Her expression sobered, chocolate-brown eyes scanning the faces around the table. "My concern lies with how easily rumors spread. The children adore the jackalopes, and while they understand the importance of secrecy..." She sighed softly. "One excited slip to a human friend could draw unwanted attention. Children mean well, but accidents happen."

Aleksei nodded solemnly, his stern expression softening for a moment. "The survival of endangered species should concern all of us, and most especially such creatures as the jackalopes. To know two still exist is indeed encouraging." The ancient vampire's gaze swept across the gathered supernaturals. "We have witnessed too many extinctions across the centuries. They'll have our protection as well."

Rising from his chair, Tyr's powerful frame drew all eyes in the room. Her pulse quickened when his intense blue gaze swept past her before settling on Jacinth.

"We can install outdoor motion detectors and sensors around the entire property," he said, his deep voice carrying easily across the table. "The latest models are virtually invisible once properly placed. They'll alert us to any unauthorized intruder, human or animal."

He turned toward Aleksei, seeking confirmation.

Aleksei nodded in approval. "I'll send Dimitri to do the initial assessment tomorrow night. He has extensive experience with wildlife monitoring systems." His accent wrapped around the words with crisp precision. "Once we know exactly what's needed, we'll put a rush order on the equipment."

Tyr's shoulders slumped slightly, a flicker of disappointment crossing his handsome features. "I wanted to see the jackalopes," he grumbled, his voice carrying a hint of petulance that seemed oddly endearing coming from such an imposing vampire.

Beth pressed her lips together, trying to suppress a smile at his obvious disappointment. Around the table, several others failed to contain their amusement. Soft chuckles rippled through the room.

Tobi elbowed his twin playfully. "Aww, does big bad vampire want to see the cute bunny?" His eyes sparkled with mischief as he dodged Tyr's retaliatory swat.

"They're not bunnies," Tyr protested, his expression growing more dignified. "They're rare magical creatures.."

The laughter grew louder, breaking some of the earlier tension in the room. Even Aleksei's stern expression softened into something approaching amused exasperation.

The moment of shared amusement dissolved, and gravity settled over the room as Joe rose to his feet. The alpha wolf shifter's grim expression matched Aleksei's as he took his place beside the vampire at the head of the table arrangement.

"The threats we face come from three distinct sources," Joe's deep voice carried easily through the quiet room. "First, we have scientific and government interests. They'll wrap their motivations in pretty phrases about research and the greater good." His lip curled slightly. "But what they really want is to study us, experiment on us, find ways to weaponize our abilities for military applications."

Ice flooded Beth's veins. Her arms wrapped around herself instinctively, as if she could shield herself from the ugliness conveyed in those words.

"Second," Joe continued, his voice hardening, "are the anti-shifter hate groups. They're driven by fear and prejudice. Their goal isn't to study us - they want to eliminate us entirely."

Beth's leopard snarled internally at the threat, even as her human side recoiled from the malice behind such sentiment. She caught Tyr's intense gaze flicking toward her, as if he'd sensed her visceral reaction to the mention of those hate groups.

"Finally," Joe's expression turned calculating, "we have collectors and traffickers. These are possibly the most dangerous because they're motivated purely by greed. To them, we're valuable commodities to be captured, sold, and displayed as status symbols among their twisted circles."

Katerina shifted in her chair, clearing her throat. "Actually, there's another category we should probably consider."

All eyes turned to the Maine Coon shifter. Beth noticed the mischievous glint in her friend's golden eyes, so different from her usual artistic focus.

"I've been getting correspondence from a group that..." Katerina paused dramatically, her wild dark hair seeming to crackle with suppressed amusement. "Er... wants to worship me as their goddess."

Beside her, Troy dropped his face into his hands with a groan. Beth couldn't help the giggle that escaped her. The tension in the room broke as others joined in the laughter. Even Aleksei's stern expression cracked slightly, though he quickly schooled his features back to professional neutrality.

Beth stifled another laugh as Tobi's hand shot into the air, his blue eyes sparkling with the same mischief she often saw in Katerina's.

"Ooh, can I go public too? I would totally be up for being worshipped as a god." He struck an exaggerated pose.

Beside him, Tyr snickered and shook his head. "They'd probably stake you instead, brother." His lips quirked in amusement. "Though that might improve your personality."

Aleksei's expression darkened, his green eyes boring into Tobi with glacial disapproval. The temperature in the room seemed to drop several degrees under that withering glare. Tobi's theatrical pose wilted slightly, though his irrepressible grin remained firmly in place.

Beth watched, intrigued, as Antonio stirred from his quiet observation. The ancient vampire opened a sleek laptop with graceful movements, his long fingers moving across the keyboard with practiced ease.

His formal bearing and impeccable Italian suit contrasted sharply with the casual atmosphere Tobi and Tyr had created moments before.

"We are establishing a contact roster," Antonio's cultured voice carried subtle hints of an Italian origin. "For each shift, we require one representative on-call from the vampires, shifters, and Djinn. While vampires cannot serve during daylight hours, we need updates about daytime incidents relayed to the vampire coming on duty at nightfall."

Beth's attention was caught by the sudden change in the twins' demeanor. The change in the brothers was instant, their matching grins vanishing as they snapped to attention, gazes locked on the ancient vampire.

Their obvious respect for Antonio made Beth wonder about the hierarchy among the vampires. Though Aleksei was officially second-in-command, something about Antonio clearly commanded a deeper level of deference from the twins.

Approval crossed Jake's face at Antonio's suggestion, Joe nodding in agreement beside him.

"I'll work up a schedule and send it to you, Antonio," Jake said, already pulling out his phone. "We can coordinate coverage across all three groups."

The three Djinn huddled together in quiet discussion. Beth's sensitive hearing caught fragments of their melodic voices, though she couldn't make out the actual words. After a moment, Arthur straightened from their huddle, his silver-streaked hair catching the lamplight.

"I'll take tonight's shift," the elderly Djinn announced, his weathered face creasing in a gentle smile. "Then we will get you a roster."

Jake glanced up from his phone. "Alex Metaxas will be our shifter contact tonight." He looked around the room. "Everyone has Alex's number, right?"

Heads nodded around the table. Beth had gotten Alex's contact information earlier that week when he'd stopped by the clinic to discuss security arrangements with Douglas.

Aleksei's stern gaze swept across the table to fix on Tobi. "You will be on call tonight," he stated, his accent giving the words a crisp authority.

"Cool, I'll be the vampire on call." Tobi's face lit up with his usual infectious enthusiasm.

"VOC!" Tyr's eyes sparkled with sudden inspiration. "We need t-shirts!"

The twins' hands met in a resounding high-five that made Beth jump slightly in her seat. Apparently catching her movement, Tyr flickered a wink her direction.

Remi practically bounced out of his chair, his youthful energy bubbling over. "Dude! We can be Djinn On Call... DOC! We'll totally do t-shirts!"

Beth snickered, she couldn't help it. She noticed Jake's inquiring eyebrow raise toward his brother. Joe's response was immediate - a distinctly wolf-like growl that rumbled through the room.

"Don't even."

Beth pressed her lips together, trying to contain her giggles as the twins and Remi continued their impromptu t-shirt brainstorming session.

"Vampire Security: We've got your neck," Tobi declared with a theatrical flourish, earning another enthusiastic high-five from his brother.

Remi leaned forward, his dark eyes dancing with mischief. "Your Wish Is Literally Our Command," he shot back, waggling his eyebrows.

Beth ducked her head to hide her smile as Aleksei's disapproving glare swept over the trio. The ancient vampire's stern expression only seemed to fuel their enthusiasm. Her sensitive hearing picked up Tyr's barely suppressed snicker.

Beside her, Katerina wasn't even trying to hide her amusement, her shoulders shaking with silent laughter. Even Troy's professional demeanor cracked as he pressed his knuckles against his mouth, clearly fighting a grin.

Beth watched in fascination as Antonio's quiet "Enough" cut through the playful atmosphere like a knife. The twins' transformation was instant - their matching grins vanishing as they snapped to attention, gazes locked on the ancient vampire. The change reminded her of watching military documentaries where seasoned soldiers responded to their commanding officer.

She could see the subtle shift in their postures - backs straightening, shoulders squaring. Even their scents changed, the playful energy replaced by sharp focus and the deep respect she'd observed earlier.

Movement caught her eye as Remi, still bubbling with irrepressible Djinn energy, caught her gaze across the table. His dark eyes sparkled with mischief as he silently mouthed "t-shirts!" at her, complete with exaggerated eyebrow waggling.

Beth pressed her lips together, trying desperately to contain the giggles threatening to escape. She ducked her head, letting her pale hair fall forward to hide her face as her shoulders shook with suppressed laughter. Beside her, she felt Katerina's silent amusement.

Beth almost had her giggles under control, when Katerina leaned close, her wild dark hair brushing Beth's shoulder.

"Don't worry," Katerina whispered, her golden eyes dancing with mischief. "The shifters won't be left out. I'm thinking 'Purr-fect Protection' for the felines." She paused, tapping her chin thoughtfully. "Or maybe 'Who's Afraid of the Big Bad Security Wolf?' for the wolves."

Oh, God, she was going to die trying not to laugh! Beth had to bite her lip hard to keep from laughing out loud, especially when she caught Tyr watching their whispered exchange with obvious curiosity. His intense blue eyes held a warmth that made her cheeks heat slightly, even as she struggled to maintain her composure.

Aleksei rose from his seat, his commanding presence drawing all eyes. "We'll break into smaller groups now to discuss specific assignments and schedules." His accent gave the words a crisp authority. "Arthur, Antonio, and I will coordinate the rotation details and get the details out to the group leaders."

The change in atmosphere was immediate. Chairs scraped back as people rose, conversations resuming at normal volume. Groups began to form—shifters gravitating toward each other, the clinic staff clustering near Douglas and Jacinth. Aleksei gestured for Dimitri and the twins to join him. The four vampires moved to a corner of the dining room, their expressions serious.

Katerina tugged at Beth's sleeve. "Let's grab some cookies before Remi inhales them all."

"I might leave one for you," Remi said, smirking as he reached for the platter.

Beth allowed herself to be pulled along, though her gaze lingered on Tyr's tall form. His casual demeanor from earlier had vanished completely, replaced by the focused intensity she remembered from their first meeting. Whatever Aleksei wanted to discuss, it was clearly important.

Tyr followed Aleksei and Dimitri to one side of the large dining room, Tobi close on his heels. Aleksei's keen green eyes swept over the twins, assessing.

"Update on the warehouse construction," he commanded, his accent giving the words a clipped precision.

Tyr straightened instinctively under that intense gaze. Even after centuries, Aleksei's battlefield presence still commanded immediate respect. The ancient Scythian warrior might be wearing modern clothes, but his bearing remained that of a general expecting reports from his officers.

"Joe's crew is making impressive progress," Tyr replied. "They've even pulled some all-nighters to expedite the vampire quarters—they know we need those ready as soon as possible. The exterior modifications are complete, and the steel shutters for the windows are installed and operational."

Tobi nodded, picking up the thread seamlessly as they'd done for centuries. "The vampire suites should be done in about a week, then they'll start on the apartments on the 3rd floor for the Companions." His usual playfulness had vanished, replaced by professional efficiency.

"The basement reinforcements are taking longer than expected," Tyr added. "The bunker specifications Lord Damien sent require additional structural supports."

"Where are the Companions staying now?" Aleksei asked, his voice maintaining that quiet intensity that only vampire hearing could detect.

Dimitri gestured toward the inn's upper floors with a subtle tilt of his head. "Here at the Inn. Angus and Renee have given them the entire third floor."

Tyr nodded, adding, "We're in regular contact with the Companions, coordinating their preferences for the permanent accommodations." He pulled his phone from his pocket, displaying a spreadsheet. "Each one's suite will be finished in the color scheme they request. Most have already submitted their preferences."

Antonio, who had been talking to Joe, crossed the room to join them. "Four vampires is insufficient coverage," he told Aleksei, his cultured voice carrying that subtle Italian inflection despite his perfect English. "Once the quarters are finished, we will need more security personnel as soon as possible. The clinic, restaurant, pack house - and soon the bank - these locations cannot be adequately secured with only the four of us."

At Aleksei's nod of assent, Tyr exchanged a quick glance with his twin. They'd been thinking the same thing but hadn't wanted to question Antonio's judgment.

"Our quarters are actually finished," Tyr offered, turning back to Aleksei. "We could temporarily double up to make room if needed."

Dimitri inclined his head in agreement, his caramel skin gleaming in the soft lighting. "I will also share quarters if needed."

Antonio's face gave nothing away, but Tyr caught the slight approving nod. The ancient warrior had never been one for effusive praise, even after millennia.

"I will contact Lord Damien tonight," Aleksei decided, his accent more pronounced as he considered the logistics. "Three more of the clan can come immediately. Once the second floor is completed next week, we can bring another half dozen."

"That should give us sufficient coverage for the current threat assessment," Antonio observed, his fingers tapping thoughtfully against his thigh. "Though I would prefer at least twelve total for optimal rotation."

Aleksei's stern gaze shifted to Antonio. "You have Shadow Guard to manage. The company's reputation cannot suffer while we handle this situation. I have conferred with Lord Damien on this matter, and we are sending Jochi to coordinate security forces."

Tyr's eyebrows rose at the mention of Jochi. The Mongolian vampire's tactical expertise was legendary within the clan. As the son of Genghis Khan, he'd commanded armies before being turned. Having him take point on security would be a significant advantage.

"That would be most welcome," Antonio said, his cultured voice carrying genuine relief. "Shadow Guard's client list has been growing just in the month since we opened our office here in the Hudson Valley. Having Jochi handle the protection details will allow me to focus on the company's broader operations."

Tyr shifted his weight, considering this new development. "Will Saikhan be coming as well?"

The corners of Aleksei's mouth twitched slightly. "Of course. Where Jochi goes, Saikhan follows." His green eyes held a hint of amusement. "They have been inseparable since he turned her eight centuries ago."

Tyr nodded, remembering the petite vampire with her elaborate braids and fierce fighting spirit. Despite her eternally teenage appearance, Saikhan was one of the most formidable warriors in the clan. The fact that she'd once been from an enemy tribe conquered by Jochi during the Mongol expansion into Siberia only added layers to their complex relationship.

Though not romantic partners, their bond was unshakeable. Jochi had recognized something in the young noble girl from an enemy tribe - a strength of spirit that matched his own. He'd offered her immortality when she lay dying from wounds sustained defending her people. Now, centuries later, they moved through the world as a perfectly synchronized unit, their shared history and cultural heritage binding them together in ways few others could understand.

"Having both of them here will be advantageous," Antonio observed, his cultured voice thoughtful. "Their tactical experience is considerable."

"I will speak with Angus tonight about reserving more rooms for the Companions who are arriving with our reinforcements," Antonio said. "The Companions will need orientation once they arrive. Tyr, you and Tobi will handle this. Ensure they understand the local dynamics with the shifters and Djinn."

Tyr nodded, accepting the assignment. "Of course. We'll make sure they're properly briefed on the situation here."

From across the room, Tyr caught Beth's scent - that unique blend of vanilla and wildflowers with the underlying notes of her feline nature. His gaze found her automatically, watching as she poured herself a steaming mug of hot cider. The fragrance of mulled spices reached him instantly - sweet apples mingled with cinnamon, cloves and nutmeg. His gaze lingered on the graceful curve of her neck as her pale blonde hair fell forward, creating an intimate curtain while she savored the warm drink.

As if sensing his gaze, she glanced up, their eyes connecting across the crowded dining room.

The jolt of awareness that shot through him was immediate and potent. His vampire senses heightened, zeroing in on her completely—the slight flush rising to her cheeks, the almost imperceptible quickening of her heartbeat, the way her pupils dilated when she met his gaze. His own body responded instinctively, a rush of heat flowing through him that had nothing to do with feeding.

Beth didn't look away as she might have days ago. Instead, she held his gaze, a small, shy smile curving her lips. His centuries of existence narrowed to this single perfect moment—her stormy blue-gray eyes holding his, the faint pink tinting her fair cheeks, the gentle curve of her smile. His keen hearing picked up the slight catch in her breathing when he allowed his own lips to curve upward in response.

An elbow jabbed into his ribs, breaking the spell.

"Earth to Tyr," Tobi muttered under his breath, low enough that only vampire hearing could detect it. "Antonio asked you a question."

Tyr blinked, dragging his attention back to the conversation at hand. Antonio's piercing gaze held no amusement, only sharp assessment.

"I apologize," Tyr said, straightening his posture. "Could you repeat the question?"

Antonio's expression remained neutral, but Tyr caught the knowing glint in the older vampire's eyes. "I asked if you've completed the security assessment of Dr. McConnell's home."

Aleksei's green eyes narrowed imperceptibly, his gaze flicking between Tyr and Beth before returning to fix on Tyr with predatory focus.

"Yes," Tyr replied, forcing his mind back to their security discussion. "We did the walk-through, and we've already ordered the necessary equipment—motion sensors, reinforced locks, and the digital surveillance package. We're just waiting on that. Tobi and I can handle the installation of the security system, once it arrives"

"Excellent," Antonio nodded, his long fingers steepling together. "Timeline?"

Tyr pulled his phone from his pocket, quickly navigating to his email.

"The equipment should arrive tomorrow," he reported, scanning the delivery details.

Tobi leaned over his shoulder to peek at the screen. "Cool. We can start tomorrow night then. Probably just two nights to complete the installation."

Aleksei's expression remained impassive, but Tyr caught the slight nod of approval. The ancient warrior always appreciated efficiency.

"We've also completed the assessment of the wolf shifters' pack house," Tobi added. He pulled up the schematics on his phone, expanding the display so the others could see. "It's going to be complex. The house itself is massive—ten bedrooms, five full bathrooms, four half-baths, and four separate entrances. And dozens of windows. And that's just the house. The property extends over five acres, heavily wooded, with multiple outbuildings and natural blind spots."

"While the alpha, Joe, and his wife are the only permanent residents, the pack house serves as both guest house and community center for the wolves," Tyr explained, scrolling through his digital notes. "Joe explained that pack members who need temporary housing stay there, and they frequently host visiting wolf shifters, as well as social gatherings for the pack."

Antonio's eyes narrowed thoughtfully. "Difficult to secure."

"Precisely," Tyr agreed. "We'll need a multilayered approach—perimeter sensors around the property boundaries, focused surveillance on the approaches to the house, and a more comprehensive system for the house itself."

"The wolves won't appreciate excessive monitoring inside their den," Antonio observed, his voice carrying centuries of diplomatic experience.

"No," Tyr acknowledged. "We've discussed this with Joe. The internal systems will focus on entry points rather than living spaces. Privacy is a priority."

Dimitri tilted his head slightly, his desert-dark eyes thoughtful. "Are any of the wolf shifters planning to come out publicly?"

Tyr watched as Antonio shook his head, the movement almost imperceptible. "No. Lord Damien and the wolf alpha have agreed that having the Maine Coon shifters as the public face of the community is strategically sound. The wolves will remain in the background for now."

"Actually," Tobi interjected, his voice uncharacteristically measured for once, "there's a connection we should be aware of." He glanced at Tyr, who nodded encouragingly. "Layla, the caracal shifter who's temporarily staying at the pack house with her young son, is the sister of Tamera Kazakis."

"Ah, yes," Dimitri nodded in recognition. "The woman who was rescued from Morocco."

"Exactly," Tobi confirmed. "And Tamera is married to Kester Kazakis, who's definitely public as the owner of the Greek restaurant."

Antonio frowned slightly, seeing the security implications immediately. "So while the wolves themselves aren't coming out, their pack house is housing someone with a direct connection to one of our public shifters."

"Which makes the pack house a potential target through association," Aleksei concluded, his military mind instantly grasping the strategic vulnerability. "Any threat researching the Kazakis family could discover that connection."

"Joe mentioned they've been keeping Layla's presence quiet," Tyr added. "She's not a Kazakis, and she's still adjusting to life outside the compound where she was held. But in today's world of social media and surveillance..."

"One photo, one mention online," Antonio nodded, "and the connection becomes clear."

"We'll need to upgrade the pack house security to highest priority," Aleksei decided. "Especially with a child involved."

Tyr nodded in agreement, his mind already calculating how they would redistribute their limited resources. "The electronic security systems will help, but with a property that size..."

"The pack house presents unique challenges," Antonio said thoughtfully. "Unlike the clinic or restaurant, it's a residence, and on a massive wooded property. Furthermore, due to it's nature as a pack house, people other than those residing there are in and out at all hours."

"We need boots on the ground," Tobi finished his thought, as he often did. "Or wings in the air."

Aleksei's gaze turned calculating. "You're suggesting a permanent night watch at the pack house?"

"Yes," Tyr backed up his brother, straightening under the ancient warrior's scrutiny. "At least one vampire on patrol from sunset to sunrise. The property has excellent vantage points for aerial surveillance. We could maintain a perimeter watch without intruding on the wolves' privacy."

Antonio's fingers tapped a contemplative rhythm against his thigh. "With only four of us currently available, a permanent night watch would stretch our resources very thin."

"True," Tyr acknowledged. "But once the reinforcements arrive next week, we'll have more flexibility in our rotation."

"The pack house has both tactical and symbolic value," Dimitri added, his voice carrying the quiet authority of centuries. "It's the heart of the wolf community. An attack there would be devastating to morale throughout the shifter population."

Aleksei inclined his head fractionally at Dimitri's assessment. "Certainly the children must be protected at all costs. The shifter communities place great value on their young ones. As they should."

"The young ones also represent our future cooperation," Antonio observed in his quiet manner. "The next generation who might grow up seeing vampires as allies rather than enemies."

Tyr felt a surge of protectiveness at the thought of the small caracal cub he'd glimpsed playing in the pack house yard two nights ago. The boy couldn't have been more than five or six, his laughter carrying across the property as he chased fireflies in the twilight.

"Until our numbers increase, perhaps we could coordinate with the Djinn," Tyr suggested. "They don't require sleep as we do. If they could provide additional coverage during critical hours..."

Antonio nodded slowly. "A reasonable proposal. I'll discuss it with Arthur before we leave tonight."

"In the meantime," Aleksei decided, "we will establish the night watch with our current personnel. Tyr, you'll take the first rotation tomorrow night. Familiarize yourself with the property boundaries and optimal surveillance positions."

"Yes, sir," Tyr responded automatically, the formal address slipping out in response to Aleksei's commanding tone.

Antonio's expression settled into quiet satisfaction. "We have a plan, then. The security installations at both the pack house and Dr. McConnell's residence will be the priority, while construction proceeds on our quarters.

Antonio looked thoughtful as he considered their limited resources. "In the meantime, we'll need to stagger roving patrols between the restaurant and pack house tonight. The clinic remains our primary concern - its public yet isolated location and the connection to Katerina makes it the most likely target. I want at least one of us there at all times. Once reinforcements arrive, we'll have someone consistently at the pack house."

Tyr nodded, already calculating patrol routes in his mind. The clinic sat exposed on the main road, its parking lot visible from multiple angles. The pack house at least had the advantage of a more secluded location, set back from the road and surrounded by dense forest.

"Dimitri will take the clinic for the rest of tonight," Antonio decided, his accent more pronounced as he shifted into tactical planning. "Tyr, take the pack house surveillance, and Tobi, you are roving."

"Yes, sir," Tyr and Tobi both responded automatically, their voices blending.

"Maintain radio contact at all times," Antonio instructed, his formal bearing emphasizing the gravity of their task. "If you spot anything suspicious, alert the entire team immediately. We cannot afford gaps in our coverage, not with so few of us available."

Tyr caught Tobi's slight nod of agreement. His twin's usual playfulness had vanished completely, replaced by the focused intensity they'd developed during centuries of working together. They'd perfected their coordinated surveillance techniques long ago, seamlessly trading positions to maintain optimal coverage while conserving energy.

Aleksei straightened, his warrior's bearing becoming even more pronounced. "I will return to New York City tonight to brief Lord Damien on our progress and arrangements. Three vampires and their Companions will arrive tomorrow evening to reinforce our numbers. Antonio, I'll send you the names of those arriving once I verify with Lord Damien."

Antonio nodded. "Understood."

"Dismissed," Aleksei said simply, his accent clipping the word.

The small group dispersed, Antonio already pulling out his phone to begin coordinating the logistics. Tyr watched as Aleksei moved with predatory grace toward the inn's entrance.

Tyr watched through the inn's front windows as Aleksei stepped onto the wraparound porch. The ancient warrior paused, his shaggy blond hair catching the moonlight. In one fluid motion, Aleksei's form shimmered and shifted. Where the vampire had stood moments before, a massive golden eagle now perched on the porch railing.

While eagles weren't naturally nocturnal hunters, the vampire magic amplified their already impressive vision. What would be merely decent low-light vision in a normal eagle became true night hunting capability in their transformed state.

Tyr had learned this from Aleksei himself, centuries ago when the ancient warrior first taught him to master his raptor form. The vampire magic didn't just enhance their physical capabilities - it bridged the gap between the eagle's natural abilities and what they needed for nocturnal surveillance.

The raptor's dark green eyes, unchanged from Aleksei's human form, swept the property in one final assessment. Powerful wings spread wide, catching the night breeze. With a single powerful thrust, the golden eagle launched from the railing, wings spread wide as Aleksei caught an updraft.

Even in the darkness, Tyr's enhanced vision tracked his commander's ascent. He couldn't help the surge of respect as he watched the eagle's form grow smaller against the star-filled sky. The golden eagle form suited Aleksei perfectly - a fierce predator that had been revered as a symbol of power and authority since ancient times, just as Aleksei himself had commanded armies for Philip of Macedon and helped shape the young Alexander into the conqueror who would change the world.

The eagle's cry echoed once across the quiet grounds before Aleksei vanished into the darkness, winging his way back to Lord Damien's clan.

CHAPTER 5

Beth stood in the quiet lobby of the Country Veterinary Clinic, breathing in the familiar scents of antiseptic and animals. The evening sun slanted through the windows, painting golden stripes across the tile floor. Whisper stretched luxuriously inside her mind, perfectly content with their new schedule.

The transition to evening shifts was a relief. Beth had always functioned better in the twilight hours, her clouded leopard's crepuscular nature making her most alert at dawn and dusk. During college, she'd scheduled all her classes for late afternoon, and even her study sessions had stretched well into the night.

A smile tugged at her lips as she remembered Douglas's pleased expression when she'd volunteered for the evening rotation. The clinic had been looking to expand their hours, and Beth's natural inclination toward night shifts made her the perfect candidate.

The familiar weight of her stethoscope around her neck and the soft scrub fabric against her skin grounded her in the moment. This was where she belonged. Whisper chuffed in agreement, contentment radiating through their shared consciousness.

The setting sun painted the clinic's waiting room in warm amber tones. A gentle snowfall had begun, flakes drifting lazily from the sky and spatting softly against the windows. Only the evening shift remained now - herself, Liam, and Layla at the front desk.

"Well, it's just you and me, kiddos." Liam's eyes crinkled with amusement as he leaned against the reception counter. "You two ready for your first evening shift?"

Layla's laugh rang out, bright and clear. "You've got this," she told them, her soft blue-grey eyes sparkling as she straightened a stack of files. "Shifters Shift at the clinic!"

"Two felines against one canine." Beth's lips curved into a playful smile as she organized supplies at the treatment counter. "Those aren't great odds for you, Dr. McConnell."

"None of that 'Dr. McConnell' business," he said, his Irish lilt more pronounced. "You're family, Beth. It's Liam when it's just us." His hazel eyes softened as he turned to Layla. "And that goes for you too, lass. You might as well be family at this point."

Layla ducked her head, but Beth caught the pleased smile that curved her friend's lips. For someone who'd spent most of her life imprisoned in that compound, being claimed as family meant everything.

Beth grinned at Liam. "You're still outnumbered though... Liam." She emphasized his name with exaggerated formality, making Layla giggle.

Layla's delighted laugh joined in from the reception desk. "And you're outnumbered as the only male too." Her blue eyes danced with mischief. "How does it feel being the minority in every possible way?"

"Aye, gang up on the poor canine." Liam's Irish lilt carried his amusement as he checked the schedule board. "Uppity felines. Though I'll have you know Great Pyrenees were bred to protect against wild cats." He winked at Beth. "Even adorable wee clouded leopards."

"Good thing we're not wild cats then." Layla's grin widened as she filed charts. "Just your friendly neighborhood domestic felines."

Liam snorted in derision.

"Domestic?" He snorted, shaking his head. "You're both wild cats - a clouded leopard and a caracal. Nothing domestic about either of you."

Pride swelled in Beth's chest at his words. Whisper preened as she lifted her chin, adopting an exaggerated haughty expression.

"I'll have you know," she informed them with mock superiority, "that the clouded leopard is actually considered to be the evolutionary link between big cats and small cats."

She enjoyed the way both Liam and Layla's eyebrows rose with interest at this fact. It felt good to share her knowledge without the usual anxiety that came with speaking up. These people were her friends, her chosen family. With them, she could relax and just be herself.

Liam's eyebrows rose with interest. "I didn't know that," he admitted, running a hand through his brown hair. "Learn something new every day."

"We're also the only cats who can climb down trees head-first," Beth added, feeling a surge of pride in her animal form's unique abilities.

"Well," Layla interjected with an exaggerated huff, tossing her red hair back, "caracals can snatch birds right out of the air. We can leap over twelve feet from a standing position." Her gaze lit with competitive spirit.

Beth huffed playfully, crossing her arms. "Well, clouded leopards have the longest canine teeth compared to the body size of any living cat." She tapped her chin thoughtfully. "Our canines can grow up to two inches long, even though we only weigh between thirty and fifty pounds. And..." Beth paused for emphasis, "our canine-to-body-size ratio is similar to prehistoric saber-toothed cats."

"Okay, that's seriously cool," Layla admitted, leaning forward on her elbows at the reception desk. Her blue eyes sparkled with genuine interest.

"Remind me never to get on your bad side," Liam's warm laugh filled the reception area. "Alright, you two. This is shifter shift, not shifter wars." He gestured for Beth to follow him. "Come on, let's make sure we're ready for our patients."

Beth paused as she began to follow Liam, glancing back at Layla. "You sure you'll be okay up here by yourself?" she asked softly. "It's your first time handling the front desk alone."

Layla's blue eyes warmed with appreciation for Beth's concern. "I'll be fine. Tamera's coming in soon to back me up." She straightened a stack of forms with precise movements. "Besides, I've got the computer system down now, and the phone scripts are right here."

"Okay, you know where to find us if you need anything," Beth said.

Beth turned to follow Liam when the clinic's front door swung open, bringing a swirl of snowflakes and two tall figures dressed in black leather. Her breath caught as Tyr and Tobi strode in, their matching outfits making them even more striking than usual. The leather pants and boots gave them a dangerous edge, while their identical grins softened the effect.

Beth's gaze caught on their matching black t-shirts visible beneath their open jackets. "Night Shift: Because Sunlight is Overrated" blazed across their chests in bold white lettering. A giggle escaped before she could stop it.

"You actually made the shirts!" she pressed her hand to her mouth, trying to contain her laughter.

Tyr's blue eyes found hers, warming with amusement.

"This is just the beginning," Tobi declared, striking a pose that showed off his shirt. "Wait until you see the rest of them."

At the reception desk, Layla blinked rapidly, her uncertain gaze darting between the twins. Beth noticed how the caracal shifter's fingers tightened on the edge of her desk, her shoulders tensing slightly. Of course - Layla hadn't met the vampire twins yet, and given her traumatic past, two intimidating male figures - looking a little like dangerous gangsters - probably triggered her anxiety.

"Layla," Beth called softly, drawing her friend's attention. "These are Tyr and Tobi. They're part of our security team." She emphasized the last words, wanting Layla to understand these men were here to protect them, not threaten them.

The brothers approached the reception desk with deliberately casual movements, their usual swagger toned down. Tobi stepped forward, his infectious grin softening into a gentle smile.

"Hi Layla, I'm Tobi," he said, keeping his voice warm and unthreatening. "And this is my slightly less handsome twin, Tyr." He gestured behind him without taking his eyes off Layla's uncertain face. "We're your security detail."

Layla's shoulders relaxed slightly, a hesitant smile tugging at her lips. Tobi winked at her, his playful manner drawing a small laugh from the caracal shifter.

Beth grinned as Tobi swept into an elegant, theatrical bow before Layla, his fair hair falling forward with the movement.

"Your Vampires On Call, milady, reporting for duty. My deepest apologies for our rather casual attire," he said, his voice carrying an exaggerated formality that made Beth bite back a smile. "We were unable to wear our long black cloaks tonight due to certain... job requirements."

Layla's tension visibly eased at his playful manner, a small laugh escaping her.

"We don't sleep in coffins either," Tyr added dryly, his blue eyes sparkling with amusement. "In case you were wondering."

"Though Lord Damien used to sleep on that stone slab in his crypt before he met Alyssa," Tobi straightened from his bow, grinning. "Remember that, brother? Talk about old school vampire aesthetics."

Layla hesitantly asked, "Who is Lord Damien?"

The playful energy drained from both brothers' faces, and their expressions had shifted from playful to profound respect in an instant. Even Tobi's mischievous smile had vanished, replaced by an expression of quiet awe that spoke volumes about their leader's significance.

When Tyr spoke, his voice dropped to a tone of deep reverence. "Lord Damien is our leader. He is one of the first vampires ever created, and - so far as we know - the oldest who still walks this earth."

Beth's voice came out soft and uncertain as she ventured, "And Alyssa is his Chosen, if I remember correctly?"

The effect was immediate - both brothers' faces transformed from solemn respect to warm affection. They nodded in perfect synchronization, their matching blue eyes softening at the mention of Lord Damien's wife.

"She is," Tyr confirmed, his usually intense expression gentling. "A Djinn who captured our lord's heart centuries ago."

"She's amazing," Tobi added, his ever-present grin returning with genuine warmth. "She completely turned our stern, brooding lord into a lovesick puppy." He chuckled. "Well, as much as an ancient vampire can be a lovesick puppy."

Tyr's gaze shifted to the clock mounted on the wall behind the reception desk. His playful demeanor faded, replaced by the focused intensity she'd noticed during the security meeting.

"We should start our patrol," he said. "We only stopped in to introduce ourselves to the evening staff."

The transformation in Tobi was striking - his ever-present grin vanishing as he shifted into what Beth could only think of as 'security mode.' His blue eyes swept over them with professional assessment.

"Everyone has the emergency number, correct?" he asked, his usually jovial voice carrying a stern edge that made Beth's spine straighten automatically.

Beth nodded along with Layla, but Tobi's serious expression didn't waver.

"Make sure it's in your speed dial," he instructed firmly. "Not just saved in your contacts. You need to be able to reach us instantly if there's trouble."

The intensity in his voice made unease ripple through her. She pulled out her phone, noting that Layla did the same. Beth quickly added the number to her favorites list, where she could access it with a single tap.

"Done!" she announced.

Layla nodded. "Me, too."

Beth gestured toward the treatment area where Liam had disappeared. "Dr. McConnell is here, too, plus a couple kennel assistants in the back. And whoever's on duty at the barn with the horses."

Tyr nodded, his leather jacket creaking softly as he shifted his weight. "Liam already knows we're here. We'll stop at the barn next."

"Well then," Tobi announced, bouncing on his toes with barely contained energy, "time to make our rounds!" He sketched an exaggerated bow toward Layla, who giggled at his theatrics.

"Stay safe," Beth called softly as the twins headed for the door.

Tyr paused, glancing back at her with those intense blue eyes. The corner of his mouth lifted in a slight smile that made her heart skip. Then they were gone, disappearing into the swirling snow.

Beth moved to Layla's side, noting how her friend's hands still trembled slightly as she straightened papers on her desk. "Are you okay?"

Layla's blue eyes lifted to meet Beth's, uncertainty flickering in their depths. "I think so." She smoothed her dark red hair back from her face with shaky fingers. "It's just... in the compound in Morocco, they never taught us about the Others. The men kept us isolated, focused only on breeding more caracal shifters."

Her voice caught slightly on the painful memories. "I only learned about them two years ago, after we were rescued and brought to the States." Layla's fingers traced abstract patterns on the desk surface. "Tamera tried to explain everything, but it was overwhelming. Vampires, Djinn, demons..." She shook her head. "Sometimes I still can't believe they're real."

"Says the shapeshifter," Beth teased gently.

Layla gave a soft laugh. "Yes, I suppose it sounds silly when you put it in perspective. And I knew we have vampires doing night security, I just... it's so weird, and I am so embarrassed! I guess I somehow never made that connection that I'd be meeting real, live vampires."

"Technically, I don't think they're alive," Beth said, snickering.

Scowling, Layla swatted at her. "Stop that! You know what I mean!"

Beth chuckled, but sobered, laying a hand on Layla's shoulder. "Just remember, they're here to help us. These vampires volunteered to leave their homes in New York City to make sure shifters stay safe at night."

Layla's tension eased further as she considered this. A warm smile spread across her face, chasing away the last traces of anxiety. "You're right. I'll remember that." Her eyes lit with sudden mischief. "Speaking of the vampires... I couldn't help but notice how often Tyr kept looking at you."

Heat rushed to Beth's cheeks. Had he really been watching her that much? She'd been so focused on not staring at him herself, she hadn't realized. "He was probably just doing his security assessment," she mumbled, tucking a strand of pale hair behind her ear.

"Mmhmm." Layla's knowing smile widened. "Is that why he smiled at you before leaving? For security purposes?"

Beth's inner cat preened internally at the thought, even as she tried to maintain her composure. "Oh hush," she said, failing to hide her pleased smile. "We have work to do."

Beth headed into the treatment area, finding Liam organizing supplies for their first appointment. The familiar routine of preparing exam rooms and checking equipment helped settle her nerves after the twins' visit. Her feline-enhanced hearing picked up the approaching sound of a car in the parking lot moments before the front door chimed.

The evening passed quickly in a blur of routine checkups, vaccinations, and one emergency visit for a dog who'd gotten into chocolate. Before Beth knew it, the clock was striking eight, and Layla had finished checking out their last patient.

The front door opened, bringing another swirl of snow and the twins' matching forms. Beth's heart skipped as she caught Tyr's scent - leather and something uniquely him that made Whisper rumble in pleasure.

"Ready to head out?" Tobi asked, his cheerful smile in place as he approached the reception desk where Layla was shutting down the computer. "I'll take you to your car."

"Oh, that's okay," Layla said, gathering her purse. "My car's just right out back in the employee parking area."

"Safety first," Tobi insisted, his voice carrying an undertone of seriousness. "Everyone gets an escort after dark. No exceptions."

Layla hesitated, glancing uncertainly between the twins.

"He's right," Liam's voice carried from the doorway to the treatment area. "Even I don't leave without an escort. Better safe than sorry."

Layla's shoulders relaxed at Liam's confirmation..

Tobi snapped his fingers, his blue eyes lighting up. "Oh! You're the one who lives at the pack house with your son, right?"

Layla's shoulders hunched, her face draining of color as her fingers clutched her purse strap. A small nod was her only response.

If Tobi noticed her sudden tension, he didn't show it. His infectious grin spread wider as he bounced on his toes. "Perfect! We're supposed to head over there tomorrow evening to start with the security installation."

Beth caught Layla's gaze. She couldn't help herself. She threw her head back and let out an exaggerated "Awwoooooo!"

Layla's musical laughter rang out as she joined in, both of them howling like wolves in the empty clinic while Tobi and Tyr watched in puzzlement.

Catching her breath, Beth wiped tears of laughter from her eyes. "Sorry, it's just... tomorrow night is the full moon."

The brothers exchanged identical puzzled looks, their blue eyes reflecting confusion.

"Joe's wolf pack goes out to run in the woods on full moon nights," Layla explained, her musical voice still carrying traces of laughter. "All of the wolf shifters."

"The midnight howl!" Beth burst out, setting both women off into another round of giggles.

Understanding dawned on the twins' faces.

Layla smiled as she explained. "Joe arranged the timing specially. The wolves always run together on full moon nights - it's important for pack bonding. But I'm not a wolf, so that means Yousuf and I will be alone in the house."

"Not anymore," Tobi declared with a theatrical flourish. "You'll have vampire protection!"

"We'll be installing security on the house, and assessing the needs for the rest of the property," Tyr explained more practically. "Motion sensors, cameras, the works. And we'll be adding a layer of cybersecurity to Joe's computer... and yours, too, if you wish. But protection detail is part of it. After we do the installation part, there'll be someone slated to stay on the property for the night, watching over things."

"That'd be me," Tobi told his brother. "Dimitri's on the clinic, and you have the deli."

"We appreciate it," Layla gave them a warm smile. "And Yousuf, my son, will be so excited to meet you. He's fascinated by the idea of vampires. He's been pestering Joe and Jake with questions ever since he learned that there were vampires."

"Well then," Tobi's grin widened impossibly further, "we'll have to put on a proper vampire show for the little guy. No scaring though," he added quickly, noting Layla's sudden concern. "Just some harmless fun. Maybe levitation tricks?"

"And proper vampire etiquette," Tyr added with mock seriousness. "Every six-year-old should know how to bow like a proper creature of the night."

Tobi shook his head, snickering at his brother.

Layla yawned suddenly. "Oops. I think I should get home."

"I'll take you to your car," Tobi said, gently taking Layla's elbow. His usual playful demeanor had shifted back to professional security mode.

"Bye, Beth!" Layla called, waving with her free hand. "See you tomorrow!"

Beth returned the wave, smiling as her friend gathered her purse and coat. "Sleep well."

Tobi guided Layla toward the back door that led to the employee parking lot, his leather jacket creaking softly as he moved. Liam gathered his coat and keys, following close behind them. The door closed with a quiet click, and the sound of their voices faded into the snowy night, leaving Beth alone with Tyr in the reception area.

Tyr's frown drew her attention. His blue eyes held concern as he studied her. "I don't like you being here in the clinic alone."

"I'll be fine," Beth assured him, straightening some supplies on the counter. "We have animals that need medication through the night, and a couple that need monitoring after surgery." She gestured toward the kennels. "The early morning staff arrives at five."

His frown deepened. "That's a twelve-hour shift."

Beth's heart warmed at his obvious concern. "I volunteered for it," she said softly, meeting his intense gaze. "Some of our regular overnight staff are out with the flu. I don't mind the quiet time with the animals. In fact, I'm going to talk to the bosses and see if I can't pull twelve-hour shifts and have more days off during the week. Besides," she teased, "you have to work twelve-hour shifts, too."

"Fair enough," Tyr acknowledged. "I'm off to do the rounds. Stay safe, and let me know if you're going to leave the building."

Beth saluted sharply, bringing her heels together. "Yes, SIR!"

"Smart ass," he grumbled.

Beth grinned as Tyr strode to the front doors, his movements fluid and purposeful. The locks clicked into place with solid finality as he tested each door handle, giving them a firm shake. Without a word, he turned and headed toward the back of the clinic, presumably to check those exits as well.

Her heart fluttered at his protectiveness, but she pushed the feeling aside and focused on her tasks. The exam rooms needed attention before morning. She moved efficiently through each one, restocking supplies and wiping down surfaces until everything gleamed under the fluorescent lights.

The kennel area welcomed her with familiar sounds and scents. On the dog side, a golden retriever's tail thumped against his cage as she approached. The sweet old guy had come through his dental surgery well, but needed monitoring overnight. Beth checked his water level and noted his bright, alert expression - good signs of recovery.

A chorus of soft whines and sleepy shuffling greeted her as she made her rounds, checking water bowls and medication charts. Satisfied all was well, she crossed to the cats' side of the clinic. Here, the atmosphere shifted to quiet purrs and occasional meows. A tortoiseshell recovering from an abscess drainage blinked lazily at her from her cozy bed. Beth paused to scratch under her chin, earning a loud rumbling purr of appreciation.

Beth grinned to herself as she finished her final checks. The night stretched ahead, quiet and peaceful. She moved through the clinic, double-checking each window shade was securely drawn. No need to startle any late-night passersby with what she planned next.

In the corner of the cat ward, she quickly shed her scrubs and underwear, folding them neatly on a shelf. The familiar tingle of transformation rippled through her body. Her bones shifted and reformed as pale fur sprouted across her skin. In moments, a clouded leopard stood where Beth had been, her coat a masterpiece of smoky swirls against pale fur.

She stretched luxuriously, extending her claws and arching her spine. Freedom! Her leopard form always felt so natural, so right. Padding silently through the kennel area, she purred deeply, rubbing her head against the cage doors. The cats inside responded with curious meows and answering purrs. Even the usually grumpy Persian seemed charmed, reaching a paw through the bars to bat playfully at Beth's tail as she passed.

Beth continued her feline greetings, sharing gentle head-butts with the recovering patients. Her sensitive whiskers picked up their improving health conditions - steady heartbeats, clear breathing, warm healthy scents, her wild instincts complementing her medical training perfectly, giving her unique insight into their well-being.

Her leopard bubbled with playful energy. Unable to resist any longer, she crouched low, her muscles coiling like springs. With a silent laugh, she launched herself down the hallway at full speed.

Sharp claws scrabbled for purchase on the slick linoleum as she rocketed past the exam rooms. The thrill of pure joy coursed through her as she took the corner too fast, sliding sideways before catching herself against the wall with her shoulder. She barely paused, using the impact to propel herself in a new direction.

Through the treatment area she flew, weaving between chairs and counters. Her powerful muscles carried her in graceful bounds, though the slippery floor made each landing an adventure. She skidded around another corner, her hip bumping the base of a cabinet as she over-corrected.

She tore down the main hallway, her four-legged form a blur of marbled fur. Her paws slipped and slid with each stride, but she didn't care. This was freedom, this was joy! Taking the turn into the lobby too sharply, her momentum carried her straight into the reception desk. She caught herself with her front paws, using them to pivot before launching herself back the way she'd come.

The cats in their cages called out encouragement as she zoomed past, their excited energy feeding her playful mood. Even the drowsy post-surgery patients lifted their heads to watch her wild run through the clinic.

Beth landed gracefully on top of the highest row of cages, settling into a comfortable sprawl. The metal surface felt cool beneath her belly as she draped herself across it, letting her tail swing lazily over the edge. Pure contentment radiated through her entire being after her wild run through the clinic.

She rested her chin on one outstretched paw, feeling it dangle slightly over the edge of the cage. Her whiskers twitched with satisfaction as she caught the various scents of the recovering cats below, their quiet purrs a soothing melody.

Her eyes drifted closed, though her ears remained perked and alert, swiveling to catch every small sound. The quiet hum of the heating system, the soft shuffling of the cats settling for sleep, the occasional whine from the dog ward - all normal, peaceful nighttime sounds that told her all was well in her domain.

Her leopard spirit practically glowed with happiness. This was exactly where she belonged - caring for these animals, using both her medical training and her shifter abilities to ensure their well-being.

Beth dozed contentedly atop the cages, the quiet purrs from below and gentle hum of equipment lulling her into a peaceful half-sleep. Her tail swayed lazily over the edge as she drifted deeper into slumber.

A presence tickled her awareness. Her eyes snapped open as her body tensed, claws automatically extending with a soft *snikt* against the metal cage top. Her ears flattened against her skull as she twisted into a defensive crouch, a warning hiss escaping her throat.

Tyr stood in the center of the aisle, his tall form casting a shadow in the dim night lighting. His leather jacket creaked softly as he raised his hands in a peaceful gesture.

Beth's racing heart slowed as recognition set in. Her hiss transformed into an irritated growl as she glared down at him. How dare he interrupt her well-deserved nap! Whisper bristled with annoyance, though she retracted her claws and settled back into a more relaxed pose. Still, she maintained her growl, wanting him to know exactly how displeased she was about having her rest disturbed.

Her tail twitched with irritation as Tyr's intense blue eyes studied her feline form. His gaze traveled over her coat, taking in the distinctive nebulous pattern that gave her species its name.

"Well, aren't you just the prettiest little clouded leopard," Tyr murmured, his voice carrying a note of genuine admiration that made her whiskers quiver.

Whisper, the hussy preened under his admiring gaze. She rose to her feet, arching her back in a long, languid stretch that rippled through her clouded coat. Her whiskers twitched with amusement as she noted Tyr tracking her every movement, his blue eyes bright with fascination.

With fluid grace, she gathered her muscles and launched herself from the cage top. She moved with perfect precision as she landed silently on the clinic's floor beside him. The familiar thrill of feline pride coursed through her - clouded leopards were renowned for their agility.

She hummed with pleasure as she wound her way around Tyr's legs, letting her fur brush against the soft leather of his pants. She couldn't resist rubbing her head against his knee, marking him with her scent. Her sensitive whiskers picked up his unique vampire essence - leather and night air, with an underlying sweetness that made her want to purr. Well, if she could. She gave a chuffing moan and preened

Tyr's hand hovered uncertainly above her head. "May I?" he asked softly, his blue eyes seeking permission.

She dipped her head in a graceful nod, her whiskers twitching with anticipation. His fingers sank into her thick fur, stroking with such perfect touch that pleasure sparked along every nerve. Typically feline, Whisper practically liquefied beneath his hands, each gentle caress igniting warmth along her spine.

A deep rumbling chuff - she'd purr if clouded leopards could purr, which they couldn't - escaped her throat as his skilled fingers found the perfect spot behind her ears. She leaned into his touch, her eyes drifting half-closed with pleasure. His gentle scratching sent waves of contentment through her entire being.

The careful reverence in his touch made her untamed spirit sing. Here was someone who appreciated both her feline grace and respected her as a person. She gave a rumbling moan as his fingers continued their delightful exploration of her ears, hitting all the right spots that made her want to puddle at his feet.

"I'll leave you to your patients," Tyr said softly, stepping back with obvious reluctance. "Stay safe, little leopard."

She watched him stride away, her leopard still rumbling in content from his touch. With a contented stretch, she leaped back to her perch atop the cages, settling in to monitor her patients through the quiet hours.

Beth stifled a yawn as she gathered her belongings at the end of her shift. The clinic's night lights cast long shadows through the quiet halls as she made her final rounds, checking on their overnight patients one last time.

Tyr materialized beside her at the back door. "Ready?"

She nodded, pulling her coat tighter against the pre-dawn chill. Their breath fogged in the frigid air as they crossed the empty parking lot, their footsteps crunching on fresh snow.

At her car, Beth fumbled with cold fingers to unlock the door. "Thanks for the escort."

"Drive safe," Tyr's deep voice carried concern as she slid behind the wheel.

Beth watched in her rearview mirror as his tall form stood sentinel, waiting for her to pull away. Her headlights carved twin paths through the darkness as she navigated around the long side of the clinic building toward the driveway.

She hit the brakes so hard her seatbelt cut into her chest. There, impossibly, was Tyr straddling a massive black motorcycle, helmet dangling from his fingers. The same Tyr who had been standing behind her car moments ago. Her brain struggled to make sense of what she was seeing. For a moment, she thought it might be Tobi - but no, she knew for certain that it was definitely Tyr.

Beth rolled down her window, ignoring the blast of cold air. "What in the world?"

Beth stared between the clinic, where Tyr had been standing behind her car on the far side, and where he now sat on the motorcycle, her mind struggling to process how he'd moved so quickly. Her heart hammered against her ribs as she gripped her steering wheel tighter.

"But you were just—" she pointed weakly toward the back of the clinic, then at him. "How could you possibly—"

Tyr followed her bewildered gaze back toward the clinic and laughed, the rich sound carrying clearly through the pre-dawn air. "Vampire speed," he explained with a wink. "Faster than a speeding cheetah, but we can maintain it over distance."

Her jaw dropped even further, the scientist in her immediately challenging the claim. "But... that's impossible! The fastest recorded cheetah sprint is..."

"Around sixty miles per hour," Tyr finished, his blue eyes dancing with amusement. "I know. And yes, we're faster. Eighty or so." He revved the motorcycle's engine. "Though this beauty helps when I want to blend in with traffic."

Beth's attention shifted to the sleek machine between his legs. The motorcycle was unlike anything she'd ever seen - all smooth lines and gleaming black chrome with subtle red accents. "Is that a Harley?"

Tyr's chest puffed with obvious pride. "No, this is one of my own designs actually. Tobi and I have our own custom motorcycle business." His gloved hand patted the fuel tank affectionately. "We've been building bikes for decades, improving the designs as technology advances. This is our latest model."

"You build motorcycles?" Beth couldn't keep the amazement from her voice. "Like, as a business?"

"Nighthawk Customs," Tyr confirmed with another grin. "Though most of our clients don't realize just how many decades of experience go into each bike."

"That's amazing," Beth breathed, her eyes tracing the motorcycle's sleek lines. The craftsmanship was evident even to her untrained eye - every detail seemed perfectly balanced and purposeful.

"Do you ride?" Tyr asked, his blue eyes bright with enthusiasm.

Beth glanced sideways at the powerful machine, her expression skeptical. The motorcycle looked like it could eat her tiny Prius for breakfast. "No, I've never ridden one. I guess I never thought about how they were made, either."

Tyr shook his head sadly, as if she'd admitted to never having chocolate. "You should come see our showroom sometime."

"You have a showroom?" Beth's interest piqued. She'd never been inside a motorcycle shop before.

"We bought an old Civil War era cannonball factory that's being renovated right now," Tyr explained, his face lighting up as he talked about the project. "Nighthawk Customs will be on the ground floor, along with the offices for Shadow Guard Security. The building has amazing bones - all brick with these incredible wooden trusses inside."

Beth rested her elbow on the window's edge, intrigued despite the early hour fatigue seeping into her bones. "A cannonball factory? That must be huge."

"Three stories plus a kind of observation level," Tyr confirmed. "The shifter construction crew is handling the renovation."

Beth perked up. The local construction business, owned and operated by shifters only, had become well-known in the area for their quality work. "I knew the vampires had bought a place and were renovating it. I didn't realize the shifters were doing the renovations."

"Makes sense to keep it in the community," Tyr said. "Plus, having an all-shifter crew means we don't have to worry about humans discovering anything... unusual during construction."

"Like vampire-specific modifications?" Beth asked, her curiosity growing.

Tyr nodded. "The upper floors are being converted into residential suites for clan members stationed here in the Hudson Valley. Some will be permanent residents, others rotating through on temporary assignments." His expression softened. "Their Blood Sworn will have rooms there too, of course. We take care of our own."

"So it's not just a motorcycle shop, but a vampire..." Beth paused, the term hovering just beyond reach before clicking into place. "A Residence? That's what they're called, right? The buildings where vampire clans live?"

Looking pleased, Tyr nodded. "Exactly. This will be the Hudson Valley Residence for our clan. Although it's not our clan headquarters, Lord Damien wants a permanent Residence for those of us relocating here to help protect the shifter community. The security offices give us a legitimate cover for being so active at night."

Beth tilted her head, curiosity getting the better of her exhaustion. "What are the Blood Sworn?"

He shifted on his motorcycle, his expression growing thoughtful. "They're human donors who've taken formal oaths of allegiance to our clan. It's not a decision made lightly - they become part of our extended family."

"They're well compensated," he continued. "Full housing, meals, comprehensive medical insurance - everything is provided. Many have been with us for decades." His voice carried obvious pride. "Some even have children who grew up in the clan and chose to become Blood Sworn themselves when they come of age."

"That's..." Beth trailed off, struggling to wrap her mind around the concept. A whole community of humans willingly living with vampires, giving their blood, raising their children in that environment? "I mean, don't get me wrong, it sounds amazing but also kind of... scary? Not in a bad way," she rushed to add, not wanting to offend him. "Just the idea of humans choosing to dedicate their entire lives to serving vampires. It must take incredible trust on both sides."

Tyr's grin widened at her reaction. "Not quite what you expected from the stories, is it?"

"Not at all!" She stifled another yawn, realizing how long they'd been talking. The sky had begun lightening ever so slightly at the horizon - dawn wasn't far off.

"You should come see the Residence," Tyr said, his whole demeanor shifting from casual to animated. "The ground floor is mostly finished now except the workshop where we actually build the motorcycles. Then living quarters on the second and third floors, which they're working on now. The observatory lounge above the third floor is finished and it's spectacular. Would you like a tour on your next evening off?"

Beth perked up with interest, pushing aside her exhaustion. "Really? That would be amazing." She dug her phone from her coat pocket, pulling up her work schedule. "I'm off tomorrow, but that's probably too soon..."

"Tomorrow works perfectly," Tyr assured her. "I'll be there anyway, overseeing some deliveries for the shop. Come by just after sunset?" His fingers tapped the motorcycle's handlebar as he gave her the address.

"Sunset's around five-thirty now," Beth mused, making a note in her phone. "So maybe six?"

"Six is perfect." Tyr's smile warmed his entire face. "I'll meet you at the main entrance... you can't miss the big roll-up bay door. The construction crews will be gone by then, so I can give you the full tour without dodging ladders and paint cans. Not to mention all the noise."

"It's a date," Beth said, then immediately felt heat rush to her cheeks. "I mean, not a date-date, just... you know, an appointment. To see the building."

Tyr's rich laugh filled the pre-dawn air, and he winked at her. "An appointment it is. Though I wouldn't object if you wanted to call it a date."

Beth's cheeks warmed, a flutter of anticipation stirring in her chest. "Six o'clock tomorrow," she managed, tucking a strand of pale blonde hair behind her ear while trying to maintain an air of nonchalance. "I'll be there."

CHAPTER 6

Beth slowed her Prius as she approached Nighthawk Customs. At the end of the street, a massive brick building loomed, set back from the road behind a curved driveway. The substantial brick structure commanded attention, its weathered red facade speaking of history and permanence. Tall, arched windows marched in symmetrical rows across both floors, their decorative stonework catching the sun. High clerestory windows running along the roof ridge softened the warehouse's utilitarian nature.

Dense woods pressed close to the back and far side of the building, their bare winter branches creating a natural barrier. The trees reminded her of protective sentinels standing guard over the property.

Despite its imposing presence, the structure maintained a welcoming atmosphere - much like the vampire twins who called it home. Beth smiled to herself as she noticed the neat landscaping around the entrance, softening the industrial structure's stern lines.

She pulled into one of the few clear spaces in the parking lot, carefully avoiding the scattered construction equipment.

The rumble of her engine died, leaving an almost eerie quiet. No sounds of hammering, no workers calling to each other, no equipment whirring - just the soft whisper of wind through bare tree branches. The last, quickly fading rays of the sun cast long shadows across piles of lumber and stacks of building materials.

Light spilled from the open bay door, creating a bright rectangle against the growing dusk. The warm glow invited her forward, promising warmth and activity within the otherwise silent building.

Her boots crunched on gravel as she made her way between a cement mixer and stacks of scaffolding. The scent of fresh sawdust and new paint tickled her sensitive nose. Whisper raised her head curiously, nostrils flaring, intrigued by all the new smells.

As Beth stepped inside the bay doors, the expanse of the newly renovated motorcycle shop revealed itself. The space retained its Civil War era industrial character, with impressive wooden cross-braced trusses forming X patterns overhead throughout the high-ceilinged room. Light from the overhead fixtures washed over the honey-colored pine flooring that had been carefully restored to its original luster. The industrial-style lighting cast a warm glow throughout the space, highlighting the rich tones of the wood.

To the left, a sleek reception desk of polished metal and reclaimed wood stood as the sole piece of furniture in the otherwise empty waiting area. The desk faced the entrance, positioned at an angle that allowed whoever would sit behind it to greet visitors while maintaining a view of the entire shop floor. A small sign reading "Custom Cycles" sat on the desk's corner, the only indication of the business that would soon fill this space.

Along the right wall, a raised platform had been constructed, its fresh wood still carrying the scent of recent carpentry. Upon this display dais sat a single custom motorcycle – a sleek café racer with matte black exhaust pipes contrasting against polished chrome details. The bike gleamed under strategically placed spotlights, drawing Beth's eye to its craftsmanship.

The center of the space stretched toward the back, open and ready for workstations and equipment. At the rear right corner, a recently installed glass partition wall created what would become a separate work area – its transparency ensuring the space would remain visually connected while containing whatever activities would take place inside.

The back left portion of the shop was similarly prepared for some purpose Beth couldn't yet determine, with newly installed electrical outlets and lighting fixtures strategically placed along the walls. Though tools and workbenches had yet to arrive, the careful planning of the space was evident in the layout.

Throughout the room, the building's heritage remained the dominant feature – the weathered brick walls and restored wooden beams created a striking contrast with the modern, polished concrete floors that gleamed under the new lighting system.

A door to the left of the large bay swung open, and Tyr emerged. She instantly knew it was Tyr and not his twin - there was something in the way he carried himself, a subtle intensity that Tobi's more theatrical personality lacked.

His face lit up as he spotted her, his serious expression transforming into a warm smile that made her heart skip. He crossed the space between them with fluid grace, his boots silent on the polished concrete floor.

"Welcome to Nighthawk Customs," he said, his voice carrying genuine pleasure at her presence. The way his gaze swept over her, an appreciative gleam in his eyes, sent a flutter through her stomach.

Beth gazed around the spacious bay, taking in the careful restoration work and thoughtful design choices. "This is incredible. You've managed to preserve the building's character while making it completely modern."

Tyr's hand swept through the air, encompassing the exposed brick walls and massive wooden beams overhead. "We're trying to maintain as much of the building's historical integrity as possible," he explained, pride evident in his voice.

"These trusses are original to the Civil War era. The floors too - though we had to replace some damaged sections."

Beth's gaze followed his gesture upward, admiring how the wooden cross-braces formed dramatic X patterns across the ceiling. Now that she knew to look, she could pick out the subtle differences between the original timbers and the carefully matched replacements. The craftsmanship was impressive - she could barely tell where old met new.

"The building has such character," she murmured, breathing in the mingled scents of aged wood, fresh paint, and something uniquely Tyr. "You can feel its history in every beam and brick."

"That's exactly what we wanted to preserve." Tyr's blue eyes warmed as they met hers, clearly pleased by her appreciation of their work. "The industrial heritage, the solid craftsmanship - it deserves to be honored while we create something new here."

"It looks impressive," Beth told him.

"Wait until you see it finished," Tyr said, his blue eyes bright with pride as he gestured toward the empty spaces. "The workstations will go here, with specialized equipment for custom builds. And inside that glass partition will be our fabrication area."

Beth followed Tyr to the glass partition, admiring how the late afternoon sunlight played across its pristine surface. His knuckles rapped against the glass with a solid thunk.

"Completely soundproofed," he explained, his voice carrying pride, gesturing with obvious pride to the enclosed space. "The fabrication work gets pretty loud - grinding, welding, that sort of thing. This way customers can still watch the process without going deaf."

Beth peered through the clear barrier, noting the specialized ventilation system and what looked like mounting points for equipment along the walls.

"The glass is specially rated to contain sparks and debris," Tyr continued, running his hand along the frame. "Safety first, but we didn't want to hide the craftsmanship. People love watching their bikes come together."

"It's like a workshop aquarium," Beth mused, earning a rich chuckle from Tyr that made her cheeks warm.

"How much of the building are you renovating?" Beth asked, her curiosity piqued by the scope of the project.

"The whole thing... all three floors, plus the gallery on the top floor. Though we prioritized the living spaces first." Tyr ran a hand through his fair hair. "The vampires' apartments are on the second floor - steel-shuttered windows to keep us safe during our day sleep. The third floor is for our Companions."

Beth's eyebrows rose in surprise. "Companions?"

"Human blood donors," Tyr clarified. "They live here voluntarily, providing fresh blood in exchange for protection and generous compensation. It's a mutually beneficial arrangement that keeps everyone safe and well-fed."

Beth blushed in embarrassment. She had totally forgotten. "Oh, that's right... you mentioned that before."

"It's better than having to hunt for our meals," he explained with dry humor. "Much more civilized. Plus, no one gets hurt or drained. We're very careful about taking only what we need."

Beth struggled to wrap her mind around the concept. The idea of humans voluntarily living with vampires, offering their blood... it challenged everything she thought she knew about vampire-human relationships.

"So they just... live here? And let you feed from them?" Her voice came out higher than intended, making her cheeks flush.

"They're more like family than food sources," Tyr explained gently. "Many have been with us for years. Some are retired military or law enforcement who appreciate our security measures. Others simply prefer the safety and stability we offer compared to civilian life."

Beth's cheeks flamed hotter as she struggled to form her next question. Her curiosity burned, but heat flooded her cheeks as her heart hammered against her ribs. The words stuck in her throat, her natural shyness warring with her intense curiosity.

"So... um... does that mean..." She twisted her fingers together nervously. "I mean, do they also...?" She couldn't quite bring herself to say the word 'sex' out loud.

Tyr chuckled warmly, amusement dancing in his gaze at her obvious discomfort. "It depends on the arrangement," he said with dry humor. "Some relationships remain strictly professional - blood donation only. Others develop into more... intimate partnerships."

He gestured toward the upper floors. "Antonio, for instance, has what we call a Consort - more what you'd think of as a steady girlfriend. They share both blood and a deeper emotional connection." His expression softened. "Most donors are what we call Blood Sworn, each one swearing fealty to one particular vampire as their lord or lady. It's a formal arrangement of mutual respect and protection."

"Our Blood Sworn aren't just convenient food sources," he said, his tone turning fiercely protective. "They become part of our world, trusted - allies, I guess you could say." He ran a hand through his fair hair, searching for the right words. "They're invested in protecting our secrets, maintaining our cover businesses, keeping the clan safe." A small smile tugged at his lips. "Some have been with us for decades. They age, of course, but they remain loyal even after they're too old and frail to donate blood. We take care of our own."

The warmth and respect in his voice as he spoke about the human donors touched something in Beth's heart. This wasn't the predator-prey relationship she'd imagined - it was a carefully cultivated network of trust and mutual support. Okay, if she was really honest, not much of what she was learning was anything like what she'd thought, or what myth and legend made vampires out to be.

Tyr's hand settled at the small of Beth's back as he guided her toward a door beside the reception desk. His touch, though light, sent sparks racing along her spine. Heat bloomed where his palm rested, radiating outward until her entire body hummed with awareness. Deep inside, Whisper stretched luxuriously under his touch, chuffing her contentment.

The door opened into a small hallway with polished concrete floors matching the main shop area. To her left, a short corridor led to the building's front entrance, its solid wood door featuring elegant brass hardware that gleamed in the overhead lighting.

Directly across from where they stood, another door caught her attention. Its glass window had been etched with the words "Shadow Guard Security" in crisp, professional lettering. The glass was slightly frosted, offering privacy while still allowing light to filter through.

Beth's sensitive nose picked up the scent of fresh paint and new carpeting from beyond the security office door, suggesting recent renovations there as well. The whole space felt both professional and welcoming, despite its obvious security focus.

Her heart skipped as Tyr's arm brushed against hers in the narrow space. The hallway suddenly felt much smaller with his tall frame so close beside her. His unique scent - leather and night air with that hint of sweetness - wrapped around her, making her feel oddly content. Safe, even.

Tyr pushed open the security office door, gesturing for Beth to enter first. Her boots sank into plush charcoal carpeting as she stepped inside. The reception area stretched before her, decorated in sophisticated greys and deep blues that spoke of understated professionalism.

A sleek reception desk dominated the space, its polished surface gleaming under recessed lighting. Two leather guest chairs sat angled toward the desk, their chrome accents matching the modern art pieces adorning the walls. A tablet mounted on a stand served as a visitor sign-in system.

Behind the reception area, another door - this one solid wood with a keypad lock - presumably led to the actual security offices. Beth's sensitive hearing picked up the soft hum of computers and electronics from beyond that barrier.

The whole space radiated competence and discretion, exactly what you'd want from a high-end security firm. Nothing about it suggested vampires or supernatural beings worked here - it could have been any upscale business office.

Whisper's keen senses detected traces of Tyr's scent throughout the room, mixed with others she didn't recognize. The space felt lived-in despite its pristine appearance, suggesting the security team had already been working here while renovations continued elsewhere in the building.

Beth gestured at the sleek office space. "So this is yours and Tobi's company, also?"

"No, this is Dimitri's operation." Tyr's blue eyes held a hint of amusement at her assumption. "Shadow Guard Security is his specialty."

"Oh!" Beth's mind flashed back to the meeting at the West Side Inn - the tall, slender vampire with caramel skin and dark eyes who'd stood quietly observing from the corner. She'd noticed how the other vampires had deferred to him, though he'd barely spoken.

"Antonio is actually our senior vampire here. The VIC - Vampire in Charge - although don't tell him I said that." He winked at her, before continuing more soberly. "Don't let his formal manners fool you though. He may look like he just stepped out of an Italian fashion magazine, but he's been around since before the Black Death."

Beth tried - and failed - to imagine living through centuries of human civilization, watching empires rise and fall.

"Dimitri serves as his second here in the Hudson Valley," Tyr continued. "He handles all our security operations while Antonio manages the financial side of things." His expression softened with obvious respect. "They're both incredibly capable. We're lucky to have their experience."

Beth's curiosity got the better of her shyness. "What about the other vampire at the meeting? The one with the shaggy blond hair - Aleksei?"

The change in Tyr's demeanor was immediate. His casual stance shifted to something more formal, his spine straightening as if at attention. Even his voice took on a tone of deep respect.

"Aleksei is Lord Damien's second-in-command," Tyr explained, his blue eyes serious. "He was one of Alexander the Great's generals before he was Turned, after Alexander's death."

Beth's head spun at the casual mention of such ancient history. Alexander the Great?

"He'll remain in New York City," Tyr continued, his voice still carrying that note of profound respect. "Aleksei is never far from Lord Damien. As his general, he ensures our lord's safety and handles any... complications that arise."

The way Tyr said 'complications' made Beth gulp. She had a feeling she didn't want to know what kind of situations required the intervention of an ancient vampire general.

Beth tucked a strand of pale hair behind her ear, processing all this information about the ancient vampires. "So, from what was discussed at the security meeting, we'll have seven vampires here from NYC?

"For now," Tyr nodded, his leather jacket creaking softly as he leaned against the sleek reception desk. "Joshi, Adele, and Saikhan should be here before long." His intense gaze swept over the modern office space. "More may come, if it becomes necessary. Time will tell."

It was amazing, she thought, how seamlessly the vampires had integrated themselves into the community. A custom motorcycle shop, a high-end security firm - they'd created legitimate businesses that served as perfect covers for their true purpose while allowing them to protect their chosen territory.

Tyr led the way back into the hallway, and approached another door, this one equipped with an electronic keypad. His fingers moved swiftly over the numbers, the soft beeps followed by a decisive click as the lock disengaged.

The door swung open to reveal a spacious foyer that seemed to serve as a central hub. The polished concrete floors from the motorcycle shop continued here, their surface gleaming under recessed lighting. To her right, a heavy door would lead back into the motorcycle shop.

The foyer managed to feel both welcoming and secure, balancing the building's commercial and residential needs. Exposed brick walls and restored wooden beams overhead maintained the warehouse's industrial heritage, while modern lighting and security features brought it firmly into the present.

Her gaze was drawn to the impressive staircase directly ahead. It curved upward, its wrought iron railings complementing the industrial aesthetic while adding an element of elegance. The aged wood of the treads had been carefully restored, maintaining the building's historical character.

Leading her toward a door set into the far wall, Tyr pushed open the door with a flourish, and Beth's mouth fell open as she stepped into what had to be the most beautiful kitchen she'd ever seen. Exposed brick walls framed a space that would make professional chefs envious. Gleaming stainless steel appliances lined one wall, their surfaces reflecting the warm light from industrial-style pendant lamps suspended from the restored wooden beams overhead.

A massive island dominated the center of the room, its butcher block top showing signs of careful restoration. Bar stools tucked beneath the overhang suggested this served as both prep space and casual dining area.

"This is amazing," Beth breathed, running her hand along the smooth countertop. Her sensitive nose picked up traces of coffee and something that smelled deliciously like fresh-baked bread. "I wasn't expecting anything like this in a warehouse conversion."

"The kitchen was one of our first priorities," Tyr explained, moving to lean against the counter beside her. "We may not need to eat, but the humans do, of course. Plus," amusement lit his features, "Tobi insists on having proper coffee-making facilities. He's developed quite the addiction to fancy espresso drinks over the centuries."

Beth laughed at that image - an ancient vampire obsessing over the perfect latte. The thought somehow made these powerful beings seem more approachable, more... human.

She jumped a little, startled, as a young man emerged from what was clearly a pantry doorway, his arms laden with supplies. His head snapped up as he spotted them, and he quickly set his burden on the counter. Hurrying over, his manner shifted to one of deep respect.

"My lord," he addressed Tyr with a slight bow of his head, his tone almost reverent. "Is there anything I can do for you?"

Tyr rolled his eyes at the young man's obsequiousness, sliding an amused glance her way.

"Beth, this is Mark, one of the Pledged. Mark, Beth Kerrigan." Tyr said warmly, despite his exasperation with the formal address.

Mark straightened, offering Beth a genuine smile that transformed his earlier reverent demeanor. "Nice to meet you. Can I get either of you something to drink?"

Tyr turned to Beth. "Coffee?"

She shook her head, tucking a strand of pale hair behind her ear. "At this time of night? I should probably stick to herbal tea if I want any chance of sleeping."

"Decaf?" he suggested.

"That's just wrong." Beth's nose wrinkled in disgust. "What's the point of coffee without caffeine? It's like..." she searched for the right comparison, "like blood without the bite."

Tyr's laugh echoed through the kitchen. "Fair enough. Mark, make mine a double espresso."

Beth's eyebrows rose in surprise as she watched Mark begin preparing Tyr's espresso with practiced efficiency. "I didn't realize vampires could consume anything besides... well..." She gestured vaguely, her cheeks warming.

"Blood?" Tyr's blue eyes sparkled with amusement. "

"We can handle any clear liquids, actually." Tyr took a careful sip. "Water, coffee, tea. Alcohol too, though it doesn't affect us the way it does humans. We can drink wine and other alcoholic beverages. Our bodies process them differently than humans do. The alcohol doesn't affect us at all. Our systems simply absorb it. But being able to share a glass of wine with companions or business associates helps maintain a sense of normalcy." His lips quirked. "Tobi finds that particularly disappointing... no buzz."

She nodded, understanding dawning. It made sense - in a world where vampires needed to blend in, being able to participate in social drinking would be invaluable.

"But... no food at all?" Beth tried to imagine existing without being able to enjoy a good meal.

"Not unless we want to be violently ill." He grimaced. "Trust me on this. Immortality grants many advantages, but vomiting remains equally miserable whether you're human or vampire."

Beth wrinkled her nose. "That's awful. I mean, no chocolate? No pancakes drowned in maple syrup?" She shook her head. "Never tasting food again seems like such a harsh trade-off for immortality."

"There are other benefits," Tyr told her, chuckling.

Mark returned, respectfully placing the steaming cup before Tyr, bowing his head. "Your espresso, my lord."

He then turned a warm smile on Beth. "What did you decide on?"

"Do you have hot chocolate?" Beth asked hopefully, her sweet tooth winning out over more sensible beverages.

"Sure thing." Mark's face lit up as he moved to the industrial refrigerator, pulling out a glass bottle of milk. "I make it from scratch - none of that powdered stuff here."

Beth observed with fascination as he poured the milk into a heavy-bottomed saucepan, then began gathering ingredients from various cupboards. Rich cocoa powder, vanilla beans, a hint of sea salt, and what looked like high-end chocolate chunks joined the milk in the saucepan.

"You're making it completely from scratch?" Beth couldn't keep the awe from her voice. Her idea of hot chocolate usually involved a packet and hot water.

"Only way to do it properly." Mark whisked the ingredients together with practiced ease, the rich scent of chocolate beginning to fill the air. "The secret is using both cocoa powder and real chocolate. It creates the perfect balance of silky smoothness and rich chocolate depth."

"Wow, you really know your chocolate," Beth approved, earning her a smile from the man.

"It was my gram who taught me."

He delivered her drink to her with the same formal reverence he'd shown to Tyr.

"Will there be anything else, my lord?" Mark's eager expression reminded Beth of an overexcited puppy.

Tyr waved him off with a slight shake of his head. "That's all, Mark. Thank you."

Mark retreated back to his earlier task of organizing pantry supplies, though Beth noticed how he kept glancing their way, as if hoping to be called upon again.

Observing Mark's deferential behavior with interest, Beth waited until he was out of earshot to ask Tyr the questions burning in her mind.

"What exactly does 'Pledged' mean? Is that different from the Blood Sworn?

"The Pledged serve the entire clan," Tyr told her. "They handle everything from blood donation to the day-to-day running of our households - cooking, cleaning, errands, messages. Having trusted humans manage these tasks keeps our existence hidden while ensuring our needs are met."

"They're our most reliable workforce. Every Pledged member has sworn oaths of loyalty and secrecy to the clan. In return, they live here under our protection, receiving generous compensation and benefits." A slight smile touched his lips. "Some have served vampire households for generations."

His expression shifted to one of fierce protectiveness. "But make no mistake - every donor, whether Pledged, Blood Sworn, or Consort, stands under our protection. They're cherished members of our clan. We take care of our own."

Beth caught the flash of something ancient and dangerous in his eyes—a glimpse of the predator beneath his charming exterior. Her leopard also recognized the predator in him, and Whisper purred in approval, rolling over like a hussy, making Beth want to roll her eyes.

"So, do the... the Pledged... do they actually swear to Lord Damien?" Beth couldn't help picturing an elaborate reception with humans kneeling before an ornate throne while the ancient vampire lord accepted their vows. Her imagination painted quite the dramatic scene.

Tyr's rich chuckle broke through her mental image. "No, usually Antonio handles that, or one of the lieutenants - Jai or Misha. They take the vows on behalf of the clan. It's more practical that way. Lord Damien has more important matters to attend to than personally vetting every potential donor."

Beth nodded, her earlier dramatic vision dissolving into something more businesslike. Of course the vampire lord would delegate such tasks - he probably had centuries of experience in efficient management.

"The Pledged are an important first step," Tyr continued. "It lets us evaluate their reliability and discretion before considering them for more... intimate arrangements." His gaze flickered briefly to where Mark worked, still clearly listening to their conversation. "Some remain Pledged indefinitely, perfectly content with their role. Others may eventually become Blood Sworn to a specific vampire, if both parties desire it."

Tyr leaned closer to Beth, his voice dropping to a low murmur that only her sensitive hearing could catch. "Some of the newer donors like Mark can be a little... overzealous. As you can see. They have these elaborate rituals and formalities they think we expect." He rolled his eyes. "The 'my lord' business, the bowing - none of that's required. They just watch too many vampire movies and decide that's how they should behave."

Beth bit back a laugh, not wanting Mark to overhear. "So they're basically vampire groupies?"

"Exactly." Tyr's blue eyes sparkled with amusement. "Most grow out of it eventually, but the new ones..." He shook his head fondly. "Well, you saw Mark. They mean well, but sometimes it's a bit much."

"You'll love the view from upstairs," he said, his expression brightening. "Come on."

Drinks in hand, Tyr led her toward what she'd assumed was another storage door, but as they approached, Beth realized it was actually a sleek elevator entrance. The doors opened silently at his touch on the call button, revealing a car finished in brushed steel and dark wood panels.

Her heart fluttered as Tyr's hand settled at the small of her back, guiding her inside. The elevator rose smoothly, and moments later they emerged onto the mezzanine level. Beth's breath caught at the stunning view through floor-to-ceiling windows. The Hudson Valley spread out before them, bathed in silvery moonlight that transformed the landscape into something magical.

They settled into comfortable chairs positioned to take advantage of the vista. The Hudson River ribboned through the darkness in the distance, its surface catching and reflecting the moon's glow like scattered diamonds. Beth wrapped her hands around her warm mug, inhaling the soothing steam, all warm and chocolatey, as she took in the peaceful scene.

"This is beautiful," she murmured, watching the play of moonlight across the water. She felt contentment wash over her, entranced by the view while acutely aware of Tyr's presence beside her.

Her gaze drifted upward, following the line of windows until she noticed they stopped short of the ceiling. A gap of several feet ran along the entire perimeter where the walls met the roof.

"What's with the open space up there?" she asked, gesturing toward the gap with her mug. "I mean... it's winter!"

Tyr's blue eyes sparkled with amusement. "Actually, it's designed that way on purpose. We vampires can shapeshift into raptors - hawks, eagles, owls, that sort of thing. The opening allows us to come and go unseen."

Beth's mouth fell open in surprise. "You can shapeshift?" She set her mug down, turning to face him fully. "I had no idea vampires could do that."

"It's not common knowledge," Tyr admitted, his lips quirking into a smile. "We prefer to keep some abilities private."

A giggle escaped Beth before she could stop it. "But not bats?"

Tyr laughed heartily. "No, definitely not bats. Hollywood got that one wrong." His eyes crinkled at the corners. "We're raptors - predators of the sky."

Beth frowned, her fingers tracing the rim of her mug as she processed this new information. "Only raptors? You can't Change into any other form?" The restriction seemed oddly specific for such powerful beings.

Tyr's playful expression faded, his blue eyes growing distant. "Lord Damien once told us it was tied to the dark magic used to create the very first vampires, millennia ago." He took a slow sip of his espresso, his broad shoulders tensing slightly. "No one really knows why - not even the ancients. The ability to take raptor form just... came with the transformation."

Beth watched his face, noting how his usual easy manner had shifted to something more serious at the mention of vampire origins. The casual mention of dark magic and ancient transformations sent a shiver down her spine, reminding her just how little she truly knew about these immortal beings.

Tyr's expression shifted to one of fond exasperation.

"Speaking of unusual raptors, my dear brother has come up with what he thinks is a brilliant plan." Tyr shook his head, though amusement danced in his expression. "He's decided to deliberately take the form of a white gyrfalcon - a species only found in the Arctic."

"The Arctic?" Beth queried, her brow furrowing in confusion.

His lips quirked into a smile. "Tobi figures any anti-shifter groups or government agencies will immediately assume a raptor who's not supposed to be anywhere near this part of the country, must be a shifter. They'll waste time and resources trying to track and trap him while completely missing the actual shifters they're hunting."

Beth couldn't help but laugh at the cleverness of it. "So he's basically creating a decoy?"

"A very obvious, very dramatic decoy." Tyr rolled his eyes. "Which, knowing my brother, he'll enjoy immensely."

Beth gazed out at the moonlit valley, imagining what it must feel like to soar above it all. Her leopard spirit stretched inside her, content with their feline form but still curious about flight.

"What's it like?" she asked softly. "Flying, I mean."

"Freedom," Tyr answered, his blue eyes distant with memory. "Pure freedom. No boundaries, no limits - just you and the wind and endless sky." His voice held such longing that Beth's heart ached in response.

She understood that feeling completely. Her four-legged form gave her similar joy - the perfect blend of power and grace, the ability to run and climb with fluid ease. But flight... that was something else entirely.

"I love being my leopard," Beth admitted. "The strength, the agility - everything feels so natural in that form." She smiled, remembering her earlier playful run through the clinic. "But sometimes I watch birds soaring overhead and wonder what that must be like."

"Each form has its own gifts," Tyr said, his voice gentle. "Your leopard is magnificent. Such grace, such perfect balance." His admiring tone made her cheeks warm.

Beth laughed, some of her wistfulness fading. He was right - each form had its own unique joys. Whisper hummed contentedly inside her, completely at peace with their feline nature.

With a grin, she couldn't resist sharing one of her favorite facts about her animal form. "Actually, clouded leopards are one of only three types of cats who can climb down a tree head first," she told Tyr, unable to keep the pride from her voice. "Our ankle joints can rotate 180 degrees."

Tyr's eyebrows rose with interest. "Really? I didn't even think that was possible."

"Most cats have to back down trees because their ankles don't rotate enough," Beth explained, warming to her subject. "But clouded leopards?" She grinned. "We can just walk straight down, face first. Our tail helps balance us, and our oversized paws grip the bark perfectly."

Beth stifled a yawn, the soothing warmth of the hot chocolate having its inevitable effect. The moonlit view had grown hazy as her eyelids grew heavy.

"I should probably head home," she murmured, lifting her empty mug. "I'm going to be adjusting for a while to my new hours, working all night."

"Leave it," Tyr said, his voice gentle. "Mark will take care of it." He rose from his chair with fluid grace, extending his hand to help her up.

Beth's fingers tingled where they touched his as she accepted his assistance. They took the elevator back down to the main level, Tyr's hand settling at the small of her back as he guided her through the now-quiet building. Their footsteps echoed softly on the polished concrete floors.

The night air held a distinct chill as they stepped outside. Beth's breath formed small clouds in the darkness as they walked to her Prius. The parking lot was empty now except for her car and a sleek black motorcycle she assumed belonged to Tyr.

Tyr waited as she unlocked her car door, his tall form casting a protective shadow in the security lights. "Drive safely," he said softly. "Text me when you get home?"

Beth nodded, touched by his concern. Her fingers lingered on the car door handle, inexplicably yearning to stay just a few moments longer. The warmth of Tyr's presence behind her made it difficult to take that final step into her car.

"I really enjoyed seeing the shop and warehouse," she said softly, turning back to face him.

"You're welcome anytime," Tyr replied, his voice carrying a note of warmth that made her heart flutter. He shifted his weight, as if he too was reluctant to end their evening.

Beth slid into the driver's seat with a small sigh, but left the door open. Tyr remained beside her car, his tall form silhouetted against the street lights. The silence between them felt charged with unspoken possibilities.

Finally, Beth pulled her door closed and turned the key. Her Prius hummed to life, the dash lights casting a soft glow across her face. Through her windshield, she watched as Tyr stepped back, giving her room to maneuver.

Beth's hands hesitated on the steering wheel as she reversed, every instinct telling her to stay just a little longer. Through her rearview mirror, she watched Tyr remain perfectly still, as if he too was reluctant to see her go. The warehouse lights cast him in silhouette until she finally forced herself to turn onto the main road, severing their connection.

CHAPTER 7

Tyr watched Beth's taillights disappear around the corner before heading back inside. The lobby's warmth enveloped him as he shut the heavy door behind him, his boots clicking against the polished concrete floor.

"So?" Tobi materialized from the shadows near the security office, his eyes sparkling with curiosity. "How'd it go?"

Tyr ran a hand through his hair, unable to suppress his smile. "She's... different. Special."

"You like her." Tobi's grin widened as he studied his twin's face.

"I do," Tyr admitted quietly. There was no point denying it - Tobi could read him too well. "She's intelligent, curious... and her leopard form is magnificent."

"Plus she's got that whole twin thing going on," Tobi waggled his eyebrows suggestively. "We appreciate that sort of symmetry."

Tyr rolled his eyes at his brother's antics. "She's been through a lot. I don't want to rush anything."

"Good." Tobi's expression grew serious for a moment. "She deserves someone who'll be patient."

The lobby door swung open, bringing a blast of cold air. Derek stepped inside, his backpack slung over one shoulder and his laptop bag clutched in his other hand. His dark hair was tousled from the wind, cheeks still flushed from the winter chill.

"Hey," Derek called out, spotting the twins. "You two lurking in the shadows again?"

"How were classes?" Tobi asked, moving to close the door as Derek juggled his bags.

"Really good actually." He shrugged off his backpack, letting it slip to the floor. "Aced my Network Security midterm. Professor wants me to consider the graduate program after I finish my bachelor's."

Tyr smiled, noting how their Blood Sworn's eyes sparkled with pride at the achievement. "Well done. Though I'm not surprised - you've got a real knack for security systems."

"Thanks." Derek rolled his shoulders, working out the stiffness from carrying his bags. "Went out with some classmates after to celebrate. This little Korean BBQ place in the East Village." He grinned. "Don't worry, I stuck to soda. Wanted to keep my head clear for the train ride home."

"Smart choice," Tobi told him. "Though you know we would've come to get you if needed."

"I know." Derek's expression softened with genuine affection. "But I can handle the train. It's only an hour from New York. Besides, dinner was great - got to know some of my project team better. We're working on this cool cybersecurity simulation for finals."

Tyr listened appreciatively, noting how their Blood Sworn had grown more confident in his studies over the past few years. The shy high school graduate who'd first joined their household had blossomed into a capable young man, equally at ease discussing network protocols or vampire politics.

Derek's gaze flickered between the brothers. "Are you two working tonight?"

"We'll be patrolling later. First, we're heading out to set up the pack house security," Tobi told him.

"Want me to come along?" Derek's eyes lit up at the possibility of a technical challenge.

Tyr shook his head. "Not tonight. We'd planned to just assess the house on this first visit, but since we've got enough equipment, we'll go ahead and install the interior system." He shrugged. "The property outside is another matter—twenty acres of dense woodland can't be secured with traditional methods. Once we survey the grounds, we'll welcome your expertise to identify the most vulnerable access points, and figure out a perimeter strategy."

"I don't have classes tomorrow or the next day, so just let me know." Derek studied their faces for a moment, his expression turning practical. "When's the last time you fed? You might want to top up before you go."

Tyr exchanged a quick glance with his brother. Derek was right - they'd been so busy with construction and security planning, they'd neglected their own needs.

"That's probably a good idea." Tobi's voice held a note of careful restraint.

Derek rolled up his sleeve, extending his wrist with quiet trust. Tobi went first, his hands cradling Derek's wrist with gentle reverence, murmuring a soft 'thank you' before his fangs extended. The bite was swift and precise, barely more than a pinprick. After a few moments, he withdrew, his tongue sealing the small wounds with tender care.

Derek turned to Tyr without hesitation, offering his other wrist. Tyr accepted the gift with equal reverence, his touch feather-light as his fangs found their mark. The blood carried traces of Derek's dinner - warm and nourishing. Tyr took only what he needed before sealing the punctures, his hand lingering briefly in gratitude.

"Thanks." Tyr grabbed Derek's arm, steadying the young man as he swayed slightly.

"No problem." Derek grinned, already recovering. "That's what I'm here for, right?"

Tobi clapped Derek on the shoulder. "Go see Mark in the kitchen for some food and juice."

"Yeah, some juice would be good." Derek gathered his bags. "Mark mentioned this morning he was going to be making lasagna. Hope there's some left, I could eat again."

Tyr rolled his eyes. "You can always eat again."

Snickering at the familiar teasing, Derek waved, and headed for the kitchen. The sound of Mark's enthusiastic greeting drifted back to them, followed by the clatter of dishes being pulled from cabinets before the kitchen door swung shut.

Turning to Tyr, Tobi dug in his pocket and tossed something that jingled through the air. "Now, ready to go check out the pack house? The truck is out back."

Tyr caught the keys one-handed, already mentally switching gears to focus on work. "What am I, your chauffeur?"

"Suck it up, bro." Tobi's grin flashed white in the dim light. He spun on his heel and sauntered toward the back door, his leather jacket creaking softly with each step.

The keys jingled in his hand as he followed Tobi out to the parking lot. His thoughts drifted back to Beth's delighted expression when he'd explained about their raptor forms. Her genuine curiosity and quick understanding had been refreshing. Most people either feared vampires or romanticized them - Beth did neither.

"Coming?" Tobi called from the truck's passenger side. "Or are you too busy daydreaming about a certain lady shifter?"

Tyr answered with a one-finger salute as he unlocked the truck and climbed into the driver's seat.

Pulling into the pack house driveway, he navigated the winding approach through the large property to the house. The full moon hung like a spotlight in the clear night sky, casting sharp shadows across the snow-covered lawn.

"Look at that." Tobi pointed through the windshield at a small figure bouncing up and down on the front porch. "Someone's excited to see us."

Layla stood in the doorway, her hand resting on her son's shoulder as the boy practically vibrated with enthusiasm. The moment Tyr cut the engine, Yousuf broke free from his mother's grasp.

"Vampires! Real vampires!" The boy's voice carried across the yard. "Mama, look! They're here!"

"Inside voice, *ibni*," Layla called after him, but her smile was warm as she watched her son race down the porch steps.

Tyr exchanged an amused glance with Tobi as they climbed out of the truck. The cold air carried the mingled scents of wolf shifters, caracal, and the lingering aroma of someone's recent barbecue dinner.

"Are your fangs real?" Yousuf skidded to a stop in front of them, snow flying from his boots. His eyes were wide with wonder as he stared up at them. "Can you really turn into birds? Do you sleep in coffins?"

"Yousuf!" Layla's cheeks flushed as she hurried down the steps. "I'm so sorry, he's been asking questions about vampires for days."

"No need to apologize." Tobi crouched down to the boy's level, his gaze twinkling with amusement. "And yes, the fangs are very real." He flashed a quick grin, letting his fangs extend just enough to be visible.

Yousuf gasped in delight, bouncing on his toes. "Cool! Mom says you can turn into birds! Can you fly?"

"We turn into raptors, not birds." Tyr moved to the truck's tailgate, hiding his own smile. "They're a lot bigger and... you know what? Maybe another night we can find a video on YouTube to show you the difference. But right now we need to get this equipment inside before it gets too cold."

"Can I help?" Yousuf was already reaching for one of the smaller boxes.

"Of course." Tobi straightened up, ruffling the boy's dark curls. "But only the light ones, okay? Some of this stuff is pretty heavy."

"I'm strong!" Yousuf puffed out his chest. "I can carry lots of things. Watch!"

Tyr watched as Yousuf carefully carried a small tub of cable connectors, following close behind Tobi, his face scrunched in concentration. The boy's excitement radiated off him in waves, making Tyr chuckle.

"Thank you both," Layla murmured as Tyr reached the porch, his arms laden with boxes. She took some of them from him, stacking them beside the front door. "He's been impossible to settle down tonight. Usually he's sound asleep by eight, but..." She shook her head, a fond smile playing across her features. "The moment he heard vampires were coming to install security equipment, he refused to go to bed until he'd seen you."

"It's no trouble." Tyr placed the rest of the boxes by the others. "Though I hope we're not disrupting his schedule too much."

"He'll sleep late tomorrow." Layla's voice carried warmth as she watched her son chattering animatedly with Tobi. "It's worth it, seeing him this happy."

"Mama, look!" Yousuf's excited voice broke through the moment. "I'm helping carry vampire stuff!"

"I see that, *ibni.*" Layla's expression brightened. "You're being very helpful."

The boy beamed at her praise, carefully placing his tub beside the growing pile of equipment on the porch. His eyes sparkled with barely contained questions as he bounced from foot to foot, clearly torn between his desire to help and his burning curiosity about the vampires.

"Ibni - that means my son, right?" Tobi asked.

"Yes," she smiled at him. "Do you speak Arabic?"

"Yes, but it's been a couple hundred years."

"One more trip should do it," Tyr told him with a shoulder bump, heading back to the truck. "Unless our young friend here wants to help with the last few boxes?"

"Yes!" Yousuf sprinted back down the steps, alight with enthusiasm.

Tyr watched Tobi and Yousuf head back toward the truck, the boy bouncing with each step. The security lights cast long shadows across the snow-dusted walkway, and Tyr noticed a telltale gleam where earlier snowmelt had frozen into a slick patch.

"Careful-" he started to call out, but Tobi was already moving.

Yousuf's feet shot out from under him as he hit the ice. Layla's sharp cry cut through the night air as she lunged forward, but her son was too far away to reach. Before the boy could hit the ground, though, Tobi's hands caught him smoothly under the arms, lifting him clear of the slippery surface.

"Whoa, watch your step there, little man." Tobi set Yousuf back on his feet on a safer patch of concrete. "Ice is tricky stuff, especially when it's hiding under the snow like that."

Tyr's enhanced vision caught the flash of fear that crossed Layla's face from the porch, quickly replaced by relief as she saw her son safely steadied by Tobi's quick reflexes. Her hand pressed against her heart, and Tyr could hear its rapid beating from where he stood.

Tyr moved closer to Layla, catching the lingering tension in her posture. "Hey, it's okay. Kids slip on ice all the time. It's practically a winter tradition."

"Yeah, remember that time in Bergen?" Tobi called over his shoulder as he guided Yousuf around the icy patch. "Must have been, what, winter of 1320? We were ten, and that merchant's son dared us to race across the frozen harbor."

"And you face-planted right into a snow bank." Tyr's lips twitched at the memory. "Father was furious when we came home soaked to the bone."

"Worth it though." Tobi grinned. "I won that bet."

"You did not." Tyr crossed his arms. "You fell before reaching the other side."

"But I got up and finished first!"

"After I stopped to help fish you out." Tyr shook his head at Layla. "He conveniently forgets that part of the story."

"Because it's irrelevant to who crossed the line first," Tobi insisted, helping Yousuf gather a few small boxes from the truck.

"We were about ten," Tyr told Layla. "Mother threatened to lock us in our room until spring thaw after that stunt."

Tobi snickered, his expression bright with mischief. "Mother was always threatening to lock us in our room. Remember that time with the baker's chickens?"

"Don't remind me." Tyr winced at the memory. "Though in her defense, we did deserve it that time."

"The baker wasn't happy either." Tobi guided Yousuf around another icy patch. "Especially when his prized rooster ended up on top of the church steeple."

"How did it get up there?" Yousuf's eyes went wide.

"That," Tyr said firmly, "is a story for another time." He could still hear their mother's exasperated lectures about responsibility and proper behavior for merchant's sons. The memory carried a bittersweet ache - she'd died barely two years later, dying in childbirth as so many women did in those days.

Tobi must have caught his shift in mood because he quickly changed the subject. "Hey Yousuf, want to see something cool?" He set down his load of equipment and crouched beside the boy. "Watch this."

With practiced ease, Tobi scooped up a handful of snow, compressing it between his palms. When he opened his hands, he'd shaped the snow into a perfect miniature bird.

"Wow!" Yousuf carefully set down his own box to examine the sculpture. "How did you do that?"

"Centuries of practice." Tobi's grin widened. "Though I'm still not as good as Tyr. He's the real artist."

The tension finally eased from Layla's shoulders as she watched Tobi and Yousuf carefully navigate back around the icy patch, her son's face bright with concentration as he carried his load.

Layla held the front door wide as they carried the last of the equipment inside. The warm air carried the lingering scents of dinner - something with garlic and tomatoes that made Tyr's nose twitch appreciatively, even though he couldn't eat it.

Tyr took in the spacious entryway with its warm amber glow from handcrafted sconces. Family photos in mismatched frames lined the stairwell, capturing generations of the wolf pack in various gatherings. The blend of modern furniture with rustic architectural elements—exposed wooden beams overhead and a massive stone fireplace visible in the adjacent room—spoke to both tradition and practicality.

"Would you like some coffee?" Layla asked hesitantly as they set down their loads. " Beth tells me you can drink that, so I made a fresh pot."

"Oh yeah, please." Tobi's face lit up. "Coffee sounds perfect."

Yousuf's expression crumpled, his earlier excitement vanishing. "But... but I thought vampires only drank blood!" His lower lip trembled slightly as he looked between them. "Isn't that what vampires do?"

"Yousuf!" Layla's cheeks flushed dark red. "That's not polite to ask!"

Tobi couldn't help laughing at the boy's crestfallen expression. "It's alright. And yes, we do drink blood."

Yousuf's eyes grew even wider, practically bouncing in place. "Do you suck their blood from their neck? Like in the movies?"

"*Ibni*!" Layla covered her face with her hands and let out a mortified moan. "Please, you cannot ask such things!"

Tobi crouched down to Yousuf's level, his expression turning serious as he met the boy's eager gaze. "Actually, that's a very good question.

And you deserve an honest answer." He glanced up at Layla apologetically before continuing. "We do sometimes drink from the neck, but only with someone we're in a relationship with - someone we care about deeply and trust completely."

"Otherwise," Tobi held up his wrist, tapping the veins visible beneath his fair skin, "we take a polite sip from here. It's much more proper, like having tea with a friend instead of a romantic dinner."

Tyr watched his brother handle the delicate subject with surprising grace. Trust Tobi to find the perfect way to explain vampire feeding habits to a curious child while keeping things both honest and appropriate.

"But," Tobi added, "we can also drink tea, water - any clear liquids really."

"Really?" Hope brightened Yousuf's face again. "So you're not mad that Mama offered you coffee?"

"Not at all." Tobi ruffled the boy's curls. "In fact, your mama's coffee smells amazing. Though I have to admit, blood tastes better to us than just about anything does to humans."

"Better than chocolate milk?" Yousuf's eyes widened in disbelief.

"Even better than chocolate milk," Tyr confirmed solemnly, fighting back a smile at the boy's scandalized expression.

Tobi caught Yousuf's contemplative expression and quickly added, "But that's only for vampires. We're different from humans - our bodies are made to drink blood."

"Right." Tyr nodded, recognizing his brother's concern that the curious child might get ideas about tasting blood. "To humans, blood tastes really icky. Like... if you ever accidentally bit your tongue or your cheek? That metallic taste?"

Yousuf's face scrunched up in disgust. "Ewww, yes! It's gross!"

"Exactly." Tyr tapped the boy's nose gently. "That's because humans aren't supposed to drink blood. Only vampires find it delicious."

"Like how cats love mice but humans don't want to eat them?" Yousuf suggested, his face brightening with understanding.

"Perfect example." Tobi chuckled. "Different creatures need different foods. Just like your caracal likes different food than you do."

"And just like chocolate milk tastes amazing to you but would make a vampire sick," Tyr added.

Layla, who'd been watching their interactions with her son with both amusement and appreciation, beckoned to them. "This way to the kitchen"

Tyr followed Layla through the entryway, his brother at his heels, their boots silent against the worn oak floorboards that carried the subtle scratches of countless wolf claws. The air held a complex tapestry of scents—woodsmoke from the stone fireplace, the lingering aroma of tonight's venison stew, and underneath it all, the distinctive earthy musk that marked this as wolf territory. From somewhere deep in the house came the soft bass rumble of a television and the rhythmic creak of a rocking chair. Despite its size, the pack house wrapped around them with the unmistakable warmth of a well-loved home.

Layla led them through to a modern kitchen, warm yellow lights casting a cozy glow over granite countertops. The coffee maker gurgled as she poured rich dark liquid into two mugs, the aroma filling the space.

"Now that you've met the vampires, *ibni*, it's time for bed." Layla handed Tyr and Tobi their coffees. "You've stayed up far too late already."

"But Mama!" Yousuf's face fell, his earlier excitement dimming. "I want to help them with the special equipment! Please?" He turned pleading eyes to his mother. "I'll be really good, I promise!"

"It's very late, *habibi*." Layla's tone carried the weary patience of a mother who'd had this discussion before. "You need your sleep."

Tyr watched Tobi set down his coffee and move closer to Layla, speaking in a low voice meant only for her ears.

"We don't mind if he helps," Tobi murmured. "We can find some simple tasks for him - holding flashlights, sorting cable ties, opening the boxes. Nothing dangerous." He smiled reassuringly. "Trust me, at his age, he won't last long once the excitement wears off. And this way, he'll go to bed feeling like he contributed something important."

Layla hesitated, her eyes moving between her hopeful son and Tobi's earnest expression. "You're sure it won't be a bother?"

"Not at all." Tobi's voice remained gentle. "Sometimes having a mission makes bedtime easier, right?"

Layla's shoulders relaxed as she looked at her son's hopeful expression. "Alright, but only for a little while."

"Yes!" Yousuf pumped his fist in the air, practically vibrating with excitement. "I get to help the vampires!"

"Inside voice, *ibni*," Layla reminded him, but her smile was fond.

They moved into the spacious living room where a stone fireplace dominated one wall, family photos arranged across the mantel in frames that ranged from sleek modern to hand-carved wood. Exposed beams crossed the ceiling, contrasting with the contemporary sectional sofa and entertainment center. The room balanced function and comfort—clearly designed for pack gatherings while maintaining a homey atmosphere.

Tyr knelt beside the scattered boxes they'd brought in, methodically arranging the equipment into organized piles on the area rug. Yousuf hovered at his shoulder, eyes wide with fascination as Tyr opened the first box.

"Here." Tyr handed the boy a package of zip ties. "Can you sort these by size? We need the small ones separate from the big ones."

"I can do that!" Yousuf plopped down cross-legged on the floor, immediately focused on his task.

Tobi started unpacking the cameras while Tyr sorted through the sensors. The quiet sounds of equipment being organized filled the room, punctuated by Yousuf's occasional questions about what different pieces were for.

"This goes by the windows?" Yousuf pointed to a motion sensor Tobi was removing from its packing.

"Exactly right." Tobi nodded at the boy approvingly. "You've got a good eye for this."

Layla settled into an armchair nearby, her hands wrapped around her coffee mug as she watched them work. The tension had eased from her posture, replaced by quiet contentment as she observed her son's careful concentration.

Tyr noticed Yousuf's movements becoming slower, his earlier boundless energy fading. The boy's eyes drooped slightly as he sorted the last few zip ties, though he fought valiantly to stay awake.

"I think that's enough for tonight," Tyr said softly, catching Layla's eye. "We've got everything organized for tomorrow's installation."

Yousuf's protest was interrupted by a massive yawn. "But I'm not tired..."

"You've been a huge help." Tobi ruffled the boy's curls. "We couldn't have done all this sorting without you."

"Really?" Yousuf's sleepy smile lit up his whole face.

"Really." Tobi helped the boy to his feet. "Now go get some rest. We've got more work tomorrow."

"Okay." Yousuf shuffled over to his mother, leaning against her legs. "G'night."

"Come on, *habibi*." Layla stood, gathering her drowsy son close. "Time for bed."

Tyr and Tobi moved their equipment outside to begin the exterior installations. The night air was crisp and clear, perfect for camera work. Tyr adjusted the camera angle, ensuring it captured both the front door and side window while remaining discreet. The moon cast enough light that he didn't need additional illumination.

Soft footsteps approached from inside - Layla returning from putting Yousuf to bed. She wrapped her arms around herself against the cold as she stepped onto the porch with him and Tobi.

"Are you really coming back tomorrow?" Her voice carried a hint of uncertainty.

"Of course." Tyr secured the final screw. "Tonight we're just handling the ground floor entry points. There's much more to do."

Tobi handed him another mounting bracket. "A house this size needs comprehensive coverage. We'll need to map out camera placements for all the hallways, entry points, and exterior perimeter."

"Plus installing sensors on every door and window." Tyr gestured at the stack of equipment they'd brought. "Motion detectors throughout, especially in blind spots."

"That sounds... extensive." Layla's brow furrowed.

"It is." Tyr moved to the next mounting point. "With ten bedrooms, we're looking at twenty to thirty cameras minimum. Then there's running cables through the walls and attic to connect everything to the central hub."

"And setting up the network for remote monitoring." Tobi grinned. "That's where it gets fun. The whole system will feed into both the pack's security network and our monitoring station at Shadow Guard."

"All that just to keep us safe?" Layla's voice wavered slightly.

Tyr paused in his work, meeting her eyes. "You and everyone else here deserve to feel secure. We'll make sure of it."

Tobi hefted another camera mount, his expression turning serious. "Better to have security and not need it, than need it and not have it." He gestured at the peaceful neighborhood around them. "Think of it like insurance - you hope you never have to use it, but you're glad it's there just in case."

Tyr noted how Layla's shoulders tensed at his brother's words, her arms wrapping tighter around herself. He shot Tobi a warning look before turning back to Layla.

"There are no plans for the wolf shifters to go public," he assured her quietly. "Joe runs a tight ship here, and there's no reason to think the pack house is on anyone's radar."

The moon slipped behind a cloud, casting deeper shadows across the porch. Tyr adjusted the camera angle one final time before stepping back.

"But having precautions in place is just smart planning," he continued. "Like locking your doors at night or having smoke detectors. You probably won't need them, but they help you sleep better knowing they're there."

Layla's posture relaxed slightly as she absorbed his words. "I suppose that makes sense." She glanced through the window where they could see the pile of equipment waiting to be installed. "And Yousuf is very excited about helping tomorrow."

Tyr chuckled, remembering the boy's careful attention to detail while sorting components. "Maybe we've got a future security expert on our hands."

"Speaking of safety," Tobi's expression grew more serious, "were all the men running that compound in Morocco caught?"

The question hung in the cold night air. The change in Layla was immediate and startling. Her uncertain posture vanished, spine straightening as steel entered her voice. Gone was the worried mother from moments before - in her place stood a survivor, someone forged by fire and emerged harder. This was the caracal shifter who had endured hell and emerged victorious.

"Yes." Her voice carried grim satisfaction. "The ones who survived the raid were captured. Or killed."

"I don't know where they imprisoned the ones caught in Morocco," she continued. "But the ones who escaped and came here to America?" Her lips curved in a cold smile. "They're in the Sanctuary in Ohio now."

"All of them?" Tobi pressed.

"All except Mahmoud." Layla's voice carried no grief - only savage pleasure. "He was the last one. Their leader." She lifted her chin. "He came to try to get me and Tamera when we were staying at the West Side Inn. The solid earth beneath his feet turned to quicksand and swallowed him."

The words carried such weight that even the night seemed to still around them. Tyr caught the flash of satisfaction in his brother's eyes, matching the fierce light in Layla's.

Tyr frowned in puzzlement. "Quicksand? In upstate New York? That's not exactly common in this part of the country."

A sly smile spread across Layla's face, transforming her features from uncertain mother to someone far more dangerous. "Let's just say... one should never wander the grounds around the West Side Inn with ill intentions."

"Oh!" Tobi's face lit up with unholy glee. "Now that's a story I have to hear! Did Angus and Renee-"

"We have work to finish," Tyr cut in, though his own curiosity burned. He gestured at the remaining equipment. "The cameras won't mount themselves."

"You're no fun." Tobi grumbled but picked up another mounting bracket. "Always so focused on work."

"Someone has to be." Tyr handed his brother the drill. "Otherwise we'd still be standing here at sunrise swapping stories."

Tobi muttered something unflattering in Old Norse as he lined up the bracket, but his movements remained precise despite his complaints. The quiet whir of the drill filled the night air as they returned to their task.

Layla's laughter echoed softly as she headed back inside, the door closing with a gentle click behind her. Tobi called after the retreating caracal shifter, "I want to hear that story later!"

Tyr shook his head at his brother's antics, but couldn't suppress his own smile. Seven centuries together meant he knew that expression all too well - Tobi wouldn't rest until he'd heard the full story about Mahmoud's demise in mysteriously appearing quicksand.

"Focus," Tyr muttered, tossing another mounting bracket to his twin. "We've got three more cameras to install before we can call it a night."

"You can't tell me you're not curious." Tobi caught the bracket one-handed, his movements fluid despite the awkward angle. "Quicksand? In New York?" He whistled low. "That's some serious magical manipulation."

"Of course I'm curious." Tyr checked the angle on the camera his brother was mounting. "But unlike some people, I can wait until after we finish the job to satisfy my curiosity. A little to the left. Yeah, that."

The next hours flowed in a steady rhythm of installations - cameras finding homes in shadowed corners of the entry areas, sensors nestling against window frames, and cables threading their way through walls like electronic veins. They moved from room to room, then outside and back again, their work illuminated by moonlight in the yard and soft amber lamps within.

The house seemed to breathe around them as they worked, creaking and settling in the dark night while their security web grew more intricate with each passing hour. Finally, with the eastern sky still dark but holding the first hint of pre-dawn grey, Tyr connected the last component. A soft chorus of electronic chirps echoed through the quiet house as the system came online, devices blinking to life in sequence.

"That should do it. Tomorrow night we'll have the stuff to do the outside and the perimeter. But this is it for tonight. "

Tobi stretched, his fair hair catching the moonlight. "Awesome. You're headed to the deli?"

"Yeah. Dimitri's on the clinic tonight."

"Cool. Okay, I'll be here. It'll be good when the others come up from the city and we can have a bit more breathing room."

Tyr snickered. "We don't breathe, idiot."

He easily dodged the punch his brother sent his way, but his thoughts had already drifted to tomorrow evening. Perhaps he could find a reason to visit before heading to the pack house. The memory of Beth's smile when he'd explained about their raptor forms lingered pleasantly.

"Earth to Tyr," Tobi waved a hand in front of his face. "You're thinking about her again, aren't you?"

Tyr didn't bother denying it. "We should get going."

Tobi's knowing laugh followed him down the porch steps, but Tyr didn't mind. For the first time in decades, he found himself looking forward to tomorrow with genuine anticipation—not just for the work to be done, but for the possibility of Beth again.

CHAPTER 8

Having seen the last client of the evening to the lobby, Beth dropped into a chair behind the reception desk. Layla was organizing the day's files with impressive efficiency.

"You look like you've been doing that all your life," she told her friend.

Layla beamed at her. "I know, I was surprised at how easy I found it. So maybe it's a little boring."

They both chuckled, then looked around as Troy emerged from his office, shrugging into his worn leather jacket. His keys jingled as he patted his pockets, doing the familiar end-of-shift check - wallet, phone, keys.

"Everything's squared away for tomorrow morning's surgeries," he said, pausing at the front desk. "Tobi's waiting for me out back. You two okay to close up?"

"We've got it covered," Beth assured him, tucking a loose strand of pale hair behind her ear. "And our security's here, too," she reminded him.

"Perfect." He smiled warmly at them both. "You're both doing great work here. Have a good night, ladies."

"Good night, Dr. Shelton," they called in unison as he headed for the back door.

The clinic's waiting room sat empty, the last patient having left thirty minutes ago. Outside, the security lights cast pools of yellow illumination over the customer parking lot, while darkness engulfed the thickly clustered trees beyond.

Beth pushed away from the counter. "Want some tea? I think we still have that mint blend you like."

"No, I'm good." Layla closed the last file drawer with a satisfying click. "I've only got fifteen minutes before I head home. Are you working all night again?"

"Yeah, until five." Beth propped her feet on a stool, shaking her head as she watched Layla fuss with things.

Layla frowned at her. "I don't know how you can work twelve-hour shifts. Just a regular shift feels long enough."

A grin spread across Beth's face. "Ah, but it means I get three-and-a-half day weekends. Four nights on, then almost four days off to do whatever I want."

Layla just shook her head, clearly unconvinced by Beth's enthusiasm for the night shift schedule.

"I've always been a night owl," Beth explained. "Okay, let's lock up and get one of the guys to escort you out."

The words were hardly out of her mouth when headlights swept across the waiting room windows.

"Oops, spoke too soon. Although, Dr. Shelton's gone."

Layla shrugged. "We can send them to the emergency vet in town."

"True."

A moment later the clinic's front door burst open, and a woman stormed in, dragging a young boy by the arm. His thin face was pinched with discomfort as she yanked him forward. The woman's features twisted into an ugly sneer as she approached the counter.

"So this is where they let animals pretend to be people." Her voice dripped with venom. "Playing doctor while decent humans trust them with their pets."

Inside Beth, Whisper bristled and snarled, the leopard's fury pulsing hot and demanding in response to the pure hatred radiating from the woman. Her hands clenched beneath the counter, nails digging into her palms as she fought to keep her voice steady. "Ma'am, can I help you with something?"

"Help me?" The woman barked out a harsh laugh. "I don't want anything from creatures like you. Hiding among decent people, deceiving everyone. You're all abominations."

The boy beside her stared at the floor, his shoulders hunched. He couldn't have been more than eleven or twelve, and Beth's heart ached at his obvious distress.

"I saw the news." Her lip curled with disgust. "All this time, monsters walking among us. Wearing our faces, living in our neighborhoods. It's disgusting."

Beth felt Layla freeze completely beside her. Her friend's hands trembled so badly she nearly dropped the file, and when Beth glanced over, Layla's face had drained of all color. With a visible effort, Layla reached for the button beneath the counter that would summon security.

Beth straightened her spine. "If you don't have any medical needs, I'll have to ask you to leave. We're preparing to close for the evening."

"Leave? Oh no, I came to make sure everyone knows what this place really is." The woman's voice rose shrilly. "A den of freaks and animals pretending to be normal. You don't deserve to walk among humans. You should all be locked up in cages where you belong."

The clinic's door swung open, a blast of cold air preceding Tyr and Tobi as they strode in. The vampire twins' faces hardened as they took in the scene.

"Is there a problem here?" Tyr's voice carried quiet authority.

The woman spun around, her fingers digging into the boy's shoulder. "More of you freaks?"

"Ma'am, I suggest you leave. Now." Tobi's tone held a menace that raised the hair on Beth's arms.

Over the woman's shoulder, Tyr discreetly made the universal "call me" gesture with his hand. Nodding her understanding, Beth slipped her phone out, dialing 911 with trembling fingers. "Yes, hello? We need police at Country Veterinary Clinic. We have an aggressive woman harassing staff and refusing to leave."

"You can't make me-" The woman's words cut off as Tyr stepped forward, his blue eyes glacial.

"Actually, we can. This is private property, and you're trespassing." He gestured toward the door. "Your choice - leave willingly or be escorted out."

The woman released the boy's arm, jabbing a finger at Tyr's chest. "Don't touch me, you monster!"

"We're security, ma'am." Tobi moved to flank her other side. "You can walk out on your own or not, but you're leaving."

The woman's expression turned vicious, and she stormed toward the door. Tyr and Tobi followed close behind, their tall forms bracketing her exit.

The 911 operator was asking if they were safe.

"Yes, the woman is being escorted outside by our security," Beth told her. "They'll hold her until the officer arrives."

The operator assured her a squad car was on the way. Thanking her, Beth ended the call.

The boy remained rooted in place, his thin shoulders hunched as he stared at the floor. "I'm sorry," he whispered.

Beth's heart clenched at the misery in his young voice. She crouched down so she was below the boy's eye level, keeping her movements slow and gentle. Non-threatening. "Hey there. I'm Beth. What's your name?"

He glanced toward the door where his mother's muffled shouts still carried through the glass. "Todd," he mumbled.

His eyes darted up to meet hers for a brief moment, then his shoulders relaxed slightly when he confirmed his mother remained outside. He met Beth's gaze, a tiny smile curving his lips. "I... I actually think shifters are way cool."

Beth's heart squeezed as Todd absently rubbed his arm where his mother had gripped him. In the fluorescent clinic lighting, faint purple bruises were already forming against his pale skin.

"That looks like it hurts," she said softly.

Todd's thin shoulders lifted in a half-hearted shrug as he picked at a loose thread on his backpack strap.

Beth kept her voice gentle, barely above a whisper. "Todd... are you safe at home?"

His fingers worried the zipper pull on his jacket. "I don't know what you mean."

"I think you do." Beth prompted softly.

Todd's jaw worked for a moment before he answered. "Yeah. For now, anyway." The words came out barely audible.

Beth's heart rate picked up, but she kept her voice steady. "Has she ever hit you?"

"Not yet." He tensed as his mother's voice carried through the glass, now arguing with the police who had arrived. "She just... grabs sometimes. When she's angry."

Beth's heart sank as she studied Todd's expression. His young face held a weariness far beyond his years, a resignation that spoke of waiting for the inevitable.

She opened her mouth to speak, to offer help or resources, but Todd cut her off with a sharp shake of his head.

"I've got it figured out." His voice dropped to barely a whisper. "The first time she actually hits me will be the last time." His small fingers tightened around his backpack strap like a lifeline. "I'll let her do it once. Just once. Then I'm gone. I'll go straight to the hospital. Let them document everything."

Protective fury surged through Beth. The casual way Todd spoke about allowing himself to be hurt, the methodical planning, the resignation in his young voice - it was all wrong. No child should speak with such calculated acceptance of violence.

"I've got clothes and stuff hidden - a go bag." Todd tilted his chin up with defiant pride, though a kind of resigned acceptance shadowed his young features.

"My friend Jim's mom works at the hospital. She already promised to help, no questions asked." He patted his backpack. "And I always carry important papers with me, just in case."

Beth's leopard growled inside her, protective instincts - both human and animal - surging at the thought of this child having to plan his own escape from the very person who should be protecting him, nurturing him.

"That's... very smart of you," Beth managed, her throat tight. "But you shouldn't have to-"

"It's okay." Todd cut her off again, his voice stronger now. "Really. I know what I'm doing."

Layla's quiet voice broke through the heavy moment. "You can come here." Her words, though soft, carried the strength of someone who understood survival. "Any time. Day or night."

Beth glanced at her friend, pride warming her chest as Layla stepped around the counter to join them.

"We have connections," Layla continued, her gentle accent more pronounced with emotion. "People who help children find safe places. Good places." She knelt beside Beth, her eyes meeting Todd's. "You do not have to wait for the bruises to prove what is happening."

Todd's shoulders tensed. "Without the bruises they'll send me back to her."

"Not necessarily," Beth said, pulling a business card from the holder. She scribbled her cell number on the back. "Here. Put both numbers in your phone - the clinic's and mine. Save them under something your mom won't question."

Todd pulled out his phone, fingers flying over the keys. "Saving it as 'Math Tutor.'" A ghost of a smile touched his lips, handing the card back to her. "She'd never check that - she thinks I'm good at everything."

"Smart thinking." Beth watched as he tucked the phone securely in an inner pocket of his backpack. "We're here every day until eight, and there's always someone overnight watching the animals. You don't have to wait for things to get worse."

"We understand about having plans," Layla added softly. "About needing to escape. But you do not have to do it alone."

Beth nodded. "If you do have to go to the hospital, call me. I'll drop everything and be there for you. I promise."

The clinic's front door swung open as one police officer entered, his face professionally neutral. Outside, his partner was speaking with the woman as Tyr and Tobi flanked her.

"I'm Officer Martinez. Can you tell me what happened here?"

"She just burst in and started calling us animals and freaks," Beth said, her voice tight with anger. "Dragging that poor boy and spewing hate about shifters for no reason." Through the windows, she could see the woman gesturing wildly.

"There was no provocation, no prior interaction. We've never seen her before."

Officer Martinez nodded, making notes. "And you said she was rough with the child?"

"Yes, she was dragging him by the arm." Beth's gaze drifted to Todd, who had retreated to sit in one of the waiting room chairs, shoulders hunched.

The woman's voice suddenly carried through the open door. "They're animals! Dangerous creatures hiding among us! You should be rounding them all up, not protecting them!"

"Ma'am, lower your voice," the second officer warned. "This is your final warning to calm down."

"Or what? You'll arrest me for speaking the truth?" She jabbed a finger toward the clinic. "They're the ones who should be arrested! Locked up before they hurt someone!"

"That's enough." Officer Martinez stepped outside. "Ma'am, if you don't settle down and leave the premises, we will have to take you in for criminal trespass and disturbing the peace."

The woman's face twisted into an ugly sneer. She stormed past the officers, seizing Todd's wrist. "Come on! We're leaving this freak show."

Todd stumbled as she hauled him forward toward the door. His eyes met Beth's for a brief moment, and she saw both fear and determination in his young face.

Beth watched helplessly as the woman marched Todd to her car, her angry muttering still audible in the night air. The vehicle's engine roared to life, and they peeled out of the parking lot, tires squealing against the asphalt.

Officer Martinez returned inside, his expression grim. "Did either of you notice anything concerning about the boy's behavior or demeanor?"

Beth met Layla's eyes, receiving a small nod of encouragement.

"Yes, actually." Beth's hands twisted together. "While his mother was outside with security, Todd told us some... worrying things."

The officer's pen hovered over his notepad. "Go on."

"You saw how she held his arm. He has bruises on his arm from when she dragged him in here." Beth swallowed hard. "But what really concerns me is that he's already prepared for things to get worse. He told us he's expecting her to start hitting him."

Officer Martinez's eyebrows drew together. "He said this explicitly?"

"Yes. He has a whole plan worked out." Beth's voice wavered slightly. "He's got a go-bag hidden away with clothes and important documents. He said he's waiting for the first time she actually hits him so he can go straight to the hospital and have the injuries documented."

Layla stepped forward. "No child should have to plan their own escape like this."

"No, they shouldn't." The officer made several notes. "Did he mention any previous incidents of violence?"

"He said she 'just grabs sometimes' when she's angry." Beth felt angry all over again at the memory. "But he's clearly expecting it to escalate."

"And you've never seen them here before today?"

"No, never." Beth shook her head. "She just burst in without warning, and started going on about shifters. Even though the shifter is Katerina, Dr. Shelton's wife. Dr. Shelton himself isn't a shifter."

The second officer joined them, flipping through his own notebook. "The mother's name is Brenda Whitfield. Address is over in Riverside. You want me to call CPS?"

"Yeah." Officer Martinez nodded. "Better document everything now before something happens to that kid."

Beth drew in a deep breath, her heart still aching for Todd's situation. "That boy is incredibly smart and resourceful. He's already thought everything through and has multiple backup plans in place."

"Still, a child shouldn't have to-" Officer Martinez began.

"No, he shouldn't," Beth agreed. "But the important thing is that he's not planning to be a victim. He made it very clear he won't let things escalate beyond that first incident. He's got a support network ready - his friend's mother at the hospital, and now us."

Layla nodded emphatically. "He knows exactly what he needs to do. Documentation, witnesses, medical records." Her voice carried the weight of someone who understood survival. "He will not stay there once she crosses that line."

"He's got our numbers saved in his phone under 'Math Tutor' so his mother won't suspect anything." Beth's fingers twisted together. "He's thought of everything, even down to hiding his important documents where she can't find them."

"Smart kid," Officer Martinez observed. "Most don't plan ahead like this."

"He'll be okay," Beth said. "He's aware, and clear-headed and practical about the whole situation. The minute she goes too far, he'll get himself to safety."

The police officers left, their squad car's headlights sweeping across the parking lot as they pulled away. Tyr and Tobi strode back into the clinic, their faces grim.

Tobi nodded. "That woman's unstable - the way she was ranting about shifters..." He shook his head. "Pure hate."

"And she doesn't even know what we really are," Tyr added, his gaze flickering to his brother. "Imagine her reaction to vampires."

"What did the kid say?" Tyr's voice was soft but intense as he approached the counter.

"Todd said he thinks shifters are cool, when his mother was outside. He's nothing like her." Beth's voice shook as she recounted Todd's carefully planned escape strategy. "He's got everything figured out - documents, witness, medical documentation. He's just waiting for her to cross that final line."

"Waiting to be hit?" Tobi's usual playful demeanor had vanished. "That's messed up."

"But smart," Layla interjected. "He knows exactly what he needs to prove abuse."

Beth nodded. "We gave him our numbers. He even saved them under a different name so his mother wouldn't suspect anything if she looks in his phone."

Tyr's jaw tightened. "Want us to swing by their house now and then?"

"Would you?" Beth asked hopefully. "Their address will be on the police report."

"We'll keep an eye on him," Tyr promised, his expression fierce. "Tobi and I can take shifts watching the house, make sure things don't escalate."

"It's past time to lock up," Layla glanced at the clock on the wall. She gathered her purse from beneath the counter, her movements still carrying tension from the earlier confrontation. "I need to get home to Yousuf."

Tobi appeared at her elbow. "I'll escort you to your car and follow you home. Just in case that woman decided to lurk around waiting."

"You think she would?" Layla's eyes widened.

"Better safe than sorry," Tobi told her, and Tyr nodded solemnly in agreement.

"It's not likely," Tyr said. "But best not to take the chance."

"Text me when you get home?" Beth touched Layla's arm gently.

Layla nodded, pulling Beth into a quick hug. "Of course. You do the same."

"Don't worry, I'll make sure she gets there safely," Tobi assured them with a wink, though his usual playful demeanor was tempered by watchfulness as he scanned the parking lot through the windows.

"Goodnight, Beth." Layla squeezed her hand one last time before following Tobi out into the darkness of the quiet hallway.

Layla's car appeared a few minutes later, driving past the clinic toward the road. Above her, a gorgeous white falcon soared, circling above the car.

"Tobi's following her?"

"Just in case that woman is lingering in the area, waiting to follow anyone who leaves. It's not very likely, but it's better to be safe."

Relief washed over Beth as she watched her friend drive away under Tobi's protection. She raked her fingers through her hair, suddenly bone-weary as the adrenaline crash hit.

"I guess I should get on with my rounds, then, and check on the animals."

Tyr fell into step beside her, his tall form casting a shadow in the dim hallway lighting.

"You don't have to stay," Beth told him, feeling guilty at keeping him from patrolling.

"I know." Tyr's voice carried a hint of amusement. "But I will. That woman's hatred ran deep - the kind that often leads to rash actions. I'm not taking chances with your safety."

Beth nodded, focusing on checking water bowls and bedding. Her hands trembled slightly as she changed out a food dish, the evening's events catching up with her.

"Hey." Tyr's cool fingers brushed her arm. "You're safe. We've got your back."

"I know." Beth managed a small smile. "I just keep thinking about Todd. Having to plan his own escape route at that age..."

"He sounds like a bright kid. Resourceful." Tyr leaned against the wall while she worked. "And now he's got backup if he needs it."

Her smile came more naturally. "Yes, he does."

CHAPTER 9

Beth glanced at the clock for the hundredth time, willing the hands to move faster. The night had dragged after that evening's drama, each creak and shadow making her skin crawl. Even the animals had picked up on her tension, their usual nighttime rustling more subdued.

When Yolanda, the veterinary assistant who covered the early shift, breezed through the door at 4:45 AM, snowflakes dusting her dark curls, Beth's shoulders sagged with relief.

"Oh thank god you're here." Beth wrapped her coworker in an impulsive hug. "I've never been so happy to see anyone."

"Whoa, rough night?" Yolanda patted her back, shooting a questioning look at Tyr who stood guard by the door.

"You could say that." Beth's hands shook slightly as she gathered her things. "I'll fill you in on the gory details later, but I just want to get out of here. The incident report's on the counter. Nothing medical, just... someone being awful."

"Got it." Yolanda's expression softened with understanding as she shrugged out of her snow-dusted coat. "Go home, get some rest. I've got things covered here."

Beth nodded gratefully, tugging on her winter coat. Through the windows, fat snowflakes swirled in the security lights, coating the parking lot in pristine white. The pre-dawn darkness felt heavier than usual, pressing against the glass.

"Ready?" Tyr's quiet voice steadied her nerves as he held the door.

"So ready." Beth pulled her coat tighter against the light, swirling snow. Her boots crunched across the fresh powder as she made her way to her car, fishing her keys from her pocket.

"There's still a couple hours before sunrise. Would you like to grab some breakfast?" Tyr fell into step beside her. "It might help settle your nerves before trying to sleep."

Beth paused, her hand on the car door. She was feeling restless and edgy, and the idea of going straight home after the night's events was unappealing. "What about the clinic security?"

"Tobi's here." Tyr brushed snowflakes from her shoulder. "He can call if there's any issue. The diner's close enough I can get back quickly if needed."

Beth's stomach growled, making the decision for her. She hadn't eaten since her lunch break, too wound up after Brenda's outburst. "Breakfast sounds perfect. Lead the way?"

The snow crunched as Tyr walked to his motorcycle parked a few spaces away, its sleek black form already dusted with snow. She watched, admiring the graceful way he swung onto the bike, his movements fluid despite the cold.

Her car's heater blasted warmth as she pulled out behind him, his taillights glowing red through the falling snow.

The diner's neon sign cast a warm glow across the nearly empty parking lot when they arrived. Tyr dismounted, snow clinging to his leather jacket and hair.

"How can you ride that thing in this weather?" she asked as they walked toward the entrance. "Don't vampires get cold?"

Tyr's laugh echoed in the pre-dawn quiet. "Oh, we definitely feel the cold. I've got a truck I'll have to switch to once the snow gets heavier." He held the door for her, warmth and the smell of coffee washing over them. "But for now, the bike handles fine in light flurries like this."

The hostess led them to a booth in front next to tall plate glass windows. Outside, snow drifted lazily through pools of streetlight. Beth slid into the worn vinyl seat, appreciating the clear view of both the parking lot and entrance.

A waitress appeared with two cups and a steaming pot of coffee. "Good morning. Coffee?"

Beth waved off the coffee pot with an apologetic smile. "No coffee for me, thanks. Just finished up graveyard shift... I'm heading straight to bed after breakfast."

"Oh honey, I know that feeling." The waitress - her nametag read 'Alice' - tucked the pot against her side. "I used to work nights myself. How about some hot chocolate instead? We make it with real milk, not that powdered stuff."

"That sounds perfect, actually." Beth smiled gratefully.

"Coming right up." Alice's pen hovered over her pad. She looked at Tyr questioningly. "And for you, Sir?"

"Coffee's good," he told her.

She filled his cup from the steaming pot and whisked away the empty cup she'd set before Beth. "You need a minute to look over the menu?"

"Yes, please."

The waitress moved away to get the hot chocolate, and Beth studied the breakfast options, her stomach growling at photos of fluffy pancakes and golden hash browns. She glanced around the nearly empty diner - just a couple truckers at the counter and an elderly man reading his paper several booths away.

Leaning forward, she lowered her voice. "Can I ask you something? About... vampire things?"

Tyr's blue eyes sparkled with amusement as he sipped his coffee. "Of course."

The waitress returned with a large mug of hot chocolate, decorated with a swirl of whipped cream and topped with sprinkles. "Ready to order, hon?"

"Yes, please." Beth smiled up at her. "I'll have the blueberry pancakes with extra butter, and a side of crispy bacon."

"Nothing for me," Tyr added, handing her his menu.

"Coming right up." The waitress topped off Tyr's coffee before bustling away.

Beth sniffed appreciatively at her cocoa, licking at the whipped cream before taking a sip, and sighed in pure appreciation. Her eyes danced and she leaned forward. "It's good... but not as good as Mark makes it," she whispered confidentially.

He chuckled. "I'll be sure to tell him that, it'll make his day. So, what is it you wanted to ask about?"

"I was just curious about the... well," she paused, looking at him doubtfully.

"The blood drinking?"

Blushing, Beth nodded.

Tyr leaned back in the booth, his long fingers wrapped around his cup. "As far as drinking blood, it's really not as bad as you might think, not for vampires. Then, too, I've had seven centuries to adjust." His blue eyes took on a distant look. "But blood... it's different for vampires. The taste is incredibly rich and complex. More satisfying than any meal I ever had as a human."

"Really?" Beth couldn't quite hide her skepticism.

"Imagine the most decadent chocolate you've ever tasted, or the perfect glass of wine." His voice dropped lower. "Blood is like that for us - layers of flavor, subtle notes that shift and change. Each person's blood has its own unique taste."

"That's... actually kind of fascinating." Beth took a thoughtful sip of hot chocolate. "I guess I never considered blood could have different flavors."

"Of course not. Why would you?" Tyr's lips curved in amusement. "Though I promise you, we're much more civilized about it these days than the stories would have you believe."

Beth sat up primly, smoothing her napkin across her lap. "I should hope so," she said with exaggerated dignity. Their shared laughter broke the tension, echoing softly in the quiet diner.

Beth wrapped both hands around her mug, gathering her courage.

"Do you..." She cleared her throat, trying to sound casual. "Do you have a Blood Sworn?"

The question came out slightly higher pitched than she'd intended. What she really wanted to know was if he had a Consort - someone who shared not just blood but intimacy and affection. The thought of Tyr being that close to someone else made her stomach twist, but she couldn't bring herself to ask so directly.

"Actually, my brother and I share a Blood Sworn - Derek. He's been with us for about three years now. We're seeing him through college - network administration. Smart kid, really gets the technical side of things." Pride colored Tyr's voice. "He works part-time for Shadow Guard while he's studying."

"That's... really generous of you," Beth managed, wrapping her hands around her mug. An unexpected sense of relief washed through her at the realization that Tyr's relationship with Derek seemed purely practical. No Consort, then. She pushed away the question of why this mattered so much—some truths were better left unexamined, at least for now.

Tyr's expression grew serious, his steady gaze taking on an ancient depth that reminded Beth he'd walked this earth for centuries.

"The thing is," he said, his voice dropping lower, "vampires were created millennia ago to be the apex predators of predators. We were created to hunt, to fight... and to win." A shadow of ancient grief flickered across his features. "It is... difficult... to control that predatory nature and not kill when feeding."

She got it. Vampires weren't tame pussycats. Inside, Whisper swiveled her ears flat, hissing. Yeah, yeah. Down kitty. Come to think of it, clouded leopards were pretty ferocious in their own right.

Beth felt Whisper surge within her, rising closer to the surface than usual. Not with fear, but with a primal recognition that made Beth's canines ache momentarily. Her clouded leopard—an evolutionary descendant of the ancient saber-toothed cats—responded with unexpected intensity, predator recognizing predator across species lines. The sensation wasn't threatening but almost... respectful.

"Whisper understands," Beth said softly, touching her fingers to her lips where she'd felt that phantom pressure of elongated fangs. "Clouded leopards are direct evolutionary descendants of saber-toothed cats, you know. They can open their jaws wider than any modern big cat, and their fangs are proportionally the largest." She gave a small, self-conscious smile. "Sometimes I forget just how much predator lives inside me too."

Tyr's eyes gleamed with interest. "I didn't know that! No wonder you understand the balance so well."

"It's different, of course," Beth continued, finding herself wanting to share this part of herself. "Whisper hunts for survival, not sport. But that ancient predatory instinct—the perfect silence before the strike, the certainty of the kill—it's there, buried deep. We've just learned to channel it differently."

"Having a donor that we're responsible for, that we're invested in - and I don't mean monetarily -" His eyes met hers, intense and unwavering. "It makes it easier to control the urges that swell up when our fangs slide down to feed."

Beth nodded slowly, processing this revelation. It made sense - having someone you cared about, someone whose wellbeing mattered to you personally, would provide a powerful anchor against darker impulses.

"Like having a family to protect," she murmured, thinking of how her own predatory nature was tempered by her bonds with Naomi and the others.

"Exactly." Tyr's shoulders relaxed slightly. "The connection helps ground us, reminds us of our humanity even in those moments when the predator threatens to take over."

The conversation had shifted to something deeper than she'd expected over breakfast, this mutual recognition of the predators they carried within. She traced the rim of her mug, curious about the practical aspects of Tyr's arrangement with Derek. "So with Derek as your Blood Sworn, how does that arrangement actually work day-to-day?"

"It works out well for everyone." Tyr shrugged. "We get blood as we need it. Derek gets hands-on experience, plus a place to live, tuition, and a steady salary, in addition to what he makes part-time with the security company. As well, we get someone we trust and who knows about us, working at Shadow Guard." His blue eyes sparkled. "Plus, when he graduates, there's a full-time position waiting if he wants it."

"So it's almost a kind of partnership?" Beth asked, fascinated by all this.

"Exactly." Tyr nodded approvingly. "When you've lived as long as we have, you learn the value of investing in people, building relationships that benefit everyone involved." He took a sip of coffee. "Derek's got real talent with computers. It would be wasteful not to nurture that. He's not under any obligation to join Shadow Guard when he graduates, but it's our hope he'll want to."

The waitress appeared with Beth's pancakes, momentarily halting their conversation. Steam rose from the golden stack, blueberries dotting the fluffy surface like tiny colorful jewels.

Beth picked up her fork, then hesitated as she glanced at Tyr sitting across from her. The steaming pancakes smelled incredible, but eating while he could only watch felt oddly rude.

"This is awkward," she murmured, setting her fork back down. "Eating in front of you, when you can't."

A rich chuckle escaped Tyr's throat. "Not at all." His blue eyes crinkled with genuine amusement. "After seven centuries, I assure you I've made peace with my dietary restrictions." He gestured toward her plate. "Please, enjoy your breakfast. Even the smell doesn't tempt me anymore - it's like looking at a painting. I can appreciate its beauty without wanting to eat it."

"You're sure?" Beth fidgeted with her napkin. "Because I could get this wrapped up to go..."

"Beth." Tyr leaned forward, his expression warm. "I invited you here because you needed to decompress after a rough night. That means actually eating the breakfast you ordered." His lips quirked. "Besides, watching humans enjoy food is one of life's small pleasures. Their expressions of delight, the way tension melts away with good food - it's rather charming."

Beth felt herself blushing at his words, but she picked up her fork again. The first bite of pancake melted on her tongue, butter and maple syrup creating the perfect balance of sweet and rich. A small sound of pleasure escaped before she could stop it.

"See?" Tyr's eyes danced. "Charming."

Beth laughed, the tension finally easing from her shoulders. She glanced around the nearly empty diner - the truckers remained focused on their meals, and the elderly man lingered over his coffee while absorbed in his newspaper. Leaning forward, she lowered her voice to barely above a whisper.

"So... how did you become a..." She glanced around again before mouthing the word, "vampire?"

Tyr's expression softened with memory, his blue eyes taking on that distant look that spoke of centuries past. "It was during the Black Death - 1347 in Genoa. My brother and I were merchants, just twenty-seven." His fingers traced patterns in the condensation on his coffee cup. "Not long after we arrived, the plague hit the city hard. First the rats died, then the people started falling ill. We thought we could outrun it, but..."

He shook his head, ancient grief flickering across his features. "Tobi got sick first. I refused to leave him, of course. By the next day, I was showing symptoms too. We both knew we were dying.

Beth's fork paused halfway to her mouth. "You had the plague? I thought that killed people within days."

"It did." Tyr's voice carried the weight of centuries. "Back then, we just called it 'the plague' - no one knew there were actually different types. What Tobi and I had was pneumonic plague."

"I thought..." Beth set her fork down, brow furrowing. "I always thought the Black Death was bubonic plague. You know, the one with the swollen lymph nodes they called buboes?"

"That was the most common type, yes." Tyr's fingers traced the rim of his coffee cup. "Bubonic plague spread through flea bites. The bacteria would travel through the lymphatic system, causing those characteristic swellings. Painful, but you could survive it if you were strong enough - maybe three in ten lived."

He took a slow sip of coffee. "But pneumonic plague was different. It infected the lungs directly and spread through the air - just breathing near someone who had it could infect you. Almost nobody survived that form."

"I've never heard of that type before." Beth wrapped her hands around her cooling mug.

"There was a third type too - septicemic plague. That one went straight to the blood." Tyr's expression darkened. "If you got that, you were dead within hours. Your skin would turn black while you were still alive, hence why they called it 'the Black Death.'"

Beth shivered, imagining the horror of watching your own body turn black as the infection spread through your blood. "So you and Tobi..."

"We had pneumonic plague. We were coughing up blood, our fever so high we were delirious." His voice grew distant with memory. "By the second day, we could barely breathe."

Beth's hand crept across the table before she could stop herself, her fingers brushing his cool skin. "That must have been terrifying."

"It was." Tyr's thumb stroked once across her knuckles, the gesture so quick she might have imagined it. "But then Antonio found us. He was an ancient vampire even then, and he saw something in us worth saving. He gave us a choice - die of the plague or live as vampires."

"Some choice," Beth murmured.

"Actually, it was." Tyr's voice carried centuries of certainty. "Antonio made sure we understood exactly what we were choosing - the need for blood, the darkness, watching everyone we knew grow old and die. He wanted us to choose with clear minds, not just from fear of death."

"But you both chose to turn?"

"We did." A smile touched his lips. "Tobi and I had already lost our mother when she died in childbirth. And a few years ago, our father's ship went down. We were all each other had left. The thought of one of us surviving while the other died..." He shook his head. "That wasn't an option we could accept."

Beth pushed a blueberry around her plate, fascinated by this glimpse into Tyr's past. "Where were you from originally? Before Genoa, I mean."

"Bergen... a port city in Norway." Tyr's eyes lit up at the memory. "It was part of the Hanseatic League - a powerful trading alliance across northern Europe. Our family had been merchants there for generations." His fingers traced the rim of his coffee cup. "We specialized in timber trade initially, but expanded into wool and furs. The profits were excellent, especially from the Russian furs."

"Wow!!! You're from Norway?"

"Yes, though of course, that was back in the 1300s." A fond smile played across his features. "The harbor was always busy - ships coming and going, loaded with goods from across the known world. The smell of salt air mixed with pine from the timber yards..." He shook his head.

"Sometimes I can still hear the creak of the wooden wharves, the shouts of sailors in a dozen different languages."

"Is that why you ended up in Genoa? For trade?"

"Exactly. We were expanding our routes into the Mediterranean." His expression darkened slightly. "The timing couldn't have been worse - we arrived just as ships arrived from Caffa, a port city in the Crimea, carrying the plague."

Beth found herself leaning forward, drawn in by the way his voice softened when speaking of his homeland. "Do you ever go back? To Bergen, I mean?"

"Sometimes." Tyr's fingers drummed lightly on the table. "Though it's changed so much I hardly recognize it now. The old Hanseatic wharf is a tourist attraction these days. But the mountains still look the same, and the fjords..." A wistful note crept into his voice. "Those haven't changed in a thousand years."

Beth speared another piece of pancake and hummed in pleasure, the blueberries bursting with sweetness. "I've always dreamed of taking one of those cruises through the Norwegian fjords." She smiled, picturing the majestic landscapes she'd seen in travel magazines. "The photos look incredible - those towering cliffs rising straight from the water, waterfalls everywhere..."

"The photos don't do them justice." Tyr's eyes lit up. "Especially at dawn, when the mist clings to the cliffs and the water turns to liquid gold. Though, I suppose the cruise ships are quite different from the trading vessels I remember."

"Indubitably." Beth grinned at him, and drizzled more syrup over her remaining pancakes. "The brochures all show these massive cruise ships with buffets and swimming pools. Probably not quite the same as medieval merchant vessels."

"Not quite." Tyr's rich laugh filled the space between them. "Though I must say, the modern amenities are a vast improvement over what we had. Sleeping on wooden planks with rats for company wasn't exactly luxury travel."

Beth wrinkled her nose, taking another bite. "Okay, maybe some changes are for the better."

"The views though..." Tyr's voice softened with memory. "Those are eternal. The way the mountains meet the sea, the play of light on the water - that hasn't changed since the Vikings first sailed those waters."

Beth sighed, a wistful sound that carried dreams of far-off places. "Definitely on my bucket list. Along with seeing the Northern Lights from one of those glass igloos in Finland."

Tyr's rich laugh echoed across the quiet diner. "A bucket list, hmm? What else is on this list of yours?"

"Learning to scuba dive. Seeing the pyramids."

"So what else?" Tyr leaned forward, genuinely interested. "Surely there's more."

"Well..." Beth pushed a stray blueberry through the puddle of syrup on her plate, watching it leave a golden trail. "Most of my dreams weren't about what I wanted to do. They were about what I desperately hoped I wouldn't become."

She took a steadying breath, her fingers tightening around her fork. "Growing up, we - my sister Naomi and I - were told it was inevitable that we would eventually become rogues. Killers without remorse. They said it was our birthright." The blueberry made another lazy circle through the syrup. "So my biggest dream was just... not turning into a psychopathic killer."

Her voice dropped lower, barely above a whisper. "Every birthday, every milestone - there was always this shadow hanging over everything. This fear that today might be the day I'd lose myself. That I'd wake up covered in blood, with no memory of what I'd done." She ducked her head. "I spent more time planning how to contain the monster I thought I'd become than actually dreaming about my future."

The cool touch of Tyr's fingers against her hand startled her. She hadn't realized how tightly she'd been gripping her fork until his gentle touch made her release it.

"That must have been terrifying for a child," he said softly.

"It was. Naomi and I swore to each other that we'd never become that - never hurt the people we loved, no matter what." Her throat tightened. "But then it happened anyway. The first time Neil and I..." She stopped, heat flooding her cheeks. "After we made love. I fell asleep in his arms, and when I woke up, I was soaked in blood. Neil was dead beside me, and I had no memory of how it happened. I remember falling asleep and then... nothing. Just a blank where my memory should have been."

"But you weren't the one who killed him." Tyr's voice carried quiet certainty.

"No." The word came out as barely a whisper. Beth stared down at her half-eaten pancakes, no longer hungry. "But I didn't know that, back then. I lived with that belief - that I'd killed the man I loved - for almost two years. That I'd become exactly what they always said I would."

Her throat tightened as the old pain washed over her. "Even now, knowing the truth, I can't..." She swallowed hard. "I can't shake those feelings. The guilt, the self-hatred, the certainty that I'm dangerous. That I'll hurt someone again."

She stared down at her plate. "Every time I close my eyes, I still see his blood on my hands. Still feel that crushing certainty that I'm a monster. And even though I know now it wasn't me..." Her voice cracked. "Those feelings don't just go away."

Cool fingers wrapped around Beth's hand, anchoring her to the present moment. Tyr's thumb traced gentle circles on her palm, the soothing motion drawing her out of the dark memories.

"Have you considered talking to someone?" His voice carried genuine concern. "A professional, I mean. Someone who specializes in trauma?"

"I am, actually." Beth managed a watery smile. "Dr. Harrison, a shifter. Well, obviously. She's been helping me work through everything. Naomi too, my sister. Sometimes we go together for joint sessions."

"Good. That's really good." Tyr's fingers squeezed hers gently. "Trauma like that needs proper care and healing."

Beth took a shaky breath, the weight of the conversation settling around them. Then the absurdity of the situation hit her, and a bubble of laughter escaped her throat. Here she sat in a diner at dawn, being counseled about mental health by a centuries-old vampire.

"What's funny?" Tyr's eyebrows drew together in confusion.

"Sorry, it's just..." Beth pressed her free hand to her mouth, trying to contain her giggles. "Here you are, a seven hundred year old vampire, giving me therapy advice."

Tyr's lips twitched.

Alice appeared beside their table, coffee pot hovering over Tyr's cup. "Top off?"

He nodded, and she filled his cup with practiced efficiency. "Anything else I can get for you two?"

Beth shook her head. "No, thank you. Could we get separate checks?"

"Just one check," Tyr interrupted smoothly.

Alice smiled and bustled away, leaving Beth staring at Tyr with wide eyes.

"I can pay for my own breakfast," she protested.

"Of course you can." Tyr's blue eyes danced with amusement. "But I invited you to breakfast."

Beth's heart skipped a beat as she processed his words. "Like..." She cleared her throat, her voice coming out barely above a whisper. "Like a date?"

"Exactly like a date." Tyr's gaze didn't waver, steady and patient.

A flutter of excitement mixed with nerves hit her. A date. The word felt impossible - like something that belonged to the person she'd been before everything shattered. Neil's memory stirred, but instead of the crushing weight she expected, it settled quietly in her chest. Different now. Manageable.

Her fingers twisted the napkin in her lap. "I... I haven't dated anyone since..."

"I know." Tyr's voice remained gentle, his blue eyes holding no pressure or judgment.

He wasn't pushing, wasn't demanding an answer, and that somehow made all the difference. Part of her wanted to flee, to protect herself from the possibility of that kind of pain again. But another part, one that had been sleeping for so long, stretched awake with tentative hope.

"The question is," Tyr continued softly, "would you like to have a second date?"

Beth's breath caught. The question hung between them in the quiet diner, weighted with possibility. Beth felt heat creep up her cheeks as she met Tyr's steady gaze across the table. Her heart fluttered, a mix of excitement and nervous anticipation dancing through her veins.

"Yes." The word came out soft but certain. "I'd like that."

Tyr's smile brightened the pre-dawn darkness, making her blush deepen. His cool fingers squeezed hers gently where they still rested on the table between them.

"I'm glad," he said simply.

Beth ducked her head, unable to contain her own smile as she toyed with her empty hot chocolate mug. The warm glow in her chest felt foreign but welcome - a sensation she'd forgotten existed in the long dark months after Neil's death.

CHAPTER 10

Tyr pushed open the kitchen door of the Residence, and stopped short. His twin brother stood at the counter, methodically loading items into a cardboard box.

Baking soda. White vinegar. Liquid dish soap.

Tyr's eyebrows rose as Tobi added red and yellow food coloring to the growing collection. A container of glitter sparkled under the kitchen lights as it joined the other items. Play-Doh and a small plastic water bottle completed the bizarre assembly.

"Have you finally lost what's left of your mind?" Tyr crossed his arms, leaning against the doorframe. "What in seven hells is all this?"

Tobi looked up, a mischievous grin spreading across his face. "Oh, hey there!"

His grin turned slightly sheepish as he continued packing up the supplies. "Did you know there are like a million videos online about cool science experiments for kids? This one's supposed to be awesome - a lava volcano - the baking soda and vinegar make it foam up, and then with the food coloring and glitter..." He gestured enthusiastically. "Instant lava!"

"And you're doing this because...?" Tyr prompted, though he had a suspicion he knew where this was heading.

Tobi ducked his head, suddenly very interested in adjusting the Play-Doh container. "I might have... offered to watch Yousuf tonight." He glanced up through his bangs. "Beth and Layla wanted to go out with Katerina - you know, girls' night or whatever."

"So you volunteered to babysit." Tyr couldn't quite keep the amusement out of his voice.

"Hey, I figured making volcanoes beats sitting around watching cartoons all night." Tobi straightened defensively. "Besides, the kid needs some fun. And what's more fun than explosions?"

"Controlled explosions," Tyr corrected automatically. "Very small, very contained explosions."

"Obviously." Tobi rolled his eyes. "Give me some credit. I got plastic sheeting to put down and everything." He paused, then added with a grin, "Though maybe don't mention the explosion part to Layla."

Tyr narrowed his eyes, studying his twin's suddenly defensive posture. "You're not... using the kid to get closer to Layla, are you?"

Tobi's head snapped up, genuine hurt flashing across his features. "What? No! How could you even think that?" He slammed the box down on the counter with more force than necessary. "Yousuf's a great kid. Smart as hell, curious about everything. And yeah, maybe I want to show him some cool science stuff, help him feel safe and have some fun. Is that such a crime?"

"Did you know what happened to him? He was four years old - four - when they crept in and stole him from his mother's side while they slept." Tobi's knuckles went white against the counter. "Snatched him and a bunch of other kids in the dead of night, loaded them into trucks, and drove them out into the Moroccan desert in the blazing summer heat. Dumped them there to die because they weren't 'worthy' of growing up to breed more caracal shifters."

His face contorted with a fury that stripped away his humanity, revealing the dangerous apex predator beneath. "They left babies to die in the desert, Tyr. Four-year-olds. Like garbage." His voice turned deadly quiet. "So, yeah, if I want to spend an evening making volcanoes explode with glitter and showing that sweet kid that not all men are monsters, I'm going to do exactly that."

Tyr flinched at the broken fury in his brother's voice. He'd known the basics of what happened at the compound, but hearing it laid out so starkly...

Clearing his throat, Tyr sought to change the subject to something lighter. He picked up a box from the counter, turning it over in his hands. 'Brownie mix?'"

Tobi shrugged, continuing to arrange his science experiment supplies. "Kids like that stuff. Figured we could make them together after the volcano thing."

"But you don't bake." Tyr stared at his brother in disbelief. In seven centuries, he'd never seen Tobi so much as boil water.

"Well, how hard can it be?" Tobi grabbed the box back, gesturing at the instructions printed on the side. "There's directions on it and everything. Add eggs, oil, water, stir, pour in pan, stick it in the oven." He grinned. "Even I can handle that."

"Says you, who once managed to burn soup," Tyr muttered, remembering their early attempts at maintaining human appearances by pretending to cook.

"That was almost seven hundred years ago!" Tobi protested.

Tyr picked up a printed sheet covered in colorful diagrams, scanning the instructions. "Volcano Science Experiment for Kids" blazed across the top in bold letters, followed by step-by-step directions and safety warnings.

"I found a different version using yeast and hydrogen peroxide," Tobi said, arranging bottles of food coloring. "But I figured vinegar and baking soda would be safer for a kid his age. Less chance of anything going wrong."

Tyr nodded absently, still reading. The diagrams showed how to build a volcano base from Play-Doh, then create the chemical reaction inside. Simple but effective. His interest piqued as he noticed additional variations listed - different combinations of ingredients to create various effects.

"This is actually pretty clever," he admitted, looking up at his brother. "Mind if I tag along? Could be fun to help out."

"Seriously?" Tobi's face lit up. "Yeah, that'd be great! Between the two of us, we can make sure nothing gets too out of hand." He grinned. "Plus, having backup means we can try multiple versions. See which one makes the best explosion."

"Controlled reaction," Tyr corrected automatically, but he was already mentally calculating the best ratios of vinegar to baking soda for maximum effect.

Tyr helped Tobi load the last of the supplies into the cardboard box, carefully arranging the bottles so nothing would spill during transport. Through the kitchen windows, they could see snow beginning to fall outside, coating everything in a pristine white blanket.

"Truck's probably smarter tonight," Tyr said, glancing out the window. "These roads will get slick fast."

"Plus we've got all this stuff to haul." Tobi grabbed the keys from the counter. "I'll drive."

The twins made their way to Tobi's black pickup, their boots crunching through fresh powder. The truck's headlights cut through the swirling snow as they headed toward the pack house where Layla and Yousuf lived.

Warm light spilled from the windows when they pulled up. Before they could reach the door, it flew open and Yousuf bounded out onto the porch.

"Tobi! Tyr!" The boy's face lit up with excitement. "You both came!"

"Careful on those steps," Tobi called as Yousuf navigated the snow-dusted porch. "They might be slippery."

Layla appeared in the doorway, wrapped in a thick sweater. "Come in, come in! It's freezing out there." Her smile was warm and relaxed.

"Thanks for watching him tonight," she said as they stomped snow from their boots in the entryway. "It means so much to have a night out with my friends."

"Our pleasure," Tobi assured her while carefully setting down the box where Yousuf couldn't peek inside. "We'll have a great time."

"What's in the box?" Yousuf tried to peer around Tobi's legs.

"Just some stuff for later," Tyr deflected smoothly. "It's a surprise."

Layla gathered her purse and coat, practically glowing with anticipation. "Beth should be here any minute to pick me up. He loves chicken nuggets, he can tell you how to make them, it's really simple. And his bedtime is-"

"Eight o'clock, we know," Tobi finished with a grin. "Go have fun. We've got this covered."

A car horn sounded outside, and Layla hurried to kiss Yousuf goodbye. "Be good for Tobi and Tyr, ibni. I love you."

"Love you too, Mama!" Yousuf waved as she hurried out into the snow.

Shutting the door, Tobi led the way to the pack house kitchen. It was large, but not so large as the Residence had.

Tobi clapped his hands together. "Okay, first things first - dinner. Can't do science experiments on an empty stomach."

"Chicken nuggies!" Yousuf bounced on his toes, darting to the freezer. He yanked open the door and pointed to a bag of dinosaur-shaped nuggets. "These ones!"

Tyr peered at them. "Dinosaur shaped?"

"Yeah, they're the best!" Yousuf enthused, grabbing a plate from a lower cabinet.

"You have to put them in the microwave for two minutes," Yousuf instructed seriously. "And spread them out in a circle."

Tyr leaned against the counter, watching as his brother arranged the frozen nuggets with exaggerated care. Tobi punched in the time - five minutes instead of two.

"Uh, Tobi..." Tyr started, but his brother had already hit start.

The microwave hummed. At the three-minute mark, a burning smell filled the kitchen. When Tobi finally pulled out the plate, the nuggets had transformed into small, hardened rocks.

"I don't think they're supposed to look like that," Yousuf said diplomatically.

Tyr couldn't contain his snicker. "Nice work. I'm sure prehistoric creatures were exactly that fossilized."

"Oh, shut up." Tobi set them aside, and pulled out the box of frozen nuggets, shaking out another bunch. "Let me try again."

This time, Yousuf supervised more closely. "Two minutes," he repeated firmly. "And you have to stop halfway to flip them over."

Under the boy's careful direction, the second batch came out perfectly golden and dinosaur-shaped. Yousuf beamed with pride as he showed Tobi how to squirt ketchup in the shape of a smiley face next to them.

"See? Not so hard when you listen to the expert," Tyr teased, ruffling Yousuf's hair.

Tyr watched Yousuf polish off the last dinosaur nugget with obvious enjoyment. The boy's table manners were impeccable - no doubt Layla's influence. He used his napkin without prompting and carefully gathered his dishes.

"Here, let me help with that." Tyr opened the dishwasher while Yousuf handed him the plate and utensils.

"Ready for the surprise?" Tobi asked, scooping Yousuf up and settling him on one of the tall stools at the kitchen island. The boy's feet dangled, swinging with excitement.

"Yes! What is it? Can I see now?"

"I'll go get it." Tyr headed to the living room where they'd left the supplies.

"Okay, close your eyes!" Tobi instructed, as Tyr returned, the box tucked under one arm.

Yousuf squeezed his eyes shut tight, bouncing a little. "What is it?"

"Keep them closed," Tobi sang out as he arranged items on the counter. "No peeking!"

Tyr leaned against the doorframe, arms crossed, fighting back a smile as his brother lined up the supplies with military precision. Food coloring, baking soda, vinegar - each item placed just so. The plastic sheeting came out last, ready to protect the counter from whatever mess they were about to create.

"Alright," Tobi announced grandly. "Open your eyes!"

Yousuf's eyes flew open, darting between the assembled items with growing curiosity. "What is all this stuff?"

"We," Tobi declared, practically vibrating with excitement, "are going to build a volcano! And then make it explode!"

"A volcano?" Yousuf's eyes went wide. "A real one?"

"Well, sort of." Tobi was already reaching for the Play-Doh. "We'll build it with this, and then use special ingredients to make it erupt. With lava and everything!"

Tyr couldn't help chuckling at the matching expressions of pure delight on both their faces. His ancient vampire brother looked every bit as thrilled as the six-year-old about their upcoming experiment.

"Can we make it big?" Yousuf asked, already reaching for the Play-Doh. "With lots of lava?"

"Oh, we're going to make it awesome," Tobi assured him, spreading out the plastic sheeting. "And wait till you see what happens when we add the glitter..."

Tyr strolled forward and picked up the printout from the counter. "Why don't I read the directions while you two artists handle the construction?"

"Yeah!" Yousuf bounced on his stool. "Can we make it really tall?"

"Hold up there, buddy." Tobi ruffled the boy's hair. "How about some milk first? Can't do proper science on an empty stomach."

While Tobi got Yousuf settled with his milk, Tyr grabbed two Cokes from the fridge. He popped the tabs, sliding one across to his brother.

"Okay, according to this..." Tyr held up the instructions. "First we need to build a base from the green Play-Doh."

Tobi and Yousuf dug into the containers, squishing the modeling compound between their fingers. Yousuf's tongue poked out in concentration as he helped Tobi flatten the clay into a circular base.

"Now what?" Tobi asked, hands covered in green.

"Start building up the sides." Tyr demonstrated with his hands. "Cone shape, but leave a deep well in the center for our 'magma chamber.'"

"Like this?" Yousuf pressed more of the colorful clay onto the sides, his small fingers carefully smoothing the surface.

"Perfect." Tyr nodded approvingly. "Make sure those walls are thick - they need to hold the liquid without collapsing."

They worked steadily, Tobi and Yousuf shaping the volcano while Tyr called out measurements from the instructions. The finished structure stood about a foot tall, with sturdy walls and a deep central chamber.

"Now we need to texture the outside," Tyr read. "Make it look more like real rock."

Yousuf's face brightened. "I know!" He slid off the stool and went to a kitchen drawer, and grabbed a fork. He clambered back up onto the stool, using the tines to scratch irregular patterns into the surface. "See? Like a real mountain!"

"You bet!" Tobi stepped back to admire their handiwork. "We've got a real Mount Vesuvius here."

"What's Mount Veh-suv-i-uhs?" Yousuf looked up from where he was still adding texture to the Play-Doh volcano.

"It's a famous volcano in Italy," Tyr explained, keeping his tone light. "A very long time ago, it erupted and covered a whole city called Pompeii."

"Really?" Yousuf's eyes widened. "What happened to the people?"

Tobi shot Tyr a quick glance before answering carefully. "They had time to leave the city. And now it's like a big museum - scientists found the whole city preserved under the volcanic ash, so we can see how people lived back then."

"Wow." Yousuf traced a finger along their creation. "Was that what made all the dinosaurs die?"

Tyr caught his brother's eye, seeing his own uncertainty reflected there. Despite their long existence, neither had actually been around for that particular event.

"You know what?" Tyr shrugged. "We're not really sure about that one. I think it might have been a different kind of disaster - maybe an asteroid hitting Earth?"

"Yeah," Tobi agreed, running a hand through his hair. "The dinosaur thing was way before our... uh, before anyone's time. Could have been volcanos, I guess."

Tyr glanced at the fossilized dinosaur-shaped chicken nuggets still sitting on the counter, and a slow grin spread across his face. He snatched up the plate and brought it over.

"Hey, looks like my brother's cooking disaster might be useful after all." He held up one of the rock-hard nuggets. "What do you think? Perfect volcanic boulders, right?"

Yousuf clapped his hands together in excitement. "Yeah! Can we stick them in?"

"Here." Tyr pressed one of the hardened nuggets into the volcano's slopes. "See how it looks like it's embedded in the rock?"

"Cool!" Yousuf grabbed another nugget-turned-boulder and carefully pushed it into place. "Like real rocks that got stuck when the lava cooled!"

Tobi snorted. "Well, at least my culinary skills are good for something."

They worked together, embedding the nuggets at different angles around the volcano's surface. The irregular shapes actually enhanced the mountain's realistic appearance, making it look more like natural rock formation than smooth Play-Doh.

"See?" Tyr stepped back to admire their handiwork. "Sometimes mistakes turn into happy accidents."

"Now it looks like a real mountain," Yousuf declared, adding the last nugget-boulder with careful precision. "With real rocks and everything!"

Tobi picks up the instruction sheet. "Okay, hang on, let me get this part done.

Tobi grabbed the plastic water bottle and carefully poured its contents into a glass. With an exaggerated wink at Yousuf, he said, "Waste not, want not!"

Yousuf giggled, his feet swinging against the stool rungs as he watched Tobi work.

Following the printed instructions with unusual care, Tobi measured out the baking soda, pouring it into the now-empty bottle. He added a squirt of dish soap, then held up the food coloring bottles.

"What color should our lava be?" Tobi asked, waggling the bottles enticingly.

"Red!" Yousuf bounced on his stool, nearly toppling over in excitement. "Like real lava!"

"Red it is." Tobi added several drops of the crimson dye, then sprinkled in a pinch of gold glitter. The mixture sparkled under the kitchen lights as he held the bottle up for them to see. He then carefully positioned the bottle in the center of their Play-Doh creation.

"That's called the caldera," Tyr explained, pointing to where the bottle nestled in the volcano's mouth. "It's the main vent where the lava comes out during an eruption."

Tobi poured vinegar into a glass measuring cup, and held it up, his eyes sparkling with anticipation. "Ready for some volcanic action?"

"Yeah!" Yousuf practically vibrated off the stool, bouncing from foot to foot. His excitement was contagious - even Tyr found himself grinning as he positioned his phone to capture the moment.

"Layla's going to want to see this," Tyr said, making sure he had a good angle on both the volcano and Yousuf's face.

"Okay, scientist Yousuf." Tobi handed the boy the measuring cup. "On the count of three, pour this right into the center. Ready?"

Yousuf nodded vigorously, gripping the cup with both hands.

"One... two... three!"

Yousuf tipped the vinegar into the volcano's mouth. For a split second, nothing happened. Then the mixture began to bubble and foam, red "lava" streaming down the slopes. Sparkles caught the light as it cascaded down, making the eruption sparkle and shine.

"It's exploding!" Yousuf screamed in delight, jumping up and down. "Look at all the lava!"

The reaction continued, foam spilling over the sides and around the chicken-nugget boulders. Yousuf's laughter echoed through the kitchen as he watched the "lava" flow, his face a picture of pure joy.

"This is the best volcano ever!" he declared, eyes wide with wonder as the last bits of foam trickled down the sides.

Tobi grabbed the box of brownie mix from the counter, waving it triumphantly. "And now, for our next scientific experiment - brownies!"

Yousuf's eyes lit up. "I love brownies! Can I help?"

"Of course!" Tobi flipped the box over, squinting at the instructions. "Okay, we need... a bowl, eggs, oil, and... what are these beater things?"

"Oh! I know where those are!" Yousuf scrambled down from his stool and pulled open a lower drawer. He emerged with an electric hand mixer, the cord trailing behind him. "Mama uses these when she makes cookies."

Tyr watched in amusement as his brother stared at the mixer like it was some alien technology. "Right. And how exactly does this work?"

"There's buttons," Yousuf pointed helpfully. "But I'm not allowed to use it by myself."

"Bowl first," Tyr suggested, opening cabinets at random. "Where would your mom keep the big mixing bowls?"

"That one!" Yousuf pointed to a cabinet near the stove. "The glass ones."

Tobi rummaged through the pantry. "Oil... we need oil. There's olive oil and something called vegetable oil. Which one?"

"The box says vegetable oil," Tyr read over his shoulder.

"There's a difference?"

"Apparently." Tyr shrugged. "Don't ask me, I haven't cooked since the 1400s."

They gathered their supplies on the counter - bowl, oil, eggs that Yousuf carefully carried from the fridge, and the mysterious electric beaters.

"Okay, plug it in," Tobi directed, holding the mixer like it might bite him.

"Maybe read the instructions first?" Tyr suggested dryly.

"How hard can it be? You just..." Tobi pressed a button. The beaters whirred to life at top speed, spraying the dry brownie mix across the counter.

"Turn it off!" Tyr ducked as powder flew past his head.

Yousuf dissolved into giggles as Tobi frantically jabbed at buttons. "No, the other one! The big button!"

The mixer finally fell silent. Tobi stood frozen, covered in a fine layer of chocolate powder. "Well," he said finally. "That was educational."

"Maybe we should add the wet ingredients first?" Tyr brushed brownie mix from his brother's shoulder, fighting back his own laughter.

"Now you tell me." Tobi glared at the mixer. "I liked cooking better in the Middle Ages."

Tyr watched as his brother and Yousuf finally managed to get all the ingredients combined into something resembling brownie batter. The kitchen looked like a war zone - chocolate powder dusted every surface, eggshells littered the counter, and mysterious splashes of oil decorated the backsplash.

"There!" Tobi declared triumphantly, pouring the mixture into the glass baking dish. "Now we just pop it in the oven and-"

"Pre-heat to 350°F," Tyr read from the box. "Did anyone turn on the oven?"

Tobi's face fell. "Oh. No."

They all turned to stare at the oven's control panel, a bewildering array of buttons and digital displays.

"Which one turns it on?" Tobi jabbed randomly at buttons. Nothing happened.

"Maybe this one?" Yousuf pointed to a knob.

Tyr twisted it, but the display remained dark. "There has to be a power button somewhere..."

"Oh, wait!" Tobi punched the air triumphantly as he discovered a button labeled 'BROIL'. He pressed it, and the oven hummed to life, the display glowing. "See? Got it!"

"Are you sure that's-" Tyr started, but Tobi was already sliding the brownie pan onto the top rack.

"It says thirty-five minutes." Tobi pulled out his phone and set the alarm. "Perfect! Who's ready for some TV while we wait?"

Yousuf bounced toward the living room. "Can we watch Paw Patrol?"

"Sure thing, buddy." Tobi ruffled the boy's hair as they settled onto the couch.

Tyr sank into an armchair, trying to ignore the nagging feeling that something wasn't quite right about their baking adventure. The smell of warming chocolate began to fill the air as Yousuf's show played on the screen.

Tyr's head snapped up from watching the cartoon. Something wasn't right. The scent of chocolate had transformed into something more... acrid.

Smoke.

The piercing shriek of the smoke detector split the air. Tyr bolted from his chair, Tobi and Yousuf right behind him as they raced to the kitchen.

Thick grey smoke billowed from the oven, filling the room with an eye-watering haze. Tobi yanked open the oven door, releasing a fresh cloud of smoke.

"Holy hell!" Tobi waved his arms frantically, trying to disperse the smoke. "What happened?"

"The broiler!" Tyr grabbed a nearby stool. "You had it on broil instead of bake! I knew that was wrong!"

Yousuf darted to the back door, throwing it open to the snowy night. Cold air rushed in, helping to clear some of the smoke.

Tyr climbed onto the stool, reaching for the still-screaming smoke detector. His fingers fumbled with the device as smoke swirled around his head. "How do you turn this damn thing off?"

"There's a button!" Yousuf called up from below. "Push the big button in the middle!"

Tyr jabbed at the center of the detector. The shrieking finally stopped, leaving them in blessed silence broken only by Tobi's coughing as he fanned away smoke from the oven.

The front door slammed open, and Antonio materialized in the kitchen doorway. His dark eyes swept the smoke-filled kitchen, taking in the disaster before him.

"What in God's name happened here?" Antonio's voice rang with authority.

Before either twin could respond, Yousuf launched himself across the kitchen, colliding with Antonio's legs.

"Hi!! Are you a vampire? Tyr and Tobi are vampires, and we made a volcano! And it exploded with real lava! And Tobi burned the chicken nuggets so we used them as rocks! And then we tried to make brownies but they caught on fire and there was all kinda smoke coming from the oven and the alarm went crazy and-"

Antonio's stern expression flickered as he looked down at the boy clutching his designer trousers.

Tyr struggled to keep his expression neutral as he watched the horror in the aristocratic vampire's eyes as he took in the chocolate fingerprints now decorating his pristine trousers. Yousuf's face and clothes were smeared with an impressive combination of Play-Doh, chocolate brownie mix, and glitter, all of which were transferring to the custom Italian wool.

"I... see." Antonio's appalled gaze shifted to the twins, one eyebrow rising in silent demand for explanation.

"We might have had a slight... cooking mishap," Tobi offered weakly, still holding the smoking brownie pan with oven mitts.

Yousuf tilted his head back, staring up at Antonio with wide-eyed fascination. His small hands remained firmly wrapped in the perfectly pressed fabric of Antonio's custom Italian suit pants.

"So you're a vampire too?" He persisted, determined to know.

Tyr caught the flash of panic in his sire's eyes as Antonio's mental voice thundered through his and Tobi's minds. *Get. This. Child. Off. Me. NOW!*

The ancient vampire stood frozen, clearly torn between maintaining his dignified composure and extracting himself from the enthusiastic six-year-old currently attached to his legs. Glitter from Yousuf's hands sparkled on the dark fabric of Antonio's trousers, and a smear of chocolate decorated one pristine cuff.

"Hey, buddy!" Tobi swooped in, scooping Yousuf up and away from Antonio. "Want to show Antonio our awesome volcano? It's still got some lava left!"

Yousuf squirmed in Tobi's arms, still focused on Antonio. "Can you turn into a bird too?"

Antonio's expression suggested he'd rather face a firing squad than discuss shapeshifting with an over-excited child covered in Play-Doh and brownie batter.

Tyr bit back a laugh as his sire discreetly tried to brush glitter from his ruined trousers. He'd never seen the ancient vampire quite so discombobulated.

Yousuf wriggled free from Tobi's grasp and bounced over to their volcano, now surrounded by dried "lava" and scattered glitter. "Look! We made Mount Ve-suv-i-us!" He pointed proudly at the chicken nugget boulders embedded in the sides. "It exploded and killed all the dinosaurs in Pompeii!"

Antonio's perfectly groomed eyebrows climbed toward his hairline as he turned to fix Tyr and Tobi with a withering stare.

Tyr spread his hands helplessly. "The explanation about dinosaurs and Pompeii got a bit... mixed up somewhere along the way."

Beside him, Tobi scratched the back of his neck, leaving a streak of brownie batter in his hair.

"We might have confused a few historical events," Tobi muttered, avoiding Antonio's gaze.

Antonio pinched the bridge of his nose, a gesture Tyr had witnessed countless times over the ages.

"Seven centuries," Antonio muttered. "Seven! And you two still manage to create chaos wherever you go."

Tyr exchanged a knowing look with his twin. They could practically mouth the words along with their sire - they'd heard variations of this speech since the Black Death.

"In my defense," Tobi offered, "the volcano part went perfectly."

"Yeah!" Yousuf piped up, bouncing on his toes. "It was awesome! Want to see it again?"

Antonio held up one elegant hand, warding off the suggestion. "Clean." He gestured at the disaster zone formerly known as the kitchen. "All of it. Now."

His gaze swept over the scattered brownie mix, the dried "lava" trails, and the liberal coating of glitter that seemed to have multiplied since its release. A particularly sparkly patch caught the light on his ruined trousers.

Without another word, Antonio turned and stalked toward the door, his usual fluid grace somewhat diminished by the way he tried to brush glitter from his clothing. His muttering carried back to them - something about "children" and "eternal teenagers" - before he disappeared into the snowy night.

"I think he likes us," Tobi stage-whispered to Yousuf, who giggled.

"He didn't even yell," Tyr agreed, surveying the chaos around them. "Must be getting soft in his old age."

Tyr caught his brother's eye across the disaster zone of the kitchen. Despite the chaos - or maybe because of it - he couldn't stop the grin spreading across his face. Tobi's answering smile was equally wide as they reached across the counter to high-five.

"Best babysitting night ever," Tobi declared, ruffling Yousuf's hair.

"Even with the brownie disaster?" Tyr asked, already grabbing paper towels to start cleaning.

"Especially with the brownie disaster." Tobi lifted Yousuf onto the counter, safely away from the mess. "Though maybe next time we stick to cold snacks."

"And more volcanoes!" Yousuf added, swinging his feet happily.

Tyr smiled, watching his brother and the young shifter start planning their next scientific adventure.

Tyr felt a surge of pride watching his brother, and he shook his head. In all their long existence, he'd rarely seen Tobi so enthusiastic about anything beyond motorcycles and mayhem.

His eyes drifted to the stove's digital display and he jerked upright. "Shi- shoot!" He caught himself just in time. "It's nine o'clock!"

Tobi's head snapped up. "What? Already?" He lifted Yousuf down from his perch on the counter and grimaced. "We can't put him to bed looking like this. He's covered in... everything."

Yousuf beamed up at them, his pajamas dusted with brownie mix and glitter. "I can take a bath by myself! I do it all the time."

"Right." Tyr headed for the bathroom. "I'll get the water started."

While he adjusted the temperature and filled the tub, he heard Tobi and Yousuf in the bedroom, rummaging for clean pajamas. Their voices drifted through the walls, Yousuf explaining his precise bedtime routine with the authority of a seasoned professional.

The twins stationed themselves in the hallway while Yousuf bathed, listening intently for any signs of trouble. Tobi paced, pausing every few steps to press his ear against the door.

"He said he does this all the time," Tyr reminded him.

"I know, but..." Tobi resumed his pacing. "What if he slips?"

"You're going to make a great dad," Tyr told him, then ducked, snickering, as his brother swung a fist at him.

Finally, the bathroom door opened. Yousuf emerged in fresh dinosaur pajamas, his hair damp and his eyes heavy with sleep. He yawned widely as they tucked him into bed, barely managing a sleepy "g'night" before drifting off.

Back in the kitchen, Tyr wrinkled his nose at the devastation before them. Dried "lava" trails decorated the counter, sparkles covered every surface, and a fine layer of brownie mix coated everything like volcanic ash. The ruined brownies sat in their pan, a blackened testament to their culinary disaster.

"This place sure looks like Pompeii after the eruption," he muttered. "Complete with fossilized remains." He poked at the charred brownie pan.

"Yeah, we better clean this up before Layla gets home." Tobi grabbed a roll of paper towels. "She might not appreciate our historical reen-actment."

They worked in tandem, ages of practice making them an efficient team. Tyr tackled the counters while Tobi handled the floor, both of them scrubbing at stubborn spots of dried "lava" and Play-Doh.

"How does this stuff get everywhere?" Tobi grumbled, finding yet another sparkly patch under the stove. "It's like it multiplies on its own."

"At least it's not blood this time," Tyr reminded him, thinking of other messes they'd cleaned up over the long course of their lives. He sprayed cleaner on a particularly stubborn chocolate smear. "Remember that time in Venice?"

"That was different. That was life or death." Tobi straightened up from scrubbing the floor. "This was just... enthusiasm."

They worked methodically through the kitchen, restoring order to the chaos. Fresh air from the still-open back door helped clear the lingering smoke smell. Tyr wiped down the last counter while Tobi put away the cleaning supplies.

Finally, the kitchen gleamed, showing no trace of their volcanic adventure or baking catastrophe. Even the glitter had been mostly contained, though Tyr suspected they'd be finding sparkly spots for weeks to come. They left the volcano, though, taking igneous pride of place in the center of the counter.

"Not bad," Tobi said, surveying their work. "Think Layla will notice anything?"

Tyr sniffed the air, and nodded. "It's still a little smoky in here. Other than that, we're golden."

And just in time, too. The sound of tires crunching on snow outside caught his attention. Through the window, he caught a glimpse of Beth's pale blonde hair shining under the porch light as she helped

Layla navigate the icy steps, both women laughing together. The sight of Beth's smile made everything else fade away, her stormy blue-grey eyes catching the light as she glanced toward the house and waved at him.

In all his long existence, he'd never expected this - somehow he'd ended up here, covered in brownie batter and glitter, teaching a six-year-old about volcanos while falling for a woman whose gentle nature and fierce heart captivated him more than any immortal ever had.

Not exactly how he'd imagined spending his immortality, but somehow, it felt exactly right.

CHAPTER 11

Beth smoothed her hands over her favorite jeans one last time before opening her front door. Tyr stood on her porch, his fair hair catching the porch light. His casual attire of dark jeans and a leather jacket made her feel better about her own laid-back outfit choice.

"Ready for an adventure?" His sapphire eyes sparkled with mischief.

"Should I be worried?" Beth grabbed her wool peacoat from the hook, shrugging into its warmth.

"Never." He offered his arm with an exaggerated flourish that made her giggle.

The drive was peaceful, classical music playing softly as they left the city lights behind. Trees crowded closer to the road until finally Tyr turned onto a narrow gravel path that led to a small parking area near a lake.

Beth emerged from the truck and paused, taking in their surroundings. Moonlight silvered the water's surface, while thick woods spread into darkness on all sides. The night air carried the crisp scent of autumn leaves and pine needles.

Tyr's smile was warm as he gestured toward the tree line. "Shall we?"

As they headed toward the woods, Beth quickened her pace, eager to explore the area around the lake. Whisper stirred with interest, sensing the wild spaces ahead. Once they were well hidden from the parking area, Tyr stopped.

"I thought we could spend some time in our other forms." His voice held a hint of uncertainty. "If you're comfortable with that?"

Something warm unfurled in Beth's chest. He understood how personal shifting was, especially after everything she'd been through. But this felt right - sharing that intimate part of herself with him.

"I'd love that." She glanced around the moonlit forest, already feeling the joyous anticipation build.

Beth ducked behind a massive oak tree, quickly stripping off her clothes and folding them into a neat pile. She closed her eyes, letting her small feline form flow over her human shape. Her whiskers twitched as she caught Tyr's scent - that unique mixture of leather and winter air that was uniquely him.

She peered around the tree trunk just in time to see Tyr's form shimmer and blur, shrinking and reshaping until a magnificent hawk stood where he had been. His clothing had simply vanished, absorbed into his raptor form through whatever vampire magic allowed such things.

Beth crept from behind the oak tree, her clouded leopard form moving with fluid grace. Her lush pelt shimmered in the silvery light filtering through the branches as she studied Tyr's transformed shape.

The hawk before her was breathtaking. Sleek feathers in shades of slate blue and cream caught the silvery light, while his razor-sharp beak and fierce yellow eyes spoke of a deadly predator. His head turned with quick, precise movements as he surveyed their surroundings, every motion displaying the perfect efficiency of a born hunter.

Beth wasn't sure if vampires could communicate telepathically like shifters could in their animal forms, but she focused her thoughts carefully, projecting them toward him.

Can you hear me?

The falcon's head swiveled toward her, those piercing eyes fixing on her feline face. *Yes, I can hear you perfectly.*

Excitement rippled through her, making her tail twitch. *You're absolutely magnificent! What kind of hawk are you?*

The falcon's feathers puffed up in clear indignation. *I am not a hawk,* he projected, his mental voice carrying an amusing mix of offense and pride. *I am a falcon. A tiercel, to be precise.*

Beth settled onto her haunches, wrapping her long tail around her paws. *What's the difference?*

A tiercel is specifically a male peregrine falcon, he explained, preening his wing feathers with his sharp beak. *The word comes from the Latin tertius, meaning 'third,' since male falcons are roughly one-third smaller than females.*

Beth's whiskers twitched with amusement. *So what do you call the females then?*

A ripple of laughter echoed through their mental connection. *Simply 'falcon.' We males get the fancy name while the ladies keep it straightforward.*

That seems rather unfair, Beth projected, her leopard making a soft chuffing sound that was her version of laughter. *Though I suppose it makes up for them being bigger and stronger.*

Indeed. Pride colored his thoughts. *The peregrine falcon is the fastest animal on Earth when diving, up to 240 miles per hour.*

Beth circled closer, admiring how the moonbeams played across his sleek feathers. *Your coloring is beautiful - your back and head have this gorgeous blue cast to them."*

Beth's whiskers twitched with amusement as Tyr fluffed his feathers, spreading his wings in an elegant display. His plumage caught the moonlight, creating an iridescent shimmer that rippled across his form. He turned his head this way and that, showing off the precise patterns of his markings.

Someone's feeling proud of himself, Beth projected, her projected thoughts carrying her laughter.

Can you blame me? Tyr's fierce yellow eyes fixed on her. *Though I must say, your form is truly breathtaking.*

Beth's ears flicked forward as warmth spread through her chest at his words. Her clouded leopard form was smaller than a regular leopard, but still powerfully muscled beneath her distinctive coat.

The way your spots create those cloud-like patterns... Genuine admiration filled his thoughts. *They're remarkable. Like wisps of storm clouds dancing across your fur.*

Beth ducked her head, suddenly shy despite being in her animal form. Her clouded coat had always felt ordinary to her - just part of who she was. But seeing it reflected in Tyr's raptor gaze made her view it differently. The complex rosettes and markings that gave clouded leopards their name did create an ethereal effect, especially in the dappled moonlight streaming through the branches above.

The way they flow along your sides, Tyr continued, hopping closer on his powerful talons. *It's like watching weather patterns form and dissolve. Absolutely gorgeous.*

Beth felt Whisper's playful nature surge forward, her feline instincts taking over. Without warning, she darted between two massive oaks, the patterns in her fur blending with the dappled moonlight. Her powerful muscles bunched and released as she wove through the undergrowth, her paws silent on the carpet of fallen leaves.

A shadow passed overhead as Tyr swooped low, his wings nearly brushing the branches. Beth's heart raced with excitement as she changed direction, zigzagging between the trees. Her wild cat was perfectly suited to this environment - equally comfortable on the ground or in the trees.

Can't catch me! Bubbling with joy, she projected the thought toward him.

Tyr's falcon shot upward, using a gap in the canopy to gain height before diving again. His sleek form knifed through the air as Beth darted beneath low-hanging branches. She could feel his exhilaration matching her own as they played this impromptu game of aerial tag.

Beth leaped onto a fallen log, using it as a launching pad to bound deeper into the forest. Tyr's shadow danced across her patterned fur as he matched her movements from above, dipping and weaving through the trees with incredible precision. His wings caught a shaft of pale lunar light as he banked sharply, anticipating her next turn.

Whisper's delight in the chase sang through Beth's blood. This was what she was made for - the perfect blend of power and agility as she navigated the forest depths. Above her, the tiercel demonstrated equal mastery of his domain, his controlled flight a testament to centuries of practice.

Beth skidded to a halt as Tyr landed gracefully on a thick branch high in a towering oak. His yellow eyes gleamed with challenge as he peered down at her, head tilted in that distinctly bird-like way.

Oh, you think you're clever up there, do you? Beth's mental voice carried Whisper's playful confidence.

Tyr's only response was to settle more comfortably on his perch, his feathers ruffling slightly in the cool night breeze. The branch he'd chosen was at least thirty feet up, but that was nothing to a clouded leopard.

Beth circled the massive trunk once, her rich fur shimmering as she sized up her path. Whisper's instincts guided her as she bunched her powerful muscles and leaped. Her sharp claws found perfect purchase in the rough bark as she scrambled upward.

Branch by branch, she climbed with fluid grace. Her long tail helped her balance as she navigated the narrowing spaces between limbs. The oak's spreading crown offered plenty of sturdy pathways for her agile form.

With one final push, Beth hauled herself onto Tyr's branch. She crouched beside his tiercel, her sides heaving slightly from the exertion as she projected smug triumph toward him. *Caught you.*

The falcon made a soft chuckling sound as he leaned down to rub his curved beak gently along the top of Beth's head. The affectionate nibbling sent tingles down her spine, making her ears twitch with pleasure. His feathers brushed against her fur, impossibly soft despite their sleek appearance.

That tickles, Beth projected, though she made no move to pull away. Whisper's contentment rumbled through her chest in a deep, throaty chuff. The simple intimacy of the moment struck her - here they were, perched high in an ancient oak, sharing affection in their most natural forms.

The stream of light filtering through the leaves cast dappled patterns across Tyr's slate-blue feathers, making them shimmer with an almost otherworldly beauty. His yellow eyes held a gentleness that seemed at odds with his fierce raptor appearance, yet perfectly matched the tender way he preened her fur.

The night breeze carried the scent of autumn leaves and pine needles, mingling with Tyr's unique winter-air scent that persisted even as a falcon.

Beth shifted her weight on the branch, settling more comfortably beside him.

Do you only have this one form? She projected the thought toward him. *Like how shifters each have their specific animal?*

Tyr's feathers rustled as he adjusted his position, turning to face her more directly. *No, actually. Vampires were created with the ability to take on any raptor form we choose. Owls, hawks, falcons, eagles - though only owls are nocturnal, and if we'll be flying where there are humans to see, I'll be in owl form.*

Beth's whiskers twitched with interest. *But you prefer the peregrine falcon?*

Indeed. Tyr spread his wings slightly, silvery beams catching the precise edges of his flight feathers. *They're incredibly sleek, built for pure speed. And their hunting abilities...* His fierce yellow eyes gleamed. *There's nothing quite like diving from thousands of feet up, reaching speeds that would make your fastest cars seem slow.*

Beth watched, impressed, as he demonstrated a quick hop-flutter along the branch, his movements displaying the deadly grace he described. Even perched beside her, every line of his raptor form spoke of lethal efficiency.

The peregrine falcon just feels right, he projected. *Like it matches something essential in my nature.*

Beth could understand that. Whisper wasn't just an animal shape she wore - it was an integral part of who she was. Her feline instincts and personality were woven through her own, inseparable and vital.

I'll be right back, Tyr projected. *Hang tight.* His wings spread wide, catching a shaft of moonlight before he launched from the branch. The downdraft from his takeoff ruffled Beth's fur as she watched the tiercel disappear into the darkness.

Beth settled more comfortably on the wide oak branch, crossing her front paws and resting her chin on them. The rough bark pressed against her belly, but her thick fur cushioned her from any discomfort. Whisper's contentment radiated through her as she breathed in the crisp night air.

Up here, surrounded by rustling leaves and the glow of the moon and stars above, Beth realized how long it had been since she'd simply enjoyed being in her leopard form. Not hiding, not running, not trapped or escaping her human troubles, but - just being. The gentle sway of the branch in the breeze felt natural, right. The markings on her fur collected patches of silvery light, creating shifting patterns that mimicked the oak's shadows.

I'm sorry, she thought to her inner cat. *We should do this more often. We will, I promise.*

Whisper's response was a wave of forgiveness mixed with lazy pleasure. Her leopard nature had always been patient, understanding that Beth's trauma made shifting complicated. But now, stretched out on this branch with the moon above and the forest below, Beth felt a pang of regret for all the nights she could have been doing this.

Her sensitive ears caught the subtle sounds of nightlife - an owl's wings brushing air, mice scurrying through fallen leaves, the distant call of a whippoorwill. These were Whisper's songs, the music of the wild that spoke to her feline soul. Beth let her eyes drift half-closed, absorbing the peaceful moment.

A flutter of wings broke the peaceful silence as the falcon emerged from the darkness. Beth's nose twitched at the rich scent of fresh meat carried on the night breeze. Whisper's interest sparked through her, making her tail twitch as she sat up on the branch.

Tyr's talons released their prize - a generous portion of deep red beef that landed with a soft thud on the wide oak branch. He settled beside it, his feathers gleaming as he folded his wings.

You brought me dinner? Beth projected, warmth spreading through her chest at the thoughtful gesture. Her keen nose picked up the quality of the meat - this was prime beef, not some random scrap.

Tyr made a soft, musical trill that seemed to vibrate through his feathers, a sound both wild and intimate. His sharp beak tore off a tender morsel which he offered to her with surprising delicacy. The gentle way he presented the food touched something deep in Beth's heart, making both her human and leopard sides purr with pleasure.

Beth delicately accepted the morsel from Tyr's beak, savoring the rich flavor as Whisper's appreciation rumbled through her chest. Her spotted tail curled with curiosity as she projected her thoughts toward him.

Where did you get this? I know you didn't take down a cow somewhere.

Tyr's mental chuckle rippled through her mind. *No aerial cattle rustling tonight. I stopped at Markus's Butcher Shop before picking you up. He always sets aside prime cuts for me.*

His yellow eyes gleamed with mischief as he shifted on the branch. *Had it wrapped in brown paper in the truck bed. Much easier for talons to unwrap.*

Beth's whiskers twitched with amusement at the image of his fierce raptor form delicately unwrapping a package of meat. *So you planned this little picnic all along?*

Guilty as charged. He preened a feather back into place. *Though I wasn't sure if you'd be comfortable shifting with me. I'm glad you were - watching you move through these trees is breathtaking.*

Beth watched as Tyr's sharp beak tore another tender piece of meat from the larger portion. His movements were precise, almost elegant as he offered it to her. Whisper's deep, rumbling chuff of pleasure vibrated through Beth's chest as she accepted the morsel. Contentment flowed through her veins like warm honey as Tyr continued to share his offering.

This is perfect, she projected, settling more comfortably on the wide branch.

Another piece of meat, another gentle exchange. Whisper's satisfied rumble echoed in Beth's mind: *Mate feeds us.*

The word hit Beth like a punch to the gut, stealing her breath. Wait, what? Her leopard's casual declaration sent her thoughts spinning. Mate? When had that happened? She hadn't even known Tyr that long, and yet...

Her gaze shifted to the tiercel beside her, noting how naturally he fit into this moment - sharing food with her under the stars, treating her with such tender care. Whisper's certainty hummed through her blood, unshakeable and profound. Her animal nature recognized something her human side was just beginning to grasp.

Are you alright? Tyr's mental voice carried a note of concern as he noticed her sudden stillness.

Beth forced her tail to resume its gentle swaying, not wanting to disturb the peaceful moment with her internal revelation. *I'm fine,* she projected, though her thoughts felt scattered. *Just... thinking.*

The night breeze rustled through the oak's leaves as Beth finished the last morsels of meat. She stretched luxuriously on the wide branch, feline contentment radiating through her.

We should head back, Tyr projected reluctantly. *You need to get some sleep, dawn will come soon.*

Beth's whiskers twitched in agreement. They descended the massive oak with fluid grace - Beth climbing down while Tyr glided between branches. At ground level, Beth padded silently through the underbrush toward where she'd left her clothes, the tiercel swooping overhead through gaps in the canopy.

Concealed behind the shelter of the undergrowth, Beth shifted back to her human form, quickly pulling on her jeans and sweater. The cool autumn air raised goosebumps on her skin until she shrugged into her wool peacoat. When she stepped out onto the path, the tiercel shimmered for a moment, the air around him rippling like heat waves above summer pavement. In the space between heartbeats, his raptor silhouette elongated and expanded, feathers dissolving into the familiar outline of his tall frame. The transformation completed with a subtle whisper of displaced air, leaving Tyr standing at the base of the tree in his human form, leather jacket and dark jeans somehow perfectly unwrinkled.

Beth glowered at him. "I'm jealous that you get to keep your clothes when you Change back."

Tyr's rich laughter echoed through the trees. "One of the perks of being a vampire."

Without conscious thought, Beth launched herself at Tyr, wrapping her arms around his neck and legs around his waist. His cool hands caught her easily, steadying her as she clung to him like an enthusiastic sloth.

"Thank you, thank you, thank you!" The words tumbled out between breathless giggles. "This was just... perfect. The most wonderful second date ever."

Tyr's rich laughter vibrated through his chest where she pressed against him. His strong arms held her securely as she buried her face in the crook of his neck, breathing in that crisp winter-air scent that was uniquely him.

"I take it you enjoyed yourself?" His voice held warm amusement as he adjusted his grip, supporting her weight effortlessly.

"Enjoyed myself?" Beth pulled back just enough to meet his eyes, her own sparkling with joy. "Tyr, this was amazing. Running through the trees, climbing, sharing food under the night stars..." She hugged him tighter. "No one's ever thought to do something like this with me before."

His cool fingers traced gentle patterns on her back through her wool coat. "I wanted to share something special with both sides of you - human and leopard."

"Well, you succeeded spectacularly." Joy bubbled up inside her, and Beth gave him a radiant smile. "Whisper absolutely loved it too."

Together they walked back to the parking lot, fingers entwined. The drive back passed in comfortable silence, classical music playing softly as the sky began to lighten. When they pulled up to Beth's house, Tyr walked her to her door.

"Thank you," Beth said softly. "Tonight was... magical."

"It was." Tyr's eyes crinkled at the corners as he smiled down at her. His cool fingers brushed a strand of hair from her cheek.

Beth's heart fluttered wildly against her ribs as Tyr leaned closer, his cool breath fanning across her heated skin. His lips met hers with exquisite gentleness, soft as a whisper yet electrifying enough to send sparks of sensation cascading down her spine. She melted into his embrace, her fingers curling into the supple leather of his jacket as warmth bloomed in her chest. The sweet tenderness of the moment wrapped around them like a cocoon, making the rest of the world fade away.

When they finally parted, the first hints of dawn were painting the sky in soft pastels.

"Good night... well, morning," Beth whispered with a small laugh.

"Good morning." Tyr's thumb traced her cheekbone. "Sleep well."

He waited until she was safely inside before heading to his car. Beth watched through the open doorway as he drove away, her fingers touching her lips where she could still feel the ghost of his kiss.

Beth closed the front door and leaned against it, her heart still racing from Tyr's kiss. Her fingers traced her lips where the coolness of his touch lingered. She couldn't seem to make her feet move from that spot, overwhelmed by the evening's revelations.

Whisper's certainty about Tyr being their mate echoed through her mind, making her knees weak. The sound of footsteps on the stairs barely registered until Naomi's voice broke through her daze.

"Beth? Are you okay?"

The warmth in her twin's voice undid Beth completely. Without warning, tears poured down her face and a sob escaped. Her whole body shook as the pent-up emotions of a lifetime broke free.

"Oh my god!" Naomi flew down the remaining stairs and wrapped her arms around Beth. "I'm going to kill him! What did that vampire do?"

Beth gave a watery chuckle and pressed her face into her sister's shoulder. "No, no - they're happy tears. I think." She drew in a shuddering breath, Tyr's gentle kiss still tingling on her lips.

Naomi held her at arm's length, studying Beth's tear-streaked face with the intense scrutiny only a twin could manage. "Happy tears or sad tears - which is it?"

Beth sniffled, swiping at her damp cheeks with the sleeve of her wool coat. "Confused tears?" Her voice wavered as she met her sister's concerned gaze. "We shifted together tonight. Whisper, she..." Beth's throat tightened. "She says he's our mate."

Naomi's eyes widened. "Oh! Oh, my!"

"Yeah." Beth leaned back against the door, her legs still feeling unsteady. "And the thing is, it felt right. Being with him in our animal forms, sharing that connection..." Fresh tears spilled down her cheeks.

"But I'm terrified. After Neil, I never thought... And I know I didn't do that, but still..."

Her voice broke as Naomi pulled her into another fierce hug. Beth buried her face in her twin's shoulder, breathing in the familiar scent of home and safety as years of conditioning, grief, guilt, and hope tangled together in her chest.

Beth pulled back from her sister's embrace, wrapping her arms around herself as guilt clawed at her insides. "There's something else." Her voice came out barely above a whisper. "Something I've never told you... or anyone."

She sank down onto the bottom step, her legs no longer able to support her. Naomi settled beside her, their shoulders touching in silent support.

"Neil..." His name barely made it past the tightness in her throat. "I don't think... I didn't really love him. Not the way I should have." The confession burned her throat like acid. "I loved what he represented - freedom, normalcy, a chance to escape." Her voice cracked. "I used him."

Tears dripped onto her clasped hands. "He was so kind, so genuine in his feelings. And I... I convinced myself I felt the same way. But really, I saw him as our ticket out - for both of us. A way to break free from the family without having to run."

"Beth..." Naomi started, but Beth shook her head.

"No, let me finish. All this time, I've been drowning in grief and guilt over his death. But the worst part?" Her voice dropped to a broken whisper. "The worst part is knowing that I didn't love him the way he deserved, and now he's dead because of me. Because I was selfish enough to use his love as an escape plan."

Fresh tears spilled down her cheeks. "If I hadn't been so desperate for us to get away, if I hadn't dragged him into our mess... he'd still be alive. His blood is on my hands, even if I wasn't the one who actually killed him."

Naomi wrapped an arm around Beth's shoulders. "You know what Liam would say if he were here? That surviving isn't something to apologize for."

"This isn't about—"

"But it is," Naomi interrupted gently. "You saw a chance to escape, and you took it. Anyone would have done the same."

Beth shook her head. "I was using him."

"Were you? Or maybe you were trying to love him the best way you knew how." Naomi's voice softened. "We never learned what healthy love looks like, Beth. How could we? But you're learning now."

She nudged Beth's shoulder with her own. "The fact you can recognize the difference between what you felt for Neil and what you're feeling for Tyr? That's growth. That's healing."

"What if I'm wrong about Tyr too?" Beth whispered.

"Then we'll face it together. But I don't think you are." Naomi smiled faintly. "Whisper recognized him as your mate. Our leopards don't lie about these things. Shadow and I both knew immediately with Liam, even when I was fighting it with everything I had."

Beth's eyes widened slightly. "You never told me that."

"Because I was terrified at the time. I was so afraid to trust," Naomi admitted. "But our leopards understand something we're only beginning to learn, because we were never taught to listen to them. They recognize what's right for us, what's true." She squeezed Beth's hand. "If Whisper knows Tyr is your mate, that's not something you need to question. It's something you can trust."

Naomi squeezed Beth's shoulder one last time before standing. "I'm going to make breakfast. You should grab a shower and get into your PJs then come eat before you try to sleep - food will help you process all this."

Beth watched her twin disappear into the kitchen, the soft sounds of cabinets opening and closing drifting back to her. She remained perched on the bottom step, her mind replaying the magical evening with Tyr. The way his falcon moved through the moonlit trees with such grace, how tenderly he'd shared that meal with her, the exhilarating freedom of running and flying together.

Her fingers drifted to her lips again, remembering the gentle pressure of his kiss. Whisper's certainty about him being their mate hummed through her blood - an unshakeable knowing that went bone-deep. For the first time since Neil's death, she felt truly alive, as if color was seeping back into a world that had been grey for so long.

The euphoria of the evening dissolved as Beth sat motionless on the step. Tyr would never age. His existence stretched beyond human comprehension, his body perpetually youthful while hers would follow the natural progression of time. The mathematical impossibility of their situation settled into her awareness, cold and unyielding.

Whisper's certainty about their mate collided with the reality of the situation. Their lifespans existed in different dimensions—his measured in centuries, hers in mere decades. It seemed a cruel irony. Shouldn't finding her mate—someone who understood both sides of her nature—bring pure joy? Why was she instead drowning in this complicated tangle of emotions?

And yet... Whisper purred softly within her consciousness, content with finding their mate, untroubled by practicalities.

The aroma of coffee and bacon drifted from the kitchen, and Beth inhaled deeply.

Beth pushed herself up from the bottom step, her muscles protesting after the evening's exertions. The wood grain beneath her fingers felt solid, real, anchoring her to the present moment despite her whirling thoughts.

The sound of Naomi humming in the kitchen brought a small smile to her face. Her sister always knew exactly what she needed - whether it was a shoulder to cry on or scrambled eggs at dawn. The familiar domesticity of breakfast preparations settled something inside her.

Her wool peacoat suddenly felt too warm, too confining. Beth shrugged out of it, hanging it on the hook by the door where traces of forest and wild places still clung to the fabric. The scent reminded her of soaring through trees with Tyr, sharing that magical connection in their animal forms.

Her feet carried her down the hall as exhaustion crept through her limbs. A hot shower would wash away the lingering forest debris caught in her hair, and maybe help clear her tangled thoughts. Maybe after some rest, she'd be better equipped to process everything. For now though, she'd focus on the basics - shower, food, sleep. Tomorrow was soon enough to face the bigger questions.

CHAPTER 12

Beth hesitated outside Dr. McCandliss's office, her hand poised to knock. Late afternoon sunlight slanted through the hallway windows, casting long shadows that stretched toward his door—shadows that seemed to mirror her own reluctance to voice what troubled her. She'd been called to a staff meeting before her shift, but she'd arrived early in hopes of a private talk with Jacinth's husband. Taking a deep breath, she tapped lightly on the door frame.

"Yes?" Douglas's voice carried through the partially open door.

Beth peeked around the edge, finding him at his desk reviewing patient charts. "Do you have a few minutes?"

"Sure, what's up?" He glanced up from his paperwork.

Warmth flooded Beth's face as she fidgeted, suddenly feeling exposed under his gentle attention. "It's... um... it's personal."

Douglas set down his pen and folded his hands on his desk, giving her his full attention. He gestured to the chair across from his desk. "Come on in."

Beth perched on the edge of the chair, her fingers twisting in her lap. The afternoon sunlight streaming through the window felt too bright, too exposing. She drew in a shaky breath.

"I... I wanted to ask you something." Her voice came out barely above a whisper. "About you and Jacinth."

"Go on," he prompted with an encouraging smile.

"What's it like?" Beth blurted, then immediately felt her face flame. "I mean... being married to someone who's immortal? When you're... not?"

Douglas's aquamarine eyes softened with understanding, and a knowing smile tugged at his lips. "Is this about Tyr?"

Beth's breath caught in her throat. Her heart thundered so loud she was sure he could hear it. She managed a tiny nod, unable to meet his gaze.

"Beth." Douglas's gentle tone drew her eyes back to his face. "How long have you been wrestling with this?"

"Since..." She swallowed hard. "Since I realized I was falling for him. But he's a vampire. He'll live forever, and I..." Her voice cracked. "I won't."

A thoughtful expression crossed Douglas's face. "You know, that was never really an issue for me. Jacinth was actually the one who struggled with it. She kept trying to push me away, for the longest time, worried about outliving me and the kids."

He smiled, the warmth of memory softening his features. "But for me? It was simple. I loved her. I wanted her in my life - in our lives. The kids adored her from day one." He spread his hands. "Everything else was just... details."

"But how?" Beth's voice cracked on the words. "How did you make peace with knowing she'd go on without you?"

"Because the alternative was living without her at all." Douglas's voice carried absolute certainty. "And that wasn't really an option that I wanted to consider."

The simple truth hit Beth like a physical blow, stealing her breath. She hadn't considered it from that angle before - that pushing Tyr away to avoid future pain meant choosing immediate pain instead.

"Look at it this way," Douglas continued. "None of us are guaranteed tomorrow, mortal or immortal. But we can choose how we spend today."

Beth felt something tight in her chest finally loosen as his words settled into place. Before she could respond, Douglas glanced at his watch.

"We should head over to Troy's office. The Chief of Police is here to talk to us about our less-than-friendly visitor the other night, which is why we asked you to come in." He stood, gathering a few folders from his desk. "Are you ready?"

"Yes," Beth said, feeling strangely lighter after their conversation. The question of immortality wasn't resolved, but somehow it felt less overwhelming now.

She followed Douglas down the hallway, her mind still processing his advice as they approached Troy's office. Douglas knocked briefly before opening the door. The space felt crowded with Troy behind his desk, Suzanne occupying one visitor chair, and a tall, broad-shouldered man in a police uniform standing near the window. All heads turned their way as they entered.

"Beth, thanks for coming in early," Troy greeted her, rising slightly from his seat. "This is Police Chief Flynn."

The chief nodded, his weathered face serious beneath salt-and-pepper hair. "Miss Kerrigan. I understand you were working during the incident the other evening."

"Yes, sir." Beth hovered near the door, wincing a bit at the chief's understatement. "I was the one who called the officers."

Troy gestured to the last vacant chair. "Please have a seat, Beth. No need to stand."

As Beth situated herself, Suzanne leaned forward. "Chief Flynn was just explaining why he came to speak with us in person."

The chief crossed his arms, his uniform crisp despite the late afternoon hour. "As I was saying, we're concerned about escalating tensions in the community since the revelation about shifters went public. What happened here appears to be the first direct confrontation we've had locally."

"It certainly caught us off guard," Troy admitted. "We've implemented security measures in anticipation of any attacks, but honestly, we weren't expecting someone to come in like she did, just ranting."

"People rarely make sense when they're driven by fear," Chief Flynn replied. His gaze settled on Beth. "I read the report from my officers.

They were impressed with how you handled the situation—especially your interaction with the boy."

Beth's cheeks warmed slightly. "I was just worried about Todd. He's clearly in a difficult situation."

"CPS is following up," the chief assured her. "But that's not the only reason I'm here. We're establishing a community response team to address potential incidents involving shifters. Given your clinic's connection to the shifter community through Dr. Shelton's wife, I wanted to coordinate directly with you."

Douglas dipped his chin in acknowledgement. "We appreciate that, Chief. We've been working on increasing security, especially for our night shift staff."

"That's why I asked Beth to join us," Troy added. "She works nights with our security team and can communicate our discussion to them."

"Security team?" The chief raised an eyebrow.

"Private security," Suzanne clarified smoothly. "Given Katerina's interview, we felt it was a prudent measure."

Chief Flynn studied each of them for a moment before nodding. "Smart move. I'd like contact information for your head of security. We should coordinate response protocols with them directly."

Chief Flynn's stern expression softened slightly. "That's not the only reason I'm here, actually." He shifted his weight, pride creeping into his voice. "My son Daniel worked here the last couple years, helping Dr. McCandliss in the barn."

"Daniel! Of course." Douglas's face lit up with genuine warmth. "He's a great kid, Chief. He really impressed me with his work ethic and how he handled the horses. We definitely feel his loss since he left for college. He has a real gift with the animals."

Beth noticed how the chief's professional demeanor had shifted when discussing his son, his broad shoulders relaxing slightly as pride replaced authority in his bearing.

"And that's why I'm here." Chief Flynn ran one hand through his short red hair. "I'm not sure if you are aware, but a couple years back, Daniel started getting into some serious trouble. Running with a bad group of kids. Skipping school, drinking and smoking, being disrespectful. That sort of thing. He had nothing but scorn for me, when I attempted to reason with him. He was on the wrong path, and I felt helpless. There seemed no way to get through to him. Then one day, he and some friends went out joyriding, fortunately in a relative's car."

Beth glanced at Douglas, noting his furrowed brow as he processed this information.

"I wouldn't have begun to think that of young Daniel," Douglas confessed. "I'm trying hard to make that connection."

Chief Flynn's fingers drummed once against the arm of his chair. "The D.A. and I sat down with the boys and their parents." His mouth quirked slightly. "These kids wanted to act like adults, so we decided to treat them like adults."

Douglas leaned forward, intrigued. "How so?"

"Simple choice," the chief continued. "Get after-school jobs - including weekends - or face felony theft charges." He shrugged. "Amazing how quickly their perspective changed when real consequences were on the table."

Troy's eyes crinkled with amusement. "Let me guess - they suddenly discovered a work ethic?"

"You could say that." Chief Flynn's stern expression cracked into a grin. "Though Daniel nearly quit after his first day here."

"Cleaning the kennels," Douglas said, understanding immediately.

"Exactly." The chief chuckled. "The kid came home reeking of disinfectant and dog hair, complaining about everything. But something made him stick it out." His expression grew thoughtful. "Then that second week, you moved him to the barn."

The chief's expression softened, pride replacing his professional demeanor. "From that day forward, everything changed." He shook his head in wonder. "Daniel came home that first evening talking nonstop about some wild mare."

Douglas's eyebrows rose. "Firefly?"

"That's the one." Chief Flynn leaned forward. "He was fascinated by how you handled her. Said you didn't just bark orders at him like most adults do." The chief's voice grew warmer. "You actually took time to explain why things needed to be done a certain way."

"He was genuinely interested," Douglas said quietly. "Most kids his age just want to get through their tasks, but Daniel asked real questions."

Chief Flynn's mouth twitched with amusement. "He spent twenty minutes at dinner that evening explaining leather conditioning to his mother and sister." He gestured expressively. "My wife was rolling her eyes, but I could see something had clicked for the boy."

Troy smiled. "Douglas has that effect on people. He makes you want to do the work right."

"The next day, he was offered the barn as his permanent assignment," the chief continued. "Daniel actually called me at work to tell me. It's the first time he'd ever reached out like that."

A smile tugged at the corners of his mouth. "And ever since, it's been 'Doc McCandliss this,' and 'Doc McCandliss that.' He hasn't been in a lick of trouble since."

Beth glanced at Douglas, who cleared his throat, a faint blush coloring his cheeks at the unexpected praise. She hadn't seen that much of Douglas, as he worked mostly with horses and livestock, but it didn't surprise her at all that he'd had such an impact on the troubled teen.

"I remember that," Troy mused. "We had a staff meeting with the partners and our office manager. Douglas, you remember? You asked us if you could have Daniel in the barn on a regular basis."

Douglas's eyes narrowed, his expression thoughtful. "I do remember. Daniel has a natural way with the horses - they responded to him immediately. And he asked such intelligent questions about their care. You could tell he was really thinking things through, not just going through the motions."

"He earned everyone's respect pretty quickly," Troy added. "Even Barbara started bragging about him to clients - and you know how particular she is about the staff."

Douglas's face softened at the memory of the mare and her foal. She'd heard snippets about that particular horse from other staff members - how dangerous she'd been when she first arrived, how no one but Douglas would go near her stall.

"Firefly was a special case," Douglas said quietly. "She'd been badly abused before she came to us as a rescue. They wanted to put her down, claimed she was too dangerous to handle. But I could see the fear in her eyes. She wasn't mean - she was terrified."

"Daniel told us how you'd spend hours just sitting near her stall," Chief Flynn continued, his voice carrying quiet admiration. "Reading paperwork or making phone calls. How you never pushed her, never tried to force her to accept you."

"Sometimes that's what healing takes," Douglas replied. "Time and patience. Letting them come to trust you at their own pace."

Beth's thought of Todd, and how carefully he was planning his own escape from an abusive situation. Some wounds needed more than just time to heal - they needed the right person to show them a path forward.

"The respect has been mutual," the chief assured him. "In great part, it was due to Dr. McCandliss's work with that mare. Daniel saw all the time he spent with her, standing outside her stall just talking to her. Putting treats on the stall door and retreating so she felt safe to come take them. Daniel had heard the stories from the other employees, of course, about how vicious she was, how she could never be tamed, but Dr. McCandliss never gave up on her."

He chuckled, shaking his head. "It made such a huge impression on Daniel, when the foal was born, he took us all out to dinner to celebrate—his mother, his little sister, and myself—and insisted on paying with the money he'd made working in the barn. He spent the entire two hours at dinner telling us all about the foal and how pretty she was, and how Doc McCandliss let him groom her."

Beth noticed Douglas's throat work with emotion as he heard how deeply the experience had affected the boy. Pride and wonder filled his features as he remembered that breakthrough.

"We were all pretty excited. None of us ever thought Firefly would come around, and now she lets my kids, Molly and Benny, sit on her back while we lead her around."

Chief Flynn's stern expression softened further. "Daniel showed us pictures on his phone. He was so proud of being part of her rehabilitation." He looked at Troy. “I know Daniel appreciates the extra hours you've given him to help out at your place as well.”

Troy smiled. “Daniel seems to have a special touch with horses.

They like and trust him. I'm glad to have his assistance. We were all sorry to lose him when he went off to college."

Chief Flynn shook his head as if in disbelief. "When I think that just a few years ago, I had despaired of my son. And now he plans to be a veterinarian himself."

Chief Flynn's expression shifted from proud father back to professional police chief, though warmth lingered in his eyes.

"Those letters of recommendation you both wrote made all the difference in Daniel's college acceptance," he said, nodding to Douglas and Troy. "The admissions board was particularly impressed by your detailed observations of his work with difficult cases."

"He earned every word," Douglas replied. "His dedication to learning proper horse handling techniques was remarkable."

Chief Flynn straightened his shoulders, authority settling back over him like a familiar coat. "Now, about the security situation. After Dr. Shelton's wife appeared on that talk show, we've been monitoring social media chatter. There's been an uptick in anti-shifter sentiment locally."

"Having private security is a smart move," he said. "Especially for your night shift staff. We've increased patrols in this area, but we can't be everywhere."

"Katerina knew going public would stir up reactions," Troy said quietly. "But she felt it was important to show that shifters are just regular people living regular lives."

"And most folks have been supportive," Suzanne added. "The hate groups are a vocal minority."

Chief Flynn nodded grimly. "True, but sometimes the loudest voices cause the most trouble."

Troy's expression was thoughtful. "Actually, Chief, we've been surprised it took this long to have any real trouble. When Katerina went public, we knew the clinic would become an obvious target."

"Exactly," Suzanne said. "That's why we contracted private security before any incidents occurred. We wanted to be proactive rather than reactive."

"The night shift was our biggest concern," Troy continued. "Fewer staff, darker conditions, more isolation. Beth and our other night employees are particularly vulnerable."

"The security team has been excellent," Beth offered. "They maintain a constant presence without being intrusive. Our regular clients don't even notice them, but they're always there if needed."

Troy's smile reached his eyes for the first time that evening. "They responded immediately when that woman started causing trouble. Within minutes, they had the situation under control, while our staff called 911."

Chief Flynn's shoulders relaxed slightly, and he nodded in approval. "Having security is a wise move. As you can imagine, law enforcement has been scrambling since the start of this, from the big cities to smaller communities like ours. Having our local celebrity coming forward as a shapeshifter made a big difference in swaying public opinion, I will say."

"We did lose some clients right away," Douglas added. "But for every one who left, we gained three new ones. People specifically seeking us out because they want to support shifters."

Beth grinned as she remembered the impact of Katerina's going public. The fashion designer's graceful revelation of her shifter nature on national television had indeed changed many minds locally. Beth had witnessed it firsthand - the way regular clients now smiled knowingly when they spotted the familiar Maine Coon lounging on the clinic's front desk, understanding it was actually Katerina in her cat form.

"The interview helped put a familiar face to it all," Troy agreed, pride evident in his voice as he spoke of his wife. "People who've known Katerina for years suddenly realized they'd been interacting with shifters all along without even knowing it."

Beth remembered Liam telling her how so many of the staff had reacted when they learned the truth - not with fear, but with delight that they'd had shifters around them all along, and finally understanding why the clinic's "resident" cats - that would be Katerina and Kester - had always seemed so intelligent and aware.

"It's certainly made our job easier," Chief Flynn continued. "When people see someone they already know and respect is a shifter, it's harder for them to buy into fear-mongering propaganda."

Beth couldn't help smiling as Chief Flynn's professional mask dropped away entirely, revealing the proud father beneath.

"My wife is a fan of Katerina's, and she's over the moon. And I must say she's quite disappointed, like Daniel, that it wasn't catching."

Troy laughed, his eyes crinkling at the corners. "Yes, that was the general consensus at the staff meeting we had when we informed everyone that we had shifters here, before Katerina's appearance on the talk show. Everyone wanted to know if they could become a shifter themselves."

Douglas chuckled. "I think every staff member had the same question that day—why couldn't they become shifters too? We had to explain it's genetic, not contagious."

"Like Daniel," Chief Flynn said, shaking his head with fond exasperation. "When he found out, all he could talk about for weeks was how cool it would be to transform into a horse. Said it would make understanding their needs so much easier."

Beth's smile widened, picturing the enthusiastic young man she'd met briefly last summer, with his shock of red hair and freckles so like his father's. She could easily imagine his disappointment at learning he couldn't simply become a shifter through exposure.

"It's funny," she said. "Most of us who are born shifters never think about how special it is until we see that reaction from humans who wish they could experience it."

Chief Flynn's gaze snapped to Beth, his eyebrows shooting upward as realization dawned. "You're a shifter, too?" He studied her with newfound interest, as if seeing her for the first time. "I wouldn't have guessed. If you don't mind my asking—" he hesitated, curiosity overtaking his professional demeanor, "what's your form?"

"I'm a clouded leopard," she answered softly.

The chief whistled low under his breath, clearly impressed. "A wild cat. That explains how you stayed so calm during that confrontation. Predator instincts."

Beth gave him a small, quiet smile, something fierce flickering in her eyes. "Let's just say I can take care of myself if needed."

Beth listened intently as Chief Flynn shifted back to official business, his posture straightening as he addressed the room.

"The police department will arrange for more patrols past the clinic," Chief Flynn told them. "You have our full support. Any shifter who feels threatened or is in danger, need only call. We'll also make sure patrols go past your home."

"It's appreciated," Troy said. "Could you include Kazakis on the patrol list?"

Chief Flynn looked puzzled. "Kazakis? The Greek deli?"

"Kester Kazakis, the owner, is Katerina's brother. It won't take five minutes on Google for someone to make that connection. So the deli will be a target also. In fact, probably more so than the clinic, since Kester actually works there, and owns the deli."

The chief pulled out his phone and made some notes. "Got it. Any others I should be aware of?"

Beth cleared her throat softly. "Carter's Bank should be on that list too."

Chief Flynn's eyebrows shot up. "The bank? Why?"

"Lydia Metaxas, the bank manager, is a shifter. She's planning to come out publicly next month." Beth smoothed her hands over her knees, remembering Lydia's determined expression at their last security meeting.

"And her husband Alex is also a shifter," Troy added. "He works at Bobcat Construction, so you might want to add them to your patrol route as well."

Chief Flynn paused in his note taking. "Are the owners of these businesses aware of the situation?"

"Yes, they all know." Douglas assured him. "The bank's CEO has been very supportive of Lydia's decision to go public. And the construction company requested additional security measures for their work sites last week, to get ahead of the situation."

Chief Flynn made careful notes about each location, his lined face set in concentration. After a minute, he turned to Beth. "Miss Kerrigan, I want to personally thank you for how you handled that situation with Todd. Having someone recognize the signs and offer support - it can make all the difference."

Emotion clogged Beth's throat, making speech impossible. "I just hope he knows he can count on us if he needs help."

"Between your clinic staff, my officers, and CPS, we'll make sure that boy stays safe." The chief's stern expression softened. "Sometimes all it takes is one person showing they care to change a life."

Chief Flynn's gaze swept the room, his expression growing more serious.

"I wish I could tell you everyone in my department was as accepting of shifters as my family," he said, his mouth tightening. "But I'd be lying. We've got some officers who are... less than enthusiastic about the situation."

"That said, the majority of my officers are at least willing to keep an open mind. My Patrol Sergeant has been instrumental in managing schedules to ensure safety for everyone."

"How so?" Troy prompted.

"He's partnering officers who support shifter rights with those who are still uncertain," Flynn explained. "And for the patrols covering shifter-owned businesses, we're only assigning officers who've demonstrated positive attitudes toward the shifter community."

The tension Beth hadn't realized she'd been carrying melted from her shoulders. It was reassuring to know they'd thought this through so carefully.

"We want to make sure any shifter who needs police assistance feels safe calling us," Flynn continued. "Having the right officers on those beats is crucial for building that trust."

As the meeting wrapped up, Chief Flynn shook hands with each of them. His firm handshake and direct gaze conveyed both authority and genuine concern for their community's well-being.

"We'll increase patrols starting tonight," he promised as he headed for the door. "And Miss Kerrigan? Don't hesitate to call if you need anything. Day or night."

"Thank you, Chief," Beth replied, warmth spreading through her chest at the sincere offer of support.

She took a deep breath as the door clicked shut behind Chief Flynn. With the chief gone, the formal atmosphere began to ease, and everyone seemed to exhale at once.

Douglas ran a hand through his toffee-colored hair. "Well, that was unexpected. When Barbara said the police chief wanted to meet with us, I thought we were in for trouble."

"Me too." Troy worked his shoulders in that unconscious way men do when stress finally lifts, making Beth have to hide a smile. "I was bracing for complaints about security overreach or demands to reduce our protective measures."

"Instead we got a proud father." Suzanne smiled, shaking her head. "Who knew Daniel's working for us would have such an impact on the situation we're in now?"

"It's nice to know we made a difference," Douglas said softly. "Though I had no idea Daniel was having problems before he came here. He was always so eager to learn, so good with the horses."

"And now we have official police support," Troy added. "That's going to make things much easier moving forward."

"Plus regular patrols." Suzanne stood, stretching. "I'd call this meeting a definite win for everyone."

The three veterinarians shared relieved looks. The atmosphere in the office had completely shifted from the tense anticipation of earlier to something lighter, almost celebratory.

"We should update Shadow Guard about this meeting," Beth suggested, her voice quiet but assured. "And Jake will want to know, too, since he coordinates the daytime security."

Troy reached for his phone. "Good thinking. The last thing we need is our security teams working at cross-purposes with the police."

"I can tell Liam when he gets home.. and Naomi too, of course," Beth offered. "And the rest of the evening shift folks. I know they're going to be relieved. We've all been a bit on edge after... well. After what happened."

Douglas smiled at her. "Thanks, Beth. That'll be great."

As the meeting broke up, Beth gathered her things. Purpose bloomed warm and steady in her chest. Two years ago, she'd been trapped in her leopard form, lost in despair at the Sanctuary. Now she sat in meetings with police chiefs, helped troubled teenagers, and served as a bridge between her shifter family and her work colleagues.

The clinic had become more than just a job—it was becoming part of her healing journey. Each day she spent here, each person she helped, each small act of courage built her confidence a little more.

Chief Flynn's words echoed in her mind: "*Sometimes that's what healing takes. Time and patience.*" As Beth made her way to the staff room to get ready for her shift, Firefly's story stayed with her. Douglas had spent hours just sitting outside her stall, never pushing, never forcing - just being present until the frightened mare learned to trust.

Beth thought about her own early days here, how she'd flinched away from kindness, certain she was too broken to heal. And now look at her - she had friends who cared about her, a job that gave her purpose, colleagues who trusted her judgment enough to include her in meetings with police chiefs. The transformation felt as miraculous as Firefly's—and just as hard-won.

Beth smiled, touching the clinic badge clipped to her scrubs. Life certainly had taken some unexpected turns, and with each passing day, she felt more eager to see what came next.

CHAPTER 13

Beth looked up from organizing the evening's files as the automatic door swooshed open. Nathan and Harper burst through, faces flushed and breathing hard. Between them, they half-dragged a massive black dog on what appeared to be a length of climbing rope. Beth had been to their home several times, visiting with their two adorable jackalopes.

"Help!" Harper's normally quiet voice carried an edge of panic.

Beth rushed around the reception desk, medical training kicking in as she scanned for injuries. But as she got closer, something about the dog made her pause. On closer inspection it appeared to be a puppy, despite the fact that it was approximately the size of a small pony.

Those paws could double as dinner plates. And despite the animal's intimidating size, there was something distinctly puppyish about its expression and movement.

"Oh!" Beth couldn't help the surprised laugh that escaped as the creature lost its balance, and flopped onto the floor with an undignified "whuff." Its shaggy black tail thumped against the tile as it grinned up at them, pink tongue lolling.

"That's... that's not a full-grown dog, is it?" Beth crouched down, keeping her movements slow and gentle. The puppy's head was nearly level with her shoulder even lying down.

"No." Harper's voice carried equal parts exasperation and amusement. "At least, you'd think?"

"It just showed up on our front porch," Nathan explained, still slightly out of breath.

The puppy rolled onto his back, long legs waving in the air as he wiggled on the floor. Despite being nearly the size of a small bear, his uncoordinated movements and goofy expression were pure baby animal.

Beth knelt beside the massive puppy, running her fingers through the thick black fur. A sudden tingling sensation, like static electricity, made her pull her hand back. Frowning, she leaned closer, parting the dense outer coat to examine the undercoat more carefully.

Her breath caught. Tiny embers danced through the dark fur, like embers caught in a breeze.

Beth straightened up slowly, keeping one hand on the puppy's shoulder to steady herself. "Nathan, Harper - I think we'd better get him into an exam room." She kept her voice deliberately calm, not wanting to alarm either the humans or the unusual creature sprawled across their lobby floor.

The couple exchanged solemn, worried glances, and nodded in agreement.

Locking the outer doors - they were officially closed now anyway - Beth watched another flicker of red dance through the puppy's fur as she led the way back to Exam Room 2. The sparks reminded her of watching a campfire, the way embers would float up into the night sky.

"Okay big guy, let's get you up on the table." Beth positioned herself at the puppy's chest while Nathan and Harper took his hindquarters. "On three - one, two, three!"

Even with all three of them working together, lifting the massive pup felt like trying to hoist a small boulder. Beth's arms strained as they managed to get him onto the exam table. She estimated he had to weigh close to a hundred pounds, despite clearly being just a puppy given his oversized paws and uncoordinated movements.

The pup's huge pink tongue darted out, catching Beth's cheek before she could dodge. His enthusiasm nearly knocked her over before Nathan managed to gently redirect the eager pup's attention.

"Ack! No, no!" She laughed, wiping puppy drool from her face. "I didn't need a bath."

"At least he's friendly," Harper commented.

"He's definitely still growing into those paws," Beth observed as she helped the gangly pup find his balance again. He rewarded her by attempting to lick her hands, face, and any other part of her he could reach. "When he does, he's going to be so enormous I can't even imagine!"

The exam room door opened as Dr. Shelton stepped in, his eyebrows shooting up at the sight of the massive black puppy taking up most of the exam table.

"What in the..." He moved closer, professional curiosity overtaking his initial surprise. "That's not like any breed I've ever seen." His hands moved with practiced efficiency as he examined the pup's ears and eyes. "The skull structure is all wrong for a Newfoundland or a Saint Bernard. A Black Russian Terrier, maybe, but..."

A red spark danced through the heavy midnight-dark fur. Troy jerked back, nearly colliding with the cabinet behind him. His moss-green eyes narrowed as he glared first at the puppy, then at Beth, Nathan, and Harper in turn.

“Oh, hell no." Troy yanked out his phone like it had personally wronged him. "Why me? Why is it always me who gets the weird ones?"

He jabbed at the screen with more force than necessary, holding the phone to his ear while keeping a wary eye on the sparking puppy.

Beth caught Harper's eye, pressing her lips together to suppress a laugh as Troy muttered into his phone. Nathan covered his mouth with his hand, shoulders shaking with barely contained mirth. The three of them shared knowing looks. Harper ducked her head, hiding her smile behind her curtain of foxy-red hair. Beth busied herself pretending to examine the climbing rope they'd used as a makeshift leash, while Nathan suddenly became very interested in studying the educational posters on the wall about heartworm prevention.

None of them dared make eye contact with each other, knowing they'd lose their composure completely if they did. The puppy's tail thumped harder against the table, sending another spray of glowing embers through his fur. Troy's exasperated sigh only made it harder for them to maintain straight faces.

"Jacinth? Clinic. Now." He paused, listening. "No, now." Another pause. "Because I've got a puppy the size of a bear, throwing off sparks like a firework show, that's why."

The puppy released a sound somewhere between a bark and a freight train's whistle.

"Yes, actual sparks." Troy pinched the bridge of his nose. "Like tiny embers. Just... can you get here?"

A soft pop of displaced air announced Jacinth's arrival in the exam room. The petite Djinn's dark eyes sparkled with delight as she took in the massive puppy sprawled across the exam table.

"Oh, aren't you just precious!" She cooed, moving closer. The puppy's tail wagged frantically, sending another cascade of tiny flames through his coat as he attempted to give her face a thorough washing.

Jacinth laughed, not bothering to dodge the enthusiastic greeting. "Such a sweet baby! Look at those paws - you're going to be enormous when you grow up, aren't you?"

She grinned at Troy. "I call dibs on telling Douglas."

Troy cleared his throat pointedly. "He's already enormous, if you hadn't noticed. What exactly is he?"

She shrugged. "I don't know. I never saw anything like this before."

"You don't know?" Troy ran his hand through his hair, exasperated. "Can you at least get someone here who does?"

"Of course!" Jacinth touched her silver bracelet, her voice taking on a more formal tone. "Kieran."

Beth watched in fascination as tiny blue symbols flickered across the surface of the bracelet, reminiscent of the red sparks dancing through the puppy's fur. The puppy seemed equally intrigued, his oversized head tilting to one side as he watched the magical display.

Beth startled as the exam room door flew open with enough force to rattle the cabinets. A tall figure filled the doorway, his white hair gleaming under the fluorescent lights.

"I was on my honeymoon," Kieran grumbled, his nordic blue eyes narrowed in annoyance. "Can this not wait?"

Despite his irritated tone, the Djinn prince managed to look both casual and regal in his cream-colored kurta - the loose-fitting tunic and straight-legged trousers adorned with gold embroidery that caught the light as he moved.

The massive puppy let out an excited bark at the new arrival, his tail wagging so hard his entire back end wiggled. More embers cascaded from his shaggy dark coat, making Troy take another step back.

"Does this look like something that can wait?" Troy gestured at the sparking puppy with obvious exasperation.

Kieran moved closer to examine the puppy, his long silver hair falling forward as he leaned in for a better look. His black eyebrows shot up. "How in the hell did you get your hands on a hellhound?"

Beth's jaw dropped. Around her, she heard Nathan and Harper's sharp intakes of breath. The puppy's tail thumped harder against the metal exam table, sending another shower of red sparks through his dense coat.

"HELLHOUND?" Troy's voice cracked as it rose several octaves.

But Jacinth seemed to have missed Troy's panic entirely. She stared at Kieran, her dark eyes widening as she replayed his earlier words.

"Wait." Jacinth held up a hand, completely ignoring the sparking puppy. "Did you say you were on your honeymoon? You got married?"

Kieran's silver eyebrow arched elegantly as he turned to face the smaller Djinn. "That is usually what a honeymoon would indicate."

Beth pressed her lips together, fighting back a smile at the prince's dry tone. The hellhound puppy chose that moment to flop onto his side, more red sparks dancing through his fur as he grinned up at them, tongue lolling.

"But... but..." Jacinth sputtered, waving her hands. "When? How did I not know about this?"

"Perhaps because I desired privacy?" Kieran's nordic blue eyes held a hint of amusement despite his stern expression. "Not everything requires a grand celebration with the entire Djinn community in attendance."

The puppy woofed, which Beth thought, with a snicker, sounded rather like a foghorn with a head cold. He attempted to roll over, his gangly legs tangling with each other in the process.

"Right," Troy said firmly. "As fascinating as your love life is, can we please focus on the HELLHOUND currently taking up my exam table?"

The puppy woofed happily at all the attention, completely oblivious to the bombshell Kieran had just dropped. His oversized paws scrabbled against the metal table as he attempted to turn in a circle, nearly sliding off before Beth and Nathan steadied him.

Another soft pop of displaced air announced a new arrival. Beth's eyes widened as an older woman materialized beside Kieran, her face flushed with excitement. She wore a flowing cream-colored galabiyya, its fabric adorned with intricate cross-stitch patterns in vibrant jewel tones that caught the light as she moved.

"Oh my God, I did it!" The woman's forest-green eyes sparkled with triumph as she steadied herself against Kieran's arm. "I actually managed to teleport on my own!"

A rare smile softened Kieran's stern features as he took her hand, his thumb brushing over her knuckles with obvious affection. "Everyone, this is my Chosen, Mandy." Pride rang clear in his voice as he made the introduction.

Troy visibly gathered himself, his professional demeanor sliding back into place despite the chaos of discovering they had a hellhound puppy in their exam room. He reached across the table and extended his hand to Mandy.

"Dr. Troy Shelton. And this is apparently the weirdest Tuesday of my career." His voice carried warmth despite his earlier exasperation. "Though I have to say, this isn't quite how I planned to spend my evening."

Beth stepped forward. "I'm Beth Kerrigan, one of the vet techs here." She gestured toward the couple who'd brought in their unusual patient. "And these are Nathan Burke and Harper O'Neill. They're the ones who found our... unexpected visitor."

Harper gave a small wave, her foxy-red hair gleaming under the exam room lights. Nathan nodded in greeting, one hand still steadying the enthusiastic overgrown puppy.

Beth watched the interplay between the Djinn with growing amusement. Jacinth's lower lip pushed out in an impressive pout as she crossed her arms, glaring at Kieran.

"I still can't believe you got married without telling anyone," Jacinth muttered.

Kieran rolled his ice-blue eyes toward the ceiling.

"We eloped," Mandy chimed in, her whole face lighting up with dimples as she grinned at Jacinth. Her forest-green eyes sparkled with mischief.

"Yes!" Jacinth wailed, throwing her hands up. "That's exactly my point! You eloped and didn't tell me!"

Beth pressed her lips together, trying desperately not to laugh at Jacinth's dramatic response. "That's... pretty much the definition of eloping," she pointed out, her voice shaking slightly with suppressed mirth.

Mandy caught her eye and delivered an exaggerated wink that broke Beth's composure completely. A giggle escaped despite her best efforts. Beth didn't know the woman at all, but she could already tell she was going to like Kieran's new wife immensely.

With amusement, Beth watched Troy pinch the bridge of his nose, his eyes squeezed shut. His chest rose and fell in a deep breath before he dropped his hand and fixed them all with an exasperated glare.

"HELLO? PEOPLE?" Troy's voice cracked with barely contained hysteria. "HELLHOUND. SPARKING. IN MY CLINIC."

The puppy's ears perked up at Troy's raised voice. His massive tail thumped against the metal surface, sending another shower of red sparks cascading through his shaggy ebony coat. He attempted to turn to face Troy, his gangly legs tangling as he nearly slid off the table. Beth and Nathan lunged to steady him.

Mandy's mouth fell open at the sight of the massive puppy sprawled across the exam table. The older woman's forest-green eyes went wide with wonder.

"Oh my God, what is this?" Mandy pressed her hands to her cheeks in delight. "Look at you, you gorgeous thing!"

The puppy's tail wagged frantically as Mandy approached. His entire back end wiggled with excitement as she wrapped her arms around his neck, completely unfazed by his intimidating size.

"Aren't you just adorable?" Mandy cooed, burying her face in the puppy's shaggy fur. "You're like a great big teddy bear! Yes you are! The sweetest, most precious teddy bear!"

The pony-sized pup attempted to give Mandy's face a thorough washing, his enormous pink tongue darting out with such enthusiasm it nearly launched her backward into Kieran's arms. She laughed and scratched behind his ears, completely unfazed by his size. More sparks danced through his coat, but Mandy didn't seem to notice or care.

"Who's the most handsome boy? You are!" She ruffled the thick fur around his neck, making the puppy wiggle with joy. "Such a good boy! Look at those big paws - you're going to be even bigger, aren't you? Yes you are!"

The hellhound puppy soaked up the attention like a sponge, his tail thumping against the table with enough force to make the cabinets rattle, the sound like a bass drum.

"It's a hellhound," Kieran told his wife, reaching out to scratch behind the pup's ears, his stern expression softening slightly, completely unfazed by the shower of sparks. "He's just a baby. He can't be more than two or three years old, I'd say. When he's full grown - in about thirty to forty years - he'll be roughly the size of a bison."

"Years?" Harper's voice squeaked. She gripped Nathan's arm, her amber eyes wide. "He's already the size of a pony!"

Nathan just stared at the Djinn Prince. "A bison? But... but that's..."

"Approximately six feet tall at the shoulder and up to twelve feet long," Kieran supplied helpfully. "Though some grow even larger, depending on their bloodline."

The puppy attempted another excited spin on the table, nearly taking out a tray of instruments with his wildly wagging tail.

"No! No!" Beth and Nathan both lunged to keep him from tumbling off, while Harper rescued the medical equipment before it could crash to the floor.

Troy slumped against the counter, looking like he might need to sit down. "Thirty to forty years to reach full size," he muttered. "A hellhound the size of a bison. Why is this my life?"

"Still new to all this supernatural stuff?" Mandy's forest-green eyes regarded Troy with sympathy.

Troy ran his hands through his hair, making it stand on end. "Been a couple years now." He gestured at the massive puppy sprawled across his exam table. "Every time I think I've got a handle on things - shapeshifters, Djinn, whatever - something new crops up." He waved helplessly at their current patient. "Case in point."

The hellhound's tail hammered rhythmically against the table, sending another shower of sparks through his thick black coat. His enormous pink tongue lolled out in a happy grin as he basked in Mandy's continued attention.

Mandy's delighted laugh filled the exam room. "Oh honey, I've only been at this a couple months." She buried her fingers deeper in the puppy's shaggy fur, completely unfazed by the tiny red embers dancing around her hands. "And I am totally loving every minute of it."

Nathan ran his fingers through his sandy brown hair, his expression a mix of concern and bewilderment. "Um, so a hellhound showed up at our door. But what are we supposed to do with him?"

"Well, first you should feed him," Kieran said, his tone matter-of-fact.

"Kieran!" Mandy regarded her Chosen in exasperation. She planted her hands on her hips, glaring up at the much taller Djinn prince. "That's not helpful. They need actual guidance here."

The prince shrugged, seemingly unperturbed. "The more pressing concern is determining where his mother is and how they became separated. A hellhound pup this young shouldn't be wandering alone. He doesn't belong in this dimension." His nordic blue eyes narrowed thoughtfully. "Jacinth, contact Kayja. As Lord Damien's demoness half-sister, she may have insights into this situation."

Kieran held out his hand to Mandy, his stern features softening as he gazed down at his new wife. "Shall we get back to our honeymoon, my love?"

Mandy's forest-green eyes lit up as she took his offered hand. "Yes, please!" She gave the puppy one final scratch behind his ears. "Be good, you adorable thing. Bye, everyone!"

The couple vanished with another soft pop, leaving behind only the lingering scent of jasmine and sandalwood.

In the sudden silence, the weight of their situation seemed to settle over the room like a blanket. They were alone. With a hellhound. A hellhound *puppy*, who would grow to the size of a bison.

Harper was the first to react. She shoved her fingers through her foxy-red hair, her amber eyes wide with dawning panic. "But what are we supposed to do with him in the meantime? We can't keep a hellhound! We've already got Jill and her mother living in the backyard!"

"We can't just abandon him either," Nathan said, steadying Harper. His normally calm expression was pinched with worry. "He's just a baby. Even if he is... well, a hellhound."

Troy sighed, rubbing his temples. "Look, take a bag of dog food to get you through tonight. At least that will keep him fed until we figure something out."

"I'll have Alyssa send Kayja to your house," Jacinth assured them, her dark eyes twinkling with amusement as she watched the puppy's antics. "She'll know what to do with this little one."

With a soft pop of displaced air, Jacinth vanished, presumably off to find her friend.

Beth couldn't help smiling as Nathan's face scrunched up in confusion.

"Wait, who's Kayja?" He glanced between them, his sandy brown hair falling into his eyes.

Harper nudged him with her elbow. "Keep up, honey. She's the vampire head honcho's demoness half-sister."

Nathan's face went three shades paler as the full implications hit him. "The vampire lord has a demon for a sister?" His voice cracked. "And she's coming to our house?"

Beth pressed her lips together, trying to maintain her composure, but Harper's snort of laughter broke her resolve. They dissolved into giggles as Nathan stared at them, his expression a perfect mix of confusion and dismay.

"Welcome to my world," Troy grumbled.

Beth slipped past Harper and Nathan as they wrangled with the uncoordinated puppy—no, hellhound—and headed for the supply closet. They kept emergency supplies for all kinds of animals, just in case clients needed something to tide them over. Beth spotted the ten-pound bag of premium kibble on the bottom shelf and hefted it into her arms.

Beth nudged the closet door closed with her hip and headed to the reception area. Tyr stood just inside the entrance, his fair hair gleaming under the fluorescent lights. The sight of him sent a flutter through her chest. Even after several weeks of working together, her reaction to him hadn't diminished.

"Tyr!" She hurried toward him, nearly dropping the bag of dog food in her excitement. "You will not BELIEVE this!"

He looked up from his phone, blue eyes lighting with interest as he took in her flushed face and the unusual burden in her arms. His lips quirked into that half-smile that never failed to make her heart skip.

"What's happened?" he asked, pocketing his phone and moving to take the bag from her.

Beth surrendered the dog food, bouncing on her toes as laughter bubbled up through her chest. "We have a hellhound puppy in Exam Room 2!"

He stared at her blankly for a moment, before asking, "How the hell did they find a hellhound?"

Beth giggled as he unconsciously echoed Kieran's words. Before she could explain, the exam room door burst open. Nathan and Harper emerged first, still wrestling with their makeshift climbing rope leash as the pup bounded between them. Troy followed after, still with that disconcerted expression on his face.

The hellhound's tail wagged frantically at the sight of a new person, nearly knocking over a display of pamphlets as he dragged Nathan and Harper toward Tyr. Red sparks showered from his thick black coat, making Troy take another step back with a muttered curse.

Tyr crouched down, completely unfazed by the magical display. He held out his hand, letting the puppy sniff his fingers before scratching behind the massive ears.

"Hey there, little guy." His voice carried the same gentle tone he used with the clinic's smallest patients.

Beth caught Harper's eye, pressing her lips together to suppress a giggle. Harper's shoulders shook with barely contained laughter as they both looked at the "little guy" who already stood nearly as tall as Tyr's waist.

"Little?" Harper's voice climbed several octaves into dog-whistle territory as she lost her battle with composure. "He's already the size of a pony!"

Beth dissolved into giggles, earning a confused look from Tyr. "Kieran says he'll grow to be the size of a bison," she managed between laughs.

The puppy woofed happily, his tail thumping against the reception desk hard enough to rattle the computer monitor. Red sparks sparked through his fur as he attempted to give Tyr's face a thorough washing.

Tyr straightened, still scratching behind the hellhound's massive ears. His blue eyes flicked to the bag of kibble on the counter.

"Yeah, that won't work," he said, shaking his head. "Hellhounds need fresh meat. A lot of it."

Harper's amber eyes went wide with alarm. "How much is a lot?"

"For a pup this size?" Tyr considered the massive black puppy, who was now attempting to climb into his lap despite being nearly as big as Tyr himself. "Probably about fifty pounds of raw meat. But he'll only need to eat every week or two."

Nathan's face went pale. "Fifty pounds?" His sandy brown hair fell into his eyes as he stared at Tyr in dismay. "Where are we supposed to get fifty pounds of meat?"

"And where would we store it?" Harper added, her voice rising in panic. She gripped Nathan's arm. "Our freezer is barely big enough for our groceries!"

"Just check with a local butcher," Tyr said, ruffling the pup's fur so it sparked even more. "Order a bunch of roasts. Tell them you're having a big barbecue or a family reunion or something."

The hellhound's tail thumped harder against the reception desk at the attention, nearly knocking over a stack of appointment cards.

Beth shrieked "No, no!" and dove forward, catching the stack of appointment cards just before they scattered across the floor. She nudged the massive puppy sideways, redirecting his enthusiastically wagging tail away from the reception desk. Harper lunged past her, snatching the container of pens before it could go flying.

The hellhound woofed happily at all the excitement, his tail now thumping against the wall instead in a thudding rhythm.

"Sorry!" Nathan grabbed the makeshift leash, trying to pull the puppy back. "He doesn't quite understand how big he is yet."

Beth straightened up, carefully setting the rescued cards back on the counter. Her heart was still racing from the near disaster. The last thing they needed was to spend an hour sorting scattered appointment cards off the floor.

The puppy attempted to turn around, his back end not quite getting the message from his front end. His oversized paws scrabbled against the tile as he nearly fell over himself, saved only by Nathan's quick grab of his shoulders.

"Careful, there." Nathan steadied the gangly pup, who rewarded him with another attempt at a thorough face-washing.

Beth couldn't help laughing at the sight of the massive hellhound trying to climb into Nathan's arms like a lapdog, completely oblivious to the fact that he was nearly as big as the musician himself. Red sparks continued to dance, creating a mesmerizing display in the fluorescent lighting of the clinic's reception area.

Nathan turned to Tyr. "That... that could actually work. About the butcher, I mean." He ran his fingers through his sandy brown hair, pushing it back from his eyes. "We wouldn't even need to worry about storage if we just bought it when it was feeding time."

Tyr nodded. "Exactly. Every week or two, just pick up what you need."

Beth couldn't help smiling as she watched the massive black puppy trying to spin in circles between them all, his oversized paws scrabbling on the tile floor. Despite his intimidating size and supernatural nature, he was still very much a baby, ungainly and sweet.

"That's actually brilliant," Harper said, her amber eyes brightening. "We can rotate between different butcher shops too, so no one place gets suspicious about our massive meat orders."

For the first time since the hellhound had bounded into their lives, the group seemed to relax slightly. They had a plan. It might be unconventional, but it was workable.

A soft pop of displaced air announced Jacinth's return, and with it, another complication. The puppy's tail wagged harder, sending another shower of sparks through his shaggy dark coat as he attempted to turn and greet her. His back end didn't quite cooperate, resulting in him nearly bowling over Harper in his enthusiasm.

"Careful!" Beth steadied the massive pup while Nathan and Harper regained their balance.

Jacinth's dark eyes sparkled with amusement as she watched their antics. "Kayja is a bit... occupied at the moment." Her lips twitched. "Apparently there's some new demon nightclub in Manhattan she simply had to check out."

Beth blinked. "Demons have nightclubs?"

"Oh yes." Jacinth's smile widened. "This one just opened last week. Something about incorporating actual hellfire into their light show?" She waved her hand dismissively. "Anyway, Kayja says she'll come by your house in an hour or so, after she's done dancing."

The hellhound woofed happily, his tail thumping against the reception desk in a steady rhythm.

Nathan's eyes went wide. "Midnight?" He glanced at Harper, who looked equally alarmed. "That's... that's really late."

"For a demon?" Jacinth laughed. "That's practically early afternoon."

"But she'll know way more than I do about hellhounds," Tyr told them. "My knowledge is pretty limited."

"Would you..." Nathan hesitated, running his fingers through his sandy brown hair. "Would you mind coming with us? Just until Kayja arrives? We've never dealt with anything like this before."

"Of course." Tyr scratched behind the hellhound's massive ears, earning another shower of sparks dancing through the black fur, creating an oddly beautiful display in the fluorescent lighting.. "I can help you get him settled in."

"Oh thank god." Nathan's shoulders slumped with relief. "Because I have no idea what we're doing here."

The puppy woofed happily, apparently approving of this plan, making them all laugh.

"Do you think he can understand what we're saying?" Beth asked, turning to Tyr.

Tyr's brow furrowed as he considered the question, his blue eyes studying the massive puppy thoughtfully. After a moment, he crouched down to the hellhound's eye level.

"Can you understand us?" he asked directly.

The puppy's response was immediate and enthusiastic. He lunged forward, nearly knocking Tyr over in his eagerness to give him a thorough face-washing. His enormous pink tongue left trails of slobber across Tyr's cheeks as his tail wagged frantically, showering red sparks everywhere.

Laughter filled the reception area. Beth covered her mouth with her hand, trying to stifle her giggles as Tyr attempted to fend off the enthusiastic puppy while maintaining his dignity. He failed at both, ending up sitting on the floor with the hellhound half in his lap, still determinedly trying to wash his face.

"I think that's a no," Harper managed between laughs.

"Or maybe it was a yes?" Beth snickered. "Hard to tell."

"Wait!" Beth stepped forward, her heart racing with excitement. "Could I come too? I'd love to meet a demoness." She bounced on her toes, grinning. "Plus, I haven't visited Jill in ages."

Troy's moss-green eyes went wide as he stared at her. "Do you know how weird that sounds? 'I'd love to meet a demoness'?" He shook his head in disbelief. "Sometimes I forget how completely insane my life has become."

Laughter erupted through the reception area.

"Welcome to the supernatural club," Harper managed between giggles, her amber eyes dancing with mirth. "Where wanting to meet demons is just another Tuesday night."

"At least she didn't say she wanted to pet one," Nathan added, his shoulders shaking with suppressed laughter.

Beth helped Harper and Nathan wrangle the pup through the clinic's front doors while Tyr held them open. The colossal puppy launched himself into the snowy night like a furry cannonball, dragging his makeshift handlers behind him as red sparks showered all around him, creating a mesmerizing display against the white snow.

"This is ridiculous." Troy locked the clinic doors behind them, his breath fogging in the cold air. "A hellhound. In my clinic."

"Could be worse." Beth grinned, watching the puppy attempt to chase his own tail, nearly taking Nathan and Harper down in the process. "At least he's friendly."

Tyr rolled his eyes at their antics. "Beth, why don't you ride with me? I'll bring you back to finish your shift after we get this sorted."

The puppy woofed happily as Nathan and Harper coaxed him toward their car, his massive paws leaving deep prints in the fresh snow. Fire motes scattered through the thick black fur, creating tiny melted spots in the snowflakes around him.

"Good luck!" Troy called after them, already heading for his own vehicle. "Text me if anything explodes! Wait... don't!"

Beth hurried to Tyr's SUV, grateful to escape the biting wind. She slid into the passenger seat, watching through the windshield as Nathan and Harper somehow managed to get the enormous puppy into their back seat. The car visibly shifted under his weight as he bounded inside, his tail still wagging enthusiastically.

"Ready?" Tyr asked, starting the engine.

Beth nodded, still grinning as she watched red sparks dance past Nathan and Harper's car windows. "This is going to be interesting."

CHAPTER 14

Beth watched the taillights of Nathan and Harper's car disappear around the corner before them, the hellhound's massive silhouette visible through their back window. Red embers occasionally flickered through their windows, creating an otherworldly light show against the dark night.

"I can't believe we're actually going to meet a demoness." Beth bounced in her seat, unable to contain her excitement. "I mean, I've met a couple of Djinn and now vampires, and whatever Angus and Renee are, but never even imagined I'd meet a demon."

Tyr's lips quirked into that half-smile that made her heart flutter as he navigated the quiet suburban streets. "Kayja is... unique."

"Is she scary?" Beth twisted in her seat to face him better. "I mean, she's Lord Damien's sister, right? And he's pretty intimidating from what I've heard."

A low chuckle escaped Tyr as he turned onto Nathan and Harper's street. "Oh, you have no idea."

Excitement buzzed through Beth as they pulled into the driveway behind her friends. The hellhound puppy bounded out of the car the moment Harper opened the door, dragging Nathan behind him on the makeshift climbing rope leash.

Red sparks showered from the pup's shaggy fur as he attempted to investigate every snow-covered bush along the front walk at once. His enthusiasm nearly knocked Harper off her feet before she managed to steady herself against Nathan.

"Easy there, big guy!" Nathan laughed, somehow maintaining his grip on the rope despite the puppy's size and strength.

As they reached the front steps, movement in the shadows of the porch caught Beth's eye. A small figure stepped forward into the porch light, and Beth's breath caught.

The woman - if she could be called that - had mottled red skin with darker patterns blending into black. Small glossy black horns curled up from either side of her head, partially hidden by long, arrow-straight hair that mixed true red and black. Black-veined red wings stretched behind her, and Beth glimpsed dainty black cloven hooves where feet should be.

But it was her eyes that held Beth transfixed - they seemed to swirl between green and blue, filled with ancient knowledge and barely contained mischief.

"Well," Kayja's smoky voice carried clear amusement as she took in their unusual group. "What have we here?"

Beth's throat went dry as she stared at Kayja's wings. The black-veined membrane seemed to pass right through the demoness's flowing dress without disturbing the fabric. She blinked hard, wondering if her eyes were playing tricks on her.

An excited bark snapped Beth from her daze. The puppy lunged forward with enough force to drag Nathan stumbling across the snow-covered yard.

"No! No!" Nathan's voice cracked as he desperately tried to maintain his grip on the climbing rope. His feet slid on the icy ground while the puppy bounded toward Kayja, showering bits of crimson flame in his wake. "Down!"

The commands had absolutely no effect. The hellhound's tail wagged frantically as he attempted to climb into Kayja's arms, apparently oblivious to the fact that he was nearly twice her size. His enormous pink tongue darted out, trying to give her face a thorough washing.

Beth watched in amazement as Kayja threw back her head and laughed, the sound like silver bells chiming. The demoness's eyes sparkled with mischief as she gazed down at the enthusiastic puppy.

Harsh, guttural syllables rolled off Kayja's tongue, the sound making Beth's ears throb unpleasantly, as if the demonic words operated on frequencies not meant for mortal hearing. She noticed Nathan and Harper both flinch at the alien sounds, Nathan's jaw tightening while Harper's shoulders hunched defensively. The language seemed to vibrate in the air, carrying otherworldly power that made the hair on the back of her neck stand up.

The change in the hellhound puppy, however, was instant and dramatic. The puppy dropped into a perfect sit, his oversized paws planted firmly in the snow. Though his entire body quivered with barely contained excitement, he remained perfectly still, staring up at Kayja with complete focus. His tail still wagged, sending more of the red embers dancing through the night air, but even that seemed more controlled now.

Beth's jaw dropped. She glanced at Nathan and Harper, finding their expressions mirroring her own shock. The climbing rope hung slack in Nathan's hands as he stared at their now perfectly behaved charge.

"How did you do that?" Harper blurted out, her amber eyes wide with disbelief.

"Oh, he's old enough to have been trained," the demoness explained, her eyes swirling oddly between green and blue. Beth found it hard not to stare. "But of course he would not understand any human language."

Another rough word rolled off her tongue. The hellhound immediately flopped onto his belly in the snow, though his tail continued wagging enthusiastically.

Kayja crouched down beside the pup, her black-veined wings folding gracefully behind her. As she stroked the thick, shaggy fur, her expression shifted to a concerned frown.

"These sparks..." She traced her fingers through another shower of red embers. "They only appear when a hellhound is distressed or agitated." She studied the puppy's face intently.

Harper shifted her weight anxiously, biting her lip. "But he doesn't seem distressed at all. He's been super happy meeting everyone. If anything, he's been trying to wash us all to death with his tongue."

The hellhound's tail thumped harder against the ground at the sound of Harper's voice, sending another shower of fiery wisps through his thick black fur. His enormous pink tongue lolled out in a happy grin as he gazed up at them adoringly.

Nathan ran his fingers through hair, mussed from trying to wrestle the oversized puppy. "If being distressed makes the fire stuff appear in his fur..." He swallowed hard. "I really don't want to see what happens when he gets angry."

"If he were angry, you'd see full-on flames." Kayja's voice was laced with humor, filling the night air as she grinned at Nathan, her pointed teeth gleaming in the porch light. The sight made Beth's breath catch - there was something both beautiful and terrifying about the demoness's smile.

Kayja's expression softened, her gaze fixed on the puppy still sprawled in the snow.

"As for being distressed..." Kayja stroked the pup's head affectionately. "He's not in his own dimension, or plane, if you will. The underworld is a very different type of place." Her voice softened, carrying a note of sympathy. "Plus, he's young enough to still need his mother."

Whisper stirred restlessly in Beth's mind, responding to the distress of a young creature separated from its pack. The thought made Beth want to wrap her arms around the enormous pup. Despite his size and supernatural nature, he was still just a baby. No wonder he'd been drawn to Nathan and Harper's love.

Nathan glanced around the quiet suburban neighborhood, his expression anxious. "Maybe we should go inside." He shifted his weight, the climbing rope still hanging slack in his hands. "Before someone notices the, uh, wings. Or the flames."

The moment Nathan opened the front door, the hellhound bounded inside with enough enthusiasm to make the whole house shake. His long tail with its feathery black fur knocked over an umbrella stand as he attempted to investigate every corner of the entryway at once.

Beth hurried in after him, not wanting to miss any of Kayja's insights about their unusual visitor. The demoness followed, her wings somehow passing through the doorframe without touching it. The sight made Beth's eyes hurt as she tried to understand how that was possible.

"Please, sit." Kayja gestured to the couches with an elegant wave of her hand. "Let me see what our young friend has to tell us."

The demoness crouched down beside the enormous puppy, who immediately stilled, his ears perked at attention, his entire body quivering with barely contained energy. Grating sounds rolled from Kayja's tongue, making Beth massage the spot just in front of her ears as the vibrations created a dull ache. To her amazement, the hellhound responded with a series of low whuffs and rumbling sounds, tilting his massive head as if truly engaged in conversation.

"Did you just... talk to him?" Beth leaned forward, unable to contain her curiosity. "And he answered you?"

Kayja's lips curved into that pointed-tooth smile that was both beautiful and unnerving. "Hellhounds are far more intelligent than Earth's animals." She scratched behind the puppy's enormous ears, earning a happy puppy groan. "While we cannot have detailed conversations, they can certainly communicate rough ideas and concepts."

The hellhound woofed again, his tail thumping against the floor hard enough to rattle the coffee table.

"See?" Kayja's eyes swirled between green and blue as she regarded the puppy with obvious fondness. "He may be young, but he understands far more than you might expect."

Fascinated, Beth watched as the demoness as she spoke in that alien sounding language again. The hellhound immediately dropped into a perfect sit, his tail still wagging enthusiastically despite his otherwise perfect stillness. More of the ruby embers danced through his thick black fur, creating tiny scorch marks on the hardwood floor.

"Sit," Kayja said clearly in English, her voice infused with command, emphasizing the word. She glanced at the puppy, who remained perfectly still except for his wagging tail.

Another string of otherworldly sounds rolled off her tongue, and the hellhound bounded to his feet, nearly knocking over a side table in his excitement.

Kayja turned to Harper and Nathan, her eyes flickering from green to blue, then back again. "Now you try. Tell him to sit."

Nathan stepped forward, gripping the climbing rope leash nervously. "Sit?"

The hellhound's enormous head tilted to one side as he stared at Nathan, his tail swishing back and forth. Then, to Beth's amazement, the puppy lowered his hindquarters to the floor in a perfect sit.

Beth couldn't help grinning as Harper's shoulders slumped with relief.

"Oh thank God," Harper breathed, making them all laugh.

The hellhound's tail thumped harder against the floor at their laughter. His enormous pink tongue lolled out in a happy grin as he gazed up at them adoringly, but he held his sitting position.

Kayja's rich laughter filled the room. "Now, let's try 'down.'" She demonstrated the command first in the gravelly demonic language, then in English. The oversized pup immediately flopped onto his belly, though his tail continued wagging enthusiastically.

The demoness ran the pup through more commands - "up" and "come" - having Nathan and Harper practice each one. The hellhound responded perfectly every time, his entire body quivering with barely contained excitement as he obeyed.

"He's a quick learner," Kayja praised, scratching behind the puppy's enormous ears. "He already knows the commands, of course, he only had to learn to recognize the English.

She had another short incomprehensible conversation with the pup, then returned her attention to Harper and Nathan, indicating the patio door with a tilt of her head. "He'll let you know when he has to go out."

"How long before we need to feed him?" Tyr asked. "They'll need to arrange something with the butcher."

Kayja's eyes swirled between green and blue as she regarded the puppy. Those otherworldly words rolled off her tongue again. The hell-hound responded with a series of low whuffs and rumbling sounds.

"He's eaten recently," Kayja translated, her pointed teeth gleaming as she looked at them. "You should be fine for another week or so."

"The most important thing now is finding his mother." The demoness's black-veined wings rustled as she straightened to her full height. She surveyed them all with those mesmerizing eyes that shifted between green and blue. "Would you be willing to keep him until I can locate her? It's not safe for a pup his age in the underworld without his mother's protection. There are... things there that would see him as easy prey. If you'll keep him safe here, I will go to the underworld myself to search for his mother."

Harper and Nathan exchanged a long look. Nathan ran his fingers through his hair, pushing it back from his eyes. "We can't just abandon him." He glanced at Harper, who nodded firmly.

"Of course we'll keep him," Harper said, her eyes bright with determination. "He needs us."

Kayja's lips curved into an approving smile, her pointed teeth gleaming in the soft living room light. The demoness's wings rustled softly.

"My brother has agreed to compensate you for feeding him," Kayja said, looking amused. "Lord Damien understands such a large puppy will require significant resources."

Harper's eyes went wide. "That's... very generous, and we definitely appreciate it." She glanced at Nathan before turning back to Kayja. "But why would a vampire lord care about a hellhound puppy?"

Kayja's eyes swirled between green and blue as her grin widened, making Beth's breath catch. There was something both beautiful and unnerving about that pointed-tooth smile. The demoness turned to Tyr, tilting her head.

"Would you like to tell them?" Kayja's honeyed voice carried clear amusement.

Tyr chuckled, his blue eyes dancing with mirth as he looked at their confused expressions. "Lord Damien is half demon himself."

Beth's jaw dropped. She stared at Tyr, then at Kayja, her mind struggling to process this revelation. The vampire lord who ruled over New York City - the Dark Lord himself - was half demon?

"We share the same father," Kayja confirmed, her chin lifting in pride. "Damien is quite a bit older than me, and his mother was human." Her eyes swirled between green and blue as she turned her attention back to the pup.

Those raw, gravelly syllables rolled off her tongue again, making Beth's ears ache again. The hellhound immediately flopped onto his belly, his tail still wagging enthusiastically despite his otherwise perfect stillness. Kayja crouched beside him, running her fingers through his coat.

Beth pressed her fingers against her ears as the demoness began speaking again to the pup, who responded with a series of low whuffs and rumbling growls, his head tilting as if engaged in serious conversation.

Suddenly, Kayja stiffened. Her pointed teeth bared in a snarl that sent chills down Beth's spine. A deep, inhuman growl rumbled from the demoness's throat as her eyes flashed dangerously between green and blue. Gone was the playful, mischievous creature who had been teaching them commands. In her place stood something ancient and terrifying, radiating otherworldly power that made the air crackle with tension.

Beth took an involuntary step backward as Kayja transformed from playful to predatory in an instant. The demoness's wings flared wide, the black veins pulsing with dark energy as her eyes flashed between green and blue with frightening intensity.

"This pup," Kayja's voice turned razor-sharp, the temperature in the room seeming to drop with each syllable, "was torn from his mother's side. Summoned by a human sorcerer who dared reach into the depths of hell itself."

Outrage for the stolen pup surged through Beth, even as every instinct screamed at her to back away from the rage radiating off Kayja in waves. Around her, she heard Harper and Nathan's sharp intakes of breath. Even the hellhound puppy went still, his tail no longer wagging as he pressed closer to Kayja's side.

A low, dangerous growl filled the room. Beth turned to see Tyr's normally gentle features transformed into something ancient and predatory. His blue eyes had taken on an eerie glow as his lips pulled back, revealing extended fangs.

"A sorcerer?" Tyr's voice carried centuries of contained violence. "How dare he!"

Kayja's pointed teeth gleamed as she snarled, the sound making Beth's skin crawl. "Someone who deeply regretted their actions, I assure you." The demoness's wings rustled ominously as she placed a protective hand on the hellhound's head. "No one steals a pup from its mother without consequences."

"Perhaps the fool thought a hellhound would be easier to control than a demon," Tyr growled, the dangerous edge to his voice carrying centuries of contained violence. "Safer."

Kayja's laugh held no warmth now. Her pointed teeth gleamed as she grinned, the expression making Beth's blood run cold. This wasn't the mischievous smile from earlier - this was the grin of an apex predator.

"Well," the demoness purred, her multicolored eyes churning faster with predatory satisfaction, "he was wrong."

Beth glanced at Harper and Nathan, seeing her own mix of horror and curiosity reflected in their expressions. She swallowed hard, gathering her courage. "How... how did the pup get away from the sorcerer?"

Kayja's pointed teeth gleamed as her lips curved into another predatory smile - one that made Beth's blood run cold. The demoness's eyes swirled between green and blue with dark amusement.

"He ate him."

Silence stretched out for a long moment. Harper's face went ashen, and Nathan's mouth dropped open. Beth swallowed, hard, her stomach churning, but looking at Tyr, she saw something different in his expression - approval.

He crouched down beside the hellhound, scratching behind those floppy furry ears.

"Awesome." His blue eyes gleamed with satisfaction as he patted the puppy's shaggy coat. "Good boy."

"Was it..." Harper's voice came out faint, her lips trembling. "Was it someone here? In our community?"

Kayja turned to the hellhound, words in her demonic language rolling off her tongue again. The puppy responded with a series of low whuffs and rumbling sounds, pressing closer to the demoness's side.

"No." Kayja's eyes swirled between green and blue as she translated. "It was quite some distance from here. This little one has been wandering for several days, trying to find his way back to the underworld." Her pointed teeth gleamed in a gentler smile. "He sensed the jackalopes, which drew him here."

Harper stared at the demoness, puzzled. "Jill and Sage?"

Kayja's expression softened as she stroked the hellhound's thick black fur. "He sensed they were Other creatures - magical beings like himself." Her eyes swirled between green and blue as she gazed at Nathan and Harper. "But more than that, he felt the love and care you give them. The affection radiating from your home drew him here, and the knowledge he would find safe harbor."

Beth's throat tightened with emotion as she met Harper's moist eyes. Both women sniffled, overcome by the thought of this lost puppy - supernatural or not - being drawn to the warmth and love they offered to magical creatures.

"That's..." Beth wiped at her eyes, her voice thick with emotion. "That's actually really sweet."

The hellhound's tail thumped harder against the floor as he gazed up at them with complete adoration. Despite his huge size and supernatural nature, in that moment he was simply a lost baby who had found his way to safety through the power of love.

Nathan stood and approached Kayja and the pup, his hair falling into his eyes as he crouched beside them.

"Kayja, could you tell him he's safe with us?" Though his voice shook slightly, his words carried firm conviction. "We'll protect him and take care of him until his mother is found."

The demoness's eyes swirled between green and blue as she regarded Nathan thoughtfully. Then more of those unintelligible words rolled from her tongue, and the hellhound's head tilted as he listened, intelligence in his coal-black eyes.

More otherworldly sounds filled the room as Kayja and the puppy engaged in what seemed like an actual conversation. Whatever the demoness was saying, was met with soft whuffs and rumbling sounds from the hellhound.

Harper squeezed Beth's arm, whispering excitedly. "Look! They're fading!"

She was right. As Kayja continued speaking in that ancient language, the red embers flickering through the hellhound's coat grew fewer and farther between. His tail still wagged, but the motion no longer sent flickers of sparks through the air.

Finally, the last tiny red spark faded from his black fur. The hellhound pressed closer to Kayja's side, his enormous pink tongue darting out to give her cheek a gentle lick. When he turned to gaze at Nathan and Harper, his eyes held complete trust.

"He understands," Kayja said, her voice firm with approval. "And he accepts your protection until I can locate his mother."

Beth felt a sudden tingle of magic dance across her skin, making the fine hairs on her arms stand up. A soft pop echoed through the living room as a young man materialized beside Kayja. He appeared to be in his early twenties, with spiky black hair and milk-white skin that seemed to glow in the soft lamplight.

"Remi!" Kayja's delighted squeal held none of her earlier menace as she threw her arms around the newcomer. Her black-veined wings fluttered with excitement.

"Hey there, trouble." Tyr grinned and stepped forward, exchanging a high-five with the young man.

"Remi!" Harper bounced on her toes, her bright eyes sparkling. "Perfect timing! Wait until you see who showed up tonight!"

"Dude! I heard there was a hellhound!" Remi's lean features lit up with pure joy. He crouched down beside the enormous puppy, completely unfazed by its supernatural nature. "Oh man, look at you! Freakin' fantabulous!"

The hellhound's tail immediately started wagging, sending tiny wisps of crimson smoke through the air - much less dramatic than the earlier sparks. His enormous pink tongue darted out, attempting to give Remi's face a thorough washing.

"Whoa there, big guy!" Remi laughed, somehow managing to dodge the enthusiastic tongue while still scratching behind those massive ears. "Easy with the kisses!"

Beth stared at Remi with fascination. Though they'd only met briefly at the security meeting at the West Side Inn, his mannerisms echoed Jacinth's so strongly she would have pegged him as a Djinn anyway. The same otherworldly grace flowed through his movements, and his eyes held that distinctive spark of ancient mischief she'd come to associate with Djinn.

His tousled dark hair fell in loose waves as he moved, his deep brown eyes alight with enthusiasm as he crouched beside the hellhound pup. The contrast between his obvious magical nature - he had literally appeared out of thin air moments ago - and his genuine excitement as he interacted with the enormous puppy made Beth's lips curve into a smile.

"Where did you come from?" Remi's voice took on that special tone people used when talking to adorable animals. "Who's a good boy? Are you a good boy?"

The hellhound's tail thumped harder against the floor as he attempted to climb into Remi's lap, apparently forgetting he was nearly twice the size of the young Djinn.

"This is so cool." Remi's grin was infectious as he stood up, moving toward the sofa and draping himself across the cushions in a lazy sprawl.

Abandoned by Remi, the hellhound bounded across Nathan and Harper's living room, his heavy tail knocking over a potted plant.

"No! No!" Harper lunged to catch the falling plant, barely managing to save it before dirt spilled everywhere.

Nathan snickered. "At this rate, he's going to think his name is 'No! No!' since that's all we seem to say to him."

The hellhound's ears perked up at the repeated phrase, his tail wagging harder as he bounded over to Nathan.

"Oh my god." Harper's eyes went wide as she set the plant safely on a higher shelf. "Did you see that? He actually responded to it!"

Beth couldn't help giggling as the puppy sat at Nathan's feet, gazing up at him adoringly. "I think he likes it."

"Nono." Kayja tested the name, the smoky tones of her voice carrying clear amusement. She addressed the hellhound. The puppy's tail thumped harder against the floor as he turned to look at her.

"It's perfect!" Tyr said, snickering. "I mean, look at him - he's basically a walking disaster area. Everything he does makes you want to yell 'No! No!'"

As if to prove Tyr's point, the newly-named Nono attempted to climb into Nathan's lap, nearly knocking him over in the process.

"Nono!" Harper laughed, the name already feeling natural. "Down boy!"

The hellhound immediately flopped onto his belly, though his tail continued wagging enthusiastically. His head tilted as he looked between them all, clearly pleased with the attention.

"Well," Tyr chuckled, "I guess that settles it. Nono it is."

Remi's expression suddenly shifted, his dark eyes lighting up with remembrance. He patted his pockets, finally pulling out a sleek black debit card.

"Oh! Almost forgot." He held the card out to Nathan. "Jacinth asked me to give you this. It's preloaded with enough to cover meat from the butcher for a couple weeks."

Nathan accepted the card, eyes widening as he stared at it. "That's... really generous."

Harper peered over his shoulder at the card. "We can't possibly-"

"Of course you can." Kayja cut through Harper's protest. The demoness's eyes swirled between green and blue as she stroked Nono's thick black fur. "I'm quite certain I can locate his mother within that time frame."

Harper narrowed her eyes playfully as she crossed her arms. "I dunno, I feel like I should be kind of offended that they think Nathan and I can't afford to feed the pup, even if it is a roast-eating hellhound."

"Oh please." Kayja's honeyed laughter filled the room as her black-veined wings rustled. "This has nothing to do with your financial situation." The demoness's eyes swirled between green and blue with amusement. "My brother simply believes in taking responsibility when supernatural creatures end up in the human realm."

"Besides," Remi added, his dark eyes dancing with mischief, "you're basically providing a supernatural foster home here. Between Jill, Sage, and now Nono?" He gestured at the hellhound, who perked up at his new name. "You're running a magical menagerie."

Beth couldn't help giggling as Nono's tail thumped harder against the floor. The hellhound gazed up at them all adoringly, tongue hanging out as he panted happily, completely oblivious to the discussion about his dietary needs.

"Think of it as hazard pay," Tyr suggested, his blue eyes twinkling. "For all the furniture he's probably going to destroy."

As if on cue, Nono's wagging tail knocked over a side table, sending a lamp crashing to the floor.

"No! No!" Nathan and Harper shouted in unison, making everyone burst out laughing.

The hellhound's tail wagged harder at hearing his new name, creating more wisps of red smoke as he bounded over to shower them with enthusiastic kisses.

"Besides," Remi added, scratching behind Nono's floppy ears, "you're doing us all a huge favor by keeping him safe. The least we can do is cover his food costs."

Beth couldn't help smiling as she watched Nathan and Harper exchange a long look. Finally, Harper's shoulders relaxed and she nodded.

"Thank you," Nathan said, carefully tucking the card into his wallet. "We really appreciate it."

CHAPTER 15

Tobi circled the pack house grounds in a wide arc, his boots crunching softly in the snow. The winter moon cast sharp shadows across the pristine snow, making it easy to spot any disturbances. Nothing seemed out of place - no unusual tracks, no unfamiliar scents. Yet something nagged at his instincts, drawing him closer to the house.

His instincts rarely lied to him. Tobi altered his path, moving in tighter circles around the building. The feeling grew stronger as he approached the east wing where most of the guest rooms were located.

He heard the usual nighttime sounds with preternatural clarity - the quiet hum of the heating system, someone's television playing softly upstairs where Joe, the alpha wolf, resided with his wife, the rustle of sheets as sleepers turned over. But there - underneath it all - a racing heartbeat that didn't match the peaceful rhythm of sleep.

Tobi stopped beneath a floor window, head tilted as he focused on the sound. Rapid breathing, small whimpers of distress. Yousuf's room.

The child's pulse hammered against his ribs, caught in the grip of terror, his breath coming in sharp gasps. Tobi recognized the patterns - nightmares had their own signature: racing pulse, strangled breathing, muffled sobs.

His enhanced hearing caught the sudden change in Yousuf's breathing - the sharp intake followed by muffled sounds of terror. The nightmare had torn him from sleep, panic flooding his small body. The boy's heart beat even faster as he buried his face in his pillow to stifle his cries.

Without conscious thought, Tobi tapped his fingers against the window pane - just loud enough for Yousuf to hear, but not enough to wake anyone else.

The muffled sounds ceased abruptly. Through the glass, Tobi saw Yousuf's head snap up from the pillow, tear tracks glistening on his cheeks in the moonlight. The boy's eyes went wide as he stared at the window, his small frame trembling.

"It's okay, Yousuf," Tobi called softly, pitching his voice to carry through the glass without being too loud. "It's just me - Tobi. The vampire security guy, remember?"

Yousuf's rigid posture relaxed slightly as recognition dawned in his eyes. He scrubbed at his wet cheeks with the back of his hand, small hiccups escaping as he fought for control.

Tobi watched as Yousuf slid out of his race car bed, bare feet silent on the carpeted floor. The boy pushed the window up, letting in a gust of cold winter air. His small shoulders shook, either from the chill or lingering fear.

"Nightmare?" Tobi kept his voice barely above a whisper, conscious of Layla sleeping in the next room.

Yousuf nodded, fresh tears welling in his blue eyes. "Bad men came. They... they took me from my bed at night." His voice quivered. "Like before."

Tobi's heart clenched at the raw fear in the boy's voice. He'd heard the stories of the compound, of children vanishing in the night, never to be seen again.

"No one can get to you now." Tobi gestured at the security cameras visible from the window. "See those? You watched us install them, remember?"

"But what if-"

"And that's not all." Tobi tapped the window frame where they'd installed sensors earlier. "These will tell us if anyone even tries to open a window. The bad guys can't get past all that fancy equipment."

Yousuf peered closely, trying to see the sensor in the dark, and Tobi noted that the boy's heart rate was finally beginning to slow.

"Plus," Tobi added with a gentle smile, "I'm right here tonight. No one gets past me, I promise. And even when I'm not here, there will always be a vampire watching over the grounds."

"Every night?" Yousuf's voice carried desperate hope.

"Every single night." Tobi nodded firmly. "Sometimes it'll be me, sometimes my brother Tyr, or Dimitri. But there will always be someone keeping you safe."

Tobi glanced past Yousuf into the darkened room, remembering how pitch black the hallway had been when they'd installed the security system. No wonder the kid was scared - even vampires preferred some light to navigate by.

"Hey, you know what might help?" Tobi kept his voice low. "We could put a nightlight in here. And maybe some small lights along the hall to your mama's room."

Yousuf's whole face lit up, fear forgotten in an instant. "Really? You can do that?"

"Of course." Tobi smiled at the boy's enthusiasm. "I know exactly what we need - special LED lights that won't disturb anyone's sleep. I can install them tomorrow night."

"Promise?" Yousuf gazed at him, hope replacing the earlier terror in his expression.

"Cross my heart." Tobi made an X over his chest. "Now, think you can get back to sleep? Your mama will have my head if she finds out I kept you up talking."

Yousuf nodded, already climbing back into his race car bed. He pulled his blanket up to his chin, a small smile playing across his face. "Thank you, Mr. Tobi."

"Just Tobi, little kitty." He tapped the window frame gently. "Sweet dreams this time, okay?"

Yousuf was already yawning. "'kay," he mumbled sleepily.

Tobi lingered by the window until Yousuf's breath grew quiet and even. Only when the boy had settled into peaceful sleep did he step back from the house. Snow crunched under his boots, his gaze still fixed on the darkened window. He pulled his phone from his pocket, the screen's glow illuminating his face in the night. His fingers moved swiftly across the keyboard.

«*Yousuf had nightmare. Scared of intruders. Priority watch on east wing, first floor, third window from left. Kid needs to feel safe.*»

He added a second message: «*Will install nightlights tomorrow. Put in order for motion-activated hallway lighting*»

The response came almost immediately: «*Acknowledged. Shifting patrol patterns to increase visibility from child's window*»

Tobi frowned, realizing Yousuf's window remained open, letting in the bitter winter air. Tobi couldn't close and lock it from out here, he'd need to go inside. He circled around to the front door. The keypad beeped softly as he punched in the numbers, and the door clicked open. Tobi moved through the darkened house with practiced silence, his footsteps making no sound on the hardwood floors. Centuries of hunting had taught him how to move like a ghost.

As he approached Yousuf's room, Tobi slowed. A shape on the floor outside the boy's door caught his attention. Layla lay curled on a makeshift pallet of blankets, her breathing deep and even in sleep. Her dark red hair spilled across the thin pillow, and one arm stretched toward her son's door, as if reaching for him even in slumber.

Tobi paused, understanding dawning on him. She slept here every night, keeping watch over her son. The faint shadows he'd noticed beneath her eyes weren't just from her traumatic past - they came from night after night on this hard floor, her body never truly resting.

He knelt beside her, studying her face in repose. Without the constant wariness she carried during waking hours, she looked younger, the lines of worry temporarily erased. But the floor beneath her thin blankets offered little cushioning against the hardwood. No wonder she moved stiffly.

Careful not to wake her, Tobi stepped over Layla and slipped into Yousuf's room. The boy remained deeply asleep, his chest rising and falling in the peaceful rhythm of childhood dreams. Tobi gently closed the window, making sure the latch clicked securely into place.

Before leaving, he tucked the blanket more snugly around Yousuf's shoulders. The boy murmured something in his sleep but didn't wake.

Back in the hallway, Tobi looked down at Layla again. This wouldn't do. She needed proper rest if she was to heal from her past. He pulled out his phone and added another message to his earlier texts:

«Need to get proper daybed for hallway outside Yousuf's room. Layla sleeping on floor every night. Also recommend baby monitor system so she can sleep in her own room but still hear him.»

The reply came swiftly: «*Will arrange delivery tomorrow. Good catch.*»

Tobi knelt beside Layla's sleeping form, hesitating before touching her shoulder. "Layla," he whispered, keeping his voice low and gentle. "Wake up."

Her eyes snapped open, body tensing as she jerked upright. A small sound of fear escaped her throat before recognition dawned in her wide eyes.

"It's just me," he soothed, giving her space. "Let's get you somewhere more comfortable to talk."

Layla glanced at Yousuf's door, reluctance clear in her posture.

"He's sleeping peacefully," Tobi assured her. "I just checked on him."

After another moment's hesitation, she nodded and rose stiffly from her makeshift bed. Tobi led her to the den, where moonlight spilled through large windows onto comfortable furniture.

Layla sank into an overstuffed armchair, pulling her knees to her chest. Her fingers twisted in the hem of her sleep shirt. Tobi studied her exhausted face, noting the dark circles under her eyes.

“How long have you been sleeping in the hallway?” he asked softly.

"Since we came here." She stared down at her hands. "I know it's foolish, but..." Her voice cracked. "I can't forget that night. Waking up to find his bed empty."

Tears slid down her cheeks. "They took him in the night, like they did with all the children deemed unworthy. The elders would decide which ones to... to cull." She wrapped her arms tighter around herself. "I awoke, and he was gone. I... I searched the house, screaming his name. But they'd already carried him out to the desert to be exposed - left to die under the sun."

She lifted her tear-filled gaze to meet his.

"Yousuf is not my first son." Her voice cracked, fresh pain etching lines around her eyes. "They took them all from me. One at a time. All of them." She wrapped her arms tighter around herself, as if trying to hold the pieces together, squeezing her eyes shut. "Yousuf... he is all I have left."

The words hit Tobi like physical blows. Seven centuries of existence had exposed him to countless horrors, but this... His throat tightened with rage.

"How many?" The question scraped past his clenched teeth.

"Yousuf is my sixth son. Five were taken to be... exposed."

"Five?" Tobi surged to his feet, unable to contain the explosion of fury that ripped through him. His fangs extended involuntarily as seven hundred years of carefully maintained control shattered. He paced across the room, and the lamp beside him flickered as his power rolled through the room in waves of cold rage.

The sheer magnitude of her loss - six children torn from their mother's arms, murdered for being "unworthy" - rage and anguish twisted in his chest. Small wonder she kept vigil. After losing five children, how could she risk closing her eyes? No wonder anxiety never left her eyes.

Tobi froze mid-stride, his mind racing through calculations. Something wasn't adding up. She looked young, but he'd assumed the trauma had aged her prematurely. Now, studying her more carefully...

"Layla." He forced his voice to remain gentle despite his growing dread. "How old are you?"

She blinked up at him, confusion crossing her tear-stained face. "Twenty-five."

The room temperature plummeted as Tobi's fury leaked into the air around him. Twenty-five. Six pregnancies. His hands clenched into fists as he struggled to maintain control.

Layla's gaze dropped to her hands twisted in her lap. "In the compound, they didn't wait. As soon as a girl had her first blood, she was... given to one of the men." Her voice grew distant, hollow. "I was thirteen. Just..." She trailed off, unable to continue.

Arctic cold radiated from his body, frost crystallizing on the windows. The lamp exploded in a shower of sparks. Thirteen years old. They'd forced a child to bear children. His vision went red as his vampiric nature surged forward, demanding violence, demanding blood."

"They said it was our duty." Layla's voice shook. "To preserve the caracal shifter bloodline. The elders chose which males would... would..."

She couldn't finish. She didn't need to. Tobi's enhanced hearing caught the spike in her heart rate, the way her breathing turned shallow and rapid as the memories overwhelmed her.

Tobi gained control over his emotions, pushing them away, and came to crouch before her, his voice gentle but firm. "Layla, look at me." He waited until her tear-filled eyes met his. "You saw the equipment we installed - cameras, motion sensors, perimeter alerts. The whole system creates layers of protection."

"But-"

"And that's just the technology." He gestured toward the window where the moon cast silver light across the snow. "From the moment the sun sets until it rises again, there's always a vampire on patrol. Always. We don't sleep at night - it's what we're made for."

Layla's fingers twisted in her shirt. "Patrol?"

"Yes." Tobi's blue eyes held steady on hers. "Sometimes it's me, sometimes Tyr or Dimitri takes shifts too. Never forget, Layla, that we are vampires. We're not simply guards - we are predators, hunters. It's what we were created for. Our senses are enhanced far beyond human capabilities. We can hear heartbeats through walls, smell strangers from a quarter mile away, see clearly in almost total darkness."

"The compound had guards too," Layla whispered.

"Guards who were your captors." Tobi's voice hardened. "We're not your jailers, Layla. We're here to be protectors. There's a difference." He gestured at the security panel glowing softly on the wall. "This technology isn't meant to confine you - it's here to protect you and Yousuf. You and Yousuf are free to come and go as you please. But anyone trying to hurt you or yours?" His fangs glinted in the moonlight. "They won't make it past the tree line."

Tobi's expression sobered. "There's something else you need to know. Yousuf had a nightmare tonight."

Layla's face drained of color. "I didn't hear him."

"He was trying to keep quiet." Tobi's voice gentled. "I heard him while patrolling. He was muffling his cries in his pillow."

"Oh, my sweet boy." Layla pressed her hand to her mouth, fresh tears welling. "He... he does that. Tries to hide them from me." Her shoulders shook. "I'm his mother. I should be the one comforting him, but he's trying to protect me instead."

"Has he talked to you about the nightmares?"

"No." The word came out as barely a whisper. "He pretends everything is fine. When I ask, he just smiles and says he slept well." She wrapped her arms around herself. "I know it's not right. A child shouldn't feel they have to protect their parent. But I don't... I don't know how to help him."

"He told me what the nightmare was about." Tobi leaned forward, resting his elbows on his knees. "He dreamed they were taking him again. Coming for him in the night, like before."

A small sound of distress escaped Layla's throat.

"I promised him we'd install some nightlights in his room," Tobi continued. "And maybe some motion-activated lights for the hallway. He seemed to like that idea."

"He's afraid of the dark." Layla's voice cracked. "In the compound, they always came in darkness. But I thought... I thought if I slept outside his door..."

"You can't heal him by breaking yourself," Tobi said softly. "Both of you need proper rest to recover from what happened."

Tobi pulled out his phone, showing Layla the earlier text exchange. "I've already contacted Shadow Guard about getting some equipment installed. We'll put gentle LED lights along the hallway between your rooms - they'll activate automatically when someone walks past, but they're dim enough not to disturb anyone's sleep."

He scrolled to the next message. "And we're getting a nanny cam system for Yousuf's room. It'll let you check on him from your own bed, and you'll be able to hear if he's having a nightmare."

"A nanny cam!" Layla's eyes widened, her hand flying to her mouth. "I hadn't even thought of that. With everything being so different here, all this technology..." She shook her head, wonder replacing some of the worry in her expression. "In the compound, we had nothing like this."

"The camera will connect to an app on your phone," Tobi explained, keeping his voice gentle. "You can watch him sleep, hear him breathe, all from your own room. And if he needs you, you'll know immediately."

"And I could actually sleep in my bed?" Layla's voice held equal parts hope and uncertainty.

"That's the idea." Tobi smiled encouragingly. "The equipment will be here tomorrow. We can have it all set up before sunset."

Layla's cheeks flushed dark red in the moonlight. "I... I'll pay you back for the nanny cam system. Whatever it costs." Her fingers twisted anxiously in her shirt hem. "I have some money saved from working at the clinic-"

"Stop right there." Tobi held up his hand. "The Shifter Council has already funded all security measures for the shifter community. That includes cameras, sensors, lighting - everything." He smiled gently at her obvious discomfort. "This isn't charity, Layla. It's protection that you and every other shifter deserve."

"But-"

"The Council set aside significant resources specifically for this, since shifters were outed to the public." Tobi kept his voice soft but firm. "They want to ensure everyone has what they need to feel safe in their homes and places of work."

Layla's shoulders slumped, relief warring with lingering embarrassment on her face. "I'm not used to... to people helping without expecting something in return."

"I know." Tobi's heart ached at the raw vulnerability in her voice. "But that's not how things work here. The shifter community - indeed, the Other community - takes care of its own. You know that, Layla."

Layla thought that over. "And someone will be here, very night?"

"Every single night, without exception." Tobi's voice carried absolute certainty. "I'm sending a request to Antonio, the head of the security company, that we include specific attention to this wing of the house. If either of you calls out, even in a whisper, we'll hear you."

The moonlight caught the moisture gathering in Layla's eyes. She blinked rapidly, trying to contain it, but he could see the gratitude shining there.

Tobi continued, his tone gentle but firm. "Lord Damien has

approved additional resources. More of our clan will be moving here in the next days and weeks, so we'll have better coverage."

"Why would a vampire lord care about shifters?" Layla asked, genuine confusion in her voice.

Tobi's expression softened. "The supernatural community may have its divisions, but we stand together against those who would harm our kind. Damien has lived for millennia - he's seen what happens when we fail to protect our own."

A tentative smile flickered across Layla's face. "I never thought I'd feel safer knowing vampires were watching me sleep."

"We're not the monsters humans make us out to be in their stories," Tobi said with a wry smile. "Well, not usually, anyway."

Her laugh was small but genuine - the first he'd heard from her. The sound lightened something in Tobi's chest.

"You should try to get some rest - in your own room," he specified, drawing another soft laugh from Layla. "I'll be patrolling until dawn, and I promise to keep a special watch on Yousuf's window."

Layla stood, her movements still stiff from hours on the hard floor. "Thank you, Tobi. For everything."

"You're welcome." He gestured toward the hallway. "And tomorrow night, I expect to find you sleeping in your own bed, not on that floor."

"I will," she whispered, the promise fragile but sincere.

As Layla padded softly back toward her room, Tobi watched her go, a fierce protectiveness rising in his chest. No one would harm this woman or her child - not while he stood guard in the darkness.

He waited until he heard her bedroom door close softly, then made his way to the front door. The winter air hit him as he stepped outside, sharp and clean after the emotional weight of the conversation inside.

He circled the house one last time, checking every entrance, every window. The pack house stood secure against the night, but he knew better than most that security systems alone couldn't keep nightmares at bay. Sometimes what children needed most was the certainty that someone was standing guard against the monsters.

He paused beneath Yousuf's window one final time. The boy slept soundly now, his breathing even and untroubled. Tomorrow, Tobi would bring lights to push back the darkness. Small gestures, perhaps, but he'd learned over his long existence that sometimes small gestures mattered most.

With a last glance at the peaceful house, Tobi melted into the night, his footprints in the snow the only evidence he'd been there at all.

CHAPTER 16

Beth hummed softly as she counted gauze packets, penciling numbers onto her inventory clipboard. She'd grown to cherish these quiet evening shifts—the clinic settled into stillness, her tasks unhurried, no emergency calls disrupting the rhythm of restocking and paperwork.

"Beth?" She heard her name called from the lobby.

Warmth blossomed in her chest at the familiar voice. She set down her clipboard and hurried through the hallway, unable to suppress her smile as she rounded the corner.

"Hi! I thought you were off tonight." Beth's greeting faltered as she noticed the two people flanking Tyr.

A man and woman stood beside him, both with striking Mongolian features. The man carried himself with quiet authority, his dark eyes alert and assessing. Though he wore modern tactical gear, something about his bearing spoke of ancient battlefields. The woman appeared younger, perhaps Beth's age, but her eyes held centuries of wisdom that contrasted sharply with her delicate features.

"Beth, I'd like you to meet Jochi and Saikhan." Tyr gestured to his companions. "They're members of Lord Damien's clan who've come up from New York City to assist with security in the Hudson Valley."

"Please, call me Sai." The woman's smile was warm despite her formal posture. Her dark hair fell in elaborate, impossibly thick braids that somehow managed to look both ancient and modern.

"It's nice to meet you both." Beth was proud her voice didn't waver, given how their presence filled the lobby with an almost tangible sense of power.

Beth tried not to stare at the two vampires, but their presence commanded attention in a way she'd never experienced with Tyr or Tobi, or even Dimitri, whom she'd met any number of times when he was on duty at the clinic. Something about Jochi's bearing spoke of ancient battles and conquest, while Sai's delicate features belied the centuries of wisdom in her dark eyes.

She made a mental note to ask Tyr about them later, when they were alone. There had to be fascinating stories behind these two.

"I wanted to introduce them personally," Tyr said, his familiar voice helping ease some of Beth's tension. "They'll be shadowing Dimitri tonight while he patrols the area."

"We appreciate all the help," Beth managed, proud that her voice remained steady. "Things have been... unsettling lately."

"Yes, Tyr told us about the incident with that hateful woman the other day." Sai's musical voice carried notes of both sympathy and steel. "Such behavior cannot be tolerated, especially not toward children."

Beth's shoulders relaxed slightly at Sai's words. Despite their intimidating presence, these vampires were here to help protect her community. Just like Tyr and Tobi.

Beth waited until Jochi and Sai's footsteps faded into the night before grabbing Tyr's arm. "Okay, spill. Who are they? And why do they make my skin prickle like I'm standing too close to a lightning strike?"

Tyr's blue eyes danced with amusement. "Remember how I told you I was considered young for a vampire at six hundred and change?" At Beth's nod, he continued. "Jochi is over eight hundred years old. He was born in the time of Genghis Khan - was actually one of his sons."

"What?" Beth's jaw dropped. "Like, the actual Genghis Khan? Ruler of the Mongol Empire? That Genghis Khan?"

"The very same." Tyr leaned against the reception desk. "Jochi conquered most of Siberia before he was turned. And Sai? She was nobility from one of the tribes he conquered. He turned her himself, back in 1224 or thereabouts."

Beth's mind reeled as she tried to process this information. "So they're... what? Master and servant?"

"No. More like partners." Tyr shook his head. "Their relationship is complicated - built on mutual respect forged from conflict. They've been working together for centuries."

"That explains the way they move," Beth mused. "Like they're always aware of each other without looking. And the power rolling off them..." She shivered slightly. "I've never felt anything like that from you or Tobi."

"You wouldn't." Tyr's expression turned serious. "That kind of presence comes from centuries of accumulated power. They're both ancient by vampire standards, and they've spent those centuries honing their abilities."

"Is that why Lord Damien sent them specifically?"

"Partly." Tyr straightened from his casual lean. "They're also extremely skilled at reading situations and people. Jochi was a military commander in life, and Sai comes from a warrior culture. Together, they'll be of real benefit should things come to an actual fight."

The color drained from Beth's cheeks. "God, I hope it doesn't come to fighting."

"So do I." Tyr's expression sobered. "But we've already had one nasty encounter here at the clinic. We've been lucky it hasn't been worse."

He saw the worry creeping back into her eyes and reached out to squeeze her hand gently. "It's not all doom and gloom though. There's an unexpected silver lining... the huge outpouring of public support for the shifter community. The pro-shifter movement is gaining momentum daily."

A grin spread across his face. "You should hear the conversations in the goth clubs in New York City these days. All anyone can talk about is how shifters are real."

Beth stared at him, her mouth falling open slightly. "Wait, what? What are you doing in goth clubs?"

"What, you think vampires only lurk in fancy penthouses and

ancient castles?" His eyes gleamed with mischief. "The music's good, the lighting's perfect for us, and nobody looks twice at someone who's a bit too pale and has fangs."

Beth's mouth fell open as she tried to reconcile the image of ancient, powerful vampires mingling with angst-driven goth club-goers in dark clothes and dramatic makeup.

"Besides," Tyr's eyes sparkled with amusement, "where do you think we find the donors who end up becoming Pledges and Blood Sworn?"

Beth stared at him as the absurdity of it hit her. All those elegant ceremonies she'd heard whispered about, the formal bonds between vampires and their chosen human companions - and it all started in gothic nightclubs?

Tyr threw his head back and laughed, the rich sound echoing through the empty clinic. His entire face lit up with genuine mirth, making him look younger and more carefree than she'd ever seen him.

"Your expression!" He wiped at his eyes, still chuckling. "You should see yourself right now."

Beth mock-scowled at Tyr, crossing her arms over her chest. "Well, how was I supposed to know? It's not like there's a Vampire Dating for Dummies guide out there." Her lips twitched, fighting a smile. "Though now that I think about it, I suppose you can't exactly walk up to random people on the street and ask if they want to be a blood donor."

"Exactly." Tyr's eyes still danced with amusement. "The goth scene works well - people there are already fascinated by vampire lore, and they tend to be more open-minded about supernatural things."

Beth chewed her lower lip, curiosity overtaking her embarrassment. "So when you feed... do you bite their neck?" Her cheeks flushed hot as soon as the words left her mouth.

Tyr laughed again, but the sound was gentle rather than mocking. "No, that's actually pretty intimate. Usually reserved for Consorts, or very trusted companions." He held up his wrist, turning it to show the complex network of veins beneath the pale skin. "Most of the time we feed from the arteries here. There's also a good vein in the forearm, but arterial blood is better - it flows faster too, so feeding doesn't take as long."

Beth stared at him, mesmerized by the casual way he discussed something so... profound. Her eyes traced the blue lines visible beneath his skin, trying to imagine what it would feel like to have fangs pierce the delicate flesh there.

Beth winced, her hand going instinctively to her own wrist. "Doesn't it hurt?" She traced the delicate network of veins visible beneath her pale skin. "And there are all these tendons and stuff right here. Wouldn't that cause damage?"

"Not where we feed." Tyr gently took her wrist, his cool fingers sliding up her forearm to rest just below the crook of her elbow. "Here, where you'd check for a pulse. The radial artery is closer to the surface, away from the tendons."

His touch sent shivers racing up her arm, even as his voice remained purely clinical.

"Besides," he continued, "vampires have kept our existence secret for centuries by ensuring humans don't remember being fed on. It's one of the first things we learn - how to feed without causing damage." His fingers remained light on her skin as he spoke. "Our saliva contains compounds that act as both a numbing agent and an anticoagulant. The bite itself is practically painless, and it heals almost instantly."

"So that's why there aren't thousands of people walking around with mysterious puncture marks," Beth mused, still studying where his fingers rested against her pulse point.

Beth felt her pulse flutter under his touch. Her mouth went dry as she tried to find the right words, heat creeping up her neck to stain her cheeks.

Tyr's blue eyes softened as he watched the play of emotions across her face. "You can ask me anything, you know. I won't be offended."

Beth gulped, her voice barely above a whisper. "Could I... I mean, would it be possible..." She ducked her head, unable to meet his gaze as the words tumbled out. "Could I try it?"

"Try being bitten?" Tyr's voice held no judgment, just gentle curiosity.

Beth nodded, still not looking up. Her pulse raced beneath his fingers, and she knew he could feel every rapid beat. The quiet hung between them. Beth's stomach dropped, and she wished she could take the words back. Had she just made a complete fool of herself?

Finally, she gathered her courage and peeked up at him through her lashes. Tyr's expression was unreadable, but his eyes had darkened to indigo, and something electric crackled in the air between them.

Beth's breath caught as Tyr's cool fingers encircled her wrist. "Of course," he murmured, his voice impossibly gentle as he lifted her wrist to his mouth.

A shiver raced down her spine as his tongue swept across her pulse point. The touch was feather-light, almost reverent. Beth's heart thundered in her chest, but not from fear. Anticipation coiled low in her belly as Tyr's gaze locked with hers, asking silent permission.

She gave a tiny nod, unable to look away from the intensity in his eyes. His fangs extended, but his touch remained impossibly gentle, as if she were made of spun glass. Beth held perfectly still as he brought her wrist back to his mouth. The sharp points pressed against her skin with exquisite delicacy before sliding home.

There was no pain, just a brief pressure and then... warmth. Heat spread up her arm as Tyr drew carefully from the artery. His eyes never left hers, watching for any sign of distress. But Beth felt only a dreamy sort of pleasure, like floating in a warm pool.

It only seemed a moment before Tyr withdrew his fangs. His tongue swept across the tiny puncture marks, and Beth watched in fascination as they disappeared, leaving her skin unmarked. Only the lingering warmth and the memory of his touch remained as evidence of what had just occurred.

Beth surfaced from the haze slowly. "I expected it to hurt, but..." She traced the unmarked skin of her wrist where his fangs had pierced just moments before.

She could almost feel a phantom sensation where his fangs had pierced her skin—his cool touch, the gentle bite. "Actually..." She ducked her head, unable to meet his eyes. "Even though it was just my wrist, that felt really..." Her voice dropped to a whisper. "Intimate."

Her cheeks flamed hotter as the word hung in the air between them. She hadn't expected such an intense connection from something as clinical as feeding from an artery. But the way he'd watched her, his intent gaze never leaving hers, the careful press of his fangs, the warmth that had spread through her body...

Beth's fingers traced absently over her wrist again, remembering the feather-light sweep of his tongue. No wonder vampires had such willing donors. If a simple wrist bite could feel like that...

Beth's fingers still lingered on her wrist, when Tyr's phone buzzed. He pulled it from his pocket, his expression shifting to focused attention as he listened.

"Yeah, sure. No problem." He ended the call and turned to Beth. "Dimitri's taking Jochi and Sai over to the pack house - there's something he wants them to see about the security setup there. He asked if I'd stay here to keep watch on the clinic."

"Oh." Beth dropped her hand from her wrist, trying to gather her scattered thoughts. "Yes, of course. That makes sense."

Tyr's thumb brushed once across her unmarked wrist before he released her hand. "I'll do a perimeter check, make sure everything's secure out there."

"Right." Beth nodded, grateful for the return to normal routine. "I should finish that inventory count anyway."

She watched as he slipped out into the darkness, her heart still racing from their earlier encounter. The cool night air swept in briefly as the door closed behind him, helping clear her head. She picked up her abandoned clipboard, determined to focus on work rather than the lingering warmth in her wrist or the memory of Tyr's gentle bite.

Tyr paced the perimeter of the clinic property, his boots crunching softly in the snow as he checked the security sensors along the tree line. The barn's dark shape loomed ahead, its weathered wood silvered by moonlight.

"So, how'd the introductions go?" Tobi's voice carried from around the corner of the barn.

Tyr glanced at his twin as Tobi fell into step beside him. "Beth was... a bit overwhelmed. You could see her trying not to show it, but Jochi and Sai's presence hit her hard."

"Really?" Tobi's eyebrows rose. "But she's met Antonio before. He's older than both of them."

"True." Tyr nodded, thinking of how their sire always kept his power carefully contained, wrapped in layers of courtly manners and aristocratic grace. "But Antonio pulls it back, keeps it controlled. You know how he is - all about proper etiquette and maintaining appearances."

"Whereas Jochi..."

"Exactly." A wry smile touched Tyr's lips. "Jochi fairly radiates power. He doesn't flaunt it, but he doesn't hide it either. And Sai isn't far behind him in that department."

"Well, they did spend years conquering half of Asia," Tobi mused. "Not much point in being subtle when you're leading armies."

"We could have used them back in Al Khair, in the 16th century," Tyr said, his voice tinged with wry amusement. "You know, when that barbarian horde would have invaded - if Jochi and Sai hadn't been off fighting with someone or other at the time. India, I think that was."

"Well, at least they weren't leading the army against us," Tobi replied.

Tyr snickered. "Truth."

The quiet night shattered as both their phones erupted in shrill alerts accompanied by urgent vibrations. Tyr yanked his phone from his pocket, his heart freezing as he read the message. Clinic. Possible intruder.

He and Tobi moved in perfect synchronization, centuries of fighting side by side making words unnecessary. They crossed the distance to the clinic in seconds, their enhanced speed eating up the ground.

Beth stood just inside the back door, her face drained of color. Her hands trembled as she gripped her phone, and he could smell the sharp scent of her fear. "I saw someone in the trees out front." Her voice quavered. "Just a shadow, but they were definitely watching the clinic."

"Are all the doors locked?" Tobi's voice carried quiet authority.

Beth nodded. "Yes. I double-checked everything as soon as I sent the alert."

"Good." Tobi's eyes scanned the tree line. "Stay inside, keep your phone in your hand. Keep away from the windows, and if you hear anything unusual... anything at all... text us immediately."

"I'll take the east side," Tyr said, already moving toward the shadowy trees.

"West is mine then." Tobi shifted his stance, ready to move. "Lock up behind us, Beth."

Beth slipped back inside. The lock clicked firmly into place as Tyr and Tobi split up, each heading to their designated search areas.

Outside, the night wrapped around them, familiar territory for creatures born to hunt in darkness. Tyr melted into the shadows beneath the trees, letting his awareness expand outward. The night air carried a complex tapestry of scents - pine needles, decaying leaves, the lingering warmth of sun-baked earth now cooling under starlight. But no human scent stood out as fresh or unusual, at least in the immediate vicinity.

He rolled his shoulders, feeling the familiar tingle as his form shifted. His body compressed and reshaped itself, bones hollowing, skin sprouting feathers. Where the vampire had stood, a large Barred Owl now perched on a low branch. Dark eyes, adapted perfectly for night vision, scanned the forest floor below.

Tyr spread his wings, each feather precisely aligned to eliminate sound. He launched from the branch, gliding silently between the trees. His owl form moved like a ghost through the forest, commanding a predator's view of the territory below. Every movement, every slight disturbance in the undergrowth registered with crystal clarity.

The owl's keen hearing picked up the scurrying of small creatures in the leaf litter, the soft rustle of wind through pine needles, the distant call of another Barred Owl establishing its territory. But nothing human disrupted the natural rhythm of the forest night.

Banking around a massive oak, Tyr rode an updraft higher into the canopy. His wings caught the moonlight filtering through the leaves, casting fleeting shadows on the forest floor. From this vantage point, he could survey a wider area while remaining virtually invisible to anyone below.

The eastern approach to the clinic lay exposed beneath his silent patrol. If an intruder lurked in these woods, they couldn't hide from an owl's superior night vision. Every shadow, every hollow between roots or behind fallen logs revealed itself to his searching gaze.

Through the owl's enhanced vision, Tyr spotted movement near a fallen oak. A man's form huddled close to the massive trunk, his camouflage clothing blending with the undergrowth and shadows. The intruder held binoculars in his left hand and, most concerning, a scoped hunting rifle in his right. The binoculars were trained on the clinic's front windows, where anyone moving through the reception area would be silhouetted against the dim lobby lights.

Tyr banked silently, circling lower for a better look. His keen eyes picked out details - military-style boots, tactical vest with multiple pockets.

The owl's wings carried Tyr in a soundless glide directly over the intruder's position. From this angle, he could see the man was well-equipped for a night operation. The rifle appeared to be a high-powered hunting model, likely capable of accuracy at significant range. The scope suggested he was prepared for a precision shot rather than random violence.

The man remained focused on the clinic, completely unaware of the predator observing him from above. Despite his clumsy attempts at stealth, his breathing came in excited bursts, his body twitching with anticipation. This was no military professional—just a backwoods hunter who'd traded deer for more dangerous game. His ill-fitting camo jacket bore patches from local hunting clubs, and a Confederate flag decal adorned the rifle stock. A half-empty beer can lay discarded by his boot, explaining his occasional muttering and the sour smell of alcohol wafting upward. The way he gripped his weapon with his right hand—white-knuckled and too tight—revealed his inexperience with human targets, though his familiarity with the woods suggested years of stalking animals through woods.

Tyr released his owl form, letting the magic ripple through him as feathers melted away, leaving him in human form once more. His hand closed around the man's throat like a steel trap before the human could even blink.

Tyr lifted him effortlessly, slamming him against the tree with bone-jarring force. The oak's ridged bark bit into the man's spine as the impact drove every ounce of air from his lungs in a strangled wheeze.

The rifle clattered, forgotten, to the forest floor as the man's hands scrabbled desperately at Tyr's iron grip. Pure terror replaced the hunter's earlier confidence as his feet kicked uselessly in the air, finding nothing but empty space. His eyes bulged, seeing death in the cold gaze of the creature that held him immobile.

"Not so fun being stalked, is it?" Tyr's voice carried the promise of certain death. His fangs slid out like ivory daggers, razor-sharp, designed for killing. "You think you're tough? Came here to hunt shifters? Amateur." His fingers pressed deeper into the man's throat until he wheezed for breath. "You're about to learn the difference between hunter and prey."

The acrid smell of fear and urine rose around them. His fingers clawed weakly at Tyr's hand, but the fight was draining from him as primal terror took hold. This wasn't how his night was supposed to go - he'd planned to be the hunter, not the prey.

"P-please," the man choked out. "Don't... don't kill me."

"Kill you?" Tyr's voice carried the chill of centuries of predatory experience. "That would be too easy." He leaned closer, letting the man get a good look at his fangs. "No, you're going to tell me exactly who sent you here. And then we're going to have a long chat about what happens to people who threaten those under my protection."

The stench of fear and alcohol rolled off the human in waves. His boots kicked helplessly a good foot above the ground, scrabbling for purchase against the tree trunk. The Confederate patch on his jacket caught the moonlight as he thrashed - a crude symbol that spoke volumes about his motivations.

"No one sent me... Please..." The word wheezed past Tyr's grip. "Don't..."

"Don't what?" Tyr leaned closer, letting his fangs extend. "Don't kill you? Like you were planning to kill innocent people?" His fingers flexed against the man's throat, feeling the rapid flutter of his pulse. "Give me one good reason why I shouldn't drain you dry right here."

The human's face had gone from red to purple, terror replacing the hatred that had driven him to stalk the clinic. His hands clawed weakly at Tyr's iron grip, but the vampire's strength rendered his struggles meaningless.

"Look at me." Tyr shook the man roughly, his supernatural strength making the human's head snap back. "Look. At. Me."

The man's terrified eyes locked with Tyr's glacial gaze. "What... what are you?"

"That doesn't matter." Tyr's voice deepened, ancient power threading through his words. "Because you won't remember me, or anything that happened after you came to the clinic tonight. Now. Who sent you?"

"N-no one. I swear, no one! It was just me, I—I thought I could—"

"Thought you could what?" Tyr's voice turned silky with menace. "Bag yourself a shifter?"

The man's face went even paler, if that were possible, and he made a strangled sound that might have been agreement or just pure terror.

"You were in the woods. Something was chasing you in the dark." Tyr poured power into his voice, weaving the false memory into the human's mind. "You came here to do something very, very bad - and now you're being hunted."

A whimper escaped the man's throat as the terror - not entirely manufactured - took root.

"The thing that hunts you has your scent now." Tyr's words fell like ice into the man's consciousness. "It will never stop hunting you. Never give up. You can hear its breathing in the dark. Smell its musk on the wind. Sense the evil. You'll never be safe again, anywhere you go. It can find you. And when it finds you..." Tyr leaned closer, his voice dropping to barely above a whisper. "It will tear you apart. Slowly."

Tyr's lips pulled back in a feral grin, moonlight glinting off his extended fangs. The man's eyes widened in absolute terror as Tyr's head snapped forward with supernatural speed. His fangs hovered a hair's breadth from the human's exposed throat, close enough that the man could feel their deadly points against his racing pulse.

The scream that erupted from the would-be hunter's throat echoed through the dark forest, a primal sound of pure horror that scattered sleeping birds from nearby trees. His eyes rolled back in his head as consciousness fled, his body going limp in Tyr's grasp.

Tyr held the unconscious man pinned against the tree trunk, satisfaction curling through him at the effectiveness of his performance.

Tyr let the unconscious man slump to the forest floor, his head lolling against the oak's gnarled roots. The stench of fear and urine still hung heavy in the night air.

"Damn, brother, that was awesome." Tobi's voice carried from behind him, rich with amusement.

Tyr whirled, scowling at his twin. "Where the hell have you been?"

"Recording you." Tobi grinned and held up his cell phone, its screen still glowing. "Had to document that performance. The whole 'something hunts you in the dark' bit?" He gave an exaggerated chef's kiss. "Pure poetry."

"You were supposed to be checking the west perimeter." Tyr's voice held equal parts exasperation and affection.

"I did." Tobi tucked his phone away. "Found nothing but deer tracks and rabbit droppings. Then I heard you going all dark and broody over here, and well..." He shrugged. "Couldn't resist capturing the show."

"Delete that video."

"No way." Tobi's grin widened. "This is prime blackmail material. Besides, Antonio will want to see how his star pupil handles interrogations these days."

Tyr groaned. Their sire would absolutely critique his technique, probably with a lengthy discourse on the proper etiquette of threatening humans. He could hear Antonio's voice now: 'Really, Tyr? Such melodrama? A simple glamour would have sufficed.'

Tyr ran a hand through his hair, glancing back toward the clinic's dimly lit windows. "Let's wrap this up. I need to get back inside and let Beth know everything's okay."

Tobi nudged the unconscious man with his boot. "I'll take this loser and dump him at his vehicle. It'll be parked out on the road nearby." He bent down and hoisted the limp form over his shoulder with casual vampire strength, not even grunting at the weight.

Tyr's gaze fell on the fallen rifle. He scooped it up, testing its weight before gripping it firmly in both hands. The expensive hunting weapon snapped like kindling across his knee, the crack echoing through the quiet woods. He handed the mangled pieces to his brother.

"Good thinking," Tobi said, tucking the broken rifle under his free arm. "He won't even know how that happened. Nice touch."

Tyr entered through the clinic's lobby doors, and Beth came running up to him, her eyes wide with worry and relief.

"Did you find anything?" Her arms wrapped around herself protectively as she held her breath, waiting for his answer?

"Yeah, we did." Tyr kept his voice calm and reassuring. "There was a solo intruder in the woods - definitely an anti-shifter hostile. But Tobi and I took care of him."

"Took care of him?" Beth's eyes widened, and Tyr's lips twitched at her horrified expression.. "You mean..." She couldn't bring herself to finish.

"We sent him on his way," Tyr clarified quickly. "No damage done. Well, physical damage, anyway."

Beth swallowed hard, her fingers still worrying at her scrubs. "What if... what if he comes back? What if he tells others?"

A predatory grin spread across Tyr's face as he let his fangs extend. "Trust me, he's not going to remember coming here tonight, or anything that happened in these woods." His eyes gleamed indigo with satisfaction. "And I can personally guarantee he won't be back. Ever."

"How can you be so sure?"

"Let's just say I gave him a very compelling reason to stay far away from this place." Tyr's fangs caught the fluorescent lighting. "Very, very far away."

Beth stared at him a moment, and her mouth fell open in amazement. "Wait, you can do that? Make people forget things?"

"Yeah." Tyr shrugged, trying to downplay the ability. "It's a kind of hypnosis, or power of suggestion. Something like that. Most vampires develop the skill pretty early - it's how we've stayed hidden for so long. Remember? People don't remember encountering a vampire."

Beth pursed her lips, processing this information. Her expression shifted from worried to fascinated, reminding Tyr of how she'd looked earlier when asking about feeding.

The back door clicked open, and Tobi sauntered in, phone already in hand. "Oh man, you have got to see this." He held the screen out to Beth. "Check out my brother going all dark and mysterious in the woods."

Beth leaned closer, her eyes widening as she watched. A giggle escaped her, quickly growing into full-blown laughter as Tyr's recorded voice intoned about creatures hunting in the darkness.

"'It will never stop hunting you,'" she quoted between laughs, her earlier fear completely forgotten. "That was... that was like something out of a horror movie!"

Tyr fixed his twin with a murderous look. "Way to ruin the moment, brother." But he couldn't entirely suppress his own smile as Beth's laughter filled the quiet clinic.

Tobi tucked his phone away, a mischievous glint in his eye. "You know, I noticed you didn't actually bite the guy. Just did your whole scary vampire routine."

"You didn't bite him?" Beth's eyebrows shot up in surprise.

Tyr's nose wrinkled in disgust. "God no. He reeked of cheap beer and whiskey, not to mention the body odor. I wasn't about to put my mouth anywhere near that."

"Plus the alcohol in his blood would have ruined the taste completely," Tobi added.

Beth's eyes lit up with curiosity. "Really? Alcohol affects the taste?"

"Makes it bitter," Tyr explained. "Like drinking watered-down coffee that's been left on the burner too long."

"Drugs are even worse," Tobi chimed in. "Cocaine makes the blood taste metallic and sharp - like licking a battery. And don't even get me started on meth."

"Generally, vampires prefer our donors clean and sober," Tobi summarized. "Makes for a much more pleasant experience all around."

Tyr grimaced at the memory that surfaced. "Remember that guy in '67? The one who practically lived on LSD?"

"Oh man." Tobi's eyes lit up with mischief. "Timothy. That dude was a trip - in more ways than one."

"LSD?" Beth perched on the edge of the reception desk, clearly intrigued.

"Hippie dude. He hung out at this coffee shop in Greenwich Village," Tyr explained. "Total stereotype - long hair, tie-dye shirts, peace signs everywhere. But he was genuinely one of the most entertaining humans we'd ever met."

Tobi leaned against the wall, grinning. "He'd drop acid and spend hours telling us about how the universe was actually a giant cosmic dance party, and all the stars were just disco balls reflecting each other's light."

"We seriously considered making him Blood Sworn," Tyr admitted. "He was just so much fun to be around when he was tripping. Had this way of seeing beauty in everything."

"But man, that blood." Tobi shuddered dramatically. "It was like drinking liquid rainbows mixed with stale incense and broken dreams. Made my tongue feel like it was trying to escape my mouth and start its own commune."

"We had to give up on the idea," Tyr said. "Even waiting for him to come down between trips, his blood was never quite palatable. Too much acid stored in his system."

"Last I heard, he opened a vegan crystal shop in Oregon," Tobi mused. "Still probably seeing cosmic disco balls everywhere."

Beth blinked. "Vegan crystals?"

"Exactly." Tyr nodded. "Guy's just not right."

Tyr looked around, coming to attention as Dimitri's familiar presence approached the clinic. The ancient vampire's footsteps were nearly silent on the tile floor as he entered through the back entrance.

"What happened here?" Dimitri's keen gaze swept over them, his expression shadowed with concern.

"We had an uninvited guest in the woods." Tobi tucked his phone away, his earlier playfulness evaporating under Dimitri's scrutiny.

"I've left Jochi and Sai watching the pack house," Dimitri said. "They'll maintain guard there while I resume my post here. Tell me everything."

Tyr stepped closer to Dimitri, pitching his voice too low for Beth's human hearing. "We had a solo intruder with a hunting rifle and scope. Military-style gear, but amateur execution. There was no association with a group that I could discover. I planted a strong aversion suggestion before we dumped him back at his vehicle."

Dimitri's jaw tightened with displeasure. "This complicates things. I'll need to speak with Antonio immediately." He ran a hand through his dark hair. "We can't put standard perimeter sensors around the property - too much wildlife would trigger false alarms constantly."

"The guy was watching the clinic through binoculars," Tobi added in the same quiet undertone. "Specifically targeting the front windows."

Beth stood a few feet away, clearly trying to follow their hushed conversation. Her brow furrowed in concentration, but Tyr knew she couldn't make out their words.

"We'll need to adjust our security protocols," Dimitri said at normal volume, his tone carefully neutral. "For now, I'll take over watch duty here. You two should report back to base and file incident reports."

Tyr shifted his weight, hesitating by the door. Something nagged at him, a tactical consideration he couldn't ignore.

"What is it?" Dimitri's attention zeroed in on him.

"I know it's not my place to make these decisions," Tyr began carefully. He glanced at Beth, still standing near the reception desk. "But the clinic sits on extensive grounds, and it's become a focal point for anti-shifter sentiment. One vampire, even one as skilled as you, can't cover all approaches simultaneously."

Dimitri's expression remained neutral, but his eyes sparked with interest. "Go on."

"I'm thinking, once we have more of the clan here, we should have two vampires on duty at the clinic each night," Tyr said.

"Makes sense." Dimitri nodded slowly. "I'll run it through Antonio. With Jochi and Sai here now, we have the personnel to implement dual coverage." He straightened his shoulders. "And Lord Damien is sending at least two more clan members by week's end."

"That would help with rotation schedules too," Tobi chimed in. "Keep everyone fresh."

"Agreed." Approval flickered across Dimitri's face. "Good tactical thinking, Tyr. I'll draft the new protocols tonight."

He turned to leave, but paused at the door. "I want both of you here for the rest of the night. Keep sharp out there. After tonight's incident, we can't assume we've seen the last of them."

CHAPTER 17

Tyr leaned against the warehouse's brick wall, anticipation humming through his veins as he waited for Beth to arrive for their third date. He'd spent weeks orchestrating every detail of tonight's adventure, his thoughts filled with Beth's smile, imagining her wonder at each carefully planned surprise.

Tonight would be magical - not through vampire glamour or supernatural power, but through the simple joy of watching her face light up with delight, showing her the magic that existed in moments shared together.

The last hues of sunset lingered on the horizon, casting a dusky glow over the asphalt as Beth's Prius glided into the parking space. His enhanced vision caught every detail as she emerged from her car. She'd followed his suggestion perfectly - dark jeans paired with an emerald sweater that brought out flecks of green in her storm-grey eyes. The oversized leather purse slung across her body spoke of practicality rather than fashion. Perfect.

He pushed off the wall, offering a warm smile. "That sweater suits you."

A blush colored her cheeks. "Thanks. I wasn't sure what you meant by 'upscale casual' but I figured better overdressed than under."

"You got it exactly right."

Tyr guided Beth around the corner of the warehouse, his hand hovering near the small of her back without quite touching. The rhythmic thrum of helicopter blades filled the air, and he savored Beth's sharp intake of breath as the sleek Bell 206B-3 JetRanger III came into view.

The aircraft's black paint gleamed in the fading light, gold trim catching the last rays like liquid metal. Its blades cut elegant arcs through the evening air, creating mini-whirlwinds that tugged at Beth's blonde hair.

"A helicopter?" Her voice carried both excitement and nervousness.

Martin, their pilot, stood beside the craft in his crisp black uniform. He acknowledged them with a precise nod, his movements economical as he stepped forward to open the passenger door.

Tyr gestured toward their pilot. "Beth, this is Martin Chen. He's been flying for Lord Damien for the past five years."

"Welcome aboard, Ms. Kerrigan." Martin's professional demeanor softened with a genuine smile. "First time in a helicopter?"

Beth nodded, her eyes shining with excitement. "Is it that obvious?"

"Everyone has a first flight." Martin extended his hand, helping Beth into the passenger compartment with practiced ease. "Let's make sure it's memorable for all the right reasons."

Tyr slid into the seat beside Beth while Martin secured her harness, checking each buckle with methodical precision. The familiar click of his own seatbelt provided a counterpoint to the steady whump of the rotors overhead.

Martin passed them both headsets before moving toward the pilot's door. Tyr helped Beth adjust hers, his fingers brushing against her hair as he settled the padded cups over her ears.

"See this control module?" He pointed to the small device attached to her headset cord. "The dial adjusts your volume, and this button here connects to the intercom so we can talk without shouting over the engine noise."

Beth ran her fingers over the sleek control module, fascination replacing her earlier nervousness. "Like a private radio channel?"

"Exactly." Tyr demonstrated with his own headset, touching the push-to-talk button. "Press once to talk, release when you're done."

Tyr enjoyed watching Beth's face as she gazed through the helicopter's window, drinking in every detail of the experience. Her eyes sparkled with delight as Martin went through his pre-flight checks, the engine's vibrations thrumming through the cabin. Her unrestrained joy was exactly what he'd hoped to see.

"So where are we headed?" Beth's voice came clear through his headset, accompanied by that brilliant smile that never failed to captivate him.

"That would spoil the surprise." He grinned back at her, enjoying the way her lips curved downward in a playful pout at his evasion.

"Not even a hint?"

"Nope." He shook his head, watching her nose scrunch up in mock frustration.

Martin's voice crackled through their headsets. "Ms. Kerrigan, I need to review some safety procedures before takeoff. Please confirm your harness is secure and tight across your chest."

Beth tugged at the straps, then gave Martin a thumbs up. "All set."

"Excellent. Now, the emergency exit release is here." Martin pointed to the red handle. "And if you need air, these vents can be adjusted."

Tyr observed Beth paying careful attention to each instruction, though her excitement remained evident in the way she kept sneaking glances out the window. Her natural curiosity shone through in every movement, every eager response to Martin's safety briefing.

The pilot's methodical review continued, covering emergency protocols and communication procedures. Through it all, Beth's enthusiasm never dimmed - if anything, each new detail seemed to heighten her anticipation of the adventure ahead.

The interior took Beth's breath away again - cream leather seats accented with polished wood trim and gold fixtures. The cabin's sophisticated lighting cast a warm glow over the luxurious space.

"This is..." Beth's fingers traced the doorframe, her eyes wide as she took in the opulent cabin.

"Lord Damien believes in traveling in style." Tyr couldn't help smiling at her awe-struck expression. The helicopter's interior rivaled many luxury cars, with all the comfort and none of the traffic.

Beth ran her fingers over the polished wood trim. Her expression shifted from awe to sudden suspicion.

"Wait... is this Lord Damien's personal helicopter?"

"It is." Tyr couldn't suppress his grin at her sharp intake of breath.

Beth stared at him, a mix of horror and amusement crossing her features. "Did you... steal it?"

From the pilot's seat, Martin made a strangled sound that quickly turned into poorly suppressed laughter. The professional demeanor he'd maintained cracked completely as he struggled to contain his mirth.

"I would never steal from Lord Damien," Tyr said, though his grin widened. "I value my continued existence far too much for that. No, I asked to borrow it, and he agreed."

"Sounds like a wise life choice." Beth's dry tone set Martin off again, his shoulders shaking as he tried to maintain his composure while running through the final pre-flight checks.

A few minutes later the helicopter lifted smoothly into the darkening sky, and Tyr caught the slight hitch in Beth's breathing as they left the ground.. The warehouse dropped away below them as Martin banked gently, setting their course north along the river.

Beth unbuckled her harness just enough to lean toward the window, her nose practically pressed against the glass as she took in the view. The Hudson stretched out beneath them like a silver ribbon in the fading light, its surface catching the last remnants of sunset.

"Oh wow," Beth breathed through the headset. "Everything looks so different from up here."

Tyr shifted closer, sharing her view. In his raptor form, he was intimately familiar with these aerial perspectives, but seeing Beth's awed amazement made him appreciate it anew. The river's familiar bends and curves took on fresh beauty through her eyes.

"Look at all the boats!" Beth pointed excitedly at the tiny vessels dotting the water below. "They look like toys from up here."

Her childlike enthusiasm warmed something deep in Tyr's chest. He'd hoped she would enjoy this surprise, but her pure, unrestrained joy exceeded his expectations. The way she pressed closer to the window, drinking in every detail of the landscape flowing beneath them, made all the planning worthwhile.

"The river really does look like silver from this height," Beth murmured, her breath fogging the window slightly. She quickly wiped it clear, unwilling to miss a single moment of the view.

The lights below grew denser as they approached the city, individual points becoming a glowing tapestry against the darkness. Tyr found himself stealing glances at Beth's profile, warmth spreading through his chest each time her eyes widened at a new vista. Her unguarded joy at the aerial view was becoming his favorite part of the flight.

"Oh my god!" Beth squealed, practically bouncing in her seat as Manhattan's skyline emerged from the darkness. "Look at all the lights!"

New York City sprawled beneath them like a constellation brought to earth, rivers of headlights flowing between towers of glass and steel. Beth's excitement was contagious, her joy radiating through the cabin as she pointed out various landmarks she recognized.

Martin's voice came through their headsets. "Beginning our approach to West 30th Street Heliport."

The helicopter banked smoothly, giving them a spectacular view of the illuminated Empire State Building before descending toward the helipad. Beth gripped Tyr's arm as they touched down with barely a bump, the concrete pad solid beneath their skids.

The rhythmic whump of the rotors slowed as Martin powered down the engine. He emerged from the cockpit, circling around to Beth's door with practiced efficiency. The door opened with a soft click, and Martin extended his hand to help Beth navigate the step down.

"Welcome to Manhattan, Ms. Kerrigan."

Tyr followed Beth onto the helipad, his enhanced vision catching every detail of her delighted expression even in the dim lighting. The night air carried a mix of jet fuel, and the ever-present symphony of city scents.

Martin secured the helicopter door with a quiet click. "Have a wonderful evening, Sir, Madam. I'll be here when you're ready to return."

"Thanks, Martin." Tyr pressed several folded bills into the pilot's hand, noting the man's slight nod of appreciation.

The soft purr of an approaching engine drew Tyr's attention. A sleek black Mercedes emerged from the shadows, its polished surface reflecting the helipad's safety lights as it glided toward them. Beth shifted closer to his side, her shoulder brushing against his arm as the sedan drew near.

The Mercedes S-Class Maybach purred to a stop beside them, its deep black paint gleaming like liquid obsidian under the helipad lights. The uniformed chauffeur emerged with fluid grace, his white gloves practically glowing as he opened the rear passenger door with a precise bow.

Beth's sharp intake of breath echoed in Tyr's sensitive ears as she caught sight of the car's interior. Cream leather seats stretched like thrones beneath soft ambient lighting, while hand-finished wood trim and polished metal accents created an atmosphere of understated luxury.

She spun to face him, her storm-grey eyes wide with disbelief. "Tyr, this is... I mean... what..."

"Your chariot awaits." He placed his hand lightly on the small of her back, guiding her toward the open door. The scent of her excitement - a mix of heightened pulse and subtle adrenaline - teased his senses.

Beth slid into the plush leather seat with careful movements, as if afraid she might somehow damage the pristine interior. Her fingers traced the intricate stitching on the armrest while her gaze darted from the champagne cooler to the entertainment screens to the starlight headliner twinkling above.

Tyr settled beside her, enjoying her wonderment as she discovered each new luxurious detail. The door closed with a solid thunk that spoke of German engineering at its finest, sealing them in their private sanctuary of leather and luxury.

"I feel like a movie star," Beth said in a hushed voice, still running her fingers along the leather trim.

Tyr chuckled at Beth's whispered observation as their chauffeur slipped behind the wheel. The Mercedes purred to life, gliding away from the helipad with silken smoothness. He reached into the champagne cooler, extracting a glistening bottle of Perrier-Jouët Belle Epoque.

The cork emerged with a soft pop as he filled two crystal flutes. The pale golden liquid caught the ambient lighting, tiny bubbles dancing upward in elegant streams. He reached for a smaller, more ornate bottle, its distinctive Art Noveau design drawing Beth's attention immediately.

"St. Germain?" He held up the artisanal bottle, watching her expression shift from wonder to curiosity.

"What is it?" Beth leaned closer, examining the elegant bottle with its long, slender styling.

"It's a French liqueur made from elderflowers," Tyr explained, turning the bottle so the light caught its elegant faceted surface. "Just a touch transforms ordinary champagne into something extraordinary." He watched her expression, cataloging each micro-reaction. "The flowers are gathered by hand in the French Alps during a brief window in spring when they're at their peak."

"I've never heard of it." Beth's gaze followed the gentle tilt of the bottle as he added a precise measure to each flute. The pale golden liquid swirled beneath the bubbles, releasing a subtle floral fragrance that even his vampire senses found appealing. "But I'm open to new experiences."

Tyr handed her one of the crystal flutes, enjoying how the ambient lighting caught both the champagne's effervescence and the sparkle in her eyes. The delicate stem looked impossibly fragile between his fingers as he raised his own glass.

"To magic hiding in plain sight." He touched his flute to hers with the softest chime of crystal meeting crystal.

Beth's smile brightened as she echoed, "To hidden magic."

The Mercedes glided through Manhattan's glittering canyons, each turn revealing another vista of lights and life. Beth leaned closer to the window, drinking in the spectacle of New York at night. The city's energy pulsed around them - crowds flowing along sidewalks, yellow cabs weaving through traffic, music spilling from open doorways.

Their driver navigated the Theatre District with practiced ease, finally pulling up before an elegant storefront. Warm light spilled from La Côte d'Azur's windows onto the sidewalk, and the subtle scent of herbs and garlic wafted through the evening air.

The chauffeur stepped out, his white gloves pristine as he opened Beth's door with a slight bow. Tyr slid out first, extending his hand to help Beth emerge from the Mercedes's cocoon of luxury. Her fingers trembled slightly against his palm, but her smile remained bright as she took in the restaurant's understated facade.

Inside, the maître d' greeted them with polished professionalism. "Good evening, sir. Reservation for two?"

"Yes, under Tyr Lindström."

"Ah, of course." The maître d' consulted his tablet before gathering menus. "Please, follow me."

They wound through the restaurant's intimate space, passing tables draped in crisp white linens. Copper pots gleamed from open shelving while sprigs of dried herbs hung from exposed wooden beams. The lighting struck a perfect balance - dim enough for romance but bright enough to read the menu without squinting.

Their waiter pulled out Beth's chair at a corner table partially screened by a tasteful arrangement of potted herbs. The location offered both privacy and a clear view of the restaurant's warm interior.

She settled into her seat, clearly pleased with the intimate setting he'd chosen.

A waiter approached with a basket of crusty French bread, still warm from the oven. Steam curled up as Beth broke open a piece, the yeasty aroma mixing with the herbs and garlic that perfumed the air. He placed two small dishes beside the bread - one filled with pale golden butter, the other with olive oil dotted with fresh herbs and cracked pepper.

"The bread is baked fresh every hour," the waiter explained, filling their water glasses. "Can I start you with any appetizers this evening?"

Tyr cocked an eyebrow at Beth, and she shook her head. “Just this bread is fine.”

The waiter left, and Beth draped her napkin across her lap, her attention fixed on the menu. "Everything looks amazing." She dipped a corner of bread into the herb-infused oil, closing her eyes in appreciation as she tasted it. "Oh, this is wonderful."

Pride and something deeper stirred within him as he watched her obvious enjoyment. He'd chosen this restaurant carefully, wanting somewhere special but not intimidating. The way Beth relaxed into her chair, savoring each bite of bread, told him he'd made the right choice.

When their waiter returned, Beth studied the menu one last time. "I think I'd like the Provençal roasted chicken, please."

"Excellent choice," the waiter nodded approvingly. "That comes with fingerling potatoes and haricots verts with garlic and almonds."

Beth looked puzzled. "What are haricots verts?"

"French green beans," the waiter explained with a smile. "Very thin and tender."

"Oh, that sounds wonderful. I'll definitely have that."

Tyr caught the waiter's expectant look. "I won't be dining tonight, but I would like the rack of lamb and roasted root vegetables to go." He paused, adding, "Also the grilled Mediterranean vegetables. Someone will collect it from the hostess station later."

"Of course, sir." The waiter made a note before departing with their orders.

Beth's eyebrow arched upward, a playful smile tugging at her lips. "Planning a midnight snack?"

Tyr couldn't help laughing at her expression. "Not quite. Our chauffeur will deliver it to Martin at the heliport while we're at our next destination." He enjoyed watching her face light up at the mention of more surprises to come.

"Next destination?" Beth leaned forward, her voice dropping conspiratorially. "Care to share where we're headed after dinner?"

"Not a chance." He shook his head, grinning at her attempted manipulation. "You'll find out soon enough."

"Not even a tiny hint?" She batted her eyelashes dramatically, making him chuckle again.

"Nope." He popped the 'p' sound, matching her playful tone. "Some things are worth waiting for."

Beth sat back with an exaggerated sigh, but her eyes danced with amusement. "You're impossible, you know that?"

"So I've been told." He watched her break off another piece of bread, enjoying how comfortable she seemed despite the upscale setting. "Usually by my brother."

BETH DABBED her lips with the napkin one final time, still savoring the lingering taste of the perfectly roasted chicken. The meal had been exquisite - every bite cooked to perfection, each flavor balanced and complementing the others. She couldn't remember the last time she'd enjoyed a restaurant meal this much.

The waiter approached with a small handheld card reader, its screen glowing softly in the restaurant's ambient lighting. Tyr tapped his credit card against the device with a quick, practiced motion, the terminal chiming softly to confirm the contactless payment.

"Ready for the next surprise?" Tyr asked, rising from his chair with fluid grace. He guided her toward the door with that same gentle almost-touch at her back that made her skin tingle. The evening air held a crisp bite, but before she could even shiver, their Maybach glided up to the curb as if summoned. The chauffeur opened their door with the same precise movements as before. Beth settled into the familiar luxury, the butter-soft leather welcoming them back. Tyr slid in beside her, bringing with him that subtle scent she'd come to associate with him - something like cedar and winter air.

The car merged smoothly into traffic, the city's lights creating patterns across the tinted windows. Beth watched in growing excitement as they turned onto Broadway, the famous street alive with theater-goers and the glow of countless marquees.

The Mercedes slowed, then stopped. Beth's eyes tracked upward to the brightly lit marquee above them and a delighted yelp escaped her lips.

"Dance of the Vampires?" She turned to Tyr, giggling. "Really? You're taking me to see a musical about vampires?"

The irony was absolutely perfect. She couldn't have planned a better reaction if she'd tried to be clever about it.

Beth followed Tyr through the ornate theater doors, still giggling at the sheer absurdity of a vampire taking her to see a vampire musical. Her amusement faded to awe as they entered the historic theater. Crystal chandeliers cast warm light over rich burgundy walls and gold trim, while plush carpeting muffled their footsteps.

An usher guided them to their seats - center orchestra, perfectly positioned. Beth sank into the velvet chair, drinking in the elaborate stage design visible through the curtain's slight gap.

As the show began, Beth found herself cycling through an emotional rollercoaster. She cringed at the campy vampire stereotypes, complete with exaggerated accents and billowing capes. A sideways glance at Tyr caught his amused smirk at particularly outlandish scenes.

During the ballroom scene, Beth's hand flew to her mouth, torn between horror and hysterical laughter as vampire couples waltzed across the stage in increasingly ridiculous choreography. The music soared dramatically while the performers executed elaborate spins that sent their capes swirling like demented bats.

Yet between the over-the-top moments, genuine heart emerged. The love story touched something deep inside her, while clever lyrics and stunning harmonies gave her chills that had nothing to do with vampire bites.

By the final curtain, Beth sat frozen in her seat, overwhelmed by the sheer absurdity of it all. She'd spent the entire show torn between cringing at the campy vampire stereotypes - nothing like the sophisticated, gentle man beside her - and being genuinely moved by the love story. The show had somehow managed to be simultaneously absurd and profound, hilarious and cringe-worthy at times, but also ridiculously heart-warming.

"So?" Tyr's voice held barely contained laughter as he turned to her. "What did you think?"

Beth opened her mouth, closed it, then opened it again as she struggled to form coherent thoughts. A hundred reactions warred for dominance - from analytical critique to pure emotional response.

Her mouth opened and closed several times before she managed an eloquent "Um..."

Tyr's rich laugh echoed through the theater lobby. "Yeah, that's about right." Watching her cycle through pure bewilderment to helpless laughter was better than any reward he could have imagined. "The first time I saw it, I spent twenty minutes trying to form a coherent sentence afterward."

A giggle bubbled up from Beth's chest, growing into full-blown laughter as they made their way through the theater's ornate doors. The cool night air hit her flushed cheeks, but she barely noticed, too caught up in the absurdity of it all.

"The capes!" She gasped between laughs. "All that swooshing and dramatic posing!"

"Don't forget the accent." Tyr's terrible imitation of the lead vampire's exaggerated pronunciation sent her into fresh peals of laughter.

The Maybach waited at the curb, its sleek black surface reflecting the theater's marquee lights. The chauffeur opened the door with his usual precise movements, though Beth caught the slight twitch of his lips as she collapsed into the leather seat, still giggling.

Tyr slid in beside her, his own shoulders shaking with suppressed laughter. "I thought you might appreciate the... unique interpretation of vampire culture."

"Unique is definitely one word for it!"

Beth slid a sideways glance at Tyr, taking in his relaxed posture against the buttery leather seats. "So... is this level of living normal for..." Her eyes darted meaningfully toward the chauffeur's pristine white-gloved hands on the steering wheel before trailing off.

The chauffeur's dark eyes met hers in the rearview mirror, crinkling with amusement. "No need to worry, miss. I'm a shifter myself."

Relief flooded through Beth as she relaxed back against the leather seat. Then curiosity sparked. "Wait, the limo service specifically offers Other drivers?"

"Shifter-owned company, actually." The chauffeur's professional demeanor warmed with pride. "All our employees are shifters. Makes things easier when clients need certain... accommodations."

Beth couldn't help giggling at the thought of a supernatural-friendly car service. Of course there would be specialized services catering to the Other community in a city this size. She settled more comfortably against the seat, tension melting from her shoulders.

"So... getting back to what I was asking before," she said with a small smile. "Is this level of living normal for vampires?"

"This?" He gestured at the Mercedes's opulent interior. "Maybe for certain types, like Antonio. He practically lives in designer suits and five-star restaurants. Me? I'm more likely to be cruising on my custom Nighthawk and grabbing a beer at a bar somewhere."

"Whew." Beth's shoulders relaxed as she laughed, the sound mixing with Tyr's deeper chuckle. The tension she hadn't even realized she'd been carrying melted away. The evening's extravagance suddenly felt less intimidating, more like a special occasion than a glimpse into an uncomfortably lavish lifestyle.

Her laughter faded into a comfortable silence as they watched the city lights blur past the windows. When Tyr's cool fingers found hers, the gesture felt natural rather than surprising. The leather seat creaked softly as he turned toward her, his gaze warm in the passing lights.

"I wanted to give you something special," he said, his thumb tracing gentle circles on her palm. "An evening that would stand out from all the others. Something magical."

The word 'magical' hung in the air between them, and her fingers tightened around his as emotion welled up in her throat. The helicopter, the champagne with elderflower liqueur, the perfect restaurant, every tiny detail planned just for her - it was beyond anything she'd ever imagined possible. No one had ever gone to such lengths just to make her happy.

"It was magical. I'll never forget this night," she whispered, her voice thick with feeling. "Not ever."

The city lights painted shadows across Tyr's face as he smiled, and Beth felt that familiar warmth spread through her chest at the sight. She'd never imagined someone would go to such lengths just to make her happy, to create memories this precious.

Beth pressed closer to the window as the Maybach wound through Manhattan's glittering streets. Every corner revealed new wonders - towering skyscrapers draped in lights, crowds flowing along wide side-walks like rivers of humanity, street performers creating impromptu shows on corners.

"Oh look!" She pointed at a man in a glittering silver bodysuit, frozen in a statue pose. "How does he stay so still?"

"Practice," Tyr leaned closer, his cool presence at her shoulder sending pleasant shivers down her spine. "Though some of them cheat and use mechanical supports hidden under their costumes."

A group of tourists dropped bills in the performer's collection box, and he sprang to life, executing a series of robotic moves that had the crowd cheering.

They passed restaurants with lines stretching down the block, their doorways spilling tempting aromas into the night air. Beth's nose twitched at the mix of cuisines - Italian, Thai, Indian, and dozens more she couldn't identify.

"The food scene here is incredible," she murmured, watching a waiter arrange sidewalk tables with precise movements. "Every block seems to have amazing restaurants."

They turned onto another broad avenue, and Beth's breath caught. Even having never visited New York City before, she instantly recognized the iconic plaza spread before them. The famous golden statue of Prometheus gleamed beneath carefully arranged lights, while the towering Christmas tree - already being prepared for the upcoming holiday season - stretched toward the sky.

"Rockefeller Center," she breathed, drinking in the sight of the Art Deco buildings surrounding the plaza. The elegant lines and detailed sculptures she'd seen in countless movies and photos were even more impressive in person.

Tourists clustered around the golden statue, snapping photos and pointing out architectural details to each other. A young couple posed for selfies with the emerging Christmas tree in the background, their faces glowing with excitement that matched Beth's own.

"It's exactly like the pictures," she said, "but somehow even better in real life."

The Maybach glided to a smooth stop at the curb, and Beth's pulse quickened with anticipation. Each surprise had topped the last - what could he possibly have planned now?

Tyr guided her toward the famous ice skating rink at Rockefeller Center. The pristine ice gleamed under the plaza's lights, reflecting the surrounding buildings like mirrors. A few late-night skaters glided across the surface in lazy circles, their blades making soft scraping sounds against the ice.

"We're going to watch the ice skating!" Her voice lifted with surprise and delight.

"If you'd like to." Tyr's smile held a hint of mischief.

Before Beth could point out they had no skates, a young woman with bright red hair approached them. She carried a canvas bag in one hand and a larger bag that was stamped with Saks Fifth Avenue.

"Here you go, Mr. Lindström." She handed the bags to Tyr with a gamine smile, then turned to Beth with a conspiratorial wink before walking away.

Beth watched the woman disappear into the crowd, then turned to Tyr with raised eyebrows. "You planned this too?"

Beth's jaw dropped as Tyr pulled a stunning metallic leather jacket from the Saks bag. The bronze finish caught the plaza's lights, creating subtle shifts of copper and gold across its surface. The leather looked impossibly soft, with just enough structure to hold its shape without being stiff.

"I didn't think to tell you to bring a coat," Tyr said.

Beth reached out hesitantly, her fingers trailing across the buttery-soft leather. The metallic finish felt smooth beneath her touch, luxurious without being flashy. The subtle distressing along the edges gave it an effortlessly cool vibe that made her heart skip.

"It's absolutely beautiful."

"May I?" He held the jacket open for her.

Beth slipped her arms into the sleeves, sighing at how perfectly it fit. The leather molded to her shoulders like it had been custom-made, while the quilted lining provided just enough warmth without bulk. She zipped it up, loving how the metallic sheen caught the light with each movement.

"The color suits you." Tyr's eyes sparkled as he took in her appearance. "Bronze brings out the gold in your hair."

Beth spun in a slow circle, feeling more elegant than she ever had before. The jacket moved with her like a second skin, its subtle shimmer making her feel simultaneously sophisticated and edgy.

"I can't believe you did this," she breathed, still running her hands over the impossibly soft leather. "Thank you!"

Reaching into the other bag, Tyr pulled out two pairs of ice skates. One was classic black, clearly sized for his feet. The other was a pristine white pair that looked exactly her size.

He led her to a nearby bench, setting both pairs of skates between them. "I got your shoe size from Naomi."

Beth ran her fingers over the smooth white leather of her skates. Even she could tell these weren't rental quality - these were professional grade figure skates.

"This is..." She swallowed hard, overwhelmed by the thoughtfulness of the gesture.

"Try them on?" Tyr was already unlacing his own skates, his movements precise and efficient.

Beth's fingers traced the pristine white skates, her stomach doing nervous flips. "I... I've never actually been ice skating before." She glanced up at Tyr through her lashes. "Growing up in Miami doesn't give you many opportunities for winter sports."

"No problem at all." Tyr's voice held nothing but warmth and encouragement. "I was born in Norway, plus, I've had centuries to perfect my technique. I won't let you fall."

His cool fingers brushed against her ankle as he helped her into the first skate. The leather molded to her foot perfectly, supporting her arch in all the right places. Beth watched in fascination as Tyr's hands moved with practiced efficiency, lacing up each skate with precise tension.

"Too tight?" He gave the laces one final adjustment.

Beth flexed her ankles experimentally. "No, they feel... really good actually."

"Stand up slowly." Tyr rose first, his own skates already perfectly secured. His strong hands gripped her waist, steadying her as she wobbled to her feet. "That's it. Just hold onto me."

Beth clutched his forearms, her knees trembling slightly as she adjusted to the strange sensation of balancing on thin metal blades. The ice stretched before her like a gleaming mirror, simultaneously beautiful and terrifying.

"Small steps first." Tyr's voice remained steady and calm. "Just shuffle forward a bit. I've got you."

Beth inched forward, her death grip on Tyr's arms gradually loosening as she found her balance. His patient guidance helped her work out the basics - how to push off, how to glide, how to stop without crashing.

"You're doing great." His praise warmed her chest as she managed a few wobbly strokes on her own. "Ready to try letting go?"

"Maybe?" Beth's voice quavered, but determination pushed through her nervousness. She loosened her grip one finger at a time until she stood independently on the ice.

Her first solo glide was shaky but successful. Tyr skated backward in front of her, close enough to catch her if needed but giving her space to find her own rhythm. Each stroke grew more confident as muscle memory began to develop.

"Look at you." Pride colored Tyr's voice as Beth completed a slow circuit of the rink. "A natural."

Tyr glided closer, his hand reaching for hers. Beth's fingers intertwined with his cool ones as they fell into a synchronized rhythm, their skates cutting parallel lines across the pristine ice. The plaza lights sparkled off the rink's surface, creating a magical atmosphere that made her heart flutter.

Beth's cheeks flushed from the crisp night air and exertion as they circled the rink together. Her earlier nervousness melted away, replaced by the pure joy of gliding across the ice with Tyr's steady presence beside her. Each stroke felt more natural, more fluid, as if they'd skated together a hundred times before.

Their joined hands swung gently between them as they moved in perfect sync. Beth couldn't stop smiling, especially when she caught Tyr watching her with that soft expression that made her stomach do little flips.

A puff of white mist escaped her lips as she laughed at a particularly wobbly turn. She glanced at Tyr, suddenly realizing something was different. While her breath created little clouds in the frosty air, his didn't.

"Hey, how come I can see my breath but not yours?"

Tyr's rich laughter echoed across the ice. "Silly girl, I'm a vampire - I don't breathe." His grin was irresistible. "Though I have to admit, watching your little frost clouds is adorable."

Beth giggled, purposely exhaling a bigger puff of mist. "Like a baby dragon?"

"Much prettier than any dragon I've ever met." His thumb traced gentle circles on her palm as they continued their graceful circuit around the rink.

Beth's eyes narrowed as she studied Tyr's face for any sign he was teasing. "Wait, you've met actual dragons?"

"Just one." His grin widened, showing a flash of fang that made her heart skip.

"You're kidding, right?" She tried to focus on both skating and processing this revelation. The combination proved too much.

Her left skate caught an uneven patch of ice. Beth's arms pinwheeled as she lost her balance, a squeak of surprise escaping her lips. Before she could fall, Tyr's strong hands caught her waist, steadying her against his chest. His rich laughter vibrated through her back.

"Careful there." His cool breath tickled her ear. "Though I do enjoy catching you."

Heat flooded Beth's cheeks, but she refused to let him distract her from this bombshell. "Seriously? A real dragon?"

"Mhmm." He guided her back into their smooth skating rhythm, his hands lingering at her waist slightly longer than necessary. "Hundreds of years ago, in another land. She lived as a healer named Kaylee, choosing to stay in her human form."

Beth's mouth fell open. Dragons were real. Actually real.

Suddenly, Lady Flora came to mind. The ancient being who'd appeared as a gentle elderly woman and taken Beth and her sister into the woods, then transformed into a breathtaking maiden before their eyes. The shimmer of magic as her form had shifted into that of a magnificent unicorn, her spiral horn gleaming like pure silver in the sunlight.

Lady Flora had confirmed for them the truth about Beth and Naomi's real family, freeing them from the lies of their supposed mother, aunt, and sisters. But Flora had also sworn them to secrecy. But yeah, okay. Unicorns were a thing, so, dragons. Okay.

"You're smiling." Tyr's observation pulled her from her thoughts. "What's going through that mind of yours?"

"Just... thinking about how much bigger the world is than I once believed." Beth squeezed his hand, choosing her words carefully to keep Lady Flora's secret. "A year ago, I wouldn't have thought I'd ever meet a vampire. Now here I am, skating with one under the stars."

His cool fingers tightened around hers as they glided in another graceful arc. "The world is full of wonders, if you know where to look."

Beth was about to respond when the loudspeakers crackled to life, announcing the rink's closing in fifteen minutes. Beth's legs wobbled slightly as she and Tyr made their way to the exit gate, his steady hand at her elbow keeping her balanced on the blades.

They settled onto the bench where they'd left their things, and Beth untied her skates, her fingers clumsy from the cold despite the warmth of her new leather jacket. A flash of bright red caught her eye, and she spotted the young woman who'd delivered their things earlier. She was perched on a nearby bench, a book open in her lap but her attention clearly on their belongings.

So that's why Tyr hadn't seemed concerned about leaving their things unattended while they skated. He'd arranged for a watchful guardian, someone to ensure their possessions remained safe while they enjoyed the ice.

The young woman looked up, catching Beth's gaze. A bright smile lit up her face as she waved enthusiastically. Beth returned the wave, warmth spreading through her chest at the woman's obvious enjoyment of her role in their evening's adventure. The redhead gathered her things and bounced over to their bench, her grin infectious.

"These fit perfectly," Beth said, running her fingers over the white skates one last time before handing them to the woman. "Thank you for getting them, and for keeping our things safe."

"My pleasure!" The redhead carefully tucked the skates into the canvas bag. "Hope you had fun!" With another bright smile and enthusiastic thumbs up, she disappeared into the dispersing crowd. "I'll drop these with your driver."

Tyr reached for Beth's hand, and as their fingers intertwined, a spark of warmth radiated between them. She met his gaze, her heart still light from their time on the ice, and an unspoken understanding danced in the space between them. They exchanged soft smiles, a fleeting moment that felt like the beginning of something deeper.

The evening had been filled with one magical moment after another: soaring over Manhattan in a helicopter, dining in an intimate French restaurant, giggling through a vampire musical, and now skating beneath the stars at Rockefeller Center. Yet something in Tyr's smile told her the night wasn't over yet.

CHAPTER 18

Tyr rose first, extending his hand to help Beth from the bench. Her legs wobbled slightly as she adjusted to solid ground again, and his steady grip kept her balanced while her muscles remembered how to work without blades beneath them. A soft laugh escaped her as she took a tentative step.

"Skating legs," she quipped, grateful for his support.

His smile warmed his eyes as he offered his arm, and she tucked her hand into the crook of his elbow. They took their time walking through Rockefeller Center, before winding their way to where the black Maybach waited at the curb, its engine purring softly in the chilly night air.

"Are you tired?" Tyr's question held a hint of something more.

Beth considered. Her body hummed pleasantly from the ice skating, but exhaustion hadn't set in. The night was so magical, she wasn't ready for it to end just yet. "Not really. Why?"

"I thought we might wind down at 230 Fifth Rooftop Bar." The familiar mischief danced in his expression. "It has the most incredible views of the Empire State Building, especially at night."

Beth nodded eagerly. "That sounds wonderful. I'm not ready for this night to end yet."

The Maybach glided up Fifth Avenue, its smooth ride letting Beth focus on the glittering storefronts passing by. Tyr pointed out landmarks as they drove, his cool presence beside her adding to the evening's magic.

"Bergdorf Goodman on your right - their holiday windows are legendary. And there's the Peninsula Hotel, where the employees all wear white uniforms and pillbox hats."

"Seriously?" Beth pressed closer to the window, peering at the doorman standing on the front steps. "Oh, wow."

Beth's jaw dropped as an enormous church loomed ahead, its twin spires reaching toward the night sky like ancient guardians. Delicate stonework caught the city lights, creating an ethereal glow around the massive structure. Elaborate stained glass windows sparkled like jewels set into the pale stone walls.

"A cathedral? Right in the middle of New York City?" Beth stared out the window as an enormous church loomed ahead, its twin spires rising like ancient guardians against the night sky.

Tyr chuckled, leaning toward her window. "That's St. Patrick's Cathedral. It was finished in 1878."

Beth stared in wonder at the intricate carvings adorning the facade. Even at night, she could make out the saints and angels watching over Fifth Avenue from their stone perches. The building seemed almost out of place among the sleek modern towers surrounding it, yet somehow perfectly at home in the heart of Manhattan.

"It's beautiful," she breathed, twisting in her seat to keep the cathedral in view as long as possible. "Like something transported straight from Europe."

"We were here when they built it," he said, his voice rich with memory. "Our clan arrived in New York City in the mid-1800s. Watching the cathedral rise stone by stone was quite something."

The car pulled up to an elegant building, and soon they were whisking up to the rooftop in a sleek elevator. Beth gasped as they emerged onto the open-air space. The Empire State Building loomed before them, its iconic shape illuminated against the night sky.

Beth spun in a slow circle, drinking in the spectacular view. The rooftop stretched before them, completely open to the night sky. Twinkling lights strung overhead competed with the stars, while lamps cast a warm glow over intimate seating areas.

"I didn't realize it would be open air!" She clutched Tyr's arm in excitement. "The views are incredible."

Her eyes landed on several clear dome structures scattered across the rooftop. "Are those... igloos?"

Amusement flickered across his features. "They keep guests warm while enjoying the view."

A hostess approached, her professional smile brightening as she took in Beth's obvious delight. "Welcome to 230 Fifth. Would you like one of our signature robes to keep warm while you enjoy the rooftop?"

Beth's eyes widened as she noticed several other guests wrapped in plush red robes. A giggle bubbled up from her chest, growing into full-blown laughter.

"Robes?" She wiped tears of mirth from her eyes. "Like a fancy bathrobe? At a rooftop bar?"

The hostess grinned, clearly used to this reaction. "They're quite popular, especially on chilly nights. Very cozy."

Beth's shoulders shook with renewed laughter as she pictured herself and Tyr - the ancient vampire warrior - lounging at this upscale bar in fluffy red robes. Her new leather jacket kept her perfectly comfortable, but the mental image was too hilarious to resist.

"Oh my god." She pressed her face against Tyr's shoulder, trying to muffle her giggles. "Please tell me you'll wear one too?"

Beth couldn't contain her grin as she watched Tyr eye the plush red robe with a mix of resignation and amusement.

"You aren't going to take pictures, are you?" His eyes narrowed suspiciously.

"Oh, absolutely I will be taking pictures." Beth bounced on her toes, already reaching for her phone. "This is too perfect to pass up."

Tyr sighed dramatically, but his lips twitched with suppressed humor. "Fine. But you have to promise you'll never let Tobi see these. He'd never let me live it down."

"I promise." Beth crossed her fingers behind her back, knowing her expression probably gave away her mischievous intentions.

The hostess helped them both into the cozy robes, then gestured toward one of the clear dome structures. "Would you like to try one of our igloos? They'll keep you warm."

Tyr glanced at Beth, clearly leaving the decision up to her.

"Would it be okay if we didn't?" Beth wrapped her robe tighter, breathing in the crisp air, redolent of snowfall. "I'm loving the sky and the breeze too much to be inside, even in something as cool as those igloos."

"Of course." The hostess led them to a prime spot near the edge of the rooftop, where comfortable seating offered an unobstructed view of the glittering cityscape. "This table has one of our best views of the Empire State Building."

Beth sank into the plush chair, unable to stop smiling as she took in Tyr's appearance. The ancient vampire warrior looked surprisingly dignified in the red robe, though his expression dared her to comment.

Beth snuggled deeper into her plush red robe, grateful for both it and her new leather jacket as another cool breeze swept across the rooftop. Most of the other patrons had opted for the warmth of the igloos, leaving the outdoor seating area practically empty. The heat lamps created pools of warmth around their table, but the knife-edge of winter air made her feel vibrantly alive.

She leaned forward, propping her elbows on the table and settling her chin in her hands. The Empire State Building's lights created a stunning backdrop, but her mind was fixed on Tyr's earlier revelation.

"So. Dragons." Beth's eyes sparkled with curiosity. "Talk."

Tyr's rich laughter echoed across the nearly empty rooftop. "What exactly do you want to know?"

Beth leaned closer, her eyes bright with curiosity. "Tell me about the one you know. What was it like?"

Before Tyr could answer, a waitress approached their table, her notepad ready. "Good evening! Can I get you started with some drinks?"

"Actually..." Tyr gestured toward the cocktail menu. "You should try one of their hot cocktails. They're quite famous for them."

Beth flipped open the menu, scanning the options. The warmth from the heat lamps and her cozy robe helped against the nip in the air, but her nose and cheeks tingled with the cold, making the idea of a hot drink especially appealing. "Oh, there's a spiced hot chocolate! What's it spiked with?"

The waitress brightened. "We can do it with either bourbon or rum. The rum adds a sweeter note, while the bourbon gives it more depth."

"Definitely go with the bourbon," Tyr recommended. "It complements the chocolate better. And I'll have the hot toddy."

Beth closed her menu and smiled at their waitress. "Okay, spiced hot chocolate with bourbon, please."

The waitress jotted down their orders with a smile. "Excellent choices. I'll have those right out for you."

As soon as the waitress disappeared behind the bar, Beth leaned forward eagerly. "Go!"

Tyr's laugh rumbled deep in his chest. "It was back in the 16th century. Our clan lived in the caverns of a mountain range on the edge of a vast desert." His gaze grew distant with memory. "The city there had originally been built as a caravanserai - a way station - for merchant caravans traveling between the Safavid Empire in Persia and the Mughal Empire in India."

Beth's gaze was distant as she imagined the ancient trade routes and mysterious mountain caves. The New York cityscape faded away as she pictured towering peaks rising from endless sand.

"Those mountains were the ancestral home for the earliest vampires," Tyr continued, his voice dropping lower. "Lord Damien was one of those first ones."

"The city became a sanctuary of sorts," Tyr continued, his voice carrying the weight of centuries. "A place where humans and Others could coexist, though not without... complications. We established a delicate balance. The vampire clan agreed never to feed on unwilling victims from within the city's walls. In return, the humans wouldn't attempt to drive us out or wage war against us."

Beth opened her mouth to ask about the complications when their waitress approached. The rich scent of chocolate and spices wafted from the steaming mug she carried.

"Here we are." The waitress set a large ceramic mug in front of Beth, the dark liquid topped with a swirl of whipped cream and a dusting of cocoa powder. "Spiced hot chocolate with bourbon." She placed Tyr's hot toddy before him, steam rising from the amber liquid. "Can I get you anything else?"

"We're good for now, thanks." Beth breathed in the heavenly aroma of chocolate, cinnamon, and bourbon, humming in pleasure.

She took a sip of her hot chocolate, savoring the rich blend of chocolate, spices, and bourbon as the waitress departed. The warmth spread through her chest, making her snuggle deeper into the plush red robe.

"Have you heard about the barbarian hordes?"

"Like Genghis Khan and Attila the Hun?" Beth's eyes widened with interest. Although a science nerd, history had always fascinated her, especially tales of ancient conquests and fallen empires.

"Yes, exactly." Tyr nodded, the blue of his eyes reflecting the twinkling lights strung overhead. "Though I'm not certain which particular horde it was...there were any number of them, throughout the middle ages." A shadow crossed his expression. "Antonio would know - he's our clan's historian. He remembers more of those dark times than the rest of us care to."

"You have to understand the sheer scale of our isolation. Six hundred miles of stark desert stretched between Al Khair and the nearest civilization, east or west. These weren't gentle rolling dunes - this was harsh, unforgiving terrain."

Beth shivered despite her cozy robe, imagining the vast emptiness. The bustling New York streets below felt very far away.

"No one simply stumbled across Al Khair," Tyr continued. "You had to know exactly where the watering holes were, how to navigate the desert. One wrong turn meant death by dehydration or exposure."

He paused, taking a slow sip of his hot toddy. "That natural barrier had protected the city for centuries. In all its history, no army had ever attempted to breach that desert wasteland. The logistics alone made it impossible."

"But the horde was coming anyway?"

"Yes." Tyr's eyes darkened to indigo at the distant memory. "When word reached us, the entire city mobilized. For the first time in history, vampires stood openly beside humans and Others, preparing to defend Al Khair together."

The image formed in Beth's mind - the vampire clan joining forces with the city's inhabitants, setting aside their differences to face a common threat. She was struck by the parallel - just as they were doing now, vampires choosing alliance over isolation when it mattered most.

Completely caught up in Tyr's tale, Beth's hot chocolate sat forgotten as she pictured the scene he described.

"We sent out advance scouts," Tyr continued, his voice dropping lower. "When the army was about... well, I forget exactly, but perhaps two days' march from the city , we found the perfect spot for an ambush. The desert cliffs created a natural funnel on one side, with the mountain range forming the other wall. A series of high dunes rose up before their army, giving us the advantage of height."

He paused, the set of his mouth stern. "I'll never forget that sight. Their army spread across the desert floor like a living carpet - tens of thousands strong. The moonlight caught their tents and supply wagons, while their beasts of burden created dark shadows between the countless campfires. It was like watching a river of light and darkness flowing across the sand, stretching as far as even vampire eyes could see."

Beth shivered, though not from the cold. Her imagination painted the scene vividly - the vast desert night, the massive army spread below, and the defenders of Al Khair preparing their trap. The glittering New York skyline seemed to fade away as she pictured the moonlit dunes and the endless sea of enemy campfires.

"How many defenders did Al Khair have?" she whispered, not wanting to break the spell of his storytelling.

Tyr breathed out a puff of air. "Almost none. The city had guards, of course, but there were no soldiers. No one had ever considered invasion possible."

"But..." Beth frowned. "How did you defend against such a huge army?"

"The vampires and a local jackal clan had plans." A hint of pride crept into Tyr's voice. "We positioned ourselves perfectly, waiting until they were exactly where we wanted them."

"Then what happened?"

"That's when Alyssa's father arrived - one of the elder Djinn, much like Kieran. His power rivaled anything I'd ever seen." Tyr's eyes gleamed with the memory. "But even more incredible was what came next."

He leaned forward, his voice dropping. "From the east, a streak of fire lit the night, racing like a bolt through the sky. Moonlight glinted off golden scales, and Alyssa cried out that it was Kaylee. She was... amazing. She swooped in, flaming those bastards."

"A real dragon," Beth whispered, eyes wide.

Tyr gazed off into the distance, eyes unfocused. "It was something to behold. The Djinn's magic created walls of white-hot flame that trapped the soldiers, while Kaylee's flames drove them into killing zones. Those who tried running found vampires and jackals waiting in the darkness. Quick, efficient - no one escaped to warn others about Al Khair's true defenders."

Tyr's expression shifted, a mix of pride and something deeper, more primal crossing his features. His smile turned razor-sharp, and for an instant Beth saw not her charming companion but something far older and infinitely more dangerous. The vampire who had helped orchestrate the annihilation of an entire army without a flicker of remorse. Then he blinked, and her Tyr was back, but Beth had seen what lay beneath.

"We could have taken that army on ourselves... the vampires and shifters." His voice held absolute certainty. "It would have taken a couple of days because of their numbers, but we had them. But seeing what an ancient, enraged Djinn can do..." He shook his head, and Beth caught a flicker of something like awe in his eyes. "A whole army, gone in a matter of minutes. Not days, not hours, but minutes. It was unreal."

"What happened to the rest of their caravan?" Beth asked. "The supplies, the animals..."

"We ran off the horses and camels before the battle began... that was easy enough in the dark while the soldiers were around their campfires. The rest... the wagons, armaments... they were melted into the sand." Tyr's expression darkened. "But there was one wagon we had to save. The scouts had reported the army was transporting slaves - males for the labor, women for the men."

Beth hugged her robe closer, a chill running down her spine. "How terrible."

His voice softened as he continued. "What with the chaos from the Djinn's fire, they never even noticed when Kaylee swooped down through the flames. Her claws closed around that wagon like it was nothing more than a child's toy. She carried them far from the battle, setting them down gently behind some dunes, where we could retrieve them after the battle was over, and get them safely to Al Khair where they'd be freed and assimilated."

"That's amazing." Beth wrapped her hands tighter around her cooling mug. "She saved them all in the middle of fighting an entire army."

"Dragons are remarkable beings." Tyr's voice held deep respect.

"But you said she spent a lot of her time as a human?"

A grin tugged at the corner of his mouth. "Absolutely. In fact, Kaylee was renowned throughout the region - her knowledge of herbs was unmatched, and everyone spoke of her gentle nature."

Beth's mouth dropped open. "Wait, what?"

"Mhmm." Tyr took another sip of his hot toddy. "She ran the healing house at the base of the Magi tower, treating both humans and Others. None of us knew what she truly was until that night. When she appeared in her dragon form, Alyssa cried out in recognition - it turned out she'd already known Kaylee was actually a dragon, apparently."

"Well, Lord Damien probably knew - he knows everything that happens in his territory. But the rest of us?" He shrugged. "We just knew her as Kaylee, the healer who lived in the city proper."

"But you must have noticed something different about her?" Beth couldn't imagine a dragon completely hiding their nature.

"Not really. Back then, vampires didn't mix with the city dwellers. We knew she was one of the Magi - magic users who helped maintain peace between humans and Others. But we had no real dealings with them."

"So she just... lived there in the city? Healing people?"

"Yes, exactly. But that night..." His expression shifted, wonder and something like awe replacing the casual tone. "When Kaylee descended from the sky and landed among us, Alyssa approached her, tried to communicate. Asked her to change so Kaylee could speak with us, but she couldn't. She was pure fury, completely consumed by her dragon nature."

"What we saw that night..." Tyr's voice held clear admiration mingled with awe. "I've never witnessed anything like it. The sheer power, the absolute fury..."

"She kept herself hidden for years," Beth said quietly. Part of her wished she could have witnessed that moment of revelation - seeing wisdom and fury combined in scaled majesty, golden flames lighting up the desert night. Living among the city dwellers, healing them, and no one knew what she really was."

A dragon living peacefully among humans and Others, only revealing her true nature when absolutely necessary to protect the city. It painted a very different picture from the fierce, treasure-hoarding creatures of myth.

Beth drained the last sip of her now-cool chocolate, savoring the lingering hints of bourbon and spice. The night had grown colder, and even the plush robe couldn't completely ward off the breeze sweeping across the rooftop.

"Ready to head back?" Tyr's voice held gentle concern as he noticed her slight shiver.

Beth nodded, though part of her wanted to stay forever in this magical evening. "Probably should. I do have work tomorrow."

They shed their robes, hanging them on the rack near the elevator. Beth smoothed her hands over her new leather jacket, still amazed by its buttery softness. The elevator whisked them down to street level, where their driver waited with the Maybach.

"Thank you," Beth said as Tyr helped her into the car. "For everything. This has been the most incredible night."

"Thank *you*... for letting me share this with you."" Tyr's cool fingers lingered against hers as he settled beside her. Something softened in his expression—a warmth lighting his ancient eyes that transformed his face from merely handsome to breathtaking.

While she'd noted that the traditional vampires of his clan seemed to maintain careful masks of indifference, Tyr had always worn his emotions openly, and now his usual playfulness gave way to something deeper, more genuine. The mischievous spark remained in his eyes, but beneath it lay an intensity that spoke of centuries of existence suddenly brightened by their unexpected connection.

The Maybach pulled away from the curb, gliding through Manhattan's still-busy streets. Beth leaned back against the leather seat, watching the city lights blur past her window. Her body hummed with pleasant fatigue from ice skating, while her mind buzzed with stories of dragons and ancient battles.

She stifled a yawn, feeling the long evening catching up with her. The car's gentle motion and Tyr's cool presence beside her created a cocoon of contentment that made her eyelids grow heavy.

"Rest," Tyr murmured, his voice soft in the quiet car. "We'll be at the helipad soon."

Beth's head drooped against his shoulder as the Maybach carried them toward the waiting helicopter, the glittering city gradually fading behind them.

CHAPTER 19

Seven centuries in Lord Damien's clan, and Tyr had never requested an audience for something this personal. He smoothed his shirt front for the third time, then caught himself and forced his hands to stillness. The ornate doors loomed before him, their carved surfaces depicting ancient battles between vampires and demons—flights of fancy that had never taken place.

He ran his fingers through his fair hair, then immediately smoothed it back into place. The heavy wood paneling of the hallway seemed to close in around him as he turned for another pass.

Lord Damien's Steward emerged from the inner sanctum, his clothing immaculately starched, as always.

"Lord Damien and Lady Alyssa will see you now." Charles's cultured voice carried the weight of decades of service.

Tyr straightened his shoulders, squaring them as he had countless times before entering his lord's presence. His hand smoothed down his shirt front one final time before he stepped forward.

Charles held the door, his silvering dark brown hair catching the lamplight as he inclined his head. A faint gleam of humor warmed the sharp hazel eyes. "He's been expecting you."

Those quiet words nearly stopped Tyr in his tracks. Of course Lord

Damien had known he would come. The ancient vampire missed little that happened in his domain, especially regarding members of his own clan.

Tyr entered the study, the massive doors closing behind him with a soft thud. The familiar scent of ancient leather-bound books and wood smoke filled his nose. Firelight danced across the room's dark wood paneling, casting flickering shadows that seemed alive.

Lord Damien and Alyssa sat together on a leather chesterfield before the stone fireplace, warm golden flames crackling in the hearth. Her presence softened the formality of the room, as it always did.

Damien's dark eyes reflected red sparks from the fire as he acknowledged Tyr with a slight nod. His arm draped possessively around Alyssa's shoulders, his pale fingers a stark contrast against her midnight hair.

Alyssa's smile lit her entire face, her blue-green eyes twinkling with genuine warmth. "Tyr! I'm so glad you came." Her enthusiasm earned a faint quirk of amusement from Damien's lips.

Tyr bowed deeply, the gesture automatic after centuries of practice. "My Lord. Lady Alyssa." His voice carried the proper formal tones, though Alyssa's presence always made these audiences less intimidating than they might otherwise be.

Damien's elegant fingers gestured for him to come closer. "Join us."

Tyr chose an armchair facing the couple, its rich leather creaking softly as he settled into it. The firelight cast shadows across Lord Damien's features, highlighting the sharp planes of his face. His trademark black attire - a fine linen button-down tucked precisely into black trousers - absorbed the golden light rather than reflecting it.

Beside him, Alyssa curled comfortably against her Chosen, her oversized blue sweater making her appear even smaller next to Damien's commanding presence. Her feet, clad in cozy Ugg boots, were tucked beneath her. The casual comfort of her pose contrasted sharply with Damien's rigid formality, yet somehow they balanced each other perfectly.

The Steward materialized at Tyr's elbow, a crystal decanter of deep red wine held with practiced grace.

"Wine, sir?" Charles's cultured voice carried centuries of proper service.

"No, thank you." Tyr told him politely.

Charles inclined his head in acknowledgment before withdrawing to his customary position near the door, fading into the shadows as only a veteran Steward could manage.

Alyssa's eyes danced with mischief. "So, I heard there was a misplaced hellhound in your community up north?"

Tyr couldn't help laughing, tension easing from his shoulders. "Thank you for sending Kayja - Harper and Nathan were completely out of their depths with that one." He shook his head, remembering the massive puppy's enthusiastic attempts to climb into everyone's laps despite being the size of a small pony. "They had no idea what to feed it, let alone how to handle those sparks shooting everywhere."

"I imagine not." Alyssa's musical laughter filled the room.

Damien's expression remained neutral, but Tyr caught the slight softening around his dark eyes as he watched his wife's amusement. Even after centuries, it amazed Tyr how Alyssa's presence could warm the ancient vampire's typically stern demeanor.

The easy moment couldn't postpone the inevitable forever. Tyr's throat suddenly felt dry as parchment as Damien's gaze shifted to his face.

"What can we do for you this evening, Tyr?"

Tyr's fingers curled into the leather arms of his chair. His throat suddenly felt dry as parchment. He swallowed hard, forcing the words past his lips. "My Lord, I... I have found my Chosen."

"Oh!" Alyssa bounced upright, her mussed hair dropping into her eyes. "That's wonderful!" Her smile lit up her entire face as she clapped her hands together.

Damien merely raised one elegant eyebrow, his expression unreadable as he studied Tyr's face.

"Who is she?" Alyssa leaned forward eagerly, her blue-green eyes sparkling with genuine joy. Her enthusiasm made the crystal decanter on the side table rattle slightly, drawing a quelling look from Damien.

"Beth Kerrigan," Tyr said, his voice steady despite the tension coiling in his chest.

A subtle shift crossed Damien's features. "One of the sisters from the rogue shifter family." Damien's voice carried neither judgment nor approval, merely stating fact.

"Yes." Tyr kept his response simple. There was no need to defend Beth's innocence in that situation - the ancient vampire's intelligence network was legendary, and Damien would have thoroughly investigated every shifter in the Hudson Valley.

Damien studied Tyr with the unhurried patience of immortality, his aristocratic features carved in stone as he let the silence build, each passing moment making his expression even harder to read than usual.

Tyr's fingers dug deeper into the leather arms of his chair. "I want to bring her over.... Turn her."The words escaped before he could cage them, seven centuries of diplomatic training crumbling in an instant. He had planned this so carefully—reasoned arguments, measured words, the respect due his lord. Instead, his heart had spoken first, blurting out his deepest desire like a fledgling.

The silence stretched, broken only by the sound of the flames in the fireplace. Damien's expression remained utterly impassive, those ancient eyes giving away nothing of his thoughts. Even Alyssa stilled, her earlier excitement settling into watchful attention, her eyes on her Chosen.

When Damien finally spoke, his voice carried the same neutral tone he might use to discuss the weather—though Tyr knew better than to mistake that calm for indifference. "And what does Beth think of this idea?"

Tyr flushed with embarrassment. "I... I haven't discussed it with her yet, my Lord." His voice dropped lower. "I wouldn't presume to offer such a thing without your approval."

Alyssa glanced up at Damien, her blue-green eyes bright with enthusiasm. "Beth already knows about keeping secrets. She's part of the Other community - it's not like she'd have to hide her immortality from her friends and family who are shifters."

Lord Damien's elegant fingers drummed a slow rhythm on the rich burgundy leather of the chesterfield's arm. The sound echoed softly in the firelit room.

"I know of no instance where a shifter has been turned, if it has ever been attempted." His unreadable gaze fixed on Tyr. "There may be... repercussions. If it can even be done at all."

Tyr's shoulders tensed. "I've thought of all these things, my Lord." He drew a deep breath, steadying himself. "I had hoped perhaps you might know of others, in your long existence."

"No." Damien's response was immediate and final. "In five millennia, I have never encountered nor heard of such a transformation."

"What would happen to her shifter animal?" Alyssa glanced between Damien and Tyr. "Would she keep her ability to shift? Would the vampire nature override it completely?"

Tyr's fingers clenched on the arms of his chair. He had asked himself these same questions countless times over the past weeks.

"I don't know." Damien's voice carried the weight of his ancient knowledge - and its limits. His expression grew thoughtful. "I will, however, contact the Shifter Council. They have been keeping extensive records on shifters for centuries. If it has been attempted, they will know."

Tyr bent his head. "Thank you, my lord."

Damien's expression remained contemplative, his dark eyes studying Tyr with the careful assessment of one who had witnessed millennia of hasty decisions and their consequences. The ancient vampire seemed to weigh something in his mind, considering implications beyond what had been spoken aloud.

The silence stretched between them, broken only by the soft crackle from the fireplace. Shadows danced across the dark wood paneling as Tyr waited, his entire body tense with anticipation. Even Alyssa remained still, her earlier enthusiasm tempered by the gravity of the situation, her blue-green eyes watching her husband's face with practiced understanding.

Finally, Damien stirred. His elegant fingers ceased their rhythmic tapping on the chesterfield's arm as he fixed Tyr with those ancient, penetrating eyes.

"You will discuss this fully with Beth." His voice carried the unmistakable weight of both permission and caution. "If the Shifter Council has no documentation on this, she *must* understand that there are no guarantees. No precedents. No way to know if her shifter nature would survive the transformation, or if the vampire blood would destroy it entirely."

His piercing gaze held Tyr's. "She needs to comprehend that she would be the first - an experiment, in essence. The consequences are..." He paused, choosing his words with characteristic precision. "Unknown. Completely unknown."

Tyr's fingers flexed against the leather chair arms. "Yes, my Lord. I understand."

"Do you?" Damien's voice carried a sharp edge. "Because Beth will need to understand fully before making such a choice. The risks. The uncertainties. Everything she might lose, as well as gain."

Alyssa's small hand settled on Damien's arm. "And everything she might gain," she added softly. "We don't know that for certain either."

Damien fixed his gaze on Tyr with laser-sharp intensity. "If Beth agrees to this transformation, she would be expected to swear fealty to me, as you have done." His voice carried the weight of centuries of tradition. "She would become part of our clan, bound by our laws and customs."

"And to me." Alyssa's blue-green eyes gleamed with mischief.

Damien sighed, pinching the bridge of his nose between elegant fingers.

Tyr fought back a smile. Even after five centuries together, Alyssa still managed to crack Damien's carefully maintained facade of formality. Their interactions gave him hope - if an ancient vampire and a young Djinn could build such a life together, perhaps his dream of sharing eternity with Beth wasn't completely impossible.

"Indeed, my treasure," Damien's voice carried fond exasperation. "Beth would be expected to swear fealty to both of us."

Tyr rose from his chair, hope and uncertainty warring in his chest. "Thank you, my Lord. My Lady." He bowed deeply, the gesture carrying centuries of ingrained respect.

"Give Beth our regards." Alyssa's warm smile brightened the formal atmosphere. "And let Jacinth know I'll be in touch soon for a Djinn night out."

"Keep me informed." Damien's elegant fingers traced idle patterns on Alyssa's arm. "Safe journey."

The massive doors opened silently as Charles materialized to escort him out. Tyr followed the Steward through the familiar corridors of Lord Damien's penthouse to the sleek elevator that would take him to the private garage beneath the skyscraper.

The elevator's soft hum filled the silence as it descended. Tyr leaned against the polished wood paneling, his mind already racing ahead to the conversation he needed to have with Beth.

How would she react to the possibility of transformation? Would she be willing to take such a leap into the unknown? The thought of sharing eternity with her made his chest ache with longing.

The doors opened to reveal his Nighthawk Custom motorcycle waiting in its designated spot. The sleek machine gleamed under the garage's subdued lighting, its chrome and midnight paint reflecting his approaching figure.

Tyr swung his leg over the seat, the familiar leather creaking beneath him. The powerful engine roared to life at his touch, echoing off the concrete walls. He guided the bike through the garage's security gates, emerging onto the rain-slicked streets of Manhattan.

Traffic thinned as he crossed the George Washington Bridge, the city's glittering skyline receding in his mirrors. The highway stretched before him, leading north toward the Hudson Valley. Toward Beth.

Cool wind whipped past his face as he opened the throttle, letting the bike's raw power surge beneath him. The midnight ride cleared his head, helping him sort through the tumult of emotions Lord Damien's audience had stirred up.

Stars peeked through breaks in the clouds overhead as city lights gave way to darker countryside. His enhanced vision picked out every detail of the familiar route - the gentle curves of the highway, the occasional deer watching from the tree line, the exit signs counting down the miles to home.

To Beth.

The bike's engine growled as he accelerated, eating up the distance between them. His fingers clenched the handlebars, anticipation churning with uncertainty in his chest. Seven centuries of existence, yet he'd never faced a conversation this important. Had Beth ever thought about becoming a vampire? Would she even consider such a transformation to be with him?

Plus, no one—not even Damien with his millennia of knowledge—could promise her leopard would survive. In all known history there had never been a shifter Turned. Tyr's throat tightened at the thought of asking her to risk Whisper's existence for a chance at forever with him.

Stars wheeled overhead as he opened the throttle wider, the bike's power surging beneath him like the emotions he could no longer contain. Every mile brought him closer to Beth - and closer to asking her to risk everything for a chance at forever.

CHAPTER 20

Tyr's motorcycle purred to a stop in front of Beth's house. He pulled out his phone to text her that he'd arrived when Nathan's message flashed across the screen.

«Nono won't settle. Keeps whining and pacing, acting anxious. Can't reach Kayja or Remi. Could use your help.»

Tyr frowned at his phone. The hellhound pup had been remarkably well-behaved from the very beginning.

He typed back quickly: «On my way. Give me 5»

The front door opened and Beth stepped out, her face lighting up when she saw him. She wore a cozy sweater in deep sea green that made her eyes sparkle.

"Hey." Her smile faltered as she caught his expression. "What's wrong?"

"Nathan just texted. Something's up with Nono." Tyr showed her the message. "I promised I'd head over."

"I'm coming too." Beth grabbed her leather jacket from the hook by the door. "That poor pup - he must be really upset if Nathan's worried enough to text you."

"You sure? We were supposed to have dinner..."

Beth was already locking up. "Dinner can wait. Nono needs help."

She pulled on her jacket as she descended the porch steps. "Besides, I love that goofball. Even if he did smoosh me, trying to sit in my lap despite being the size of a pony."

Tyr couldn't help smiling as he handed her the spare helmet. Her genuine concern for others, even a lost hellhound pup, was just one of the countless things he loved about her.

"Hold on tight," he said as she slid onto the bike behind him, her arms wrapping securely around his waist. The familiar warmth of her body pressed against his back made his chest tighten with emotion.

The motorcycle roared to life, and they headed toward Nathan and Harper's place, the cool night air whipping past them. Beth's arms tightened slightly as they took the curves, her trust in him evident in the way she moved with the bike.

Tyr pulled his motorcycle into Nathan and Harper's driveway, the headlight sweeping across the front of the house. Before he could even cut the engine, Harper burst through the front door, her foxy-red hair glowing in the porch light.

"Thank goodness you're here." Harper wrung her hands, her usual calm demeanor clearly shaken. "We fed him a couple days ago, and he's not acting hungry. He just won't settle down."

Beth swung off the bike, already heading for the door. "Have you called the vet?"

"There's no point taking him to the vet again." Harper shook her head. "He's a hellhound, not a dog. They wouldn't know what to do."

Nathan appeared in the doorway, his phone in hand. "Still no answer from Kayja or Remi. I've tried calling and texting both of them multiple times."

Tyr's enhanced senses immediately picked up Nono's distressed whining from the living room. He followed Beth into the house, where the oversized pup paced back and forth, his claws clicking against the hardwood floors. Tiny flames shot from his fur with each turn, singeing small marks into the baseboards.

Beth knelt down, opening her arms. "Hey sweetie, what's wrong?"

Instead of his usual enthusiastic greeting - which typically involved trying to wash Beth's face or squash her in an attempt to sit in her lap -

Nono just pressed against Beth's legs. Beth's expression shifted from concern to alarm.

"He's shaking," Beth said, running her hands over Nono's trembling form. "Like he's terrified of something."

Tyr tensed as Nono suddenly lurched to his feet, his head swinging toward the front door. The deep bark that erupted from Nono's chest shook the house to its foundations, windows rattling in protest. Each successive bark grew louder, more intense, until the entire house seemed to shake with the force of them.

Harper lunged for a Tiffany lamp on the end table as it wobbled precariously. "What in the world?"

Hellfire erupted through Nono's coat, painting the walls in eerie crimson shadows. His barks transformed into thunderous growls that made Tyr's vampire instincts surge to the surface. Whatever had triggered this reaction in the hellhound was powerful enough to set every supernatural nerve ending on high alert.

Suddenly, Nono's massive head tilted, his growls taking on a different quality - recognition mixed with desperate longing.

Three sharp knocks cut through Nono's growls. The hellhound hurled himself at the front door, leaving scorch marks on the hardwood where his flaming paws touched down. The door shuddered in its frame as he slammed against it repeatedly, whining eagerly.

Everyone froze, staring at the door. Tyr shifted slightly, positioning himself between Beth and whatever waited on the other side. His enhanced senses picked up a familiar energy signature just as Kayja's voice rang out.

"It's okay! Open up - everything's fine!"

Tyr tensed as Harper rushed to unlock the door. The moment the latch clicked, Nono burst through like a black meteor, leaving scorched pawprints in his wake.

Where Nono's fur flickered with mere embers, this new presence blazed like an inferno. An enormous hellhound, easily four times Nono's size, stood beside Kayja. Living flames rippled through her midnight fur, casting a red glow across the entire yard. Her presence radiated ancient power that made even Tyr's centuries-old vampire instincts urge him to retreat.

"Don't worry about the neighbors," Remi called out cheerfully from where he stood beside Kayja, his dark eyes twinkling with mischief. "I've cast a glamour over the whole property. No one will see or hear anything unusual."

Nono pranced around the larger hellhound, his entire body wiggling with pure joy. His earlier distress had vanished completely as he bounced and yipped, red sparks shooting from his fur in celebration. The adult hellhound lowered her huge head, gently nosing every inch of Nono's form as if checking for injuries. Her inspection was thorough but tender, a mother's careful examination of her lost pup.

Tyr watched in fascination as tiny flames jumped between them where they touched, creating intricate patterns that danced through both their coats. The larger hellhound's fire seemed to respond to Nono's excitement, dimming from its initial inferno to a warmer, more controlled glow.

"Well," Beth breathed beside him, "I guess we know why Nono was so anxious earlier. He must have sensed his mother approaching."

Kayja's growl resonated through Tyr's bones, making his vampire instincts surge to high alert. Even Remi took a step back, his usual mischievous expression replaced by wariness.

"No." Kayja's voice carried dangerous undertones that made the air crackle with demonic energy. "What Nono sensed was another sorcerer attempting to summon him."

Harper gasped, instinctively moving toward Nono as if she could shield him from the very idea of being summoned.

Kayja's mottled red skin darkened with anger, the patterns shifting to deeper crimson as she continued. "I'm guessing the first one must have had a partner. The same way they separated him from his mother originally. They wanted a hellhound puppy. I don't know why, though."

"Maybe they thought it would be less dangerous?" Beth ventured to ask. "Easier to control?"

The adult hellhound's fiery fur sparked brighter, her head swinging toward the demoness. A low rumble of confirmation vibrated through the ground.

"Partners working together." Tyr's jaw tightened. His gaze swept the darkness beyond the glamoured yard, reaching with his vampire senses for any hint of magical interference. "They're powerful enough to attempt summoning a hellhound pup - and apparently succeeding at least once. That's no small threat."

Kayja's swirling eyes shifted from green to stormy blue, then back again. Her black horns seemed to absorb the hellhounds' flames, creating strange shadows. "We know Nono somehow broke free before they could bind him, and put an end to the summoner. But he didn't return to Hell, which should have happened when the summoner died. I have no idea how Nono ended up here in the Hudson Valley."

The group exchanged puzzled glances. A hellhound pup, separated from Hell and his mother, somehow finding his way to their small supernatural community? The odds seemed impossible.

"Hold on. Wait." Harper's face drained of color, her freckles standing out starkly against suddenly pale skin. "So there's still a sorcerer out there trying to summon him?" Her voice trembled as she hurried to Nono's side, her arms going about the pup's neck.

A wicked smile curved Kayja's lips, her whirling eyes gleaming with satisfaction. The black patterns in her mottled red skin seemed to writhe with pleasure.

"Not anymore." Kayja's tone dripped with dark amusement. "We were on our way here when the mother felt the tug of the summoning. Nono is still young enough to have a mystical connection with her, so she felt it and followed it back to the summoner."

Nono seemed oblivious to the grim undertones of the conversation, still prancing around his mother's legs with puppyish enthusiasm. Sparks shot from his fur with each bounce, creating a mesmerizing dance of flames between mother and pup.

Tyr felt Beth shift closer to him, her warmth pressing against his side as she rose on tiptoe. Her breath tickled his ear as she whispered, "I probably shouldn't ask what happened to the summoner, should I?"

Before he could respond, Remi's rich laugh rang out. Obviously he had overheard her question, because the young Djinn's dark eyes sparkled with mischief as he grinned at Beth. "Probably not, no. It's safe to guess he went the same way as the first one."

Nathan drew Harper close as they both knelt beside Nono, wrapping a comforting arm around her shoulders. Nono's tail wagged madly as he tried to lick both their faces at once.

The mother hellhound lowered her enormous head, and she nuzzled first Harper, then Nathan. Her touch left faint traces of warmth on their skin, but no burns.

"She wants you to know how grateful she is," Kayja translated, her whirling eyes softening. "You gave her pup safety and love when he needed it most."

Beth reluctantly let go of Tyr's hand to give Nono one last hug. The pup's whole body wriggled with excitement as he pressed against her, nearly knocking her over in his enthusiasm. Tyr caught her shoulder to steady her, then reached down to ruffle the pup's fur.

"Goodbye, little one," Beth whispered, her voice thick with emotion.

The mother hellhound touched her nose to Nono's head, and both their flames began to pulse in sync. The red glow intensified, building to a brilliant crimson that lit up the night sky. In a rush of heat and light, both hellhounds vanished, leaving only scorched pawprints in the grass as evidence they had ever been there.

Kayja's form shimmered, the mottled red patterns in her skin writhing like living shadows. "Well, my work here is done." Her whirling eyes shifted from stormy blue back to their usual green as she faded from sight, leaving only a trace of demonic energy crackling in the air.

Remi's dark eyes sparkled with their usual mischief as he swept them an elaborate courtly bow, complete with flourishing hand gestures. "Ladies, gentlemen - it's been a pleasure. Try not to acquire any more supernatural pets while I'm gone." He winked, his grin widening. "But if you do, call me right away!"

With a shimmer of Djinn magic, he vanished.

The sudden silence felt heavy after all the excitement. Beth's shoulders slumped slightly as she stared at the scorched pawprints in the grass. Harper knelt beside the marks, her fingers hovering just above the singed grass but not quite touching.

"I'm going to miss that goofball," Nathan said, his voice thick with emotion, his arm tightening around Harper's shoulders.

Tyr understood completely. Despite only having known Nono for a short time, the hellhound pup had carved out his own special place in their lives with his enthusiastic affection and playful nature.

"At least we know he's safe now," Beth said, leaning against Tyr's side. "And back where he belongs, with his mother."

Harper nodded, rising to her feet. "That's what matters most."

Tyr squeezed Beth's hand gently. "We should let them get some rest. It's been quite an evening."

"Of course." Beth hugged Harper, who still looked a bit shaken. "Call if you need anything, okay?"

Nathan ran his hand through his already tousled hair. "Thanks for coming over so quickly. Both of you."

"Anytime," Tyr assured him. He meant it - the music teacher and the fox shifter had become good friends over the past months.

Harper managed a small smile. "Drive safely."

Beth slipped her hand into Tyr's as they walked back to his motorcycle. The night air carried a hint of autumn crispness, and the stars twinkled overhead through breaks in the clouds. Tyr helped Beth with her helmet before swinging his leg over the bike.

She settled behind him, her arms wrapping securely around his waist. The familiar warmth of her body pressed against his back centered him, helping push aside the lingering tension from the evening's events.

The motorcycle's engine purred to life. As they pulled out of the driveway, Tyr caught one last glimpse of Nathan and Harper standing in their doorway, arms around each other as they watched their unexpected foster pet's scorched pawprints slowly fade from their lawn.

CHAPTER 21

Beth hummed softly as she stacked bags of prescription diet food on the metal shelving unit. The last light of day cast purple shadows through the lobby windows, and peaceful quiet had settled over the clinic, broken only by Tamera's rustling papers at reception.

"Almost done with those notes, Liam?" Tamera called over her shoulder.

"Just finishing up Mrs. Harrison's chart," Liam's voice drifted from his office. "That cat of hers is going to need dental work soon."

Beth shifted another bag of kidney diet onto the shelf, mentally calculating how many more they'd need to order. The familiar routine of end-of-day tasks felt comforting after the chaos of their busy afternoon.

Whisper's ears pricked in alert just as the front door burst open with such force it slammed against the wall. The sharp scent of adrenaline and lethal focus flooded Beth's shifter senses as she dropped the bag of food, whirling to face the entrance. Dimitri stood in the doorway, his caramel features stark in the fading light, every line of his body radiating predatory intensity.

"Get to an inner room. Now." His voice cracked with command. "We're about to be under attack."

Cold dread punched through Beth's chest. Inside her, Whisper came alert, a warning growl rumbling through her mind. "What-"

"No time." Dimitri cut her off, already moving to secure the door. "Backup's coming, but we need to move. Now."

Tamera's files scattered across the reception desk as she bolted upright. "Liam!"

"I heard." Liam emerged from his office, his face grim. "Treatment room three - no windows, solid walls, single access point."

"Move!" Dimitri's sharp command galvanized them into action. He herded them toward the treatment area, his dark eyes constantly scanning the windows. "Stay low, stay quiet, and stay together."

Beth crouched low as they hurried down the hallway, her heart hammering against her ribs. Liam pulled out his phone, his fingers flying across the screen as they moved. "Calling Jacinth," he told them.

Power shimmered through the air like heat waves, making Beth's skin tingle as Djinn magic poured into the room. A flash of blue light erupted in the hallway, and Jacinth materialized before them, her dark eyes fierce and alert. Another surge of power brought Arthur beside her, the elderly Djinn's usual gentle demeanor replaced by focused intensity.

"Multiple hostiles approaching down the drive," Dimitri reported, his voice clipped. "Three trucks, with at least eight, possibly more. Well-armed."

Jacinth's lips curved into a dangerous smile. "Come on back to the lobby," she invited, her voice carrying absolute certainty. "You guys are going to want to see this."

Dimitri's brow furrowed. "With all due respect-"

"I've got this." Jacinth's smile turned predatory, blue fire dancing in her eyes. The casual confidence in her voice brooked no argument.

Arthur stood silently at her side, but power radiated from him like heat from a furnace. His weathered features held the calm certainty of someone who had faced far worse threats in his centuries of existence.

"Hit the lights."

Beth hurried to the light switches, and a moment later the lobby descended into darkness.

"Now we can see them, but they can't see us." Jacinth winked, her dark eyes sparkling with mischief despite the tension. "Arthur and I have been practicing," she said, her lips curving into a knowing smile.

The two Djinn moved in perfect synchronization, their hands weaving intricate patterns through the air. The magic hit Beth like static electricity, making her skin prickle and her hair stand on end. Yet she saw nothing - no flashes of light, no visible barriers forming.

"Look." Jacinth pointed toward the lobby windows. Beth squinted, finally noticing a faint shimmer in the air, like heat waves rising from hot pavement. The distortion curved upward, forming what appeared to be a massive dome over the entire clinic.

"Protective barrier," Jacinth explained, satisfaction evident in her voice. "Nothing and no one can get through without our permission."

Liam stepped closer to the windows, studying the barely visible shield with professional interest. "Nothing? Even bullets?"

"Even bullets." Arthur's weathered features creased in a slight smile, the first expression Beth had seen from him since he arrived. His quiet confidence was somehow more reassuring than Jacinth's overt enthusiasm.

Jacinth turned to Dimitri, who still stood alert near the door. "Have your vampires wait in the woods," she instructed. "Let's see how this plays out before anyone intervenes."

Beth's breath caught as twin beams of light pierced through the darkened trees. The vehicles' approach seemed agonizingly slow as they wound their way up the clinic's long drive, their headlights sweeping across the building's front windows.

Her fingers pressed against the cool glass, the invisible shield tingling against her skin like static electricity. The barrier shimmered faintly where her hand touched it, rippling like water disturbed by a gentle breeze.

A soft chime broke the tense silence. Dimitri glanced down at his phone, his brow furrowing as he read the message.

"Arthur." Dimitri's voice was low but urgent. "Can you create an opening in the shield at the back door? Tyr's here and..." A faint smile touched his lips. "Well, he's rather insistent about getting in."

Arthur's weathered features creased in understanding. "I assume he's in his raptor form?"

"Yes."

"Tell him to come to the back entrance." Arthur's hands traced a subtle pattern through the air. "I'll let him through."

Beth's heart skipped at the mention of Tyr. She turned away from the window, her gaze drawn toward the back of the clinic where she knew he waited, somewhere in the darkness beyond the shield.

A rush of winter air announced Tyr's arrival as he burst through the back door, his vampire speed carrying him straight to Beth. Familiar arms enveloped her, bringing the scent of leather and winter pine she'd come to associate with him. The desperate relief in his embrace told her everything - this ancient, powerful vampire had been genuinely afraid for her safety.

He'd been terrified something would happen to her.

"Are you alright?" His voice rumbled against her ear, low and urgent.

Beth nodded into his shirt, her fingers curling into the soft fabric. The tension in her shoulders eased, replaced by a profound sense of security. She trusted Jacinth and Arthur's magical barrier completely - she'd seen enough of Djinn powers to know they were well-protected. But having Tyr here, solid and real against her, settled something deep in her chest she hadn't even realized was unsettled.

"I'm okay," she whispered. He drew her more securely against his chest, and she felt him press a kiss to the top of her head.

The approaching headlights grew brighter, but Beth found she didn't care quite as much anymore. Tyr's presence grounded her, pushing back the fear that had been threatening to overwhelm her since Dimitri's warning. She breathed in his familiar scent, letting it calm her racing pulse.

"The barrier will hold," Tyr murmured against her hair, though whether he was reassuring her or himself, Beth wasn't sure. "Jacinth's magic is strong, and Arthur... well, he's forgotten more about protective spells than most Djinn will ever learn."

Beth nodded again, not quite trusting her voice. She knew all this, but hearing Tyr say it somehow made it more real, more certain. She stayed within the circle of his arms, drawing strength from his solid presence as they waited to see what their attackers would do next.

Three large pickup trucks rumbled to a stop in front of the clinic. Her fingers tightened in Tyr's shirt as men spilled out of the vehicles, their movements a mix of aggression and disorganization. The clinic's floodlights glinted off metal as they pulled rifles and handguns from the truck beds.

"Look at them," Tamera's voice dripped with disgust from her position near the reception desk. "They're not even trying to hide what they're up to."

Beth counted at least twelve men, most dressed in mismatched tactical gear and camouflage. A few wore red armbands with some symbol she couldn't quite make out. They moved with the confidence of predators, but lacked the discipline of true soldiers—some wielding their weapons with practiced ease while others handled them awkwardly, compensating with extra aggression.

"Of course not." Jacinth's tone remained casual, almost bored, as she watched the men coordinate their positions. "They want us to be afraid." She leaned against the wall, examining her perfectly manicured nails as if the armed men outside were nothing more than a minor inconvenience. "That's the whole point of this little display."

Beth felt Tyr's chest rumble with quiet agreement. His arms remained secure around her as they observed the scene unfolding before them. Through the invisible barrier, she could hear muffled voices as the men called out positions and commands to each other, organizing themselves for what they clearly expected to be an assault on the clinic.

Beth's breath caught as several men hauled red plastic containers from one of the truck beds. Her stomach dropped as she recognized the distinctive shape of gas cans.

"They're going to set fire to the clinic!" The words came out in a horrified gasp. Her fingers dug deeper into Tyr's shirt.

"They can try." Tyr's voice held dark amusement.

Jacinth stepped closer to the window, pointing to where the barrier shimmered faintly in the air just beyond the glass. "Shielding, remember?" Her dark eyes danced with mischief as she turned to face the gathered shifters. A grin spread across her face, making her look more like an impish teenager than an ancient Djinn.

Tyr's lips curved into a predatory grin that made his fangs gleam in the fading light. "Besides, Tobi and Antonio are out there in the woods right now, watching their every move."

Beth's gaze darted to the treeline, though she couldn't spot the vampires in the growing darkness. The knowledge that they were out there, unseen guardians ready to intervene, sent a wave of relief through her tense muscles.

"So..." Jacinth's eyes sparkled with barely contained glee as she moved toward the front door. "Who wants to volunteer?"

Tamera bounced on her toes, practically vibrating with excitement. "I do! I do!" Her hand shot into the air like an eager student.

"Absolutely not." Liam's voice carried the stern authority he usually reserved for difficult patients.

Tamera planted her hands on her hips, red hair flying as she whirled to face him. "You're not the boss of me, Dr. McConnell." Her stormy blue eyes flashed with determination.

"Actually, I am."

"Oh, right." She narrowed her eyes at him. "But you still can't stop me."

“Fine." Liam's jaw set in a stubborn line. "Then I'm going too."

Beth felt Tyr's arms tighten around her waist, his chest rumbling against her back. His cool breath tickled her ear as he growled, "Don't even think about it."

She hadn't been planning to volunteer, but his protective response made her smile despite the tension. She leaned back against him, watching as Jacinth strode confidently toward the front door. The ancient Djinn's movements were fluid and graceful, power radiating from her petite frame.

Tamera hurried after Jacinth, with Liam close behind. They stepped out onto the concrete walkway, remaining safely within the shimmering barrier that Beth could now see more clearly in the trucks' headlights.

A sudden flurry of movement erupted from the armed men as they spotted the trio standing there. Rifles snapped up, voices shouted commands, and bodies scrambled for better positions. The chaos of their response only highlighted how unprepared they were for their targets to simply walk out and face them.

Beth held her breath as Jacinth stepped forward, her casual demeanor making Beth's stomach flutter with nervous anticipation. The Djinn was definitely up to something—but what? Beth pressed closer to the window as Jacinth's musical voice carried clearly through the evening air.

"Hi there, boys!" Jacinth waved cheerfully, as if greeting friends at a backyard barbecue. "What can we do for you tonight?"

The men shifted uneasily, their weapons wavering slightly. Confusion rippled through their ranks at this unexpected welcome. After a moment of awkward silence, one man stepped forward. His red armband marked him as some kind of leader.

"We're here for the shifters," he declared, trying to sound authoritative despite his obvious uncertainty.

Jacinth blinked at him with exaggerated surprise. "Oh! You want a shifter?" She turned to Liam, her expression comically wide-eyed. "They want a shifter!"

"Well," Liam drawled, his hazel eyes glinting with dangerous humor, "I guess we'll have to give them one then."

Beth felt Tyr's arms tighten around her as Liam's form blurred and expanded. Where the veterinarian had stood moments before, a massive white Great Pyrenees now towered, his impressive bulk somehow even more intimidating than the men's weapons. The dog's thunderous bark shattered the night air, making several of the armed men stumble backward despite their firearms. Others started yelling "Shifter! It's a shifter!"

The rest of them panicked at the sight of Liam's transformation, their formation breaking as several bumped into each other. Beth couldn't help snickering as she watched these supposedly tough guys retreat from a single dog. Beside her, Tyr's chest rumbled with quiet laughter.

"Not quite what they were expecting, I'd say," Tyr murmured against her ear, his amusement evident in his voice.

The leader—the man with the red armband—recovered first, raising his rifle to shoulder height.

"Stay where you are!" he shouted, voice cracking slightly. "All of you!"

Jacinth tilted her head, examining him with the casual interest one might give a mildly interesting insect. "Or what?" she asked, her tone light and curious.

The man's jaw tightened. "We want the shifters. Hand them over, and nobody gets hurt."

Liam's massive canine form moved forward, head lowered, his eyes fixed unflinchingly on the leader. He placed himself protectively in front of Tamera and Jacinth, and a low, rumbling growl vibrated from his chest, the sound carrying across the parking lot with unmistakable menace.

"I don't think he likes your offer," Jacinth said, patting Liam's broad white head. "And frankly, neither do I."

The leader's eyes darted between Liam and the clinic building. "This whole place is lousy with shifters." He took a step forward, stopping abruptly when Liam's growl intensified. "This doesn't have to get messy. Just send the rest of them out."

"And why exactly do you want them?" Tamera demanded, her voice carrying despite her smaller stature. "Who sent you?"

"That's not your concern," the leader snapped, though Beth could see his confidence wavering. "Last chance. Send out the rest of the shifters, or we start shooting. And you," he waved his gun toward Liam. "Get over here. Now."

From inside the clinic, Beth felt Tyr's muscles tense. His arms tightened around her waist, ready to move at superhuman speed if necessary. She knew without asking that he could have her safely away in less than a heartbeat.

"You could try shooting," Jacinth offered helpfully, examining her nails again. "But I wouldn't recommend it."

The leader's face flushed with anger. He gestured sharply to his men. "Spread out! Surround the building!"

As the men moved to comply, Jacinth sighed dramatically. "Now you're just being rude."

Beth pressed closer to Tyr as she watched the scene unfold. The leader turned to a stocky man beside him, jerking his head toward Liam's massive white form.

"Take it out," he ordered.

The stocky man raised his rifle, but before he could aim properly, several others pushed forward, brandishing baseball bats and crowbars.

"Hold up!" A tall man with a red bandana waved his bat. "Let us have a go at him first. Been waiting to crack some shifter skull."

"Yeah," another chimed in, slapping his bat against his palm. "Save the bullets for when we really need 'em."

Beth's stomach churned as more men crowded forward, their weapons glinting in the headlights. The casual way they discussed violence made her skin crawl.

"What about the women?" A voice called from the back of the group. "Don't forget why we came here."

"Right." Another man stepped forward, leering at Tamera. "We can have some fun once we clear out the freaks."

Murmurs of agreement rippled through the group.

Beth shuddered, and felt Tyr's arms tighten around her protectively as several men's gazes swept over the clinic windows, searching for more targets.

"They're just sick," she murmured.

"Save the redhead for me," someone called out, triggering crude laughter from his companions.

Beth's fingers dug into Tyr's forearms as she watched these men discuss their friends like pieces of meat. Her heart pounded against her ribs, fury mixing with fear as she realized just what kind of monsters they were dealing with.

Tamera stepped forward, her lips curved in a dangerous smile. The redhead's eyes glinted with barely contained fury as she faced down the leering men.

"Good luck with that," Tamera called out, her voice ringing with challenge.

Before the men could respond, Tamera's form blurred and shifted. Where the petite receptionist had stood moments before, a sleek caracal now crouched, her tufted ears laid flat against her skull. The wild cat's muscular form tensed, powerful haunches coiled and ready to spring.

The men's laughter died in their throats, replaced by startled shouts as they stumbled backward. The caracal's lips pulled back, revealing impressive fangs as she released a bone-chilling hiss that echoed across the parking lot.

Beth's breath caught in her throat as she watched Tamera stalk forward, every movement radiating lethal grace. The caracal's golden eyes blazed with intelligence and fury, fixed on the men who had dared threaten her.

"Wow," Beth breathed, unable to contain her admiration. "Tamera rocks!"

"She certainly knows how to make an entrance," he murmured, his cool breath tickling her ear.

The leader's face contorted with rage. He jabbed his finger toward Tamera's caracal form and Jacinth.

"Get them!" he barked at his men. "Grab the woman and the cat, you can do what you want with the dog!"

The men with bats surged forward, cruel grins spreading across their faces as they closed in on Tamera and Liam. Even knowing Jacinth and Arthur were keeping them all safe, Beth's heart hammered against her ribs as she watched them approach her friends, their weapons raised high.

But just as the men came within striking distance, things suddenly turned bizarre. The baseball bats seemed to waver, like heat mirages on hot pavement. Their dark wooden surfaces began to shift and transform, bleeding into bright neon colors - hot pink, electric blue, sunshine yellow. The rigid forms softened and expanded until each man found himself holding nothing more threatening than a pool noodle.

Shouts of confusion erupted from the group as they stared at their transformed weapons. Men cursed and threw the foam tubes aside and scrambled away, stumbling into each other in their haste to escape.

"What the hell?" one man yelped, jumping backward. "What kind of freaky shit is this?"

Beth couldn't help the giggle that bubbled up from her chest. She turned in Tyr's arms, eyes sparkling with delight.

"I'm so sorry," she told him, trying and failing to contain her laughter, "but Jacinth is officially my new number one hero."

Tyr's lips curved into an amused smile as he watched the chaos unfolding outside. "I'm going to have to agree with that," he admitted.

Beth pressed closer to Tyr as another man jerked his rifle up, stumbling backward. His finger squeezed the trigger, and Beth's heart lurched—but instead of the expected gunshot, a powerful stream of water burst from the barrel, arcing through the air like a super-soaker.

The man's eyes widened in disbelief as he stared at his weapon, now transformed into something more suited for a pool party than an attack. Water continued spraying everywhere, soaking his tactical vest and boots.

A piercing scream cut through the chaos. Beth's attention snapped to one of the men near the trucks as he dropped his rifle, clutching his hands. The weapon clattered to the pavement, its metal surface glowing an angry cherry-red in the darkness.

"What the—" Another man yelped, frantically trying to maintain his grip on his own rifle. But Beth could see the metal beginning to shimmer with heat. One by one, the weapons grew too hot to hold, forcing their owners to release them or risk severe burns.

The parking lot filled with the sound of metal hitting concrete as rifles dropped, accompanied by pained curses and shouts as the men waved their scorched fingers in the air. Some blew on their hands while others stuck their fingers in their mouths, trying to cool the burns.

"My hands!" one of them wailed, his tough-guy facade crumbling as he hopped from foot to foot. "They're burning!"

Beth felt Tyr's silent laughter vibrating against her back as they watched the scene unfold. From here, she could see Jacinth's satisfied smirk as the Djinn observed her handiwork. The ancient being's dark eyes sparkled with mischief while beside her, Arthur maintained his serene expression, though Beth caught the slight upturn at the corners of his mouth.

Beth leaned back against Tyr's solid chest, watching the chaos unfold outside. She'd bet everything she owned Arthur had heated those weapons—it matched his precise, practical style perfectly. The pool noodles though? That had Jacinth written all over it.

"Uh oh." Tyr's arms tightened around her waist.

"What?" Beth scanned the scene, trying to spot what had caught his attention.

"Over by the truck on the left."

Beth's gaze snapped to the indicated vehicle. In the headlights' glare, she caught the distinctive flare of a lighter. Her breath caught as a makeshift projectile sailed through the air—a Molotov cocktail, its burning rag trailing fire as it arced toward the clinic.

Her fingers dug into Tyr's forearms as she watched the flaming bottle approach. Just before it hit the barrier, the cocktail's trajectory suddenly reversed. The bottle hung suspended in midair above the attackers' heads for one perfect moment before exploding.

Instead of fire and glass, a shower of rainbow glitter and confetti rained down on the men. The colorful paper pieces settled in their hair, stuck to their tactical gear, and coated their already-soaked clothing in a layer of sparkles that caught the headlights like tiny stars.

Beth burst out laughing, unable to contain her mirth at the sight of these would-be tough guys covered head to toe in glitter. Through the window, she could see Tamera doubled over, back in human form and clutching her sides as she laughed. Liam's massive white form shook with canine chuckles, his tongue lolling out in a doggy grin.

Outside, Jacinth wiped tears of mirth from her eyes, while beside her, Arthur's weathered features creased in quiet amusement as he watched their attackers try futilely to brush the sparkles from their clothes.

"I think," Beth managed between giggles, "this might be the best night ever."

Beth's laughter died in her throat as primordial magic crackled through the air. Even through the protective barrier around the clinic, she felt the crushing presence of something ancient and vast. Close to the surface, Whisper's ears swept back and she howled in dismay. A blinding flash of blue-white light illuminated the clinic's entrance, and Kieran materialized beside Jacinth like a force of nature taking physical form. His pure white hair gleamed in the headlights, a stark contrast to his black linen clothing and severe expression.

Tyr's arms tightened fractionally around her waist. Even vampires treated the ancient Djinn prince with cautious respect, and Beth understood why. Raw power radiated from his tall frame, and his glacier blue eyes held the weight of millennia as he fixed Jacinth with a stern look.

"Jacinth," Kieran's deep voice carried easily across the parking lot. "What have I told you?"

Jacinth's expression transformed into one of exaggerated innocence, though her dark eyes still sparkled with barely contained mischief. She clasped her hands behind her back, looking for all the world like a schoolgirl caught passing notes in class.

"Not to play with my food?" she offered sweetly.

Beth pressed her lips together, fighting back another giggle at Jacinth's impish response. The ancient Djinn might be one of the most powerful beings she'd ever encountered, but she still managed to make everything feel like a game.

Kieran released a deep, weary sigh as he turned his attention to the glitter-covered attackers. His icy blue gaze swept over the scene - the scattered pool noodles, the men still nursing burned hands, and the rainbow sparkles catching the light everywhere.

Tyr pulled her closer as Kieran's voice thundered across the parking lot, the sound seeming to shake the very air around them.

"SILENCE!"

The effect was instantaneous. Every attacker froze mid-motion, their mouths hanging open as they turned toward the ancient Djinn prince. Beth watched in fascination as several tried to speak, their jaws working soundlessly. No words emerged - not even whispers.

Kieran's frosty eyes blazed with cold fire as he addressed the now-silent mob. "You will return to your vehicles. You will leave this place. And you will never return." His voice carried absolute authority, brooking no argument.

At Kieran's slight nod, Arthur stepped forward to stand beside him. The two Djinn moved in perfect synchronization, their hands weaving intricate patterns through the air. Power crackled between them, making Beth's skin tingle even through the protective barrier around the clinic.

Beth's breath caught as she watched the attackers' expressions go blank. As one, they turned and walked to their vehicles with mechanical precision. No shouting, no resistance - they simply climbed into their trucks and drove away, leaving only tire tracks and scattered pool noodles behind.

"What just happened?" Beth turned in Tyr's arms, staring up at him in bewilderment. "How did they just... leave like that?"

Tyr's brow furrowed as he watched the taillights disappear down the drive. "I don't know," he admitted, his arms tightening fractionally around her waist. "Djinn magic is... complex. Even after centuries, I've never fully understood its limits."

Beth turned as Kieran strode into the clinic, his silvery hair gleaming in the fluorescent lights. The others filed in behind him, Jacinth still radiating mischievous energy while Arthur maintained his usual serene expression.

Beth let out a shaky breath she hadn't realized she'd been holding. Around her, she could see the same relief on everyone's faces - the immediate danger had passed. A collective sigh of relief went up.

"I've removed all memory of tonight's events from their minds," Kieran announced, his gaze sweeping over the gathered group. "They'll remember only finding the clinic locked and dark, and deciding to leave."

"Nor will they be able to find their way back here," he continued, his deep voice resonating through the lobby. "Even with GPS coordinates, the clinic will remain hidden from them."

Jacinth bounced on her toes, dark eyes sparkling with barely contained glee. Her lips curved into an impish smile that made Beth instantly suspicious.

Kieran released a long-suffering sigh as he caught Jacinth's expression. The grave atmosphere in the room eased as everyone recognized that look.

"What now?" he asked, his tone carrying centuries of weary experience with her antics.

"Well..." Jacinth clasped her hands behind her back, the very picture of exaggerated innocence. "I might have added a teensy little something as a goodbye present."

Kieran pinched the bridge of his nose between elegant fingers. "What did you do?"

Jacinth's grin widened. "I magicked a bunch of shrimp into their trucks' ventilation systems."

Tyr burst out laughing. "That's pure evil," he managed between chuckles.

Pure glee filled Beth as she imagined the smell that would soon permeate those vehicles. No amount of air freshener would cover that up!

"Plus they still had the confetti and glitter on them," Jacinth said with a merry wink.

Beth leaned back against Tyr's chest as Antonio swept into the clinic, his elegant movements a stark contrast to Dimitri's more aggressive stride. Tobi bounded in behind them, practically vibrating with excitement.

"That was amazing!" Tobi's eyes sparkled with barely contained glee. "Did you see their faces when the guns started spraying water?"

Antonio's lips curved into a slight smile as he brushed an imaginary speck of dust from his impeccable silk sleeve. "I particularly enjoyed the pool noodles. Most... creative."

"The confetti was a nice touch," Dimitri added, his caramel skin gleaming in the fluorescent lights. "Though I must admit, the superheated weapons were my favorite."

Tyr laughed. "The way they dropped those rifles, hopping around and blowing on their fingers..." He shook his head, still chuckling. "Priceless."

"And then the Molotov cocktail!" Tobi bounced on his toes, reminding Beth strongly of an excited puppy. "The way it just hung there before exploding into glitter? Pure genius!"

"Indeed." Antonio's cultured voice carried dry amusement. "Though perhaps next time we might consider a less... flamboyant approach?"

"Where's the fun in that?" Tobi protested, earning an exasperated look from his sire.

Antonio inclined his head toward Kieran in respect, his movements carrying centuries of practiced grace. "I suspect we have you to thank for their peaceful departure, Prince Kieran?"

"A simple memory modification." Kieran shrugged. "They'll

remember only finding an empty clinic. Nor will they be able to find it again, should they seek to return."

Jacinth bounced forward, dark eyes sparkling. "Time to go! Arthur promised to help me practice some new spells." She grabbed Arthur's arm, and they vanished in a flash of blue light.

Kieran shook his head, a fond smile touching his severe features before he too disappeared.

"We should return to our patrols," Antonio announced, his cultured voice carrying quiet authority. He turned to Dimitri. "Make sure no one harmed Kazakis Restaurant, although no one was there this time of night."

Dimitri nodded, and the two vampires slipped out into the darkness.

"I should head home too." Tamera gathered her purse from behind the reception desk. "Early shift tomorrow."

"I'll walk you to your car." Tobi stepped forward. "Then I'll do a sweep out front, make sure none of those idiots are lurking around. I mean, just in case."

Hugging Tamera tightly, Beth turned back to the scattered files on her desk, knowing she still had work to finish. Tyr's cool presence remained close behind her as she began organizing the chaos.

"I need to complete Mrs. Harrison's charts," Liam called as he walked back toward his office.

"Take your time." Tyr's voice carried quiet certainty. "I'm not going anywhere."

Beth turned toward the reception desk, intending to organize the scattered files, but her hands trembled as she reached for the papers. The adrenaline crash hit her suddenly, leaving her legs wobbly and her breathing shallow. She gripped the edge of the desk to steady herself.

"Hey." Tyr's cool fingers encircled her wrist, his voice gentle. "Sit down before you fall down."

She sank into the reception chair, the reality of what had just happened washing over her in waves. They'd faced men with guns—men who'd talked about hurting them as casually as discussing the weather. The memory of their cruel laughter made her stomach clench.

"I thought I was fine," she whispered, staring at her trembling hands.

"It's okay." Tyr crouched before her, his eyes steady on hers. "You're allowed to not be fine for a while."

He brushed a strand of hair from her face, his touch achingly tender. "The files can wait until tomorrow."

"But—"

"I'm not going anywhere," he repeated, his voice carrying quiet certainty. "Not tonight. I'm not leaving you alone."

Beth leaned forward until her forehead rested against his shoulder, drawing comfort from his solid presence as the night's events caught up with her. Right now, she was simply grateful for his strength.

CHAPTER 22

Tyr kept his arm around Beth's shoulders as Liam emerged from his office, shrugging into his coat. The veterinarian's hazel eyes swept over them both, his expression brooking no argument.

"That's it for you tonight, Beth.." Liam's tone was gentle but firm. "Go home and get some rest."

"Aleksei's on his way down from the city." The doctor's gaze fixed on Tyr. "He wants to meet with you and Tobi as soon as he arrives, for a full report. Antonio is on his way as well."

"I'll see Beth home safely," Liam assured Tyr, his expression softening. "I'll be right behind her all the way."

Tyr's jaw tightened. The thought of leaving Beth right now... but he knew this meeting was crucial after the night's events.

"Go," Beth touched his arm gently. "I'll be fine with Liam."

Tyr caught her hand, pressing a kiss to her palm. "I'll see you to your car?"

At her nod, he reluctantly released her and headed for the door. He paused in the doorway, watching as Liam helped Beth gather her things. Only when they were both ready to leave did he finally step out into the night.

The back door closed behind them with a soft click as they emerged into the employee parking lot. The night air carried a sharp chill, though Beth seemed unfazed by it. Moonlight bathed the lot in silvery radiance, casting long shadows between the scattered vehicles.

Liam broke away from them, heading toward his charcoal grey Jeep at the far end of the lot. Tyr's hand settled at the small of Beth's back as he guided her toward her dark green Prius.

"See you at home, Beth!" Liam called from his Jeep. "And so you know, I didn't call Naomi and wake her to tell her about this, so she'll be all over it in the morning."

Beth turned, her pale hair catching the moonlight as she grimaced. "Oh, boy! I can see we're going to have an interesting morning."

The sharp crack of gunfire came without warning, impossibly loud in the still night.

Beth's body jerked, her eyes going wide with shock as crimson bloomed across her stomach, spreading rapidly through her light blue scrub top. Her knees buckled.

Tyr lunged forward, catching her before she could hit the pavement. A second report rang out as he cradled her against his chest, and Liam's pained shout echoed through the parking lot.

The third shot slammed into Tyr's chest, the impact barely registering through his rising panic as he carefully lowered Beth to the ground. The bullet meant nothing - vampires couldn't die. But Beth...

"Beth!" Liam's voice cracked as he sprinted toward them, blood streaming from his shoulder. The veterinarian dropped to his knees beside them, his hazel eyes wild with fear as he pressed his uninjured hand against the wound in Beth's abdomen.

Another shot cracked through the night, another bullet slamming into Tyr's arm. He barely registered the impact, his entire focus on Beth's pale face and ragged breathing. Blood soaked through her scrubs, the metallic scent filling his nose and triggering his vampire instincts. He ruthlessly suppressed the urge to feed, channeling the surge of power into action instead.

In one fluid motion, Tyr scooped Beth into his arms and darted around the far side of her Prius. Liam followed close behind, his own wound forgotten in his concern for his sister-in-law. The car's metal frame wouldn't stop a bullet, but it provided some cover while they assessed Beth's condition.

Tyr gently laid Beth on the asphalt, his hands steady despite the rage building inside him. Her skin had taken on a greyish tinge that made his heart clench.

Liam immediately pressed both hands against Beth's wound, his medical training taking over. "Go," he ordered, his voice tight with pain and worry. "I've got her. Find whoever did this."

Tyr hesitated for a fraction of a second, his protective instincts warring with the need to eliminate the threat.

"Go!" Liam snapped. "I can handle this. You're the only one who can catch them."

Tyr raced between the trees. His heightened senses tracked the shooter's scent - gunpowder, sweat, excitement, and fear creating a clear trail through the woods behind the clinic. The man's rapid heartbeat thundered in Tyr's ears, growing louder with each stride.

About three hundred yards in, Tyr spotted movement high in a massive oak tree. The sniper was hastily climbing down, his rifle slung across his back as he descended branch by branch. The man's breathing came in sharp pants, his muscles trembling with mingled triumph and exertion.

Tyr didn't hesitate. He launched himself at the tree, his body slamming into the shooter with bone-crushing force. They hit the ground together, fallen leaves exploding around them as Tyr pinned the man beneath his superior strength.

The sniper's eyes went wide with horror as Tyr let his fangs extend, deliberately slow and menacing, the sharp points gleaming. Tyr savored the man's rising panic, the way his pulse raced beneath the thin skin of his throat.

A whimper escaped the shooter's lips as Tyr lowered his head, fangs grazing the tender flesh of his neck. The man's terror was intoxicating, a fitting punishment for what he'd done to Beth.

With a growl of rage, Tyr dove his fangs into the man's neck. He didn't stop even when the man's struggles became weak and the man slumped in his grip

"Tyr."

It was Aleksei.

"Tyr, stop."

Tyr snarled, blood dripping from his fangs. "He shot Beth!" The words came out guttural, barely human through his extended fangs.

"Nonetheless." Aleksei's tone held centuries of authority, brooking no argument.

With a snarl of rage, Tyr flung the unconscious man away from him. The shooter's body tumbled across the fallen leaves, coming to rest against a gnarled oak root.

Tobi materialized from the shadows, anger radiating from him as he knelt beside the shooter. "We'll handle this one, brother." His fingers traced the puncture wounds on the man's neck, sealing them with vampire magic. "Go to your Chosen."

A faint whisper brushed against Tyr's mind, delicate yet unmistakable. His name, carried on a thread of desperate need.

Tyr.

The single utterance echoed with a depth of need that sent a jolt of raw fear through him. "Beth!" he shouted, the name tearing from his lips like a prayer. Panic surged in his chest as he bolted back toward the clinic, vampire speed transforming the forest into a blurred tapestry of moonlit shadows. Each heartbeat echoed in his ears, urging him onward, driven by an instinctual need to reach her before it was too late.

He burst through the trees into the parking lot, anguish flooding through him at the sight of her life force bleeding away around them. He dropped to his knees beside her and Liam, his hands shaking as he reached for her.

Liam looked up, his face a mask of agony. Blood pooled around them, spreading across the asphalt in an ever-widening circle. "The bullet went through her liver," he choked out. "I've called for an ambulance, but..." His voice trailed off, the unspoken words hanging heavy in the night air.

Beth's skin felt cold beneath Tyr's fingers, her pulse weak and thready. Her clouded leopard spirit flickered dimly, struggling to maintain its connection to her failing body. The metallic scent of her blood filled his nose, triggering every predatory instinct he possessed. He ruthlessly suppressed them, focusing instead on her face, willing her to hold on.

Her eyelids fluttered, a soft whimper escaping her lips. The sound tore through him like a physical blow. In all his centuries of existence, Tyr had never felt so helpless.

Tyr's hands trembled as he cradled Beth's face, his entire being consumed by helpless rage. The universe's cruelty burned through him like acid. After everything - the years of abuse, the false accusations, being locked up as a rogue - she'd finally started to believe she might have a future. She'd begun to heal... to trust.

And now this.

Minutes ago she'd been practically bouncing on her toes, looking forward to telling Naomi about the evening's events. She'd been so alive, so vibrant.

And now... Each labored breath she took reminded him how fragile her human life was. He ached with the need to hunt down whoever was responsible, to make them suffer as she suffered. But he couldn't leave her. Not now. Not like this.

A soft whimper escaped her lips, and Tyr's fingers tightened around hers. Sweet Beth didn't deserve this. She deserved the chance to build the life she'd been denied for so long. To work at the clinic. To spend time with her sister. To learn who she really was without fear shadowing her every move.

His fingers brushed her cooling cheek as another wave of fury crashed through him. It wasn't fair. None of it was fair.

Aleksei's voice cut through Tyr's anguish, calm and certain. "You know what must be done."

Tyr lifted his head to face Aleksei, seeing centuries of wisdom in those stern features. His Commander gave a slight nod, granting permission for what they both knew was forbidden except in the most dire circumstances.

With trembling fingers, Tyr lifted Beth's limp form. Her blood stained his shirt as he cradled her against his chest. His fangs extended, and with infinite gentleness, he pierced the delicate skin of her throat.

Her blood flowed into him, carrying the essence of her spirit, her memories, her very being.

When he felt the connection forge between them, he pulled back. Using his fangs to tear open his own wrist, he pressed the bleeding wound to Beth's pale lips. "Drink, little cat," he whispered. "Please."

Her throat moved weakly as she swallowed, each drop of his immortal blood carrying the power to anchor her to life.

"Enough." Aleksei's command snapped Tyr back to awareness. "The EMTs and police will arrive soon. You must take her away from here now." His eyes held Tyr's with fierce intensity. "She will need four more exchanges before dawn."

Tyr gathered Beth closer, her body limp in his arms. Her breathing seemed steadier, though her skin remained deathly pale. The first exchange had bought them precious time, but they weren't safe yet.

Tobi emerged from the shadows, his twin's expression one of grim determination. "I am with you, brother. The prisoner is secured and unconscious."

Aleksei stepped closer, his commanding presence brooking no argument. "Liam and I will handle things here. The police will need a plausible explanation." His voice carried the calm certainty of someone who had spent centuries managing such situations.

Tyr looked down at Beth's pale face. They had to move. Now. She needed to be somewhere safe for the remaining exchanges. Time was running out. "I'll take her to the Residence."

Liam tossed his keys to Tobi, his face tight with pain from his own wound. "Take my Jeep. It's faster than trying to get her into the Prius."

Tobi caught the keys one-handed and sprinted toward the charcoal grey vehicle. The engine roared to life as Tyr carefully settled into the back seat with Beth cradled against his chest.

The Jeep's tires squealed as Tobi accelerated out of the parking lot. Tyr pressed his wrist against Beth's lips again, letting a few drops of blood pass between them to maintain the tenuous connection keeping her alive. Her spirit flickered weakly, but it was still there, still fighting.

Tobi took the turns at dangerous speeds, but Tyr trusted his brother's driving implicitly. Minutes later, they screeched to a halt outside the warehouse's private entrance. Tobi had the security door open before Tyr could even shift Beth in his arms.

Bypassing the elevator, they raced up the wide, curving stairs to the second floor, and into Tyr's apartment. Beth's pulse fluttered against Tyr's fingers, each beat a reminder of how precarious her situation remained.

Tyr gently laid Beth on his bed, crimson immediately spreading across the grey comforter. She looked impossibly small against the dark fabric. Her pulse beat weakly, but it was there. Four more exchanges. They had to make it through four more.

"I'll get towels and some clean clothes for her," Tobi said, already moving toward the door.

Tyr barely registered his twin's words as he took more of her blood, before biting into his wrist again. The wound from earlier had already healed, but fresh blood welled immediately from the new punctures. He pressed it to Beth's lips, his other hand supporting her head.

This time, she responded more strongly, her throat working as she swallowed. Her spirit flared a bit brighter with each drop of his immortal blood.

Beth's eyes fluttered open, focusing on his face with effort. Her lips curved into a weak smile as she whispered, "Tyr."

The sound of his name, barely audible even to his vampire hearing, nearly undid him. Tears he hadn't shed in centuries threatened to fall as he cradled her head more securely. Her trust in him, even now, made his chest ache with emotions he couldn't begin to process.

"I'm here, little cat," he murmured, his voice rough with suppressed emotion. "I'm here."

Tyr watched as confusion flickered across Beth's pale features. Her blue-grey eyes darted around his bedroom, trying to make sense of her surroundings.

"What happened?" Her voice came out barely above a whisper. "I remember waving to Liam, and then..." Her hand drifted to her blood-soaked scrub top, fingers probing gently at her stomach. "Pain. Just pain."

Tyr caught her hand before she could touch the wound directly. Her skin felt warmer now, though still cooler than normal. While her pulse beat stronger with each passing minute, she still remained dangerously weak.

"You were shot," he told her softly, his rage at the sniper carefully contained beneath a calm exterior. "The bullet went through your liver. You were dying." His voice roughened on the last word, the memory of her life slipping away still too fresh.

"Dying?" The word came out strangled.

"Yes." His voice was gentle but honest. "I had to give you some of my blood to keep you alive."

Beth's eyes widened slightly as she processed this information. Her fingers tightened around his, seeking reassurance or comfort - he wasn't sure which. But he squeezed back gently, letting her know he was there.

Her fingers tightened around his, her voice barely above a whisper. "B-blood?"

Tyr brushed a strand of pale hair from her face. "I need to give you my blood, if you want to live."

Tyr watched as she struggled to process everything. Her blue-grey eyes, still clouded with pain and confusion, fixed on his face.

"I would be... vampire?" Her voice trembled slightly.

"Yes." Tyr's hand cupped her face, his thumb brushing her cheek. "I'm asking you to trust me with forever, Beth."

A beat of silence as the word hung between them. "If you don't want this life with me, now is the time to tell me."

She was quiet for a long moment, her gaze searching his face. Then her eyes dropped to his chest and widened in sudden horror. "You've been shot too!"

Tyr glanced down at his blood-soaked shirt, having completely forgotten about the bullets that had struck him in the parking lot. "It's fine," he said, shrugging. "Just a through-and-through. I'll be healed completely by tonight."

Tobi returned, his arms laden with towels and fresh clothes. He took one look at his twin and shook his head. "Get that shirt off, brother. You're a mess."

Tyr reluctantly released Beth's hand and peeled off his ruined shirt, revealing the already-healing bullet wounds in his chest and arm. Tobi quickly wiped away the blood with efficient movements, then tossed him a clean black t-shirt.

Tyr shrugged into the fresh shirt, his attention never straying far from Beth as she lay, still and quiet, on the massive bed. She wasn't out of danger yet. Wouldn't be, unless she accepted the Turning.

Tyr watched as his twin moved to Beth's other side, taking her small hand in his. The uncharacteristic gentleness from his usually boisterous brother made Tyr's throat work silently.

"You'll be welcome among us, little sister," Tobi said softly, his usual mischievous demeanor replaced by sincere warmth. "You will be family."

Beth's fingers curled weakly around Tobi's hand as tears gathered in her blue-grey eyes.

Tyr felt his own throat tighten at his twin's immediate inclusion of Beth into their supernatural family. Trust Tobi to cut straight through any awkwardness or uncertainty with his characteristic directness. His brother might play the fool, but he had an uncanny ability to say exactly what someone needed to hear.

Beth's voice wavered. "I would have to drink blood?" The words came out somewhere between a statement and a question, her blue-grey eyes searching Tyr's face.

Tyr nodded solemnly. "When you're a vampire, you won't mind it at all. The thirst becomes natural, like breathing."

Beth was quiet for a moment, and he could almost see her mind working through what this meant. What she would become. What she might lose. There were so many implications, so many considerations. But without his blood, she would die.

Sudden alarm flashed across Beth's pale features, her hand tightening around his. "Wait - will I lose my leopard?"

Tyr met Tobi's equally uncertain gaze across the bed. Neither of them had an answer. In all their centuries, they'd never encountered a shifter being Turned. The situation was completely unprecedented.

A tear slid down Beth's cheek, leaving a glistening trail through the smudges of blood and dirt from the parking lot. "I've always had my leopard with me," she whispered, her voice breaking. "I-I don't want to lose her."

Tyr rubbed at the dampness on her cheek with one thumb. "Beth... if you're not Turned, you'll die, and she will die with you." His voice carried the weight of harsh truth. He continued, more gently, "I would give you assurances, if I could, but the plain fact is, we just don't know."

He lifted her delicate hand to his lips, pressing a gentle kiss against her cool skin. Her pulse fluttered beneath his touch like a trapped butterfly, each beat precious and fragile. His chest ached with emotions he'd thought long buried during his centuries of existence.

"Choose life, Beth," he whispered against her fingers. "Stay with me. Be my Chosen." The words emerged rough with intensity, carrying the weight of their kind's most sacred bond, as well as his own desperate need to keep her in his world.

Her blue-grey eyes widened at the term, recognition flickering across her pale features. Even half-conscious and gravely wounded, she understood the significance of what he offered. Not just immortality, but a permanent bond - the deepest connection possible between supernatural beings.

"Your... Chosen?" Her voice came out barely above a whisper, but he heard the wonder in it.

"Yes." Tyr brushed another kiss across her knuckles. "I knew from the moment I saw you. I just... I wanted to court you properly first. Give you time." His voice roughened with self-recrimination. "I didn't expect this."

Beth's fingers tightened weakly around his. "You want me?" The vulnerability in her voice made his ancient heart clench. After everything she'd endured, she still struggled to believe anyone could truly want her.

"More than I've wanted anything in centuries," Tyr admitted, letting her see the truth in his eyes. "Choose life, little cat. Choose to stay with me."

Beth's eyelashes fluttered, her already pale skin taking on an alarming grey tinge. She was dangerously weak, barely hanging on to life. Time was running out.

But then - the tiniest of movements. A slight nod, so faint he might have missed it without his vampire senses. Her fingers tightened weakly around his, and relief swept through him with such intensity his hands shook.

She had chosen. Chosen life. Chosen him.

Her blood called to him, even as she grew weaker with each passing second. The metallic scent filled his nose, triggering every predatory instinct he possessed. But this time, he embraced those instincts, channeling them into the ancient magic of the Turning.

Tobi's presence across the bed anchored him, his twin's steady support a reminder that Beth wouldn't face this transformation alone. She would have both of them to guide her through what was to come.

CHAPTER 23

Dawn was less than an hour away, and Beth lay fighting for her life in his bed. Tyr forced himself to remain seated at the West Side Inn's dining table, every instinct screaming to return to her side.

Aleksei commanded the head of the table, his presence immediately focusing everyone's attention. The attack on Beth had left its mark on everyone—Jake and Joe showed signs of wolfing out, their alpha tension barely contained. Katerina's usual feline grace looked brittle, while Tobi fidgeted restlessly and Antonio studied his tablet with grim focus. Jacinth's magical energy shimmered with barely contained concern, and Remi sat vibrating with agitation. Only Aleksei maintained his composure, the general who once served under Alexander the Great well accustomed to conflict.

Tyr fought to keep his expression neutral, but rage still burned through his veins like molten silver. His thoughts kept drifting to the warehouse where Beth now lay in his bed, yet he understood this security meeting couldn't wait—not when the threat that had nearly taken her from him might still endanger others.

Aleksei's voice cut through the tension like a blade. "We have little time - barely an hour before dawn." His fierce gaze fixed on each of them in turn. "Last night, a sniper targeted Beth Kerrigan and Liam outside the veterinary clinic. Liam and Tyr were wounded but will recover. Beth..." He paused, his gaze meeting Tyr's. "Beth required emergency Turning to save her life."

"The shooter has been apprehended," Aleksei continued. "He's in police custody, charged with Liam's attempted murder. Under the circumstances, it seemed best to leave Beth out of the official picture entirely."

Remi ran his hands through his spiky black hair, making it stand up even more wildly than usual. "How did this happen?" His dark eyes blazed with frustration as he looked at Tyr. "I've known you vampires for centuries. There's no way you missed the presence of a human near the clinic. It simply isn't possible."

Joe leaned forward, his expression grim. "The shooter was positioned in a tree well beyond clinic property, about three hundred yards into the forest." The wolf alpha's hands clenched into fists on the polished table. "He used a high-powered sniper rifle with a scope. From what we can tell, he'd been up there for hours... long before those idiots in the trucks came to attack. No one could have anticipated that."

Jake nodded at his alpha, his deep blue eyes intense. "We'll expand our patrols immediately. My pack can cover the surrounding woods during daylight hours - we know every tree and hollow within ten miles of here."

"The elevated positions are our primary concern," Antonio added, his aristocratic features grave as he gestured to a map displayed on his tablet. "The shooter picked his perch like a professional - that particular oak gave him a clear sightline to the clinic's rear entrances and staff parking."

Antonio's face was set in stern lines, radiating both anger and power. "We'll identify and monitor all potential sniper positions in the surrounding areas."

Aleksei nodded. "I've already alerted Lord Damien. He's sending another half dozen vampires to reinforce our numbers." The stern lines of his face hardened. "We will not allow such an attack to happen again."

Across the table, Jacinth caught Remi's eye, a silent communication passing between the two Djinn. Her fingers traced invisible patterns on the polished wood as she leaned forward.

"Physical protection is crucial, but we might offer magical defenses as well," Jacinth suggested, her voice carrying the subtle musical quality unique to Djinn. "Perhaps a glamour over the clinic grounds? Something to obscure people from outside observation."

Remi nodded eagerly, his youthful energy barely contained despite the somber meeting. "We could create a perception filter. Anyone looking in from outside the property would see an empty parking lot, even when it's full."

Jacinth's expression turned thoughtful. "Sustained glamours of that scale aren't simple for Djinn magic. Our powers excel at transformation and manifestation, not persistent illusions." She drummed her fingers on the table. "We should consult with Angus and Renee."

"Good thinking," Antonio interjected. "Their protective wards around this inn have never failed."

"They might know how to adapt similar principles for the clinic," Jacinth continued. "A collaborative working could prevent another attack from a distance. Anyone wishing harm would need to physically enter the property—"

"Where they'd face our combined strength," Remi finished, his dark eyes gleaming with anticipation.

Katerina leaned forward, her golden eyes bright with concern. "What about the police? What story did they get?"

Aleksei's expression remained impassive. "As far as law enforcement is concerned, Liam was the only victim - shot in the shoulder while leaving work. Jake happened to be on patrol nearby and apprehended the shooter."

Katerina shifted in her chair, her brow furrowing. "But won't the shooter tell them about Beth? About Tyr?" Her voice carried the edge of genuine worry.

Across the table from Tyr, Aleksei's lips curved into a smile that held no warmth - the kind of expression that reminded everyone why vampires were apex predators. "The shooter is... quite confused about what happened. He seems convinced he was attacked by a vampire - that blond French one from the movies. Most entertaining."

The tension in the room broke as Jacinth's musical laugh rang out. "You mean Lestat?" Her brown eyes sparkled with amusement. "You made him think he was attacked by a fictional character?"

A rare chuckle escaped Aleksei, the sound somehow more unsettling than laughter should be. "He is absolutely convinced Lestat de Lioncourt personally drained him almost dry."

Appreciative laughter rippled around the table. Even Joe cracked a smile, though his alpha presence remained alert and protective. Tobi's shoulders shook with barely contained mirth as he caught Tyr's eye across the table.

Tyr remained stone-faced while others around the table relaxed. His thoughts never strayed from Beth, recovering at the warehouse under Liam and Naomi's watchful care. The shooter's fate meant little to him now—all that mattered was returning before Beth woke to her new existence.

Despite his preoccupation, he couldn't help but acknowledge Aleksei's tactical brilliance. No authority would take seriously a criminal ranting about being attacked by a famous—or infamous—fictitious vampire. The ancient vampire had efficiently eliminated any threat to their secret while maintaining their cover, but such victories felt hollow with Beth undergoing her transformation miles away.

Tyr's attention snapped to Jacinth as she leaned forward, her brown eyes filled with concern. "How is Beth doing?"

The question hit him like a physical blow. "She's fighting through the worst of it," he said, his voice rougher than intended. "The Turning accelerates healing, but it's not instantaneous. Liam has her on morphine, but transforming while healing from a mortal wound..." He stopped, taking a moment to gather himself before continuing.

"She'll be fine though," he added, forcing his tone to remain steady. "The worst should pass within the next day or so."

Katerina's golden eyes fixed on him with feline intensity. "What about her leopard? Will she keep her ability to shift?"

The question he'd been dreading since the moment he'd begun Beth's transformation. His hands clenched beneath the table as uncertainty churned through him.

"We don't know," he admitted, the words tasting bitter on his tongue. "There's no record of a shifter ever being Turned before." His voice roughened with emotion he couldn't quite suppress. "Her leopard is still present - I can sense it within her. But whether she'll retain the ability to shift after the transformation is complete..." He spread his hands helplessly.

Katerina bit her lip, the worry clear on her face.

"Beth was terrified of losing her," he continued quietly. "It was the first thing she asked about when she understood what was happening, that she needed to be Turned if she were to survive. But she chose to live anyway." Pride and pain mingled in his chest at the memory of her courage.

The weight of that choice—her trust in him, her willingness to risk everything for a future together—settled over him. Looking around the table at his supernatural family, Tyr realized there was no point in hiding what everyone already suspected.

"Beth is my Chosen," he announced, his voice carrying both pride and tenderness. The words felt right, natural, as if he'd been waiting his entire immortal existence to speak them.

Jacinth's delighted gasp broke the momentary silence. Katerina's golden eyes lit up with genuine joy, while Joe and Jake exchanged knowing grins. Even Aleksei's usually stoic expression softened slightly.

Tobi beamed at his twin from across the table. "I already told her she'd be family," he said, practically bouncing in his seat. "Though you might have mentioned the whole Chosen thing before she was bleeding out in a parking lot, brother."

Tyr shot his twin a mock glare, though he couldn't maintain it in the face of his own happiness. "I was planning to court her properly," he admitted. "Take her to dinner, maybe dancing." His voice softened. "Show her she deserves to be cherished."

"Well," Jacinth said, her brown eyes twinkling, "you'll have eternity to make it up to her now."

Tyr glanced at the lightening sky through the inn's windows, his heightened senses already detecting the approaching dawn. Every vampire in the room shifted restlessly, their bodies responding to the primal urge to seek shelter from the sun.

Aleksei rose from his chair with fluid grace. "We're done here.

Everyone knows their assignments." He looked around the table one final time. "The wolves will handle daytime patrols. Vampires, to your sanctuaries."

Tyr didn't wait for further dismissal. He burst through the inn's front door at vampire speed, the pre-dawn air cool against his face as he raced on his motorcycle, Tobi at his side, toward the warehouse. His entire being focused on returning to Beth's side.

The security door barely had time to register his palm print before he yanked it open. He took the stairs three at a time, his enhanced hearing already picking up Beth's steady heartbeat from his apartment above.

Liam looked up as Tyr entered the bedroom, his hazel eyes tired but alert. The veterinarian's injured shoulder had been properly bandaged, though spots of red showed through the white gauze.

"She's resting more comfortably now," Liam said softly, gesturing to the IV stand beside the bed. "I wasn't sure if standard pain medication would work, given the transformation to vampire, but I set up a morphine drip anyway. It seems to be helping - she's finally sleeping."

Tyr's chest tightened as he gazed at Beth's peaceful face. The grey pallor had faded somewhat, replaced by the marble-like complexion of a vampire in transition.

Tyr's gaze shifted to Naomi, who sat vigil at her twin's bedside. Her pale blonde hair - so like Beth's - hung in disheveled waves around her tear-stained face. Despite her obvious distress, she managed to summon a tremulous smile as she looked up at him.

"Thank you," she whispered, her voice rough from crying. "For saving her life." Her fingers tightened protectively around Beth's limp hand. "When Liam called to tell me..." She drew in a shaky breath. "I thought I'd lost her. After everything we've been through, after finally finding our real family..." Fresh tears spilled down her cheeks.

Tyr's chest tightened at the raw emotion in her voice. The bond between the twins was powerful - he could sense it even now, a subtle thread of energy connecting their spirits. Just as he could sense Beth's clouded leopard spirit still flickering within her transforming body.

"I couldn't let her die," he said simply, his voice rough with his own barely contained emotions. The memory of Beth's blood pooling on the asphalt, her life slipping away with each heartbeat, still haunted him. "She means too much to me."

Naomi's blue-grey eyes - identical to Beth's - studied his face intently. Whatever she saw there made her nod, acceptance and understanding softening her features. "You'll take care of her?"

"Always," Tyr promised, the word carrying all the weight of his centuries of existence. "She's my Chosen."

Tyr staggered back a step as Naomi launched herself at him, her slender arms wrapping around his waist in a fierce hug. Her tears soaked into his clean black t-shirt as she pressed her face against his chest, her shoulders shaking with a mixture of sobs and laughter.

For a moment, Tyr froze, unused to such spontaneous displays of affection. But then he carefully returned the embrace, mindful of his vampire strength as he patted her back awkwardly. The scent of her tears carried notes of both joy and relief, and her clouded leopard spirit - so similar to Beth's - radiated happiness.

"Welcome to the family," Naomi mumbled against his shirt, her voice muffled but sincere.

Liam's warm chuckle drew Tyr's attention. The veterinarian leaned against the wall, his uninjured arm crossed over his chest as he watched them with obvious amusement.

"Congratulations," Liam said, his hazel eyes twinkling despite his obvious exhaustion. "Though I have to say, I never imagined having a vampire for a brother-in-law."

Tyr felt the first tendrils of lethargy creeping through his limbs as pre-dawn light began filtering through the warehouse windows. His muscles grew heavy, the pull of the day sleep tugging at his consciousness.

"You need to leave now," he told Liam and Naomi, his voice already thick with approaching torpor. "The sun's rising."

He guided them downstairs, each step requiring more effort as dawn approached. At the security door, Naomi hugged him once more before following Liam out to their car.

Tyr barely made it back up to his apartment before the sun's influence really hit. He stumbled to the bed where Beth lay peaceful in her morphine-induced sleep. With the last of his strength, he settled beside her on the bed, carefully arranging his body so he wouldn't jostle her healing wound. Beth's fingers found his even in sleep, twining together as if seeking comfort.

The lethargy of day sleep crashed over him like a wave as the sun crested the horizon. His last conscious thought was of Beth's hand in his as darkness claimed them both.

CHAPTER 24

Beth's eyes snapped open, consciousness returning between one heartbeat and the next. No gradual awakening, no lingering drowsiness - just instant, crystal-clear awareness.

Soft sheets draped over her body, and she lay still, processing her surroundings. The room felt unfamiliar, yet safe. Memories of the previous night filtered through her mind, though they seemed distant, wrapped in a haze of searing pain.

The parking lot. Waving to Liam. The sharp crack, and the agony that had torn through her body.

And Tyr...

Her hand drifted to her stomach where the bullet had struck. The wound that should have killed her. Would have killed her, if not for Tyr's choice. His blood. The Turning.

The memories crystallized: his desperate plea for her to choose life, to become his Chosen. The fear of losing Whisper warring with her will to survive. The burning pain as his vampire blood transformed her, cell by cell.

Beth turned her head on the pillow, registering Tyr's presence beside her. He lay on his side facing her, propped up on one elbow, studying her face with an intensity that would have made her blush before. Now, instead of embarrassment, she found herself cataloging every detail of his features with equal fascination - the precise shade of his fair hair, the subtle variations in his skin tone, even the barely perceptible rise and fall of his chest as he breathed out of habit rather than necessity.

She couldn't help smiling as their gazes met.

"So is this like..." Beth's voice came out stronger than she expected as she gestured between them. She couldn't resist breaking into song, remembering the musical they'd seen together in New York City. Her newly transformed voice carried the melody of "Vampires in Love" from Dance of the Vampires with surprising clarity: "Forever's going to start tonight..."

Tyr's rich laughter filled the room as he shook his head, his eyes sparkling with amusement. "I can't believe you went there!" He propped himself up on one elbow, still chuckling. "You do know, it was originally written as a vampire love song before Bonnie Tyler made it famous as 'Total Eclipse of the Heart.'"

"No way!" She stared at him. "Seriously?"

"Yeah, seriously."

Beth's own laughter joined his, the sound startling her slightly with its musical quality. Everything felt different now - sharper, clearer, more intense. Yet somehow, teasing Tyr felt completely natural, as if her heart recognized what her body was still adjusting to.

"How are you feeling?" he asked, his voice gentle despite the concern evident in his expression.

Beth started to push herself up - and found herself already sitting upright, sheets pooling around her waist. She blinked, startled by the fluid speed of the movement. One moment she'd thought about sitting up, the next she simply was sitting.

Beth's triumph at her newfound vampire speed turned to agony as white-hot pain lanced through her abdomen. A whimper escaped her lips before she could stop it, her hands instinctively clutching at the wound site. The pajama top she wore - not her bloodied scrubs, someone must have changed her clothes - felt impossibly soft against her heightened sense of touch.

"Easy, little cat." Tyr's hands steadied her shoulders, his touch both gentle and grounding. "You had a mortal wound. Vampire healing is remarkable, but not instantaneous."

Beth drew in a shaky breath, surprised to find she didn't actually need it. The pain ebbed slowly, settling into a deep, persistent ache. "How long until it's completely healed?"

"A few more days." Tyr's fingers traced soothing patterns on her shoulders. "The Turning accelerates healing, but bullet wounds are tricky. The internal damage takes time to repair, even with vampire blood."

Beth nodded, carefully easing back against the headboard. Every movement sent little sparks of pain through her midsection, but it was manageable if she moved slowly. The wound that should have killed her now felt more like a particularly bad bruise - painful, but no longer life-threatening.

She detected the lingering scent of her own blood, along with antiseptic and fresh linens. Beneath it all, she detected Tyr's unique scent - something like winter air and cedar wood, but more complex than her human nose had ever detected.

Her hand drifted to her stomach. Where the bullet had torn through her body, she expected to find bandages and agony. Instead, only the faintest raised mark remained - a small pink patch that would have been barely noticeable to human eyes.

"Vampire healing," Tyr explained, his voice warm with approval. "Even that tiny mark will fade completely within a day or two." His fingers brushed against hers where they still rested on the barely-there scar. "Your body is still completing the transformation, but the major healing happened while you slept."

Tyr reached for something on the bedside table. He produced a sleek remote control and pressed a button. The head of the bed began rising smoothly, gently shifting her into a more upright position. Once she was comfortably reclined, he placed the remote in her hand.

"Adjust it however you like," he said. "The controls are fairly intuitive."

Beth stared at the remote in her hand, then looked at Tyr with bewilderment. "An adjustable bed? For a vampire?"

"What?" Tyr's expression remained perfectly serious. "I enjoy watching TV in the early morning hours while waiting for the day sleep to take hold."

He retrieved another remote from the bedside table and pointed it at the imposing mahogany wardrobe across the room. The double doors swung open silently, revealing a massive flat-screen television mounted inside.

Beth couldn't help herself. The absurdity of a vampire with an adjustable bed and a hidden TV struck her funny bone just right, and she burst into giggles. The laughter sent sharp stabs of pain through her healing wound, making her clutch her abdomen as she tried desperately to stop.

"Ow, ow, ow," she gasped between giggles, pressing one hand against her stomach while the other still gripped the bed remote. "Please don't make me laugh. It hurts."

As her laughter ebbed, Beth took a moment to really look around the room. The furniture was unlike anything she'd ever seen - heavy, dark wood pieces that radiated quality and timelessness. The massive four-poster bed she lay in dominated the space, draped with rich velvet hangings in deep forest green that matched the window treatments.

The duvet covering her was a stunning brocade in dark green and gold, with gold trim catching the dim light. Two armchairs flanked an antique settee, their cushions matching the duvet's fabric perfectly. Even the drape pull cord was carefully chosen - dark forest green with ornate gold tassels.

Beth ran her hand over the brocade duvet, marveling at how her heightened sense of touch could distinguish every thread in the intricate pattern. "This is all so beautiful," she murmured. "I feel like I'm in a museum."

Tyr looked momentarily self-conscious, running his hand along the ornate bedpost. "I embrace modern times. But in my private chambers..." His voice trailed off, and he shrugged, looking completely at ease among the museum-worthy pieces. "When you've lived as long as we have, you treasure the things that anchor you to your past."

Beth's gaze swept pointedly around the room - the heavy carved wood, rich velvets and brocades, the obvious expense of every piece. She raised an eyebrow at him.

"So... you lived like royalty back then?"

He winked at her. "What can I say? We had a good eye for profitable ventures."

'I bet even royalty didn't have sheets like this,' Beth said, running her hand over the fabric beneath her. She peered closer at the incredibly soft material that seemed to flow like water beneath her fingers.

"Are these... silk?" she asked, fingering the delicate fabric. She'd heard of silk sheets, of course, but she'd never known anyone who actually had them.

Tyr nodded, a pleased smile tugging at his lips. "The finest available."

"I've never felt anything like this," Beth murmured, completely entranced by the way the fabric slipped between her fingers. Her heightened senses detected subtle variations in the weave that would have been impossible to perceive before. "It's incredible."

Beth closed her eyes, focusing inward. The familiar presence of her leopard still prowled through her consciousness, a warm golden glow in her mind. Whisper stretched and yawned, content despite the changes wrought by the Turning.

"She's still here." Beth's voice cracked with relief. "I still have Whisper."

Tyr cupped her face, leaning in to kiss her softly.

"You will be unique among the clan. Like you've always been unique to me."

A sharp knock preceded Tobi's entrance. He carried a steel thermos, his expression brightening at seeing Beth awake. "Perfect timing. Breakfast is served."

The copper scent hit her before he'd even opened the container. Beth's new fangs dropped, sharp and insistent against her lower lip. Her stomach clenched with a hunger unlike anything she'd experienced before.

"Easy," Tyr murmured, accepting the thermos from his brother. "Small sips at first. Your body needs to adjust."

Beth's hands trembled as she reached for the container. The first taste flooded her mouth with flavors she'd never detected in blood before - sweet, salt, iron, life itself distilled into liquid form. She picked up subtle variations that spoke of the donor's health, age, even emotional state.

"Donated blood," Tobi explained, perching on the edge of the bed. "Not as satisfying as fresh from the vein, but it'll do for now. You'll learn to feed properly once you've stabilized."

Beth lowered the thermos, licking a stray drop from her lip. "Will I be able to control myself? Around humans?"

"With training." Tyr's hand squeezed her shoulder. "The clan helps new vampires adjust. You won't have to figure this out alone."

"And you've got the advantage of your shifter discipline," Tobi added. "Most new vampires struggle with their predatory instincts, but you've already mastered one set of animal urges, living with your leopard."

Beth nodded, taking another careful sip. The blood settled her trembling, easing the hollow ache in her core. Each swallow felt like strength flowing into her limbs, awakening new abilities she'd have to learn to control.

"Naomi and Liam?" she asked, suddenly remembering her sister and brother-in-law.

"They stayed with you all night, and went home at dawn," Tyr answered. His arm wrapped around her waist, holding her steady. "They should be here pretty soon. For now, let us take care of you while your body completes the change." His lips brushed her temple. "You have eternity to adjust to your new life. Take it one night at a time."

Before Beth could respond, a sharp tap on the doorframe made her jump, nearly spilling the thermos of blood. Tyr and Tobi leapt from the bed with inhuman speed, their postures snapping to rigid attention.

A tall, elegant woman stood in the doorway, her steel-gray hair pulled back in an immaculate French twist. Black horn-rimmed glasses studded with diamonds perched on her nose, connected by a delicate silver chain that draped around her neck. Her tailored black suit and pencil skirt radiated authority.

"Ma'am," the twins said in perfect unison, their usual playful demeanors completely absent.

Beth stared in fascination. She'd never seen the vampire twins show such deference to anyone, not even Antonio.

"Beth, this is Margot," Tyr said, his voice carefully formal. "She's in charge of the Residence."

"The majordomo," Tobi added, still standing at attention. "She keeps everything running smoothly."

Margot's piercing gaze catalogued every detail - from Beth's borrowed pajamas to the thermos of blood clutched in her hands. Though clearly human, she radiated an authority that had even these powerful vampires showing deference. Beth found herself both amused and intrigued, and had to bite back a smile.

"So this is our newest vampire," Margot said, her crisp tone carrying decades of authority. "Welcome to the family, dear. Once you're settled, we'll need to discuss your wardrobe and other requirements."

Beth watched in fascination as Margot's piercing gaze shifted to Tyr. Even with her newly enhanced vampire senses, she couldn't detect any supernatural power emanating from the elegant woman - yet both twins remained frozen in place like schoolboys caught misbehaving.

"I suppose you two will be handling her training?" Margot's tone, tinged with faint disapproval, carried the weight of someone accustomed to managing supernatural beings far more powerful than herself. Her diamond-studded glasses glinted in the dim light as she studied Tyr. "The basics of vampire etiquette, feeding protocols, proper behavior in clan gatherings?"

"Yes, Ma'am." Tyr's response came out slightly strangled, as if his throat had suddenly gone dry.

Margot's perfectly shaped eyebrows rose a fraction of an inch as she considered his response. After what felt like an eternity, she gave a slight nod of approval. Without another word, she turned and swept from the room, her heels clicking precisely against the floor as she disappeared down the hallway.

Beth couldn't help noticing how both twins' shoulders slumped in relief once Margot's footsteps faded away.

Beth waited until Margot's footsteps faded completely before turning to the twins. "What was that about?" Her new vampire senses still tingled from the commanding presence the elegant woman had projected.

Tyr settled back on the bed beside her, though Beth noticed he kept glancing toward the doorway. "Margot volunteered to be majordomo of the Residence when she heard about the renovation project. She... has very definite ideas about how things should be run."

"Volunteered?" Beth raised an eyebrow. "She seems more like someone who'd be recruited."

Tobi sprawled across the foot of the bed, his usual mischievous grin returning now that Margot was gone. "Oh no, she marched right up to Antonio and informed him she'd be taking the position. Said the place clearly needed a proper manager if we were planning to house clan members here."

"Lord Damien won't let her take over the NYC Residence," Tobi added with a snicker. "You should see her butting heads with Charles? It'd be worth selling tickets just to watch those two try to out-organize each other. Lord Damien probably cheered when she said she was coming here."

"Charles?" Beth asked, taking another careful sip from the thermos.

"The NYC Majordomo," Tyr explained. "He's been running that household for decades. Very traditional, very proper. The unstoppable force meeting the immovable object."

Beth couldn't help giggling at the twins' reactions to Margot. "So is she one of the Blood Sworn?" The words slipped out before she could stop them.

Both brothers literally turned pale - a feat Beth wouldn't have thought possible. Tyr actually gulped, his usual confidence completely vanishing.

"I would not DARE!" His voice cracked on the last word.

Tobi sprawled more comfortably across the foot of the bed. "Her grandson Gabe is one of our Blood Sworn. And when Margot found out-"

"Wait," Beth interrupted, her brow furrowing in confusion. "How did she find out? I thought vampires were supposed to be kept secret from humans?"

The words had barely left her mouth when another sharp tap echoed from the doorway.

All three vampires froze, turning as a young man with tousled light brown hair popped his head around the frame, his face splitting into an enormous grin. "Hey everyone! How's our new vampire doing?"

Beth felt the twins relax on either side of her, their postures losing the rigid attention they'd shown with Margot.

"That's Gabe," Tyr explained, his voice warm with affection. "Margot's grandson."

"Welcome to your new life!" Gabe's enthusiasm bubbled over as he gave her an enthusiastic wave. "This is so exciting! We'll have to-"

"Out!" Tobi interrupted, rising from the bed with fluid grace. "She just woke up, you overgrown puppy."

Tyr joined his brother, both of them herding the still-grinning young man back toward the hallway. "She needs time to adjust before meeting everyone."

"Oh yeah, got it... c'ya around!" Gabe's cheerful voice echoed down the corridor as he disappeared from view.

The twins turned back toward Beth, identical expressions of exasperation on their faces as they pressed their palms to their foreheads in perfect synchronization. The sight was so comical that Beth couldn't help giggling, the sound surprising her with its musical quality - another change from the transformation.

Beth watched the empty doorway, struggling to connect the intimidating Margot with this enthusiastic puppy of a person.

"That's Margot's grandson?" The contrast between the stern, commanding woman and the exuberant young man seemed impossible.

"Yeah, we all wonder about that too." Tyr shook his head, settling back beside her on the bed.

Tobi sprawled across the foot of the bed again, his eyes twinkling with the same mischief as his twin's. "Odds are on that he's a changeling. No way that much cheerful energy came from Margot's bloodline."

Beth had to agree. "He gives off some serious golden retriever vibes."

A shoe flew across the room, smacking Tobi square in the face. "Getting back to Beth's question," Tyr said, ignoring his twin's theatrical yelp, "Gabe is Blood Sworn to Adele, one of our clan. He was hit by a car in NYC, had some pretty grave wounds."

"Adele was giving him blood in the hospital to help him heal when Margot walked right in," Tobi added, tossing the shoe back at his brother. "And Adele - who never loses her cool about anything - explained the whole vampire situation..."

"But Margot just took the whole thing in stride," Tyr finished. "Didn't even blink. Just started organizing everything right then and there from Gabe's hospital room."

Tobi's eyes sparkled with mischief. His theatrical gestures matched his animated storytelling style. "So then Gabe was all healed up and was released from the hospital. The next day, Margot marched straight into the NYC Residence like she owned the place."

Beth's mouth fell open. "She didn't!"

"Oh, but she did." Tobi's voice dropped dramatically. "Lord Damien himself appeared in the foyer, all ancient power and darkness, demanding to know who dared enter his domain uninvited."

"And Margot?" Tobi paused for effect. "She lifted that elegant chin of hers, looked right at him and said, 'Now see here, young man, I'm here to ensure my grandson is properly cared for, and I won't have any argument about it.'"

Beth's mouth fell open. "She didn't." The words came out in a shocked whisper. "To Lord Damien?"

"She did." Both twins nodded simultaneously, their expressions filled with remembered awe.

"Young man," Tobi repeated, mimicking Margot's crisp tones. "To a vampire who's over five thousand years old."

"And he just... let her?" Beth couldn't quite wrap her mind around anyone speaking to the powerful vampire lord that way.

"Let her?" Tobi's laugh held a note of remembered disbelief. "He actually backed down. The Dark Lord himself, ruler of the most powerful vampire clan in existence, took a step back from this human woman with her diamond-studded glasses."

"Oh, but it gets better," he said, his eyes sparkling. "Lady Alyssa was there too - she nearly collapsed against the wall, laughing so hard she could barely breathe. And Margot just sailed past Lord Damien like he was a doorman, demanding to be shown to her grandson's quarters immediately and asking where the linens were kept."

"And Charles!" Tobi shook his head. "You should have seen his face! It was priceless."

"Charles is very... traditional," Tyr explained to Beth. "He's been running the NYC Residence for decades. Think of the most proper British butler you've ever seen, then multiply it by a thousand."

"Watching them try to out-organize each other is better than any entertainment we could pay for," Tyr added. "They're both absolutely convinced their way is the only proper way to run a vampire household."

Beth frowned, thinking that over. "But if she came here to manage the Residence, she left her grandson back in New York City?"

Tobi's shoulders shook with barely suppressed laughter. Tyr pressed his lips together, clearly fighting to maintain his composure.

"Oh no," Tobi managed between snickers. "Margot informed Adele they were coming here."

"Informed," Tyr emphasized, his blue eyes dancing with amusement. "Not asked. Not requested. Just stated it as fact."

"And they did!" Tobi spread his hands in a 'what can you do' gesture. "Adele had the Pledges pack up her household within a week. Didn't even bother to argue."

Beth tried to imagine the scene - the elegant vampire being essentially ordered to relocate by a human woman. Her new vampire hearing picked up Tobi muttering something that sounded suspiciously like "probably safer that way" under his breath.

Beth settled more comfortably against the headboard, fascinated by these glimpses into vampire society. "So Margot just... took over?"

"Actually," Tyr said, his expression growing more serious, "Margot and Adele see eye to eye on most things. They're both incredibly strong, independent women who know exactly what they want. Adele was Turned in the 1920s," he explained. "It was an amazing era for women breaking free of social constraints, and she embraced that spirit completely."

"She's Swiss." Tobi added, his tone deeply respectful. "She was part of the Resistance during World War II, helping people escape Nazi Germany. Even as a vampire, she refused to stand idle while such atrocities occurred."

"That must have been incredibly dangerous," Beth said.

"It was," Tyr agreed. "But Adele has never been one to let fear stop her from doing what's right. She and Margot share that quality - that absolute certainty in their convictions."

Tobi nodded from his position at the foot of the bed. "You should see them together at the planning meetings. They're terrifyingly efficient. Between Adele's decades of tactical experience and Margot's organizational skills, nothing gets past them."

Beth could picture it - the elegant vampire and the commanding human woman, both refusing to be limited by anyone's expectations of them. No wonder they worked so well together.

"Lord Damien and Charles probably threw a celebration when she announced she was coming here instead," Tobi added with another snicker

TOBI STRETCHED LANGUIDLY and slid off the foot of the bed. "Well, I'll leave you two alone." His eyes sparkled with mischief as he backed toward the door. "I'll be in my chambers if you need anything."

"Speaking of which..." Tyr reached over to the wall beside the bed and tugged on an ornate twisted cord Beth hadn't noticed before. The braided tassel swung gently, catching the dim light.

Beth blinked in surprise. "Is that... actually a bell pull? Like in Downton Abbey?"

Tyr shrugged, looking a bit sheepish. "We're kind of old. Some things are harder to let go than others. One pull summons me, two pulls for Tobi."

"And because shouting down the hallway would be unseemly," Tobi added in a perfect imitation of Margot's crisp tones before disappearing through the doorway.

Tyr reached for the bedside table and picked up Beth's phone and purse. "I took the liberty of programming Derek's number in your contacts. If you need anything, from blood to information, and all you have to do is call. We'll give you his college and work schedules so you'll know where he is at all times."

Beth accepted the familiar items, surprised by how different they felt to her enhanced sense of touch. The leather of her purse held subtle variations in texture she'd never noticed before, while her phone's screen seemed almost too bright to her sensitive eyes.

Tyr's hand covered hers, his touch gentle. "Are you really okay?"

Beth met his concerned gaze, taking in every subtle shade of blue in his eyes. A smile curved her lips as she realized that despite all the changes - the transformation, her new abilities, the entire supernatural world she'd entered - she felt more right than she had in a long time.

"Yes," she said softly. "I really am."

Tyr shifted his weight, an oddly human gesture for a vampire. His fingers traced abstract patterns on the bed covers.

"So..." he began, oddly hesitant.

"Stop." Beth caught his hand in hers, marveling at how she could detect the subtle variations in his skin temperature. "I'm fine with all of this. No regrets." She squeezed his fingers, smiling at him. "How could I regret being alive? Being here with you? Still having Whisper?"

Tyr's shoulders relaxed slightly, though tension still lined his face. "I should tell you... I spoke with Lord Damien weeks ago. Asked his permission to Turn you, if you were willing." His gaze met hers. "I just hadn't found the right moment to have that conversation with you."

A laugh bubbled up from Beth's chest, surprising them both with its musical quality. "That's funny, because I actually talked to Douglas weeks ago about what it's like being married to an immortal." Her smile widened at Tyr's startled expression. "I wanted to understand how a human handles being with someone who'll outlive them by centuries."

"You did?" Tyr sounded both wondering and relieved.

"I did." Beth traced her fingers along his palm, following the lifelines that would now stretch into eternity. "Though I guess that particular concern is moot now."

Beth settled more comfortably against the mattress, letting her fingers trail over the fabrics. She still marveled at how her new sense of sight and touch picked up every subtle variation in the silk of the sheets, and the duvet's lovely brocade. "So what else do I need to know?"

"Actually..." Tyr's lips curved into a slight smile. "You'll probably get a written exam from Margot tomorrow night. She's very thorough about these things."

A musical laugh escaped Beth's throat. "Let me guess the first rule - don't let anyone know vampires exist."

"True, though you've had a lifetime of experience with that as a shifter." Tyr's fingers traced idle patterns on her palm. "What else?"

Beth's brow furrowed in concentration. "Number two... don't kill while feeding?"

"Exactly." Tyr nodded approvingly. "And we cannot Turn a human without explicit permission from Lord Damien. That's absolutely forbidden."

"No problem there." Beth shuddered slightly. "I wouldn't want that responsibility anyway."

"For now, we'll provide donated blood." Tyr gestured to the thermos beside her. "Until you're ready to feed from a live person. Derek has volunteered and will be available when you're ready. I'll supervise your first few feedings to ensure you don't cause any harm - hitting the right vein or artery can be tricky for beginners, and you also need to learn to know when you've taken enough."

Beth's eyes widened in alarm. "Oh no, we definitely don't want any accidents! I'd never forgive myself if I hurt someone."

Beth twisted her fingers in the soft sheets. "I've never fed from someone before. What if I mess up?"

"You won't." Tyr's voice held absolute certainty. "I'll be right there to guide you through it. Vampire instincts are actually quite precise when it comes to feeding - you'll know exactly where to bite and how much to take."

He paused, his fingers drumming an irregular pattern on the bedspread. "Speaking of which... I have you here in my chambers for now." His voice took on a hesitant quality she'd never heard from him before. "They're preparing a chamber for you, but with the renovation work still ongoing, it may be a few days before it's ready."

Beth's breath caught in her throat as Tyr continued, his words coming faster now. "You're more than welcome to stay here in my chambers, with me... if you want to, that is."

Heat flooded Beth's cheeks - apparently vampires could still blush, which was good to know. She wanted to stay, wanted it more than she'd ever admitted to herself. But saying it out loud felt overwhelming.

"Well," she said softly, studying the intricate pattern of the brocade rather than meeting his eyes, "we do have a few days before the other chamber is ready. Maybe I could think about it?"

The tension in Tyr's shoulders eased slightly at her words. "Of course. No pressure. Take all the time you need to decide."

A shadow filled the doorway, drawing Beth's attention from the duvet's intricate patterns. Tyr rose smoothly to his feet, his posture shifting to one of deep respect. She detected subtle changes in the air - an ancient power that made her skin tingle, similar to her awareness when she was in her animal form but far stronger.

Antonio stepped into the chamber, his long black hair flowing around his shoulders. His impeccably tailored suit emphasized his tall, slender frame. She'd seen him before, of course, but now she was struck by the aura of power emanating from him, something she hadn't been able to sense when she was human.

His dark eyes, the color of dark chocolate, studied her face with gentle consideration as he inclined his head toward Tyr. When he spoke, his voice carried the cultured tones of old-world European nobility.

"Welcome, little sister." Antonio's smile held genuine warmth. "Are you well? The Turning can be... overwhelming, even under the best circumstances. We had no idea if it was even possible for a shifter."

Beth found herself automatically sitting straighter against the headboard, flushing faintly. "I'm doing well, thank you. There's still some pain where the bullet hit, but..."

"The wound has healed remarkably well," Tyr interjected, his hand settling protectively on her shoulder. "She's adjusting faster than expected."

Beth nodded, grateful for his supportive presence. "Tyr's been explaining the rules to me - about feeding safely and keeping our existence secret." She straightened slightly, wanting to show proper respect to the ancient vampire. "I already understand the importance of secrecy from being a shifter."

Antonio nodded in approval. "Excellent. And I understand you've met our... formidable majordomo?"

Beth caught the flash of humor in his gaze, a surprising glimpse of mischief in his otherwise formal demeanor. The corner of his mouth twitched slightly as he mentioned Margot.

"Yes," Beth replied, fighting back a smile of her own as she remembered the twins' reaction to the commanding woman. "She was quite the personality. I almost jumped off the bed and stood at attention."

"Indeed." Antonio's rich voice held carefully controlled amusement. "Margot has that effect on everyone. Even those of us who have lived for centuries."

Antonio inclined his head gracefully to them both. "I'll leave you to your discussion. Rest well, little sister." His presence lingered for a moment after he glided from the room, like the echo of distant thunder.

Beth released a breath she hadn't realized she'd been holding. "Is every vampire going to drop by to check on me?" She heard multiple sets of footsteps in the hallway outside, along with whispered conversations just beyond her new ability to distinguish words.

"Very likely." Tyr's fingers traced soothing patterns on her shoulder. "They all know you, or at least know about you. And a new vampire in the clan is rare enough to cause excitement." His voice held a note of pride at the words. "They'll want to make sure you're adjusting well. And the Blood Sworn and the Pledges are going to be even more curious, probably." Tyr settled beside her on the bed. "Most of them have never met anyone newly Turned before. It just isn't done - the clan leader's permission is required, and it's rarely granted."

"Why not?"

"Too risky. Too many ways for things to go wrong, and now in these days, it's even more risky between social media and surveillance cameras everywhere." Tyr's expression grew serious. "A new vampire who loses control could expose us all."

Beth absorbed that, understanding the weight of trust that had been placed in her. "But he approved me?"

"He did." Tyr's smile returned, warming his eyes. "He knows you already understand the importance of keeping supernatural secrets, given your life as a shifter. And..." He hesitated slightly. "He trusts my judgment where you're concerned. His main concern was that you consented."

Beth studied Tyr's troubled expression as his words trailed off. His shoulders tensed, and he turned away slightly, his gaze distant.

"I don't know what I would have done if you hadn't been conscious," he admitted, his voice rough with emotion. "If you hadn't been able to give permission..." His fingers clenched into a fist. "I'm afraid I might have Turned you anyway. The thought of losing you..."

The raw pain in his voice made Beth's chest tighten. She reached up, cupping his cheek with her palm.

"Hey," she said softly, turning his face back toward her. "I did agree. I chose this. Chose you." Her thumb traced along his cheekbone. "And I'd make the same choice again."

The tension in Tyr's shoulders eased slightly under her touch, though worry still clouded his eyes.

"You don't understand," he whispered. "The laws about Turning without permission are absolute. If I had..." He swallowed hard. "Even to save your life, it would have been unforgivable."

Beth kept her hand against his cheek, anchoring him to the present moment. "But you didn't. You asked, and I said yes." She held his troubled gaze. "That's what matters."

Beth's eyelids grew increasingly heavy as exhaustion took hold, the healing process demanding rest. Muscles relaxed into pleasant languidness while she sunk deeper into the luxurious mattress. The transformation and day's events had taken their toll.

"You should sleep," Tyr said softly. "I'll be just a phone call away if you need anything."

A sleepy giggle escaped her lips as she pressed the button to recline the head of the bed. She snuggled deeper into the silk-covered pillow. "Or a pull of the bell cord."

Tyr chuckled, pulling the covers over her. "That too."

Beth frowned slightly as she shifted position, noticing how the mattress seemed to cradle her body perfectly. "Is this memory foam?"

"It is." Tyr's grin held a touch of pride. "With a cooling gel layer."

Beth stared at him, momentarily stunned by this modern convenience in his otherwise antique-filled chamber.

He shrugged, looking almost sheepish. "Vampires have low body temperatures. I hate getting too warm when I sleep."

"Is that why vampires are often shown sleeping on top of crypts and marble slabs in movies and stuff?" Beth asked, curiosity temporarily overriding her exhaustion.

"Yeah." His grin widened. "When they're not shown sleeping in coffins, which by the way was never a thing. That's pure fiction."

Beth's eyelids grew heavier as exhaustion pulled at her consciousness. Even with her eyes closed, she could track Tyr's presence at the bedside. Her new vampire senses picked up the steady rhythm of his unnecessary breathing, matching the rise and fall of his chest. The sound anchored her, familiar yet different through her transformed hearing. Her own chest rose and fell in unconscious synchronization with his.

The last remnants of pain from her healing wound faded into a distant ache as sleep crept closer. Whisper stirred lazily in her mind, the leopard's presence a warm golden glow beneath her consciousness. Her animal spirit settled into a contented purr, completely at ease with both her transformation and Tyr's protective vigil.

The last thing she registered before surrendering to slumber was the soft press of his lips against her forehead and his whispered, "Rest well, my Chosen."

CHAPTER 25

Beth sat cross-legged on the bed, watching intently as Tyr demonstrated the mental visualization needed for the raptor transformation.

"It's different from your leopard shift," he explained, his gaze intent on her face. "You need to hold the form in your mind - see every feather, feel the hollow bones, imagine the way air moves through them."

Beth closed her eyes, trying to picture a small hawk she'd seen when hanging out as her clouded leopard in the back yard. The mental image came easily - delicate head, curved beak, wings folded against its sides. She could almost feel the individual feathers, the way they'd overlap and shift.

"That's it," Tyr's voice encouraged softly. "Now focus on the size - hawks are much smaller than leopards. Feel how light the bones are, how the wings want to catch the air."

The familiar tingle of the Change rippled through Beth's body. It felt similar to her shifter transformation, yet somehow lighter, more ethereal. Where the shifter Change felt like liquid gold flowing through her veins, this was more like static electricity dancing across her skin.

"Good," Tyr murmured. "Let it build naturally. Don't force it."

The sensation intensified, and Beth felt her body beginning to shift.

The Change moved through her differently than her accustomed shifter Change - less muscular power, more hollow-boned delicacy. Her newly enhanced vampire senses made her even more aware of each subtle alteration as it happened.

Whisper stirred in her mind, curious but not threatened by this new form. She seemed to understand that this was just another aspect of what they were now - vampire and shifter combined into something unique.

Beth ruffled her new feathers, reveling in the strange yet exhilarating sensation. The world looked different - sharper, more vibrant. The raptor's natural acuity, amplified by her vampire transformation, created an almost overwhelming level of detail. She could see individual dust motes dancing in the air, count every thread in the brocade duvet beneath her talons.

A movement caught her attention, and she turned her head to find Tobi staring at her, his eyes wide with astonishment. His mouth hung slightly open, an expression she'd never seen on the usually composed vampire's face.

Feeling rather pleased with herself, Beth preened her wing feathers, smoothing them into perfect alignment. The gesture came naturally, as if she'd always known how to do it.

Tyr looked equally thunderstruck, his hands suspended mid-gesture, matching Tobi's stunned stillness.

The identical looks of awe on their faces made her want to laugh, though it came out as a soft purrup instead. Here were two ancient vampires, who'd seen centuries of supernatural phenomena, looking completely thunderstruck by her transformation.

Tobi turned to his brother, his voice barely above a whisper. "Have you ever seen anything like that?"

"No." Tyr's response came out hoarse, his startled gaze still fixed on her transformed form. "Never."

Beth tilted her head questioningly, wondering what had the usually unflappable vampire twins so stunned. Her new raptor vision caught every nuance of their expressions - the slight widening of their pupils, the way their shoulders tensed with surprise.

Tyr finally broke from his frozen state, crossing the room in that fluid vampire grace to pull forward an ornate cheval mirror. He turned it to face her, and Beth tilted her head, studying the strange creature in the reflection.

Where had this winged cat come from? It looked like a miniature leopard—a delicate thing about the size of a house cat, with the most exquisite fur-covered wings she'd ever seen. The creature's head tilted at the same moment Beth tilted hers, and familiar blue-grey eyes stared back at her.

Reality hit her like a sledgehammer. That impossible creature was *her*.

She leaned forward on her forepaws to study her reflection more closely. Her coloring wasn't exactly the same—the usual bold clouded leopard markings had transformed into something ethereal - soft café au lait tones with the signature pattern rendered in subtle, dreamy shades that reminded her of watercolors bleeding together. The wing tips faded to a delicate dove grey, while the leading edges near her ribs carried just a whisper of darker brown, echoing her original markings but in this mystical, muted palette.

It was as if someone had taken her fierce predator form and transformed it into something out of a fairy tale - still unmistakably her, but rendered in shades of mist and moonlight.

Beautiful. Impossible. *Hers*. The emotions crashed over her in waves. With a startled *mroww* at her reflection, Beth lost her grip on her shifted form. She tumbled back into her human shape, landing on the bed with a soft thump. She looked down in amazement, realizing she was still fully dressed in her comfortable loungewear.

"Wait, what?" She patted her clothing in amazement, her voice rising with excitement. "How am I not naked? Shifting always leaves me tangled in my clothes. I've spent my entire shifter life planning around clothing - stashing spare outfits, explaining torn fabric, praying I wouldn't have to shift in an emergency because I'd end up naked and arrested!" She laughed, almost giddy. 'This is incredible!'"

Tyr's lips curved into a slight smile. "It's a vampire thing. We can maintain our clothing and possessions through the transformation. Anything we're carrying shifts with us. Mythicals can do it, too—dragons, unicorns, and so forth."

Beth perked up, curious. "I wonder..." She closed her eyes, reaching for that familiar golden warmth in her mind. Whisper responded eagerly, and Beth felt the familiar liquid flow of the Change rippling through her body.

When she opened her eyes, relief flooded through her as she found herself standing on four powerful paws—full-sized, solid, *real.* Her clouded leopard form stretched magnificently across the bed, no longer the delicate miniature creature but her fierce, familiar self. Instead of being surrounded by her clothing as would have happened before, they had simply vanished.

Focusing on her human form, Beth shifted back. Her clothes reappeared seamlessly in place, not a wrinkle in sight.

"Oh thank god, I still have Whisper!" The words tumbled out as relief crashed over her. "I was so afraid I'd lose her when I was Turned. But she's still there, still perfect." She smoothed her hands over her shirt, marveling. "And no more trying to hide clothes in bushes before shifting!"

Beth grinned, practically vibrating with excitement. "The other shifters are going to flip when they find out about the clothes thing! No more strategic planning around shift locations or explaining mysterious nudity."

Her excitement dimmed slightly as she remembered her unusual transformation. "But what about... the mini leopard with wings? I mean, I was supposed to shift into a raptor form, wasn't I?"

The brothers exchanged a look that said they were completely out of their depth.

"Yeah, you have three forms," Tobi said, shaking his head in disbelief. "Human, clouded leopard, and the winged kitty. I've never heard of anything like that. It shouldn't even be possible."

"This is completely outside our experience," Tyr agreed. "All I can think is that it must be some unique interaction between vampire and shifter abilities. Three distinct transformations? That's unprecedented."

"Antonio will definitely want to know about this," Tobi said. "He'll need to report it to Lord Damien for the knowledge base."

Beth couldn't help snickering. "Wait, vampires have a knowledge base? Like, what - an ancient tome filled with supernatural discoveries?"

"Actually, it's a secure cloud server now," Tyr corrected with a slight smile. "But you're one to talk. Don't the shifters maintain their own database of information?"

"Well, yeah," Beth admitted, feeling her cheeks warm slightly.

"Pot, kettle," Tobi sang out, dodging the pillow Beth threw at his head.

"Centuries of supernatural observations don't document themselves," Tyr added with a grin. "Though I bet Antonio still keeps his original hand-written journals somewhere. He's old school like that."

Beth bounced on the bed, bubbling over with enthusiasm. "I want to try again. See if it was a fluke or if I'm really some kind of winged cat."

Closing her eyes, she reached for that new sensation - the static-electricity tingle of the vampire. The Change flowed through her smoothly, and she opened her eyes to find herself back in that magical form. The muted, dreamy colors of her coat seemed to shimmer in the dim light.

Crouching low on the bed, Beth gathered her muscles and sprang upward. Her new wings spread instinctively, catching the air with surprising ease. She soared around the high-ceilinged room, reveling in the incredible sensation of flight. The world sharpened around her with crystal clarity - she could feel every air current, sense the exact balance needed to maintain altitude.

"Oh my god, she's adorable!" Tobi's voice rang out below her. "I just want to hug her and squeeze her and call her George!"

Beth's ears flattened against her head in annoyance. Wheeling around mid-flight, she dove straight for Tobi's head. Her small but sharp claws extended as she landed right on top of his intricate Viking-inspired hairstyle, snagging and twisting in the complex tapestry of thin braids woven through his longer hair, disrupting hours of careful work.

"Ow ow ow!" Tobi yelped, ducking and trying to dislodge her. "Get her off! This isn't funny!"

Tyr's rich laughter filled the room as he watched his brother dance around, trying unsuccessfully to remove the winged mini leopard from his head without getting scratched.

"He said that about you the first time he saw you in your shifter form, too," he told her.

With a tiny roar of triumph, Beth launched herself off Tobi's head and fluttered over to land neatly on Tyr's shoulder. She settled into place, her miniature self nestling snugly against his neck as if she'd perched there a thousand times before. Her velvet-soft wings folded gracefully against her sides as she lifted one diminutive paw, proceeding to wash it with exaggerated care. Her tail, a perfect miniature of her clouded leopard's, curled possessively around Tyr's neck.

His shoulder shook with quiet laughter beneath her small form. The scent of his skin filled her nostrils - a complex mixture of leather, night air, and something uniquely him.

"Serves you right," Tyr said to his brother, reaching up to scratch behind Beth's ears. His fingers found exactly the right spot, making her purr despite her attempts to maintain her dignified pose. "Calling a fierce predator 'adorable' - what did you expect?"

Tobi shot them both a wounded look as he attempted to salvage his thoroughly mussed hair. "My braids - they're ruined! Do you know how long it takes to get these things done?"

Beth paused in her grooming just long enough to give him her best feline smirk before returning to meticulously cleaning her paw, her tail tightening slightly around Tyr's neck in smug satisfaction.

Tyr nudged her. "Okay, Change back. There's more we need to show you."

After nipping his ear to show her displeasure, Beth leaped off Tyr's shoulder, and shifted back to her human form. He steadied her with one hand as she regained her balance.

"Okay, pay attention, this is important," Tyr said, moving toward the ornate wardrobe that dominated one wall. He pulled open a drawer and revealed a sleek keypad that seemed oddly modern against the antique wood. His fingers danced across the numbers in a practiced sequence.

A soft click echoed through the room, and the entire wardrobe began to swing away from the wall with silent precision. Beth's eyes widened as she stepped closer.

"Cool! A secret passage?"

Tobi's grin widened. "Even better. Just wait."

Beth peered into the revealed opening. What initially appeared to be a dark shaft resolved into a circular space with a gleaming metal pole running vertically through its center. The polished surface caught the dim light, disappearing into shadows below.

Before she could ask what it was for, Tobi launched himself at the pole. His hands gripped the metal as he swung his body around it with fluid grace, vanishing downward with a whoop of joy.

Beth ran to the opening, laughter bubbling up as she looked down. "A firehouse pole? Seriously?"

"After you." Tyr's eyes sparkled with amusement as he gestured toward the pole.

Beth grabbed the cool metal with both hands, the thrill of adventure coursing through her as she let herself slide into the darkness below.

Tobi's hand shot out, yanking Beth aside just as Tyr slid down the pole behind them. His quick movement saved her from being knocked over as Tyr landed with vampiric grace.

A soft click drew Beth's attention to where Tobi pressed a recessed button on the wall. Above them, metal whispered against metal as the wardrobe slid back into position.

"Security measure," Tyr told her, noting her curious expression. "That locks the entrance upstairs. Even if someone manages to crack the keypad code up there, they can't get in until I enter the release sequence down here."

Beth turned in a slow circle, her mind reeling. The underground expanse stretched before them - impossibly vast, easily the size of the warehouse above. She'd expected a simple basement. Not this massive complex. High ceilings disappeared into shadows despite the excellent lighting, making her feel tiny in comparison, and the air held a pleasant coolness that reminded her of wine cellars she'd visited.

Multiple doors lined the walls at regular intervals, their solid metal surfaces marked with subtle symbols she didn't recognize. Each door seemed to lead off in a different direction, creating the impression of a hub with many spokes radiating outward.

"This is amazing." Beth turned slowly, catching the faint hum of hidden ventilation systems, the way sound bounced differently in the vast space.

She ran her hand along the nearest metal door, marveling at the cool, smooth surface beneath her fingertips. Subtle variations in the metal hinted at reinforcements or security measures.

"How far down are we?" she asked, still taking in the vast underground space.

"About fifty feet," Tyr replied, his voice echoing slightly in the cavernous room. "Every vampire and Blood Sworn chamber has an escape leading here. This is our emergency escape route if needed."

Beth looked about her. "This is incredible. How did you manage to build all this without anyone noticing?"

"The building already had a cellar." Tyr gestured at the expertly finished walls. "The construction crew just dug deeper, using the old Prohibition tunnels to remove the dirt and rock."

"Prohibition tunnels?" Beth's curiosity peaked. "Like bootlegger smuggling routes?"

Tobi nodded enthusiastically. "Those same tunnels now connect to our network. The woods provide perfect cover for the original exit points." His eyes sparkled with amusement. "After more than a hundred years, those exits are completely hidden by natural overgrowth. You'd never find them unless you knew exactly where to look."

Beth pictured the dense forest surrounding the property, understanding how effectively time and nature had concealed the old smuggling routes. "That's brilliant - using existing tunnels instead of having to create everything from scratch."

Beth followed the twins through one of the metal doors, which opened into a long corridor. The industrial-style lighting cast a warm glow over polished concrete floors and expertly finished walls.

"This is our main living area," Tyr said, gesturing to a series of rooms. "In case we have to be down here for any extended period."

The first room contained neat rows of bunk beds, reminding Beth of military barracks she'd seen in movies. "How many people can you house down here?"

"About fifty," Tobi said, leading them past modern bathrooms and a fully equipped professional-grade kitchen.

"Fifty people?"

“The Residence houses about fifteen vampires," Tyr explained with a grin at her stunned expression, "plus roughly twice that many Companions. We needed emergency capacity for everyone." He gestured around the space. “This isn't just a hideout - it's a serious military-grade compound, capable of sustaining an entire community indefinitely."

They entered a massive walk-in refrigerator, and Beth's nose twitched at the unmistakable scent of blood. One entire wall was lined with neatly organized medical coolers.

"Emergency supplies," Tyr indicated the coolers. "The Pledged rotate the stock regularly, replacing older donations with fresh ones. Nothing goes to waste - the older blood gets donated to local hospitals."

"The generator keeps everything running," Tobi added as they exited the refrigerator. "Completely silent and undetectable from above ground."

Beth's amazement grew as they showed her several communal spaces, furnished with plush sofas and chairs. Flat-screen TVs hung on the walls, and she spotted high-end sound systems tucked discreetly into custom cabinets.

Beth ran her hand along the butter-soft leather armchair, then sank into it with a sigh. "It's like an underground luxury hotel bunker."

"We try to make it comfortable," Tyr said, his fingers brushing her shoulder. "Being trapped underground during an emergency is stressful enough without having to deal with uncomfortable surroundings."

Beth settled deeper into the soft leather, still gazing around in awe, processing the scale and sophistication of the facility. The thought and planning that had gone into creating this safe haven staggered her.

Beth leaned forward in the comfortable armchair, fascinated by the layers of security surrounding them. "So no one can detect this place at all?"

"Not a chance." Tyr's voice held quiet pride. "The entire facility is soundproofed and built to withstand practically anything - even nuclear blasts, theoretically. Though I'd rather not test that particular feature."

"The thermal shielding is perfect too," Tobi added, sprawling across a nearby sofa. "You could have fifty vampires down here doing the Macarena, and infrared sensors wouldn't pick up a thing."

Beth snorted at the mental image. "The Macarena? Really?"

"Hey, some of us appreciate the classics." Tobi's grinned. "But seriously, this place is basically a natural Faraday cage. All the steel reinforcement means even ground-penetrating radar can't see us, especially with all the old tunnel networks creating interference."

"What about staying connected to the outside world?" Beth asked, glancing at her phone which showed no signal.

"Hardwired internet through the tunnels." Tyr gestured toward a sleek monitor mounted on one wall. "We can access all our security cameras, keep tabs on what's happening above ground. Complete surveillance coverage without anyone knowing we're watching."

The screen flickered to life, showing multiple camera views of the property - the warehouse exterior, parking areas, and surrounding woods. Beth saw a deer wander past one of the cameras, completely unaware it was being observed.

"So you can see everything happening up there while staying safely hidden down here," Beth said, recognizing the magnitude of their surveillance network. "This is cutting-edge stuff."

Beth followed Tyr's gesture to another doorway. "That's just a quick-look station. Antonio has a full command center set up through there."

Her curiosity piqued, Beth peered through the doorway, her gaze sweeping the impressive space beyond, catching every detail. Floor-to-ceiling monitors covered three walls, displaying everything from thermal imaging to satellite views. Several workstations held sophisticated computer equipment, their sleek modern designs contrasting with the industrial aesthetic of the bunker.

"Wow," Beth breathed, taking in the scale of the operation. "This is like something out of a spy movie."

"Antonio doesn't believe in doing things halfway," Tobi said with a grin. "Wait till you see the armory."

"We've got enough firepower stored down here to overthrow a small country," he continued, leading them down another corridor. "Though hopefully we'll never need it."

Beth's attention caught on a large garage-like space branching off from one of the main tunnels. A dozen rugged ATV's sat ready, their dark paint absorbing the overhead light.

"Emergency vehicles for our humans." Tyr indicated the rows of keys hanging on a board. "If we ever need to evacuate, they can take these through the old bootlegger tunnels. The routes come out miles from here, completely hidden in the woods."

"What about the vampires?" Beth asked, picturing the logistics of an evacuation.

Tyr smiled at her, taking her hand, his fingers threading through hers. "We've got it easier. If it's night, we can either ghost out - you'll learn that trick soon - or shift to our raptor forms and fly away. These are mainly for the humans who look after us."

Beth nodded, impressed by how thoroughly they'd planned for every contingency. The level of detail in their preparations spoke volumes about how seriously they took their responsibility to protect both vampires and humans.

Beth bit her lower lip, a thought occurring to her as she studied the emergency vehicles. "But what happens if it's daytime? The vampires can't escape."

Tyr's fingers squeezed hers gently as a knowing smile crossed his face. "Don't worry - we have that covered too." He guided her toward what appeared to be a blank section of wall. "There's a hidden room down here that even the Blood Sworn don't know about. It can't be discovered, nor broken into."

His blue eyes held a serious glint as he continued. "That's where we would wait for sunset. Being trapped in the daytime is something no vampire ever takes lightly." His thumb traced idle patterns on her palm. "We have layers of protection at all times in any Residence."

The weight of that reality settled over her. As a shifter, she'd always had to be careful about protecting her secret, but vampires faced an additional deadly threat every single day. No wonder they took such elaborate precautions.

CHAPTER 26

Today was moving day. After three days of staying in Tyr's chambers while the construction crew worked, Beth was finally getting her own belongings moved into the Residence. Well, temporary belongings anyway, until her and Tyr's connecting suite was finished.

Beth bounced on her toes as the elevator doors opened. Her sister emerged, along with several bobcat shifters carrying boxes of Beth's things.

"Someone's eager to get settled," Naomi teased, stepping out of the elevator.

"You have no idea." Beth said, practically vibrating with excitement. "Wait until you see what they've done."

She led the way past ornate wall sconces and richly detailed tapestries, noting textures and details she'd never noticed before her Turning. The men followed carefully with their burdens, their movements precise despite the awkward size of some of the boxes.

"Right here." Beth pushed open the door to a spacious guest chamber in soothing green and gold. "It's just temporary until the renovation is finished, but isn't it gorgeous?"

Beth gestured to the shifters as they brought in her boxes. "Just line those up along that wall, please."

Stronger than humans, the shifters made the heavy boxes look deceptively light as they carried them in. The scent of cardboard and packing tape made her want to sneeze—the intensity of ordinary smells still caught her off guard.

"Miss Kerrigan?" One of the men - Mike, she remembered from one of last summer's barbecues at Katerina's and Troy's house - straightened up after setting down his box. "Where would you like the desk positioned?"

Beth pointed toward the alcove in the corner. "That spot would be perfect. The recessed lighting makes it ideal for studying."

Mike nodded, exchanging glances with another shifter named Dave. "We'll head down and grab it next. Shouldn't take but a minute with the two of us."

The men headed out, their footsteps nearly silent on the thick carpeting despite their size. Their footsteps faded down the hallway toward the elevator, along with their quiet conversation about maneuvering the desk through the doorway.

Naomi turned in a slow circle, taking in the elegant guest chamber. "I can't believe how much progress they've made in just three days. They must be working around the clock to create your connecting suite."

"Oh, they're definitely not thrilled with us," Beth snickered. "You should hear them grumbling about having to redo work they just finished."

Her sister studied Beth's face with a knowing smile. "You look more at home here than I expected."

Beth sank onto a plush bench seat. "I feel more at home here than I ever have anywhere else. Which is strange, considering..." She gestured vaguely at herself, encompassing her recent transformation. "Everything."

"What about Whisper?" Naomi asked, settling beside her. "How's she handling all the changes?"

Beth laughed. "She's absolutely delighted with her new home. You should see her exploring the Residence, sniffing out every corner and climbing everything she can reach." Her smile widened. "Actually, Tyr's having them install floating shelves all along the tops of the walls - like a feline highway just for her. He says she should have her own territory to patrol."

"He's building her a highway?" Naomi said with a grin. "You've got yourself a keeper."

"Right? He can be just ridiculously sweet." She smiled softly. "Sometimes I can't believe this is actually my life now."

"Tyr's been amazing through all of this," Beth said, settling onto the bench. Her smile softened as she remembered their second date. "Did you know that when male raptors court females, they bring them food?"

Naomi's brows rose, her eyes gleaming with interest. "Really? I didn't know that."

"Exactly." Beth grinned at her sister. "When we're out together - him as a tiercel and me as Whisper - he'll often bring me something to eat. The first time, I thought he was just being nice, but then he explained it's actually a courtship ritual for raptors."

"Oh my god, that's adorable!" Naomi clasped her hands together. "So even in his bird form, he's trying to take care of you?"

"He is." Beth felt warmth spread through her chest at the memory. "And now that I understand what it means, it's even more special. He's literally showing me he can provide for me in any form."

"That's so sweet," Naomi sighed. "Who knew vampires could be such romantics?"

A gentle smile curved Beth's lips, warmth spreading through her chest as she thought of Tyr. "I know, right? The stereotype is that they're all dark and brooding, but Tyr's actually incredibly thoughtful. He pays attention to all these little details that matter to both sides of me - human and leopard."

A loud crash from the hallway made them both jump. Beth poked her head out to see a bobcat shifter apologizing profusely to Margot, who stood surveying a toppled box of Beth's clothes.

"Perhaps," Margot said, her crisp voice carrying that unmistakable note of authority, "we should be more careful with Ms. Kerrigan's belongings."

The burly shifter seemed to shrink under her stern gaze. "Yes, ma'am. Sorry, ma'am."

Beth bit her lip to keep from laughing as Margot supervised the cleanup with military precision.

"I never knew anyone as intimidating as Margot," Naomi whispered, watching the scene with a mix of amusement and awe. "Are you sure she's a human?"

"Yes, she is. And you're not the only one," Beth replied. "She terrifies me! You should see Tyr and Tobi around her. They practically stand at attention whenever she enters a room."

Even so, Beth felt warmth spread through her chest at Margot's unexpected support. Despite the majordomo's stern exterior, she'd been surprisingly welcoming of Beth's presence in the Residence.

Liam appeared in the hallway, carrying a box labeled "BOOKS – ESSENTIAL" in Beth's neat handwriting. "Where do you want this?" he asked, peering over the top of his burden.

"On the desk, please," Beth said, stepping aside to let him pass. "Those are the ones I want to have accessible while I'm off work this week."

"So, what's it like being a lady of leisure?" Naomi asked, settling beside her.

Beth huffed out a breath. "Weird, honestly. I've never been good at doing nothing. But Tyr insisted I needed to take at least a week to adjust to this whole vampire thing—the feeding, the speed, heightened senses, the all of it."

"It's probably wise," Liam said, his hazel eyes warm with understanding. "Your body's still adapting to the transformation. I imagine it's overwhelming, even for someone who's already supernatural."

Beth nodded, grateful for his medical perspective. As both a physician and veterinarian, Liam had a unique understanding of her situation. He'd been monitoring her recovery since the shooting, consulting with Antonio on the unprecedented aspects of her hybrid nature. The two, shifter and vampire, could often be seen with their heads together, sharing observations and trading theories.

A young man with tousled light brown hair popped his head around the doorframe, his face splitting into an enormous grin. "Hey everyone! How's the move going?"

"Gabe!" Beth's face lit up at the sight of Margot's grandson. "Come in. You remember my sister Naomi and her husband Liam from their visits."

"Of course!" Gabe bounded into the room with puppyish enthusiasm, shaking hands with both of them. "Great to see you guys again! Beth talks about you all the time."

"How's Adele?" Naomi asked, referring to the vampire Gabe was Blood Sworn to.

"She's awesome," Gabe replied with his characteristic enthusiasm. "She's still in Manhattan, wrapping some stuff up and will be here soon. She says to tell you hello, by the way, and that she can't wait to meet you."

"And wait till you see what Grandma has them doing with your sitting room," Gabe continued, his eyes bright with excitement. "Custom bookshelves built into the walls, a comfortable seating area, and this fabulous fireplace with hand-carved stonework. It's going to be incredible."

"It sounds lovely," Naomi said, unpacking a framed photo of the twins from their college days and placing it on the nightstand. "You've certainly come up in the world since our last visit. From recovering in Tyr's chambers to having a whole suite built for you."

"Hey, Naomi. I figured you'd be here," came Tyr's voice from the doorway. His fair hair was slightly tousled, and a fine layer of plaster dust covered his dark henley. He crossed the room to drop a kiss on Beth's lips.

Beth frowned, brushing plaster dust from his shoulders. "How's it going in there?"

"The wall's down," he reported, slipping an arm around her waist. "They're framing the archway now, and the built-in bookshelves should be ready by tomorrow evening."

A sharp tap on the doorframe made everyone turn. Margot stood in the entrance, her clipboard clutched to her chest, her expression as stern as ever.

"The construction foreman would like a word, Mr. Lindström," she announced. "Something about load-bearing concerns."

Tyr sighed, pressing a quick kiss to Beth's temple before releasing her. "Duty calls. I'll be back shortly."

As he followed Margot into the hallway, Beth couldn't help smiling at the way his shoulders straightened in the majordomo's presence.

"So," Naomi said once they'd gone, settling onto the edge of the bed beside Beth. "How are you really doing? And don't give me the 'everything's fine' version."

Beth glanced at Gabe and Liam, who both immediately took the hint.

"I should probably get back to work," Gabe said, sliding off the desk. "Grandma will have my hide if I'm late for inventory duty."

"And I'll help unpack those essential books," Liam added, moving to the box on the desk. "Over here, out of earshot."

Once they had relative privacy, Beth turned to her twin. "It's... an adjustment," she admitted softly. "The whole vampire thing is actually easier than I expected—the blood, the night schedule, even the enhanced senses." She chuckled suddenly. "I'm still running into walls unexpectedly, because I wasn't paying attention to my speed, and suddenly, bam!"

Naomi's face scrunched in sympathy. "Ouch. That sounds painful."

"It was, but..." Beth grinned, rolling up her sleeve to show perfectly unmarked skin. "The bruises vanish like magic. One minute I'm sporting this huge purple mark, the next - poof! Gone. Tyr says it's because vampire healing kicks in almost instantly for minor injuries."

"I am so envious," Naomi groaned, absently touching a fading bruise on her own arm from a recent mishap at the library. "Do you know how many times I've banged my shins on those stupid book carts? And I have to wait days for the bruises to fade."

Beth laughed, the sound echoing musically in the elegant room. "Trust me, the quick healing is definitely making up for my complete lack of grace with these new abilities. Though Tyr swears I'll get better at controlling the speed once I'm more used to it."

"You're telling me the graceful, elegant vampires actually have a clumsy learning period?" Naomi's eyes sparkled with amusement.

"Oh yeah. You should have seen Tobi's face when I told him about walking into walls. Apparently, he spent his first week as a vampire accidentally launching himself through windows because he couldn't control his strength."

Naomi snickered. A comfortable silence fell between them, broken only by the sounds of Liam quietly arranging books on the desk and the muffled construction noise from the other side of the wall.

A soft tap at the door interrupted their conversation. Layla burst into the room, her red hair flying as she rushed to embrace Beth.

"Oh Beth! I've been so worried!" Layla wrapped her arms tightly around Beth. "Are you really okay? When I heard..."

Beth hugged her back carefully, mindful of her new strength. "I'm more than okay. Being a vampire is incredible, Layla. Everything is so vivid now - I can hear heartbeats, smell emotions, see details I never noticed before."

"And the strength!" Beth grinned, gesturing to the heavy boxes lining the walls. "I could probably lift all of these at once if I wanted to. Though Tyr keeps warning me to be careful until I get used to it."

Layla pulled back slightly, studying Beth's face with wonder. "You look different - there's this glow about you. And your eyes..." She tilted her head. "They're still the same color but somehow more intense?"

"Vampire thing," Beth explained, touching the skin beneath her eyes. "All our features get enhanced during the transformation. But the best part is I still have Whisper!"

"Nobody knew if I would keep her when I was Turned. The thought of losing Whisper..." Beth's voice caught. "It would have been like losing half my soul."

Layla touched Beth's arm, her eyes soft with understanding. "I would have been so scared. The thought of losing my caracal... I can't even imagine."

"Me either." Naomi's fingers found Beth's, squeezing gently. "Shadow is such a part of me. The idea of living without her..."

Beth nodded, remembering the fear that had gripped her in those crucial moments. "But Tyr made me realize—if I died, Whisper would die with me anyway. At least this way, we both had a chance."

"Well, there is that," Naomi said softly, her grip tightening on Beth's hand.

The memory of that night sent a shiver through Beth - the searing pain of the bullet, Tyr's desperate race to save her, the terrifying choice she'd had to make. But here she sat, very much alive, with both her leopard and her mate.

Beth shook off the dark memory, her expression brightening. "But enough about that scary stuff. I almost forgot - I have something incredible to show you! You're simply not going to believe this. I swear."

"What is it?" Naomi asked, shifting eagerly.

"Just watch." Beth closed her eyes, reaching for that unique combination of vampire power and shifter magic that she was starting to recognize. The familiar tingle of the Change rippled through her, but lighter, more ethereal.

When she opened her eyes, she found herself perched delicately on the bed, her miniature winged form barely making a dent in the plush comforter. Her dreamy, muted coat caught the light as she stretched her wings, showing off the subtle gradients of color.

Layla's mouth dropped open, and she stared. "Oh my god," she breathed, one hand covering her mouth. "You're... you're... wow!!"

"Beth... what the hell?" Naomi leaned closer, staring at toy-sized winged leopard. "How is this even possible?"

Even Liam abandoned his book organizing to gape at Beth's unique form. "Well, that's completely insane," he said, shaking his head. "Naomi, your sister is officially the coolest person I know."

Beth preened under their admiring stares, her miniature tail curling with satisfaction. She spread her wings wider, letting them admire the delicate fur-covered appendages that somehow merged perfectly with her regular coat.

Beth shifted back to her human form, landing gracefully on her feet beside the bed. Her comfortable loungewear remained perfectly intact, not a wrinkle in sight.

"Wait - your clothes!" Naomi jumped up, circling her sister with wide eyes. "They shifted with you! How did you do that?"

Layla reached out to touch Beth's sleeve in amazement. "I've never seen anything like it. Usually when we shift..."

"We end up naked or tangled in shredded clothing," Beth finished with a laugh. "I know! It's incredible, right? Apparently it's a vampire thing - they can maintain their clothing through transformations."

"That's so unfair," Naomi groaned, tugging at her own shirt. "Do you know how many outfits I've ruined?"

Beth smoothed her hands over her perfectly preserved outfit. "No more hiding spare clothes in bushes or worrying about emergency shifts. Everything just... vanishes when I transform and reappears when I shift back. Even jewelry!"

"Seriously?" Naomi grabbed Beth's hand, examining the delicate silver bracelet on her wrist. "That is so unfair!"

Beth giggled and bounced on her toes, still excited about this new ability. "Tyr says it's because vampires can sort of... fold their possessions into their transformation somehow. They've been doing it for centuries."

Beth turned to Layla, taking her hand. "How are you doing? I've been so caught up in all these changes, I feel like I've lost track of everyone."

Layla's whole face lit up, her blue eyes sparkling. "Oh, Beth, things are going so well! Yousuf started kindergarten last week, and he absolutely loves it."

"Really? That's wonderful!" Beth remembered their earlier conversations about Layla's fears of separation from her son.

"He's made three friends already," Layla continued, practically glowing with maternal pride. "And his teacher, Ms. Reynolds, is amazing with him. She understands about his... background." Layla's smile softened. "She lets him keep his comfort toy in his desk, just in case he gets anxious."

"And you're doing okay with the separation?" Beth asked gently.

"Actually, yes. I'm volunteering in his classroom twice a week - Tuesdays and Thursdays. It helps, being able to see him thriving in his new environment." Layla beamed, her voice full of maternal pride. "And the children are so precious. They've started calling me 'Miss Layla' and always want me to read stories.

"That's perfect," Beth said warmly. "You get to be there for him while still giving him space to grow independently."

"Exactly!" Layla nodded enthusiastically. "And you were right about the therapy helping. Dr. Martinez suggested the classroom volunteering as a way to ease both of us into the transition. It's working beautifully."

"Speaking of kindergarten..." Layla glanced at her watch. "I need to go pick up Yousuf from school. I just wanted to check on you, make sure you were really okay after everything."

"I'm perfect," Beth assured her, pulling her friend into a careful hug. Her new vampire strength still required conscious control, especially with more delicate humans. "Give Yousuf a big hug from his Aunt Beth."

"I will." Layla squeezed back. "He doesn't know about... well, everything." She laughed suddenly. "He'll be thrilled that you're a vampire now, though! I think Tobi is his new hero."

"Tell him I'll come by soon," Beth promised. "Once I'm more used to..." She gestured vaguely at herself, encompassing her transformed state.

"Of course." Layla gathered her purse, the leather soft and worn. "Text me!"

Beth walked Layla to the door, touched by her friend's concern. "Drive safe. And thank you for coming to check on me."

"That's what family does," Layla said simply, her smile warm as she headed down the hallway toward the elevator.

Beth watched until Layla disappeared around the corner, her enhanced hearing picking up the soft ding of the elevator arriving. The familiar scents of her friend - jasmine perfume and the lingering aroma of the herbal tea she favored gradually faded from the air.

"Oh!" Beth suddenly remembered something, and turned to her sister. "I have news. Lord Damien wants to meet me."

Naomi's eyes widened. "When?"

"Tomorrow night," Beth said, nerves fluttering in her stomach again at the thought. "He's coming up from New York. Apparently, it's customary for newly Turned vampires to be formally presented to the clan leader."

"Are you nervous?" Naomi asked, studying her face.

"Terrified," Beth admitted with a shaky laugh. "He's over five thousand years old, Naomi. He's one of the first vampires created... like, ever. Even Tyr and Tobi—both of them—go all respectful, even reverent, when they talk about him. What do I even say to someone like that?"

"Hello would be a good start," her sister suggested with a grin.

Beth swatted her arm playfully. "Very helpful, thank you."

"What are sisters for?" Naomi's expression sobered slightly. "Seriously though, you'll be fine. If he approved your Turning in the first place, he obviously thinks you're worthy of joining his clan."

"That's what Tyr says too," Beth sighed. "I just... I don't want to embarrass him. Or myself."

"You won't," Naomi assured her. "Just be yourself. That's always been enough."

Beth leaned over to hug her sister, breathing in Naomi's familiar scent. Her heightened sense of smell picking up new layers she'd never noticed before - the subtle notes of Liam's aftershave lingering on Naomi's clothes, the fresh spring air clinging to her hair, even traces of the coffee she'd had that morning.

"You're the best sister ever," Beth murmured, tightening her arms around Naomi's shoulders. "I don't know what I'd do without you,"

Naomi returned the embrace just as fiercely. "Good thing you'll never have to find out," she whispered back, her voice thick with emotion.

Beth smoothed her hands over her silk blouse for the hundredth time, trying to calm nerves that shouldn't exist anymore. Five thousand years old. How did you prepare to meet someone who'd witnessed the rise and fall of entire civilizations?

"Stop fidgeting," Tyr murmured, his hand settling at the small of her back. "You look perfect."

Beth shot him a grateful smile, though her stomach still churned with anxiety. "I'm meeting the oldest vampire in existence. I think I'm entitled to a little nervousness."

"Lord Damien isn't as intimidating as you might think," Tyr said, his fingers tracing soothing circles against her silk-covered spine.

"Unless you get on his bad side." Tobi said, lounging against the door frame.

"Not helping," Beth muttered, resisting the urge to tug at her skirt.

Tyr turned to scowl at his brother. "Get lost, Tobi. You're not helping."

"Just keeping things real," Tobi said with a grin, pushing off from the doorframe with fluid grace. He spun on his heel and strolled away down the corridor, whistling a tune that echoed off the stone walls.

Beth's enhanced hearing picked up the subtle crunch of tires on gravel outside, the quiet purr of an expensive engine approaching the Residence. Her fingers clutched at Tyr's arm, her supernatural strength making the gesture firmer than intended.

"Breathe," Tyr whispered, covering her hand with his. "Remember what I told you—just be yourself."

Beth forced herself to release her death grip on his arm, smoothing out the wrinkles she'd created in his sleeve. "Sorry," she murmured.

"Don't be." Tyr's gaze warmed. "You're adorable when you're nervous."

"I am not adorable," Beth protested automatically. "I'm a fierce predator. In three forms now, thank you very much."

Beth and Tyr waited in their newly finished salon, sitting together on a deep forest green loveseat. A stone fireplace crackled nearby, its flames casting dancing shadows across the room.

"This is our place now," Tyr murmured, his arm around her shoulders pulling her close. The familiar weight helped calm her anxiety as they waited for Lord Damien's arrival.

Margot appeared in the doorway. "Mr. Lindström. Ms. Kerrigan." Her cultured voice carried precise formality. "Lord Damien and Lady Alyssa."

Tyr rose from the loveseat, and Beth hastily copied him, standing by his side.

Lord Damien entered the room with fluid grace. Beth had expected someone physically imposing, but the ancient vampire was of average height—and somehow that made him even more terrifying. His compact build belied the power she could feel radiating from him. She found herself unable to look away from his eyes—dark as midnight, with occasional flickers of red like embers in a dying fire.

Beside him was a woman of ethereal beauty, her blue-green eyes sparkling with welcome. Her midnight hair seemed to shimmer as she smiled, the gesture transforming her delicate features into something even more breathtaking.

"Tyr." Lord Damien's voice carried the weight of ages - deep, commanding, and unmistakably ancient. "And Beth Kerrigan."

Tyr bowed deeply, a gesture of respect that Beth hastily mimicked. "My Lord. Lady Alyssa"

"I've been looking forward to meeting you, Beth." Lady Alyssa's musical voice held genuine warmth as she came forward to embrace Beth in a gentle hug. "Please, sit."

Beth settled back onto the loveseat beside Tyr, her initial nervousness easing as she studied Lady Alyssa more closely. The Djinn's eyes held a mischievous sparkle, so similar to Jacinth's that Beth immediately warmed to her, feeling as if she knew her already. The same playful intelligence shone in those aquamarine depths, along with that distinctive otherworldly quality Beth had come to associate with the Djinn.

Beth settled back on the loveseat, perched on the edge of the cushion, trying not to stare at the ancient beings before her. Lord Damien's presence filled the room like a physical force, yet there was something almost gentle in the way he regarded her.

"So," he said after a moment, studying her face. "You are our newest vampire. And, I understand, quite unique."

"Yes, my lord." Beth's voice emerged steadier than she expected. "I seem to have retained my shifter abilities after the Turning."

"Antonio has kept both Aleksei and myself well-informed of your unique situation." There was a gleam in his expression that she thought might have been humor. "I imagine the scientific community will be quite interested in studying your case."

Beth couldn't hold back a grimace. "They already are. Both the vampire and the shifter science teams keep calling and texting."

"Not to mention the emails," Tyr added, his thumb stroking

soothing circles on her shoulder. "Our phones haven't stopped buzzing since word got out."

"They all want interviews and blood samples and various tests," Beth said, unable to keep the exasperation from her voice. "One team even suggested a full physical evaluation under laboratory conditions." She shuddered slightly at the thought of being treated like a specimen.

The temperature in the room plummeted as a growl tore from Lord Damien's throat. Beth's breath misted in the suddenly frigid air as his face transformed into something from nightmares—five thousand years of predatory rage focused into a single, terrifying expression.

"They dare to treat you like a laboratory specimen?" His voice held the weight of ages, crackling with barely contained fury.

Beth felt Tyr's arm tighten protectively around her shoulders as Lord Damien's anger filled the space between them. Damien's growl subsided, though his expression remained fierce.

"I will contact Maroulla immediately. Between us, we will put a stop to this harassment. No one, human or Other, has the right to intrude upon your privacy this way."

"If I may suggest," Alyssa said, her blue-green eyes thoughtful, "both communities could appoint a single representative to act as liaison. That person could coordinate any questions or research requests, presenting them to Beth and Tyr only when they feel ready to address them."

Beth brightened at the suggestion. "That would be so much better than dealing with dozens of different researchers."

"And this way," Alyssa continued with a gentle smile, "you maintain control over how much information you choose to share, and when. The decision remains entirely yours."

Ancient power filled the room like a gathering storm as Lord Damien's expression darkened further, what looked like literal flames leaping in his eyes.

"No." The single word held the weight of millennia. "There will be no tests. No examinations. No blood samples." Each word fell like a hammer strike. "Beth's unique nature is not for their scientific curiosity."

"But surely some basic information—" Tyr began diplomatically.

"No." Damien cut him off with a sharp gesture. "They may document that a shifter was successfully Turned. Nothing more." His dark gaze fixed on Beth. "You are not a specimen to be studied. You are a vampire—a member of my clan and a shifter—not a lab rat."

Beth's hands trembled as relief swept through her. The constant pressure from researchers had been suffocating her—phone calls, emails, demands for her blood, bone marrow, xrays—making her feel like... well, like a lab rat. But Lord Damien's absolute authority lifted that crushing burden from her shoulders.

"Thank you," she told him gratefully.

"The scientific community will simply have to accept that some mysteries remain unexplained," Alyssa added, her blue-green eyes twinkling. "It will do them good to remember that not everything in our world can be reduced to data points and laboratory analysis."

Damien nodded in agreement, his fury settling into something more controlled but no less adamant. "You are what you are. That is enough."

Alyssa changed the subject, leaning forward, her blue-green eyes warm with interest. "And how are you adjusting to your new existence, Beth?"

"Better than I expected, actually." Beth relaxed slightly, finding it easier to talk about practical matters. "The blood drinking was strange at first. I mean, as a shifter I've hunted prey, but this is different." She glanced at Tyr beside her. "Derek's been really patient, helping me learn the proper technique for feeding from humans. I'm getting better at hitting the artery, and closing the bite wounds."

Tyr's hand squeezed her shoulder encouragingly. "You're doing remarkably well for someone so newly Turned."

Beth nodded, then paused, her fingers twisting in her lap as she gathered her thoughts. "The hardest part..." Her voice caught slightly. "The hardest part is knowing I'll outlive Naomi. We're twins - we've been through everything together. All the good and bad, we've always had each other." She swallowed hard, the emotion thick in her throat. "And now I'll have to watch her grow old without me."

"That is the burden all immortals bear," Lord Damien said, his voice softening slightly. "Watching those we care for age and pass while we remain."

"But you still have her now," Lady Alyssa pointed out gently. "And memories of loved ones never truly fade, not for us."

Beth nodded, taking comfort in the thought. "I'm grateful for that. And for the chance to build a new life with Tyr."

Lord Damien's dark eyes seemed to look through her, as if assessing her very soul. After a moment, he nodded, apparently satisfied with what he found.

"You have adapted well," he said. "Many newly Turned struggle far more with the transition."

"I had excellent teachers," Beth said, glancing at Tyr with affection. "And having been a shifter helped, I think. I was already accustomed to having two natures."

"A reasonable hypothesis." Lord Damien studied her with keen interest. "I understand you have developed quite an unusual form. A winged leopard, I'm told."

Heat rushed to Beth's face as she ducked her head, guilt washing over her. She hadn't meant to develop such an odd hybrid form - it had just happened during her first attempt at the raptor transformation. "Yes, my lord. I'm sorry if it's..."

A musical laugh from Lady Alyssa cut through Beth's apology. "Oh, don't apologize! You should hear the vampires talking about it. It's all anyone can discuss lately." Her blue-green eyes sparkled with delight. "Everyone wants to see this tiny winged leopard for themselves."

"My treasure," Damien said, his stern features softening as he looked at his wife, "you are no different. When Antonio first told us, it was all I could do to keep you from transporting yourself to the Hudson Valley on the spot."

Alyssa's grin widened, unrepentant. "Can you blame me?"

Beth felt Tyr's silent laughter vibrating through his chest where she leaned against him. His arm tightened around her shoulders in quiet support as she squirmed under the attention.

Beth shifted in her seat, eager to share her latest achievement. "Actually, I finally managed another form last night."

"Did you now?" Alyssa leaned forward, her blue-green eyes sparkling with interest.

"Yes, I finally achieved an actual raptor form." Beth couldn't keep the pride from her voice. "An owl."

"The cutest little owl you've ever seen," Tyr added, grinning.

Beth kicked his shin, which only made his grin widen.

"She transformed into a Northern Saw-whet Owl," Tyr explained to Damien and Alyssa, clearly enjoying himself. "Only about eight inches high, with these adorable round-"

Beth clapped her hand over his mouth, but he simply removed it, his eyes dancing with mischief.

"And she whistles," he finished wickedly.

"I do not whistle," Beth protested, feeling heat rise to her cheeks.

Beth huffed, crossing her arms over her chest. "Just you wait. Now that I've got the hang of it, next time I'm going to transform into a peregrine falcon." Her eyes sparkled with challenge as she lifted her chin. "And I'll be a lot bigger than your tiercel form."

Tyr placed his hand dramatically over his heart, his eyes widening in mock distress. "Ouch. You wound me, my love."

Looking amused, Lord Damien rose with fluid grace, holding out his hand to his Chosen. The ancient vampire's dark eyes settled on her one final time, a hint of approval in their depths.

"Welcome to our clan, Beth Kerrigan," he said formally, his voice carrying the weight of ages.

Lady Alyssa embraced Beth warmly. "We'll talk more soon," she promised, her blue-green eyes twinkling. "I still want to hear more about this winged leopard form of yours... and see it for myself!"

After they departed, Beth sagged against Tyr's side, relief flooding through her. "That went better than I expected." She frowned suddenly, a thought occurring to her. "But... I thought he'd want to test me on all the vampire laws and protocols you and Antonio's been teaching me. Isn't that part of being formally accepted into the clan?"

Tyr chuckled, pulling her closer. "No, love. That's Antonio's responsibility. Damien is excellent at delegating - he's had millennia to perfect the art of leadership. He trusts Antonio's judgment completely when it comes to educating and evaluating new vampires."

Beth stared at him for a moment, then her relief began turning into indignation. "Wait. Why didn't you tell me that before? I was terrified he was going to quiz me on everything!" She gave his shoulder a solid punch, her vampire strength making the impact more solid than intended.

Tyr's hand covered her mouth, cutting off her anxious rambling. His eyes sparkled with amusement as she glared at him over his palm.

"Because," he said, his voice rich with suppressed laughter, "watching you study so diligently was adorable. You created color-coded flashcards, love. For vampire etiquette."

Beth's eyes narrowed above his hand, but she couldn't hide her grin pressing against his palm. She considered biting him, but given they were both vampires now, it wouldn't have quite the same impact as it might have a week ago.

Tyr slowly removed his hand, still chuckling. "Besides, all that studying wasn't wasted. You'll need to know those protocols eventually. Just not for your first meeting with Damien."

CHAPTER 27

The night air carried the crisp scent of fresh snow as Beth soared above the forest. Her small winged form caught the moonlight, casting a fleeting shadow over the treetops below. The sensation of flight still thrilled her—the freedom, the perspective, the sheer joy of defying gravity.

Next to her, Tyr's peregrine falcon form cut through the air with practiced precision. His sleek feathers gleamed in the silvery light as he banked and dove, showing off his centuries of experience with aerial acrobatics.

Beth chirped in challenge, tucking her velvet wings close to her body as she dove toward the clearing below. The wind rushed past her sensitive whiskers, her wild instincts perfectly balanced with her new flying abilities. She pulled up at the last moment, her paws skimming the tall grass before she ascended again in a graceful arc.

Tyr's tiercel shot past her, his wings barely visible as he demonstrated a perfect hunting dive. Beth couldn't help the purr of appreciation that rumbled through her small chest. Even after weeks together, watching him fly still took her breath away.

They circled the clearing once more before descending to the frost-laden grass below. Beth shifted back to her human form, the transformation as natural as breathing now. Her clothes reappeared perfectly in place—a convenience she still appreciated every time she Changed.

Tyr landed beside her, his feathers blurring as he returned to his vampire self. His eyes sparkled with exhilaration as he pulled her close.

"Show-off," Beth teased, wrapping her arms around his waist.

"Me?" Tyr's eyebrows rose in mock offense. "I wasn't the one doing loop-the-loops over the lake."

"I was practicing," Beth insisted, failing to keep the grin from her face. "Antonio says I need to work on my maneuverability."

"Mmm-hmm." Tyr's cool lips brushed her forehead. "And I'm sure the audience of astonished campers on the far shore had nothing to do with it."

Beth laughed, the sound carrying through the quiet clearing. "They couldn't see me. If they had, they'd probably have thought I was some kind of exotic owl. Or a confused bat."

"A very cute confused bat," Tyr corrected, earning himself a playful swat on the arm.

Tyr led her to a fallen log at the edge of the clearing, brushing the snow from its surface before they settled onto the makeshift seat. Beth leaned back against his chest as they gazed up at the star-filled sky. These quiet moments had become precious to her—time away from the Residence, from their responsibilities, from navigating her new existence. So many adjustments, including living separately from her twin for the first time in months.

"It's strange living apart from Naomi," Beth said softly. "I keep expecting to hear her voice in the next room. We were never apart growing up, until... everything that happened. And ever since the Sanctuary, we've been together again."

Tyr's arms tightened around her. "You know we can visit them whenever you want. She's not more than a few miles away."

"I know." Beth hummed in contentment, turning her head to rub her cheek, cat-like, against his shoulder. "It's just... different now. Good different, but still different."

"I was thinking," Tyr said, his voice carefully casual, "we could take a trip soon. Somewhere you've always wanted to see."

Beth twisted to look up at him, curiosity piqued. "Like where?"

"Anywhere." His gaze held nothing but sincerity. "Europe, Asia, South America. The world is open to us now."

The possibilities made Beth's head spin. As vampires with the clan's resources behind them, they could go anywhere, see anything.

"Norway," she said suddenly, the word escaping before she'd fully formed the thought. She wanted to trace his beginnings, to stand where the boy who would become her eternal love had once breathed mortal air. "I want to see where you grew up. The fjords you told me about."

Tyr's expression softened with surprise and something deeper. "Bergen has changed a lot since my time."

"I know. But still... it's where you began." Beth reached up to touch his face. "I want to see it through your eyes."

His cool lips found hers in a kiss that made her newly immortal heart race. The world around them—the wooded hills, the winter night, even time itself—seemed to fade away until there was only this: Tyr's gentle hands in her hair, the soft press of his mouth against hers, the perfect rightness of this moment. Above them, the stars witnessed their quiet declaration of forever. When they finally parted, his azure gaze held a depth of emotion that still took her breath away.

"Then Norway it is," he promised. "We'll sail the fjords under the midnight sun. Okay, well, in the moonlight, anyway. We'll have to time it right."

Laughing, Beth settled back against his chest, contentment washing over her. The future stretched before them, limitless and full of possibilities. There would be challenges, of course—adapting to her unique hybrid nature, navigating vampire politics, finding her place in this ancient society. But with Tyr beside her, those challenges felt manageable.

The night sounds shifted—a branch creaking where no wind stirred it, the soft scuff of a boot against bark. Beth's newly sharpened senses picked up the disturbance, her body tensing until she recognized the familiar presence lurking in the shadows.

"Tobi's here," she murmured, not bothering to turn her head. "Three o'clock, by the big oak."

Tyr sighed, his breath stirring her hair. "I told him to give us some privacy."

"Since when has Tobi ever listened?" Beth laughed softly. "Besides, he's just checking that we're safe."

"We're vampires," Tyr grumbled. "We're the apex predators."

"And yet you insisted on security cameras everywhere," Beth reminded him, poking his ribs playfully.

"That's different." Tyr's voice took on that protective edge she'd come to both appreciate and find amusing. "After what happened at the clinic..."

Beth sobered, understanding his concern. Though weeks had passed since the shooting that had necessitated her Turning, the memory remained raw. The sniper had been just one of many anti-shifter extremists who'd emerged since the supernatural revelation, and while Beth was no longer vulnerable to bullets in the same way, the threat to their community remained.

"I know," she said softly. "And I appreciate the precautions. I just think it's sweet that Tobi worries about me, too."

A rustle in the underbrush signaled Tobi abandoning any pretense of stealth. He emerged from the trees with his fair hair tousled and a sheepish grin spreading across his face.

"Don't mind me," he called, dropping onto the grass a respectful distance away. "I'm just out enjoying the night air."

"Right." Tyr's voice dripped with skepticism. "The night air. A full five miles from the Residence, exactly where we happened to be having some time alone."

Tobi brushed that off with an airy wave. "Pure coincidence."

Narrowing his eyes, Tyr glared at him. "You do realize Beth's senses are better than yours now, right? She heard you coming from half a mile away."

Tobi's grin widened. "Fine, I was totally following you. Sue me."

Beth laughed, the sound echoing through the clearing. "Since you're here, you might as well join us properly."

Tobi needed no further invitation. He bounded over like an eager puppy, flopping onto the grass next to them. "So, what are we talking about? World domination? The meaning of life? The absolutely ridiculous hairstyle Derek was trying out earlier?"

"Norway, actually," Beth said, still chuckling at his enthusiasm. "Tyr's going to take me to see the fjords."

"Ooh, yeah." Tobi's face lit up. "You should go in winter, when the Northern Lights are visible. It's spectacular, and there'll be the polar night."

"I've always wanted to explore the boreal forests in Siberia," he murmured, his voice taking on that distant quality it got when he was remembering something from his centuries of existence. "The vast wilderness, untouched by human development. And the Carpathian Mountains in Romania..." He paused, his fingers absently tracing patterns on her arm. "There are ancient vampire clans there who still maintain the old ways. Living in remote castles, keeping to themselves."

Beth's enhanced hearing caught the subtle shift in Tyr's voice as he spoke of other destinations. His arms tightened around her waist, his cool breath brushing her ear. She leaned back against his chest, picturing the landscapes he described. Her shifter instincts thrilled at the thought of running through pristine forests, while her vampire nature was intrigued by the possibility of meeting these ancient clans.

"The territories are so vast," Tyr continued, his voice warm with enthusiasm, "we could fly for hours without seeing another soul. Just endless forest and mountains stretching to the horizon."

Beth closed her eyes, letting his words paint pictures in her mind. She could almost feel the crisp mountain air beneath her wings, see the untouched wilderness spreading out below them. The thought of exploring these remote places with Tyr, both of them free to shift between their forms at will, made her dead heart flutter with excitement.

"Both," Beth decided, cutting off their budding debate. "We have time for it all, don't we? Norway. Siberia. Romania."

The brothers exchanged looks, identical smiles spreading across their faces.

"She's got a point," Tobi conceded. "Eternity is a long time."

"Eternity," Beth repeated softly, the reality of it still hard to believe.

She gazed up at the stars, trying to wrap her mind around the concept. Not just decades or centuries, but millennia stretching before her. She would see technologies develop, nations rise and fall, history unfold in real-time rather than through textbooks.

And through it all, she would have Tyr at her side. Tobi too, with his irrepressible humor and loyalty. The clan, with its ancient traditions and surprising adaptability. And she had Whisper, too, who had survived the transformation to become part of her new hybrid nature.

"Penny for your thoughts?" Tyr's breath stirred her hair.

Beth smiled, leaning into his embrace. "Just thinking about time. How different it feels now."

"It never stops being strange," Tobi offered, plucking a blade of grass to twirl between his fingers. "Even after centuries, I still find myself surprised by how quickly decades pass."

"But some moments," Tyr added, his arms tightening around Beth, "feel like they could last forever."

Beth turned in his embrace, her heart hammering against her ribs. When she met his eyes—those impossibly blue eyes that had seen centuries pass—her voice came out barely above a whisper. "Like this one?"

"Exactly like this one." His cool lips found hers in a kiss that promised countless such moments to come.

Above them, the stars wheeled in their ancient patterns, marking time as they had for billions of years. Beth watched them with new eyes, still amazed that she existed at all—a shifter/vampire hybrid that should have been impossible, yet here she was, embracing the endless night that had become her domain.

Not an ending, she realized, but a beginning. An eternal beginning, with infinite possibilities stretching before her like the star-filled sky.

And for the first time in her life, with Tyr at her side, she had all the time in the world to explore them.

Books by Allie McCormack

Wishes & Dreams

Paranormal Romance Series

Wishes in a Bottle

A Gift of Jacinth

A Cat for Troy

Coveted Mate

Reluctant Rogue

A Witch in Time

Foxy Lady

A Prince of the Djinn

Night Shift

Wishes & Dreams Boxed Set #1 (Books 1-3)

Wishes & Dreams Boxed Set #2 (Books 4-6)

Wishes & Dreams Boxed Set #3 (Books 7-9)

When Darkness Falls Trilogy

When Darkness Falls: Book I: The Palace

When Darkness Falls: Book II: The Dark Lord

When Darkness Falls: Book III: The Prophecy

When Darkness Falls: The Trilogy (Boxed set)

Sons of the Desert

Contemporary Romance Series

SwanSong

Castles in the Sand

Medieval Fantasy

Short Story Collections

Legends of Shon-Dar: Lady Chantalle

Legends of Shon-Dar: Trinket

Single Titles

Truck Stop

Nonfiction

(Writing as Deb Fletcher)

Conversations with Claude

Beloved Family Favorites

(Public Domain)

Dear Guest and Ghost

By Sylvia Dee

The Little Hunchback Horse

By Ireene Wicker

ABOUT THE AUTHOR

Allie McCormack is a disabled U.S. military veteran who has transformed her life-long dream of writing into reality. Having lived across the United States and spent memorable years in both Cairo, Egypt as an exchange student and Saudi Arabia working at a hospital in Riyadh, Allie now crafts her stories from the beautiful California wine country she calls home, accompanied by her family and two rescue cats.

When not weaving tales of romance and adventure, Allie explores the intersection of art and technology through AI-generated artwork, finding new ways to express her creativity. Her passion for storytelling drives everything she does, bringing to life the countless characters and worlds that populate her imagination. Whether through words or images, Allie believes in creating works that touch hearts and spark joy.

You can connect with Allie on social media, visit her author website (http://www.alliemccormack.com) for book updates and news, and browse her AI art on DeviantArt (https://www.deviantart.com/alliemccormack/gallery).

facebook.com/AllieMcCormackK
x.com/AllieMcCormackK
amazon.com/Allie-McCormack/e/B00JJG8ULM
goodreads.com/alliemccormack
bookbub.com/authors/allie-mccormack

www.ingramcontent.com/pod-product-compliance
Lightning Source LLC
LaVergne TN
LVHW020653110826
845149LV00012B/1984

* 9 7 8 1 9 5 5 7 1 6 3 6 9 *